Rise Fall Rise Again:

A New York Zombie Encounter

C.S. Leon

DEDICATION

First and foremost this work is dedicated to my family and friends who
have contributed to this work more than they know.
For Kathleen-who is so many things- Mother, Instigator, Lover & Friend
and so much more - you know why.

ACKNOWLEDGMENTS

I would like to express my humble and heartfelt Thanks to the men and women in uniform who keep us safe I hope those of you who read this enjoy it

This book is an original publication of Shrunken Head Press

This is a work of fiction, Names, Characters, places, and incidents either are the product of the authors imagination or are used fictitiously, and any resemblance to actual persons living or dead, business establishments, events, or locales is entirely coincidental.

Copyright ©2011 by C.S. Leon

C.S. Leon

Prologue

"This is crazy man… I mean it, this is no good. We are never gonna get out of here. We should just dig in like ticks. This is just fucking crazy." Upon exiting the far end of the tunnel into 'C' pump room Duncan stood and stretched his back, then moved towards his brother and Pete who were near the door to the hallway. Don's complaints preceded him out of the tunnel by at least tthirty seconds, and loud enough to be heard over the din of the pumps and compressor that are always running or cycling.

Liam had his ear to the door, attempting to hear anything in the hall; which was an exercise in futility with the noise from the equipment within the room? They quickly decided not to silence the equipment; they feared that it may draw attention *to* where they were hiding. Cautiously, Liam took the knob in hand and prepared to open the door a crack: Duncan lowered his bags, took up his ice chopper in both hands and stepped opposite his brother to a better vantage point to strike from if need be. Liam nodded a count of three then turned the knob. Nothing came bursting in through the door, so he opened it just enough to see a slice of the hallway without. Not seeing anything, he chanced to increase his field of view a little more. Still they seemed safe, emboldened by these minor successes, he chanced to stick his head out to scan the hallway. Satisfied that there were no new creeping monsters within view, they exited their temporary haven.

Don looked to the others and said, "You know we are trapped in here. Why did I leave the engine room to follow you guys on this fool's errand?" As if in answer to his question the radio broke silence, sounding as if someone had fallen and the transmit button were stuck. You could hear screams and groans fighting for dominance; you could hear Leneau pleading with Greg to stay back followed by more screams, some of pain some of terror. Then nothing as silence returned.

C.S. Leon

1

"...in summation this new equation has proven string fact as it is no longer a theory, as we can now extrapolate beyond the singularity. We have proven the Big Bang and String theory, not bad for a guy who was wait listed by MIT." He waits for the applause to die down. "Now I must sally forth to Geneva to see firsthand how my equation plays for the predictions of locality apply at CERN, then it's off to Mirni and then Tunguska to continue my latest theory." Again, he waits for the applause, takes a bow and makes his way off of the stage.

Greeted by his research team, Dr. Romero starts to collect his papers when a journalist from Discover magazine approaches. "Doctor, may I have a minute? This revelation is amazing, and I think that you are sure to be back here in Oslo as the next Laureate."

The doctor pauses and looks at his watch..." We ran a little long here, and we are in a hurry to make our train... do you want to come with us to Geneva, I can give you an interview on the way?"

The team takes their seats on the train as it pulls out of Oslo. Outside the air is cold, and the sky threatens snow; winter doesn't seem ready to relinquish her hold in these Northern reaches. Dr. Romero sits in a private car with John Roberts, a journalist with Discover magazine. The high-speed train is relatively quiet, and runs along its rails with only minor vibration and rocking. The journalist plugs his digital voice recorder into his laptop and sets himself up for his interview with Dr. Romero. Oddly enough, he also takes out a steno pad and pen, a bottle of water and a bag of trail mix. Now ready he turns to the doctor and asks, "Dr. Romero, your shocking discovery of your equation has been covered very well, what I would like to ask you about is your latest theory. Why are you so obsessed with an event that happened in nineteen-oh-eight? Why travel to the middle of Siberia? What is it that you intend to find proof of?"

Dr. Romero smiles arrogantly and sits back, making a show of crossing his legs. "When I was a little boy, I saw something that altered my life and the world as well... I saw a Tesla Coil. Seeing those brilliant flashes of "lightening" made me want to be a scientist. So I approached my studies with fervor and eventually got into MIT albeit via wait list, but I digress... you see I learned an awful lot about Tesla; I was fascinated by his theories, especially his concepts pertaining to wireless transmission of energies. I also became aware of the Tunguska Event, and the speculation on whether Tesla was truly involved trying to demonstrate his inventions for Admiral Perry to witness. Others have suggested that it was an air burst meteor or perhaps a comet that laid waste to that region on June third, Nineteen-oh-eight. So as my work in physics continued I thought what if Tesla did attempt this, and the electromagnetic field was affected by extra dimensional matter? Is it possible that matter from another dimension in the multiverse pass through a rip in the fabric of space-time? ...It seemed plausible to me, and it seems that the radiation could have been left in that other dimension. That is what we are looking for. Our modeling suggests that conditions are correct for re-creating that event ... granted on a smaller scale and more controlled."

2

Duncan punches in for another lack luster day at a job that at one, point was fun and rewarding, but now he dreads. Was it not for the benefit package he would have long since tendered his resignation. Walking down the hall past the endless number of Co-Eds, the Goths, the Bimbetts, the artsy types, they don't notice him as he makes his way to the Engine room stairwell. Removing the absurdly large key ring from the hook on his belt for perhaps the fifty thousandth time he opens the door to his own personal hell with a sigh.

His first stop was at the coffee pot for the first of many cups of the shift. Disappointment is not a strong enough word to describe what he felt when he saw the conditions of the coffee maker. Not only was there none of that hot nectar but the whole pot was filthy as if it had never been cleaned since the first day out of the box.

Walking into the control room, he saw the guys gathered as was the norm at shift change. Lineau was at the BMS (building management system) going through the shift paperwork and perusing the log book.

"I'm going across the street for coffee anyone else want one?" he asked of the collected engineers.

He jotted down their orders, so he would get them all correct and proceeded up the stairs, out the lobby door and across the street, pausing only long enough to give a wave to Charlie the hot dog vendor.

There were a myriad of smells to be sampled but the one that stood out from the rest was his heart's desire. That slightly acrid aroma of coffee that had been brewed strong and left on the warming pad too long, but this was not gourmet coffee, this wasn't Starbucks or any of the others that required the services of a barista. This was just plain old coffee, from the local bodega. It was exactly what he was looking for.

"The scent of coffee... is there a better smell?" he ruminates as he fills four

3

paper coffee cups, "Do you have the lottery results? Oh and pack of Denteen Ice, and three buttered rolls."While leaving the store he looks at the lottery results and nearly drops the bags when he suddenly realizes he hit the Mega Millions for 185 million dollars. He snatches his phone and calls his wife, "Hey Honeybaby, we're rich! We hit it ... all our dreams are plans! No more putting 'em off. I'll be home after work, I am gonna write my resignation and give it to the shift supervisor right away. No I can't just quit that wouldn't be ethical and besides it's gonna take a few days to get this all straightened out anyhow; look, I'll see you when I get home. " He narrowly misses death having to dodge a cab due to his being preoccupied.

He made his way down to the engine room and shared his good news with his co-workers. What started as a dismal day turned into nirvana; he spent the remainder of his shift talking about all the things he's going to do with his new wealth.

He reached the clock and punched out fifteen minutes early. "Let 'em dock me" he said to no one, in particular, and rushed down the three blocks to Penn Station and caught the early train.

When he got to his station he practically flew down the stairs to his car and raced home, to be met at the door by his wife dressed to kill holding a bottle of champagne. "Took you long enough... I almost had to start celebrating without you;" said Kate as she greeted Duncan when he walked in. Her red-ish blonde hair catching the candle light.

Excitement takes any hope of sleep away he keeps looking at the clock knowing that the lottery office does not open until nine am. At seven am he calls the Manager of the McMichael's yacht sales, "Irwin, Hey this is Duncan MacGregor; I was looking at your used Tartan... yeah that's me, well I just hit the Mega Millions, so I want to come in and buy that new Tartan fifty-three ...please tell me you still have it. Great I'll drive right up after I get to the lottery office. Yep I can have a certified check for that amount can you have it ready for me to sail off with it this afternoon? Great I'll see you soon."

"Honey... I'm calling out for the next couple of days, so we can spend the day shopping and what not, oh by the way, I just bought my dream boat... we are going to go up to Mamaroneck from the lottery office. I'm gonna call my Dad and let him know he can meet us there."

He dials his father's number and impatiently waits for his dad's voice on the other end. "Hey Dad, cancel whatever plans you have for this afternoon; I just hit Mega Millions, and well, I just bought the Tartan fifty-three… yeah over at McMichael's in Mamaroneck. Gonna sail it straight out of the yard."

"Sure mom too… I need to talk about how best to set up a trust or foundation for all the kids etc." "Ok I'll call you when we finish at the Lottery office" hanging up the phone he turns to his wife, "Let's wait till we get back to tell the kids, we'll bring home some surprises for them and then tell 'em." walks into the kitchen grabs his coffee cup off of the counter and inhales the aroma of Kona.

They pull into the marina's parking lot and park right next to his father's Cadillac. They got out of the vehicle and look around, Kate takes in all the tall masts and rigging and knows that this is her husband's dream. Even when they were dating he talked about retiring onto a big sail boat and sailing the Caribbean and the Mediterranean. The sky is that shade of blue you only see in early spring or late autumn. The gulls coasting on the wind currents, seeming to almost hover until they spot something to eat, and then they swoop down.

Duncan makes his way into the showroom to find his father and Irwin the Manager of McMichael's Yachts. He walks up to the pair of men embraces his father and shakes the hand of the manager. "Is she ready?" he asks as he looks at the tide clock on the wall.

"We should be able to finish up the paperwork just in time for the tide. Do you want to finish it up on the boat?" he stops momentarily at the teak desk and grabs a folder. The group emerges from the building, and they are joined by Kate as they make their way down the gangway to the boat slips. Irwin leads the assemblage to the boat moored at the outermost slip.

There before them was a handsome vessel, sleek and skillfully balanced. The teak bright work varnished lovingly, as they climbed aboard and made their way to the salon, they each noticed small beautiful details that was testimony to how well this boat was made.

"Well Dad we can sleep seven people in beds and another couple in the salon if need be. I'm a little concerned that it is a little too big for just us, but Duncan loves this boat. "Babe... what are we going to call it?"

"Her" he calls up "her name is going to be registered as "S.V. Persistence." What do you think?"

"She's your boat seems like a fitting name to me... hey it just occurred to me how are we getting the car home if we are going to sail her home?" she asks her husband aware that she had been snookered.

" I kind of figured you would go shopping with Mom and spend some money shopping in Greenwich Ct. Then she can pick up his car and follow you home, we could all go out to dinner. I will call Liam and Kyle and make arrangements" he says a little sheepishly. She

She thinks; I let him have this one, one; he's been working so hard, for so long he deserves a little self self-indulgence, besides, he did say I could go shopping and money is no object. "Sounds like a plan call me later sweetheart and let me know when and where to pick you up."

Duncan signs the last page, gives Irwin the check, and shakes his hand.

"She's all yours" he reaches into a cupboard and pulls out two bottles of Moet champagne. "One for Christening, the other to celebrate, with our compliments."

 He climbs off of the boat and walks back to the show room with Kate. The Diesel engines start with a low rumble. Jacob unties the bow line and then slips the stern line. Duncan engages the bow thruster and puts the boat into gear and pulls away from the dock. He punches into the Navigation computer, his destination and the boat begins to pick up speed. Never had there ever been a bigger smile upon Duncan's face aside from the births of his children, and even that one is too close to call. "Yeah perfect sailing conditions Dad... I'm glad you're here for her maiden voyage."

The trip across the Long Island Sound went without a hitch or hiccup. Duncan called both of his brothers after letting his dad take the helm, and told them of his great news, and how they can both quit their jobs and do whatever venture they want with him to bankroll. It was decided that a late dinner with the whole clan would be had at Smith & Wollensky's in their wine cellar private room. The room's walls were lined with wine racks behind tempered glass. The whole seemed very cozy with a genteel ambiance. The tables were set up as a horse shoe in the center, one of the families filling each section.

On the left leg you had Liam, who at thirty-eight years of age, presently is the GM of the W Hotel in Times Square, along his wife Erin, who works as a nurse at Presbyterian Hospital. They sat with his parents Jacob and Marie since he, and Erin didn't have any children yet.

On the right leg sat Kyle the eldest brother at forty-five, his wife Pam and their two sons Patrick age twenty-one and Kevin nineteen. Patrick being home on Leave from the Navy; is stationed upon the Ronald Regan aircraft carrier. While Kevin serves in the Coast Guard and lives in Long Beach.

At the head of the table sat Duncan and Kate, along with their children Sean(a high-school senior and somewhat of a local celebrity for his prowess on the Ice as a hockey player)and their two daughters Kaitlyn fifteen and Kristen twelve who are athletes in their own right both being competitive swimmers.

The only ones missing were his sister Carrie and her family, twin sons Keith and Christopher, who both serve in the Guard, and her new husband, however, they live in Georgia and weren't expected to make the trip in such short notice.

Duncan taps his spoon against his water glass to gain everyone's attention, "I've asked you all here to help celebrate our great fortune. I will be setting up a trust and foundation so that all of your kids can go to any college you want, or have the money to buy your first home. Liam you and Kyle along with Carrie your mortgages will be paid off in full, Mom and Dad you will never have to worry about money ever again. I know dad that you, and mom aren't hurting but since you retired the market has taken some hits, and your annuity has to have suffered some. I already gave my notice at work, and Kate has too."

The wait staffs were a true credit to their profession as they were near invisible yet everything asked for seemed to suddenly appear when sought. The meal itself was sumptuous starting out with three tiers of shellfish on ice, followed by a delightful soup and miraculous cuts of steak with crème spinach and smashed potatoes, along with numerous bottles of wine from this very cellar.

"Hey guys, remember when Dad took over as scoutmaster? And they were all afraid that he would be too strict what with his military bearing and all… look at him now 72 years old granted he doesn't look it, but now he is a little thicker around the middle as well as softer around the edges… hey Dad was it the grand children who did it to you. Turned you into the *'Devine Patriarch'* out of the former Special Ops warrior. I never cease to be amazed at the dichotomy you are …" "anyway, this weekend, I want to take you all sailing on my new boat" "Kyle, when will you be able to start collecting from Railroad Retirement? You've been on the railroad for 25 years now is it? Can you put your papers in now?" "Liam your passion has always been cars …err and your wife, do you want to start some sort of business that allows you to tinker till your heart is content?"

By the conclusion of the meal, everyone was feeling fatted up and happy, so they all returned with Liam to the Penthouse of his Hotel where he, and Erin live for drinks and to let the younger children crash.

3

"Another resounding success Doctor!" shouted Samuel over the din of machinery as he poured over the numbers on the printouts. "Every locality pinpointed as expected. It displays complete certainty; any doubters now will be viewed like flat Earthers." Samuel Griffin is a research assistant who is on sabbatical from the NSA where he works as a UN weapons inspector his expertise in radiation detection and particle physics shortlisted him for Doctor Romero's team. His fellow assistant Changming Tao, the son of the Chinese Ambassador to the United States is a graduate student from St. John's, who studied under Dr. Romero during his undergraduate days, confirms the result and says to the doctor, "I think we have empirical evidence that allows us to move forward."

John Roberts and Dr. Romero look at each other and share a smile. The journalist looks a little pale, due to his knowledge that he is one- hundred meters underground. However, apart from that unsettling fact, he knows that he has witnessed firsthand one of the most important moments in mankind's history. "Well Doctor, I have to go back stateside, and you are off to Siberia. I will send you a copy of my article before publication. I want to thank you again for all your help and access to your experiments." They shake hands and get onto the elevator to bring them back to the surface. As John gets into the car that will take him to the airport he rolls down the window and waves farewell.

Dr. Romero responds in kind and surveys the surrounding mountains noting the majesty that they can't help but instill. He turns to his aide, "Changming... have you arranged for the transport of the equipment, and have all the documents in order?"

The Chinese graduate student affirms and busies himself wrapping things up, " when is he going to learn that in Chinese, Tao is how he should call me... he is the dumbest smart man I know, or maybe he just doesn't care, arrogant S.O.B. that he is." He completes his tasks meticulously, knowing it's all in the details. The vapor from his breath demonstrates just how cold it is, and he wishes not for the first time that these experiments could have happened in July. "I have been in contact with Dr. Kasheyev, the Director of the *INR of RAS*, (Institute for Nuclear Research of the Russian Academy of Sciences) He is going to meet us in Moscow and fly with us the rest of the way to Mirni. He seems very excited to be part of this even in an ancillary fashion. He has offered us the use of any resources at his disposal. That should help the grant money go a little farther."

"With everything that has happened over the past couple weeks, today included, I don't think we will have to worry about grant money ever again." He chuckles to himself as he makes his way to the vehicles. His infatuation with his new celebrity had his phone in his hand calling John Roberts not ten minutes after his departure, "John why not come with us to Tunguska, not only will you have more for your article, but you should be able to speak with Dr. Kasheyev too. This could be quite a coupe for you... exclusives on ground breaking science? Isn't that what Discover is all about... Great I will see you at the airport."

4

The flight from Switzerland was uneventful, thankfully so thought the research team. As they disembarked from the jet way, they were each surprised to see that this airport was much the same as any airport found in any city anywhere in the world. The same molded plastic chairs and laminate topped counter surfaces, Kiosks, even a McDonald's was visible, granted the signage was in Cyrillic, but apart from that you would never know where you were by looking around. There was a delegation of people gathered round a man, whom the doctor recognized to be Dr. Kasheyev, holding a sign bearing Dr. Romero's name.

The research team walked over to the delegation and introduced themselves, offering handshakes and smiles. "Dr. Romero, your picture does not do you justice, in person you look more like a movie star than the academian that shows with your paper publish in the scientific journals I have read. The rest of your team is already at the site working with some of my colleagues. Please excuse my English is school taught, never really practice with an Amerikan" The director made hasty introductions to his colleagues and guided them through the check points handling everything at customs. Taking charge of the group, he guided them to a lounge where they were able to refresh themselves. "You must tell me how went things at CERN? I fear that there are many of my colleagues who are very sad that you made the discovery before them. You don't have any Russian ancestry do you?" he asked hopefully. Tao handed over a large folder with copies of the results from the CERN LHC* experiments. "Yes, yes, thank you, I will look it all over on the flight to Mirni; we have a long flight ahead, and in fact, we must hurry to the gate to boarding."

The plane left Moscow and five hours and fifteen Hail Mary's later arrived in the tiny airport in Mirni. When the door opened and the stairs were rolled into place, the research team realized they were not in Kansas anymore. The tarmac if indeed, it were tarmac was in sorry need of repair. A cargo plane was being unloaded, the crates and boxes being loaded into what appear to be old Soviet military trucks albeit with great care. Dr. Kasheyev had made all the arrangements, which in itself was a godsend, since Dr. Romero had gotten a little caught up in his new celebrity. He now became very aware just how out of his element, he truly was. He is a physicist; he has always done his work in laboratories and lecture halls. He wasn't what you would call a field researcher. However, if his theory was going to prove anything, he was going to be there when it was proven.

The immensity of Siberia is beyond what the feeble brain can truly imagine. It alone is why they used to say that the sun never set upon the Soviet Union. The director and the doctor spoke at length during the long bumpy ride. The director provided immeasurable help with the logistics of this venture. "This is a unique view…err… theory you have come up with," said the director "and with these new facts you have uncovered… you could be *onto* something. I must confess I have done much research on Tesla myself at behest of Mother Russia. During the cold war, much research was done trying to recreate some of his designs and weapons. I myself worked on trying to build his earthquake machine, using sympathetic harmonics." The doctor realized how naïeve he truly was. Being a theoretical physicist, he didn't really give much consideration to the weapons applications of his discoveries.

"Well we now know that certain subatomic particles can be in two or more places at once, and we have mathematically shown the multiverse has eleven dimensions as was speculated by those other M-Theorists. Now what could be earth shattering, and I mean literally, is the possibility of extra dimensional matter occupying the same space as matter in our own dimension. This could possibly have similar effects to nuclear fission. Add to this speculation, immense electromagnetic fields and the massive amounts of energy that Tesla was using, is it that far out of belief that all these things combined to make a "perfect storm" to risk using pop culture, and maybe that is what happened in Tunguska?"

After the convoy arrived, the Russian technicians set to work setting up the various equipment and running the electrical feeds from the semi that held the generator banks, and testing all the equipment. Finally, they began to assemble the transmission tower which looked like something from the Frankenstein films. These feats took the better part of three days. The doctor and his team allowed themselves to relax at the inn about thirty miles away. As promised, John interviewed Dr. Kasheyev, getting his take on not only this experiment but on the "genius" that is Dr. Romero and the results from CERN.

When at last all was ready to recreate the famous *event,* they all drove to the site. Dr. Romero's team double-checked the work done by the technicians and was satisfied. Dr. Romero himself took in the scenery around him, being very familiar with the photos taken of the aftermath of the original *event.* Over one hundred years had passed and although the forest grew back, there was an eeriness' about the place. The "new growth" forest had reclaimed the valley but somehow the trees "felt" tortured. He shrugged off the uneasiness. "Tomorrow we make history... yes?" Dr. Kasheyev exclaimed. They all retired to the inn to rest up for the early start.

At five-thirty AM, the team departed for the site for shortly after seven AM the test will begin in earnest. The technicians and team members alike shared a sense of excitement. Dr. Kasheyev and Dr. Romero were engaged in theoretical discussions centering on whether or not this could result in a worm hole or perhaps even a subatomic singularity. "Given that best estimates of the original event put the force yield to be in the neighborhood of 185 Hiroshima bombs, prudence would suggest that work with a fractional percentage of what Tesla's device yielded. If we were to use point zero one percent, the yield should be approximately one-twentieth of the Hiroshima bomb with a correspondingly smaller blast radius." The technicians make the adjustments to the equipment ... the time approaches and at seven-seventeen AM, the button is pushed. Blinding light, followed by buffeting hot wind of the shockwave blasts from the epicenter of the site. Trees are knocked flat as before, in the same radial pattern, however, instead of 800 square miles of destruction. This blast leveled just short of one square mile of forest. Where the sky had been slightly overcast before the test, the shockwave blew the clouds away allowing the sun to shine down unimpeded. Sensors captured all the pertinent data. The EMP detected was larger than expected by a factor of 1three.2, but with no detectable radiation. However, conflicting data on if there was any at all but certainly nothing exists at present. Debris rained down in the area for quite a while. When the dust settled it was clear even from this distance, there was no crater, in fact, it was just as in the photos from the famous original event.

"Well, shall we go for a closer look gentlemen?," said Dr. Romero as he shouldered a pack with some portable equipment and sensors. The rest was dispersed between the remainder of the party, and they began the trek over marshy bog towards the epicenter. Communication with the base provided results as the information was processed. "So far it seems we succeeded Yuri, wouldn't you say?" Dr. Romero said to Dr. Kasheyev over the radio.

As they moved closer to their destination, they noticed the wildlife was running away from the center as fast as their wings, feet, and hooves could carry them, the flight response in full effect. The team separated and moved to the various sensor posts. Dr. Romero continued to the edge of the devastation where he noticed that much of the wildlife nearest him was laying upon their sides having convulsions. He relayed this information back to base and suggests that some technicians or staff come and collect some specimens for further study. He continues into the blast radius and collected additional data from the next senor post, one more to go as they were laid out in concentric circles. Each of the sensor pods was housed in shielded boxes protecting them against possible radiation and electromagnetic pulse. The final sensor pod was destroyed by the force of the blast.

Returning to the base station, he was glad to see that and an impromptu surgical theater had been erected for dissection of some of the deceased animal specimens. As he inspected the area, he noticed most of the animals were shaking off their seizures, but many still remained in a catatonic state. There were numerous breeds of animals, from reindeer to foxes, badgers to lynx, a regular menagerie of animals. The initial causes of death for the first group of specimens were from the concussive force of the blast; however, what piqued his curiosity most was what caused the convulsions of those in the outer regions of the blast radius. He was amazed at the resources that were at his disposal out here in the wilderness; Dr. Kasheyev was as good as his word in that regard. The lab he had assembled did not lack for much of anything, possessing a wonderful array of equipment, from spectral analysis to gas chromatograph, to hematology instruments, as well as the more mundane microscopes and test tube centrifuges.

The field work at the site stabilized on the fourth day. The readings all returned to normal ambient levels. John Roberts made his way over to Dr. Romero's quarters to say good bye again. His editor had called him and told him if he still wanted his job, he was to return stateside as fast as humanly possible, and with the article in hand. He planned on completing it on the flight back. He knocked on the door and entered, finding Dr. Romero pouring through the data. His first thought was that field work did not suit the man; he noticed that the man's clothes did not fit him like they did when they first met. "Well I am being called back stateside. My editor has ideas of installing a chain at my desk that only he has the key to."

Dr. Romero laughed and shook his hand. "E-mail me the article and stay in touch, there is sure to be some fascinating developments from this experiment." They exchanged pleasantries and contact information, feeling a bit of déjà vu Roberts picked up his carryon and walked to the car, got in and left.

Dr. Romero's eyes were beginning to get blurry. He sat backward and stretched his back, raising his arms and yawning in a hope of providing greater oxygen levels to his brain. He decides to get up and go for a walk to get the blood moving rather than pooling in his extremities. The dusky sky and chill air do wonders for reviving his energy levels. His boots crunch the snow as he walks in the direction of the laboratory trailers. Listening to the night sounds and the wind he draws closer to the animal sheds and hears whines of fear from some of the animals within. Opening the door, the smell of urine and feces assaulted his olfactory senses. He slowly made his way down past the lines of cages, most of the animals seeming alert and normal albeit definitely frightened. Some of the animals seemed to have succumbed to death having never recovered from the initial trauma.

In the last cage on the left at the ground level was a lynx, making strange feral noises, its muscles twitching spasmodically. It seemed almost lost as it smashed its head into the cage door over and over. It seemed that this animal was the source of the unrest in the pens. The doctor decided to end the specimen's suffering and have it dissected and autopsied. Grabbing a hypodermic containing ketamine and a delivery rod, he administered the drug to the miserable creature. The cat collapsed, and its breathing slowed. Opening the cage door, the doctor reached in and picked up the cat, he noticed that the cat felt excessively warm. He brought it to the lab to be euthanized and autopsied. As he got it out into the chill air, the animal regained some of its consciousness and tried to escape by biting and scratching at the doctor but in its weakened condition, it finally expired in the doctor's hands. He continued to the lab and left it with the veterinary tech to process, then returned to his quarters to clean and dress the punctures and scratches on his hands.

During the second week, Samuel Griffin got a telephone call from his superiors in Washington DC; he was to be recalled to service by the NSA. He was to lead a reconnaissance team into Tehran to garner evidence that they were actively enriching uranium. Secondly, he was to obtain evidence that the dual-use equipment was being actively used for the weaponizing of said uranium, thus violating the UN accords. With the no-fly zone over Libya, and the various regime changes, the Middle East was a pressure cooker that threatened to blow up in the worlds face. So with some trepidation he agreed that he would indeed return in two weeks time reporting directly to command in Egypt.

After three weeks of the camp's routine, the team members were beginning to tire of the living conditions. The lack of creature comforts is not something that the team from St. Johns was used to; add to that the camp seems to be overrun with fleas. Everybody is scratching and generally miserable. Fortunately, the field work was nearing completion, the last of the flora and fauna samples collected and categorized. Even the conversations, although congenial had changed, containing less camaraderie, more of the "*we will stay in touch*," as they busied themselves preparing for the departure home.

The final day in camp was more of the same that is until the vet tech came in, to report his findings. "It seems that the lynx you brought in was a very sick animal. It was suffering from toxoplasmosa gondii* virus. However, it appears that this virus underwent some radical mutation as a result of the experiment. You see here are some copies of the slides." He passes over a flash drive that was quickly loaded *onto the* screen.

"Here you see numerous cells loaded to the gills with a normal toxoplasmosa gondii virus. The cell walls are about to explode spreading the virus to additional cells. Now this next image shows what looks like a chain. This is made of toxoplasmosa gondrex virus or at least that is what I intend to call it. The virus has centralized itself in the brain stem of the lynx, and each of its replications link together growing atop the nerves throughout the body, essentially creating a secondary nervous system. The virus is virulent in its replication. The host T cells prepare to replicate, to drive off the invader, or in this case, any ancillary infections. Only now some chemical machinery is taken over by the new DNA and instead of two new T cells, it creates two of the toxoplasmosa gondrex, and so on. This virus seems to prevent the body's ability to absorb and or utilize serotonin and other neurotransmitters, thus shutting down higher brain function. I have already sent my findings to the virologists at the RAS. They have requested the subject animal, and any specimens be frozen and sent on. We also have noticed that some of the other animals in the pens behaviors are altered, the virus may very well be spreading. We have taken blood samples from the rest of the specimens. Toxoplasmosa gondii virus is usually found in rodents and felines, although it is occasionally found in humans as well. There does not seem to be any markers for it to be an airborne virus. In fact, exposure to air, temperature fluctuations, or exposure to acidic or conversely alkaline environments seems to kill the virus, but we will learn more after the virologists complete their study."

Dr. Romero asked them to forward their findings along with anything else to him at St. John's University. "It has indeed been a privilege to have worked with you all on this, but I have to return home and the rest of my team is aching to get home too. Be sure to stay in touch; I hope to be able to collaborate on the application of what we found here." He shakes the hands of all the men in the meeting and heads for the door.

Leaving the trailer he stops at his quarters to grab his luggage and looks around the camp once more. His adventure nearing its end, he greets the rest of his team. They load their belongings into the truck, then make their way to their transport and climb in. The long drive back to Mirni found the doctor feeling a little off as his nose began to run. "Great a cold… just what I want." Thinking the last thing he wants to do is travel on various planes for the twenty plus hours with a cold. "Well maybe I will drink enough scotch on the flights to make me not care how I feel." The bumpy ride finally ends at the Mirni airport, where they said farewell to the driver who had made sure all their equipment and luggage was passed through check in, and then headed for the gate.

Boarding of the plane was uneventful. Dr. Romero found his seat and sat down hard, his cold like symptoms progressing to that of the flu. "Screw field research!" he exclaimed to himself aloud. "I hate being sick"' he thought "but then again, who likes feeling like shit" he mused repressing a chill. He hunkered down into the seat pulled a blanket up to his chin and dozed until the plane taxied to its gate in Moscow.

The team exited the plane and made straight for their connecting flights. Samuel Griffin said his good-byes to the team and made his way through the busy airport to catch his flight. Meanwhile, Dr. Romero stopped at a kiosk and purchased some Nyquil in hopes of passing the remainder of the journey stateside in symptom-free sleep. The others were unaware that they too would soon be feeling the coming on of illness. At the gate counter Dr. Romero upgraded his ticket to first class, dreading the idea of such a long flight in the cramped confines of coach.

The others remarked among themselves about what a baby the doctor was acting like. Remarking on how his behavior on the flight home was dramatically different from the man who they left New York with a month earlier. Truth being told they were happy that he was not going to be sitting with them. It was remarked that maybe the Doctor's new fame was beginning to get to him, and perhaps there were even greater pressures acting upon the man.

The doctor aware of the two fluid ounce limit on liquids allowed on the plane drank the entire contents of the Nyquil bottle, and then boarded the plane. Sitting down in his comfortable and spacious seat, he took out his laptop to continue his study of the data gained from Tunguska. The rest of the passengers boarded; it was a full flight. The Flight attendants moved through the cabin busily making sure that all was ready for takeoff. Irritably, Dr. Romero stowed his computer. He was having difficulty concentrating on the data anyway. "This Nyquil acts fast...or maybe I overdosed... hell with it, maybe it will put me out of my misery" he thought. With all seats upright and all tray tables in their locked positions, with all the overhead compartments closed and locked, the plane taxied out to the runway, then raced down it and began its steady climb into the sky. The seatbelt and no-smoking lights went out as they reached cruising altitude and the flight attendants returned to moving through the cabin taking drink orders. The Doctor thought *"in for a penny … in for a pound"* "I'll have a double Chivas."

No sooner was the drink delivered when the doctor threw it back in a single gulp, "If I am not awake when you come for meal orders, I will have the steak as rare as you can make it. I want it so that a good vet could revive it." He smiled to the flight attendant, his pale color and sweaty brow being the only visual manifestation of his illness. She nodded politely and continued on with her business. Anyone more familiar with the doctor would have thought his meal request extremely odd; being that he was a vegetarian for several years now. He closed his eyes and drifted off into a fitful slumber.

Two hours into the ten and a half hour flight, the doctor awakened to the scent of food. His first thought was "prey!" He shook his head and thought "not prey..." searching for the word "dinner... yes dinner, why was it so hard to think of that?" Feeling as weak as a kitten, he stretches, gradually becoming aware that his symptoms have worsened but at the same time not "feeling" them as much. "Should have taken the correct dosage... and probably shouldn't have had the Scotch as a chaser" he thought almost absently.

The attendant brings him his meal, and his salivary glands kick into overdrive. He smells meat, but when she lifts the lid, his nose is assaulted by the smell of overcooked meat. The smell that had wakened him was not of what was being served, but of the flight attendant herself. Mechanically, he forced himself to eat. The combination of the Nyquil and the liquor's soporific effect reasserted themselves, and the Doctor slipped from consciousness again. The mutated virus, has been replicating itself at a pace not matched by any other known virus, rapidly altering the doctor's physiology, much the same way as it did in the lynx. Five hours in, again he awakens, but he has extreme difficulty putting thoughts together in a cogent manner. He had a "feeling," a sense of falling away. His body was failing him, fever sky high, muscles beginning to react to stimulus along a different route than his nervous system. His last lucid thought was "fucking Nyquil!" before he slipped into a coma where he remained until his death nine hours and forty-five minutes into the flight.

Twenty-three minutes later, the body of Dr. Romero began to move of its own accord. The limbs moving in a jerky uncoordinated manner, a haunting groan issuing from his throat. The scent of feces from the physical act of death fouled the air around it. Just as the body reanimated, the voice of the pilot came over the loud speaker. "We will begin our final approach shortly. I have turned on the fasten seatbelts and no-smoking signs. The local time in New York is three twenty seven PM, and it is an unseasonably warm seventy four degrees Fahrenheit. We thank you for flying Lufthansa and hope you have enjoyed your flight."

The reanimated corpse struggled to stand. The flight attendant came over to "it," telling "him" he must return to his seat and fasten his seatbelt. As she put her hand upon his arm to assist him, *"it"* grabbed and bit her exposed forearm. She screamed in pain and surprise and struggled, trying to escape its grip. Another flight crew member tried to assist her in escaping the violent attack. He too was scratched and bitten, as the zombie's grip was broken. The virus needed the protein in the blood and tissue to fuel its reproduction and to sustain its ability to animate the body. The creature lunged for a nearby passenger, who was belted in and unable to escape the thing's teeth, as it quickly took a large chunk of flesh from the victim's cheek. Mayhem and panic ensued.

A sky marshal stood up, shouted a warning as he identified himself and drew his firearm. The creature paid neither him, nor his gun any mind and continued attacking anybody near enough to sink his teeth into. With the safety of the flight being his responsibility, the sky marshal shot the creature first in the leg, then getting no reaction, he then put two more shots in the torso, yielding the same result. His final shot in the head finally brought an end to the attack.

Meanwhile in the back of the plane, the team from St. John's, like everyone else, believed the plane was being hijacked or a terrorist was trying to crash the plane. They stayed in their seats absently scratching at the flea bites as they cowered in fear, praying for safety as the shots rang out. They would never have guessed the truth. The pilot made an emergency radio call, stating that shots were fired on the plane. He received emergency landing instructions and safely brought the plane down where emergency vehicles as well as an assault team waited.

5

Samuel's flight arrived thirty minutes early; he was met by a man from the consulate and quickly whisked away in a diplomatic car. A dossier containing his team members and satellite images of the site complete with radiological as well as thermo graphic imagery was waiting for him as he climbed into the back seat. "Hit the ground running... hoorah" the thought entered his brain as swiftly as a sniper's bullet. The car sped through the streets of Cairo to the consulate. His identification was checked by the marines at the gate, then he continued through and reported to the section chief.

"Say what you want about Government inefficiencies, but putting together a quick clandestine op requires mountains of logistics, and they do that better than anyone," said the master sergeant. The team briefing was scheduled. The "techno goodies" were checked, and the operation was scheduled for wheels up three hours later. Samuel was feeling poorly, but he chalked that up to pre-ops jitters.

"No matter how many times you do this, you never quite shake that lump in your stomach." His four-man squad, was comprised of veteran spec. Warriors, they all knew their jobs and the jobs of their teammates.

The team infiltrated via HALO* (High Altitude Low Opening) insertion and made their way to their objective on time. Samuel's physical condition began to deteriorate. His temperature shot up in excess of one hundred and four degrees, accompanied by sweats and chills; but being an operator you have to work through it. The team checked in over their coms, they were to link up and then breech the compound's security, make their way to the reactor area, gather the requested intelligence, and then ex-filtrate and make their way over land to their extraction point.

Things began to go badly when Sam lost some motor control over his extremities, this happened as they reached the reactor's command and control room. He collapsed into a seizure. The corpsman of the team reacted quickly, by trying to insert something into Samuel's mouth to prevent him from swallowing his tongue, and was rewarded with a bite to his hand. The two other team members were able to secure confirming evidence of Iran's failure to comply with the nuclear proliferation accords and transmitted the data via burst transmitter, a device that transmits encoded data via satellite in a small packet, reducing the chance of discovery due to radio signal monitoring.

Things went from bad to worse; the security force caught onto a breach of their security and swarmed. Sam's team was surrounded and apprehended, but by this time, Samuel had slipped into a coma that he would never wake from. The Iranian facility had medical facilities on location, and it was there that they brought the unconscious foreigner. CPR was administered, but they were unable to revive him. Mouth-to-mouth, resuscitation resulted in the virus passing from one to the other.

The virus underwent yet another mutation. The result is that its assimilation, and its replication capacities increased significantly. The incubation time decreased from days to hours. It still required fluid exchange but the ramifications of the changes are unfathomable, and as yet no one was even aware that Armageddon was at hand.

Back in DC, the Joint Chiefs received the transmission from the team in Tehran, confirming what they all *"knew"* would be the result, the conclusive evidence that Iran was actively becoming a Nuclear threat, finally allowing the US to push the UN Security council to move beyond sanctions. When the team failed to check in and contact was lost, the US State department had to fear the worst. The President was briefed, and never was his lack of foreign policy experience as apparent as now, his inaction and failure to initiate the contingency plan. A stealth bomber was standing by waiting for the go ahead to drop its payload; a bunker busting high-yield device. His lack of action was to have devastating results, as millions of people would die horribly, painfully, and in abject terror.

The team was kept in a cell. They were bound at hand and foot. They were not allowed to sit or lay; their interrogators were methodical, and not adverse to using torture. Not a single one of them remained unscathed. The corpse of the team leader lay unceremoniously on the floor in a corner, behind their tormentors, its arms and legs akimbo. The corpsman's chin against his chest, unaware of the changes the virus was affecting, had thought the pain the result of his tormentor's attentions, he vomited all over himself and his team mates. The interrogator's laughter made them fail to notice the horror reflected in the eyes of their captives, as the dead body of their leader began to stand. It was not until they heard the haunting moan from behind them that they turned to face the zombie. The closeness of the room rewarded the creature with all the meat it could eat. The screams went unheeded until the guards realized that the screams of terror were, in fact, screamed in Arabic.

The corpsman succumbed next to this "new and improved" strain of the virus. Having no pain response, it strained tirelessly at its bonds struggling to get its share of the meat. The corpsman's wrist eventually gave out and with a sickening ripping to sound like the flesh parted. It fell to the ground unable to free its feet; it crawled along and sank its teeth into another victim. When the guards finally opened the door, they went in with assault weapons leading the way, the staccato sound of fully automatic fire in the confined space was deafening; they did not even recognize that the bullets were having no effect. The zombie's nails and teeth found even more places, the wounded guards fled and the zombies were able to escape the cell, looking for more fresh meat. The remains of the partially eaten victims were not spared transformation by the virus. After a time, they too reanimated and began their quest to devour living flesh and blood. Within twenty-four hours, there were no living people remaining at the nuclear plant, the zombies wandered out of the compound sniffing the wind for new prey.

Back in the 'War *Room'* the latest satellite reconnaissance is being displayed, and nothing seems to fit their expectations. "There is absolutely no activity… nada…zip… thermals show the plant is still online, but it seems like no one is minding the store," said the chairman in his briefing of the President. "No new information on our men. All we know is that they were captured. Sir … the contingency plan is still on the table. The bomber is on station and with what we know now …" he left the thought unfinished as he saw that this President was not going to do anything. He was too concerned with his image, a little more than two years into his first (and hopefully only) term and was already consumed with his legacy.

Iranian military vehicles move in around the plant to investigate the lack of communication. As the soldiers disembarked from their transports, the few remaining zombies in the area caught their scent and began to close in. The soldiers, seeing the gore of the slaughter pulled back to their vehicles and requested orders from command. They had yet to notice the walking dead that were coming their way. The plant left unattended for so long began to fail. The fuel rod cooling system failed completely. The water temperature past its boiling point; a meltdown was imminent. There were no alarms sounding, no strobes flashing, this was of course because the control room housing those systems were where the plant workers made their last stand against the zombies, and those systems did not respond well to gunfire. The soldiers were caught by surprise as the zombies struck, fortunately for them their pain and terror were short lived. The reactor core breached; the pressure vessels exceeded their limits and blew. Oblivion ended their torment.

Radiation was detected in the atmosphere; the satellite imagery confirmed the explosion and subsequent radioactive fallout. The Nuclear agencies in countries around the world were alerted to the event. The UN immediately began prepping for relief efforts, resources were being gathered; personnel allocated and reassigned. All of these actions happening so swiftly, that little attentions were being paid to the actual weather patterns, reports were beginning to trickle in informing of refugee activity.

6

Back in New York, the flight crew opened the doors, and EMTs quickly entered the plane. The corpse of the doctor was removed, the more seriously injured were given first aid and then removed by ambulance to area hospitals. The less serious wounds were cleaned and dressed. Some of these passengers elected to go home rather than to the hospitals figuring that they would see their personal physicians after meeting with their lawyers. The authorities were taking statements. The news crews were kept at a distance, but many of the passengers made their way over to them eager for their fifteen minutes of fame providing sound bytes aplenty, although the news reporters seemed a tad let down that this was not some terrorist action but rather a lone nut job losing it up in the air. Meanwhile within the cargo hold of the aircraft fleas from Tunguska were finding their ways into the luggage of other passengers.

Lufthansa, in an effort to alleviate some of the bad press, not only offered to cover any and all medical expenses but to put those passengers who missed their connecting flights up in area hotels. Surprisingly few were overly upset about the events, knowing that there really was nothing done wrong by the flight crew or the sky marshal, the whole affair was handled swiftly and professionally. The last of the antibiotic ointment was applied, the last of the gauze dressings secured and band aids applied. The passengers and flight crew left the airport. Some sought needed rest at neighboring hotels where hungry bedbugs waited, others went to their own destinations, many carrying the virus already in their systems, still others within their luggage. It would not take long for this virus to reach epidemic proportions due to the speed of its transmission with the help of vermin and insect life that is hidden in this city. Bedbugs, rats with fleas, and even mosquitoes in the unseasonable warm weather make it easy for blood to blood transfer of this pathogen. All you have to do is look at the recent headlines to see just how scary this could be: West Nile Virus transmitted by mosquitoes. The city's bedbug epidemic, those little critters can be picked up anywhere, and they travel with you. They can be found in the finest hotels as well as in the lowest flop houses, in your hospitals and your places of employment; these little vampires drink their fill then return to or join a new colony spreading the wealth per say. Then you have those brazen rats in this city. Who among us has not seen countless rats in the subways and even on the street in broad daylight?

Ten hours after the plane landed; Erin MacGregor was looking in on her newest patient at Presbyterian Hospital, one of the passengers from the Lufthansa flight that was all over the news. She felt somewhat relieved at the change. When her shift started she had to deal with three junkies, who were displaying drug seeking behavior, and several gang toughs who were loitering around due to one of their members having been brought in with GSW (gunshot wounds). The stresses were building upon her over the last three months, there were nine incidences of violence in the workplace that resulted in lock down procedures being implemented on six of those occasions. She had almost been assaulted in the parking garage just two weeks earlier.

 The patient, a thirty-four-year-old woman named Carole Rogers was admitted with bite wounds to her face and deep scratches to her neck and arms, came through surgery well enough. Although it will take a gifted plastic surgeon *to* handle the facial reconstruction, she was sleeping albeit fitfully. Erin noted that she had an elevated temperature and a lower than a normal pulse ox level. She noted such in the charts, and called the attending physician. The information that the monitors were telling here made her get a crash cart ready. In the few minutes that passed, the patient's temperature shot up another two degrees into the danger level at one hundred-five degrees and exhibited signs of respiratory distress, as well as a change in responsiveness. The monitors showed *VTac**; Code was called, and a whirl of activity was suddenly surrounding the patient. The attending physicians gave orders for additional blood work and started the patient on broad-spectrum antibiotics. Erin turned to the doctor to ask a question. At that moment, while Millie another nurse, was drawing blood, the patient started to have convulsions. Millie yelped due to a needle stick, sure enough a droplet of blood could be seen through her glove. Orderlies assisted restraining the patient while Millie withdrew. The patient started to crash, but the team, consummate professionals all, into bated and brought her back to stable condition. The patient had slipped into a coma. The prognosis was not good. Down in the ED* two other passengers from the

Lufthansa flight came in with complaints of flue like symptoms as well as inflammation and puss oozing from the scratches they received on the flight. At New York Hospital Queens, Alison Genoa, the flight attendant that was bitten on the arm, was fighting for her life at the same time; her symptoms were identical to the patient at Presbyterian.

At the Peoples Republic of China's consulate on Twelveth Avenue in Manhattan, Changming Tao, the eldest son of the ambassador, returned home, after a harrowing flight. His father was quite anxious due to the breaking news coverage; his concerns were assuaged when his son called from the car. He shouldered his carry on and entered the consulate proper leaving his other bags to be brought in by another.

 His father embraced him and took note of his son's sallow complexion and runny nose, enough so that he commented upon it. Tao said it was nothing, that he was coming down with a cold or something and dismissed his father's concerns away. The ambassador, not one to be dismissed thought his son's behavior odd. He was not as respectful as he should have been, almost brazen, so he summoned his personal physician, an eastern medicine practitioner and asked him to look in on his son.

Tao was feeling extremely run down. When he got to his rooms, he dropped his gear on the floor, collapsed onto his bed, and crawled under his blanket to fight off the chills that he was suffering. He fell asleep quickly and began having terrifying dreams.

 He was glad to be awakened from his terrors by the doctor who knocked rather heavily upon his door. His first thought was to attack his victim and eat, but he regained his composure and remembered where he was. The doctor came in with tea and an assortment of herbs and unguents on a tray. "Your father has concerns for you… he bade me to come and put you right again." Setting down the tray the doctor started to examine Tao as much by touch as by sight. He asked of him many questions that to western eyes would seem a little absurd, such is how the two types of medicine differ. The doctor lit some incense, mixed some of his components into the tea, and had Tao drink it all. "There is much that is not right in you, but this tea will help and the incense should help you have calmer sleep," said the doctor as he gathered his things and exited. Tao's thoughts were a little confused; he was beginning to feel separation from himself, almost a sense of slipping away. He assumed it was the effect of the tea acting quickly upon his exhausted body.

A couple of hours later, the ambassador stopped by to check on his son and found him unresponsive and bathed in sweat, shivering so badly that the bed itself was shaking. Without any thought, he moved to his son's side, put his hands on both sides of his son's face and began to shake him while he called, "Son, son wake up!"

Tao's eyes opened but did not seem to recognize his father; he turned his face and bit his father's hand as he reached out to claw at his father's hands. Suddenly, he came to his senses, and in a weak voice made apologies to his father, groaned then passed from consciousness again. The ambassador, in the grips of fear that only a parent with a sick child could know left the room calling for the doctor again and went to make arrangements to get his son the medical attention he needed. Changming Tao never regained consciousness again, in fact, as a living being he never got out of that bed again; however, the body did rise and when the doctor entered the room again to check on his patient, he was fallen upon by the zombie who was Changming Tao.

Screams shattered the calm of the consulate living quarters. Security members responded to the scene swiftly and found Tao covered in the doctor's blood, chewing upon the doctor's forearm that was no longer attached to the doctor. Not knowing how to react, the security members followed their training and tackled the zombie and secured its limbs with zip ties since it didn't seem to respond to pain, and kept attempting to bite them, they each removed their belts, one was wound up and forced into the creature's mouth while the other was secured around its head effectively gagging the monster. The zombie Tao never ceased attempting to free itself, straining at its bonds and trying to bite through the thick leather belts. The security officers were joined by others, and so they had the opportunity to address the cuts and scrapes, they received trying to restrain the ambassador's son.

The ambassador himself had a lot on his plate with an emergency session being called at the UN due to the nuclear incident in Iran, and now this shameful event in his own house, not understanding the insanity that gripped his son. He was aware that the political climate in China would not accept knowledge of this incident to escape the consulate's walls; he was forced to forget he had a son named Tao and made the sacrifice of having him returned to Beijing in secret and under guard. He needed to calm his mind; he wasn't due at the UN for a few of hours yet so he changed the dressing on his hand and then sought out the tranquility of his study to pass the time in meditation.

7

Back in Iran, over the dunes the shambling of the undead went unnoticed. Small villages and towns lie unsuspectingly in the path of destruction. The few swiftly becoming many as the zombies continued their quest for flesh and blood. The winds blowing across the dessert carrying the scent of prey to the horde, they moved towards the unsuspecting communities in eerie silence, that is until they get closer and the moans of the undead predators disrupt the silence. The virus gained better control of motor skills as more of the chains develop. The movements of these older zombies, although not as quick or dexterous as when they were living, were evident; the fresher ones shuffled along in their wake. Soon larger towns will fall to the growing horde, and still no one is aware of the coming apocalypse.

In Moscow, within the RAS, the earliest mutation is working its way through the systems of those whom were exposed to the virus via flea bites. These carriers, unknowing of the death housed within their blood went about their normal lives. The kisses shared by lovers claim more victims. The visits to the brothels claimed even more. One could play six degrees of separation, with each person coming into contact with friends and neighbors, a shared drink; a taste of another's food is enough for this virus to gain access to another host. As the days passed with the virus replicating, the first of the victims began to fall, slipping into death only to return as monsters. It was then that the scientists took note that all the victims had Tunguska in common. Quarantines were put into place. However, it already slipped beyond the net. The second mutation happened here too; the same vectors exist here as in New York, it only took fourteen days to turn Moscow into a city of walking cadavers the virus spread out faster than the news of it; town after town, city after city, the virus traveled in hosts by plane, boat and train to different cities and nations. The deceased were walking on five continents within thirty days of Dr. Romero's death.

8

Carole Rogers crashed three more times over the next two hours. The medical staff at Presbyterian were neither able to arrest the fever, nor were they able to identify what was causing the infection. The blood work was unable to yield any cultures; the hematologist was able to find the chains of the virus but had never seen anything remotely like it before. The fact that there appeared to be very little brain activity led them to believe that the fever, left unchecked for so long, had left the patient in a persistent vegetative state, with the body failing.

Everyone knew the outcome, and they all felt impotent to stop it. Erin finally took her break begrudgingly and when she returned was informed by the attending that Carole Rogers had died, and her body was being taken to the morgue for a post mortem. She quickly caught up with the orderlies doing the transfer and rode the elevator with them. The M.E. was waiting for them at the elevator bank; he wanted to get started right away since there was such a mystery afoot.

As the body was moved into the room and transferred to the examiner's table, the M.E.* (medical examiner) turned on the voice recorder and began giving the patient summary as he gowned and gloved himself. After the cursory inspection of the body, he began his incision of the torso, Erin was turning away to return to the nurse's station, when Carole Rogers suddenly sat up and grabbed at the ME while opening her mouth and releasing a spine-tingling groan that would haunt them both for the rest of their days. The corpse flopped to the floor as it started to rise, giving them both a chance to escape. Erin ran as fast as she could straight up the stairs and out of the Hospital, leaving her clothes behind.

She just knew she had to get out of there while she still could. She got to the W Hotel as fast as the cab could get her there. She walked into the lobby as the doorman opened the door with a smile; she barely noticed as she blew right by him headed for the elevator. The wait seemed interminably long but when it arrived, she took out her key and rode the car to the penthouse where she lived with her husband Liam, the hotel's General Manager.

She texted him with a nine-one-one as soon as she got into her home and locked the door. Liam was in a meeting, but seeing the nine-one-one and knowing that Erin's shift wasn't due to end for another three hours, he asked his AGM to take over the meeting and went upstairs. He tried to open the door, but the privacy lock was engaged so he called through the three-inch gap for Erin to come open the door. She rushed to the door to let him in, fear written as plain as day across her features. A slight woman to begin with, the fear made her look childlike. As soon as Liam entered, she slammed the door, double locked it, and began to sob uncontrollably. Liam's first thought was sexual assault; he didn't like her working at the hospital. She had escaped a couple of sticky situations already, but as she was able to get a few words out between sobs, he realized it was something entirely different. He just hugged her close and tried to calm her down.

Twenty minutes and a glass of brandy later, she began to regain control of herself enough to relate the events of the day. Once she started, she told the story in quick concise points, a carryover from her job as a nurse. She began with Carole Rogers' arrival at the hospital listing the injuries she had; she followed with the complications and the symptoms, and then moved onto her death. Liam assumed the age of the woman, and the brutality of the assault might have been the source of his wife's disquiet, but Erin continued with the trip to the morgue and then the reanimation. She eyed him suspiciously to see if he believed what she had a hard time believing with her rational mind, but knew deep inside herself with sort of a sixth sense was gospel. Liam took a deep breath to buy some-time before responding, but she was looking for that. She insisted that it was true; she repeated the whole series of events over again; she desperately needed him to believe her. He wanted to believe her, he could see her need as clearly as her fear, but what she was saying required complete suspension of disbelief. His wife's need won out over his rational mind; he was able to suppress enough of his skepticism to satisfy his wife. He told her that she should go spend some time with his folk's upstate, where she would be safe. She needed some time to decompress; he said he would join her there in a day two at the maximum. To convince her, he invoked the name of her contact with the EAP (employee assistance program), who has been trying to get her to take some time off, afraid she would burn out from the pressures of working in a city hospital ED.

9

In another borough, at another hospital, Alison Genoa met with the same fate as Carole Rogers: the fever, the crashes, the death, followed by reanimation. However, Alison managed to catch hold of some victims to eat along the way, the first being a police suspect whom had both hands cuffed to a Gurney, not only did she take a bite out of crime but one out of the suspect's forearm. The second being the orderly tasked with taking said suspect to radiology, and lastly, the arresting officer, who then pulled his firearm and shot the creature in the head. Rational excuses were sought in both hospitals, but over the next day and a half more passengers from Lufthansa's ill-fated flight started to turn up with symptoms that followed the same progression. Some of the Russian fleas found their way onto New York rats and the virus spread like wildfire through numerous rat colonies. The bedbugs in the city also contributed to the viral transfer, as in the original virus this one shares the ability to alter the behavioral patterns of its host organism.

The bureaucracy held true to form, in that each hospital was unaware of the identical plight shared by the other. Many of the earliest victims were misdiagnosed and sent away having been told it was the flu. Some, while in fever delirium, lashed out and bit or scratched others within reach. There was little accurate news related to this in the headlines or on the box, just status quo in ole New York, just a slight up-tick in violence, but it was getting warmer and as the heat rises the tempers follow. Violence between vagrant folks didn't sell papers, nor did stories of homeless with altered cognitive states, after all if they didn't have altered mental states most of them would not be homeless. Amusingly enough, the ones who were closest to getting to the story were the tabloids that were following up on a body snatcher story. It has been reported that on numerous occasions lately the police have been called about bodies: some torn apart, some merely dead. However, when the police arrive there are no bodies to be found; Notably, the body of a passenger on that Lufthansa flight was stolen from a hospital morgue. It seems the consensus was that there is a ring of black market organ thieves working in the boroughs. Besides the big news of the day in the main stream media, was the nuclear explosion in the Middle East, along with the radiation sickness that was spreading throughout the region. Amazingly enough, they still had yet to notice that the radiation was following the wind, but the reports were that the sickness was moving against the wind. Things were about to change.

 Police Officer Juan Ramirez of the ninth precinct while walking his beat in Alphabet City, Third Street and Avenue B, heard sounds of a conflict in an alley way; he radioed in and went to investigate. He heard a terrifying scream, and a number of haunting groans. The hairs on his neck stood up; he drew his pistol and flashlight and crept closer. His eyes moving back and forth in constant surveillance, he slowly made his way towards the scream he heard.

Keeping close to the building on his right, he quietly approached the dumpster that could easily hide an assailant, all his senses at their highest sensitivity, moving carefully forward. When he got as close as he dared, he paused for a three count, drew in a deep breath, then he sprang across the alley flashing his light on the other side of the dumpster. He found no assailants. What he did find were the remains of a victim who appeared to be torn apart, with a piece or two missing. He fought hard to keep his gorge down; he then called in what he found.

 In Central Park, a jogger was accosted by a group of vagrants who appeared homeless, the jogger said that the group appeared to be quite drunk by the lack of coordination in their movement and the lack of any intelligible speech. There were nine-one-one calls coming in from all over: most of the domestic disturbance variety, along with quite a few attempted assaults.

It was truly amazing how the rise in violence did not draw more attention; perhaps it is true that the unwashed masses became invisible to most people. There were more reports of bodies being found whole or in pieces at multiple locations between Manhattan and Queens. Over the next couple of days the number of these violent incidences grew at a near geometric progression.

10

Kyle MacGregor and his son Patrick who was home on leave from the Navy where he was stationed on the Ronald Regan, were just arriving at Madison Square Garden in time to see the Islanders play the Rangers in the Stanley Cup playoffs, and as fortune would have it, it turned out to be stick night... the first five hundred ticket holders were given hockey sticks to commemorate the event. To New York Hockey fans this was even more important than the actual cup as this is a rivalry of epic proportions.

After the game, they were going to hook up with Duncan and Liam for drinks at the Molly Wee pub, as this was Duncan's last day working at FIT, the fashion institute of technology. Hell it was his last day working period; God Bless the Mega Millions. They had ridden the railroad in from Long Island where the three brothers grew up and still lived; Kyle boring his son with details about the railroad, "...this block house this... that head quarters that...the logic controllers that work the pneumatic switches..." Patrick humored his father with feigned interest, owing to the fact that his father worked hard all his life to provide for his family so that his wife could stay home for the kids. "...I spent the first twelve years of my career at Jamaica, but these last thirteen are here at Penn. Signal men have to know the tracks better than anyone every tunnel, every junction, every switch, every signal. It's an entirely different world down here, more than one body has been disposed of down here."

Pat went to their seats while Kyle stops at the concession stand for four beers and then joins his son eager for the start of the game. They were in enemy territory, and they knew it but they proudly wore their Islander jerseys. The Ranger fans would be eager to give them some shit for entering their hallowed halls in those colors, besides that was half the fun of a local rivalry.

Kyle touched base with both of his brothers on his cell phone to confirm the post game festivities. He first got a hold of Liam, "So Pat and I are at the game. We should get to the pub around ten-thirty PM; Duncan should be getting there right around the same time."

Liam paused before speaking. Kyle figured he was going to beg off again, just like last time and the time before that, but then he started to speak, " I am real worried about my wife; I need to talk to you guys I think she is on the verge of a mental breakdown; she has had a real tough go at work for the past couple months and, well, we have been trying to get pregnant and well still not happening, and she is afraid to go to the OBGYN and find out she can't conceive, but she might well be losing it, she says she saw a corpse get up off a morgue slab and try to attack her and a doctor. I just don't know anymore. I sent her to stay with Mom and Dad for a few days; I was supposed to join her today, but I'll be going up tomorrow after work. I think that Dunk's offer may be just the answer, you know let her be a home maker and if the kids don't come we can always adopt. Well, I'll see to you guys later at Molly Wee's. That's on thirtieth and Eighth?"

"There abouts" said Kyle "See you then" and then disconnected the call.

Three blocks away, Duncan punched in for the last time on the basement level of 'A' building, nigh on dancing down the hall with a jaunty tune whistling out of his mouth. He had given serious thought to just blowing off his last day, but he could hear the voice of his father in his head talking about ethics, not to mention that he did have some personal effects in his locker that he wanted to bring home, plus he did have to turn in his keys, radio, I.D. badge, and there were the guys to say good bye too. A couple of them had become pretty good friends over the years. He had no illusions though, things had changed when he had hit the lotto. Sure there would be calls from time to time maybe a get together or two, but let's face it the thing that they shared in common, the job, was gone. He thought about asking a couple of the guys if there were some business that they wanted to go into thinking he could be a silent partner and provide the capital. He figured he would have to broach that subject delicately.

 As he walked passed Eric something or other, a security guard, he gave a sort of mock salute as he walked by. He noticed that Eric didn't look well; he seemed awfully pale. His blue uniform shirt was sweat stained, and his breathing seemed labored. Duncan was about to stop and ask if he was alright when Eric sat down on his stool, gave him a weak but genuine smile, and waved him by saying, "last day mister Duncan?"

"Sure is Eric eight more hours, and I am gone. Hey, good luck, Are you sure you're all right?"

"I'll be fine just a little under the weather is all. I'll be fine." Duncan continued on his way to 'D' building basement, where he unlocked the door to the engine room and descended the stairs.

Breezing into the control room, he nodded to the guys, Pete, Leneau, George, Henry, and Don. "Where is Greg?" he asked.

"He is up in medical. Get this, he got bit by a student" laughed George.

"You've got to be shitting me, was he… you know doing something he shouldn't have been? You guys are going to be awful shorthanded if he gets canned" said Duncan.

"No, no, nothing like that… he said he was out behind Charlie building looking for a chair to bring down to the engine room, and well, some kid came out of nowhere and attacked him and bit him on the arm. The guard came down out of the cage and grabbed the kid… I think the guard got bit too, for some reason, anyway they threw the kid out of the gate and shut it right away … the kid got picked up by the cops just standing at the gate… the cops told him to get on the ground, and the kid didn't even turn around… then I heard that when one of the cops tried to grab the kid, he spun around and growled at the cop…yes growled… and tried to attack the cop. The cop gave him a taste of his baton and took him away. Kid had to be on some fucking drugs to pull that shit, but anyhow Greg is at the infirmary. He'll be down soon."

"No matter," matter" said Duncan, "Listen guys, I was thinking that since this is my last day and all, that I would order in a whole spread from Brother Jimmy's BBQ. We can clear a space on the work bench and set it up buffet style, and if you guys want to join my brothers and me at Molly Wee's after work I'm buying. I bribed the chief with a catered lunch so that we wouldn't have any P.M.s today, I told him I wanted to hook you guys up and all. He was all for it."

Free food would not be turned down by these guys "Too bad you couldn't have gotten him to let us have beers today too" laughed Henry, until he noticed he was scheduled to be up in Alumni Hall this shift.

"Hey Henry, just record your readings and come back down, then do your next readings two hours later."

"I'll come down around 6PM for a while then I'll go back up. I don't want any of these supervisors busting my balls if they come down but thanks Duncan. It's bad enough that they took away the television. I don't need a write up to go along with the rest in my file, but that's really nice of you." The rest of the crew agreed.

Duncan called the restaurant and placed the order; he went up to the lobby and out of the doors with the idea of grabbing a cup of coffee before he has to go and pick up the food. He heard sirens wailing, in the distance, but thought nothing of it. This was New York after all; he crossed the street to the Chinese Bodega and tried to open the door but found it locked, the lights inside were still burning, and he could see people within. A man popped up from behind the counter, holding a sawed-off shotgun and shouted, "Go away!" in heavily accented English. Duncan didn't have to be told twice. He retreated back across the street and reached for his cell phone but realized he had left it down in the engine room. As he was walking back to 'D' building, he noticed a distinct lack of traffic; the streets were almost deserted apart from a couple of homeless guys shuffling their way up the street in his direction. He was not in the mood to deal with pan handlers; a chill raced up his spine like someone just walked over his grave. He quickened his pace and went back into the lobby and then down the stairs. He wasn't sure what it was that was driving him. He just knew with a sixth sense that he needed to get out of there.

Back at the Garden, Kyle and Pat were enjoying the first period of the game, while down below in the mechanical spaces a few of the walking dead were trying to find sustenance. By the loading dock area, a larger group was massing drawn by the sheer number of people in the Garden and at Penn.

There were a few of the creatures who managed to get onto some subway cars for some canned meat. The operators of 911 and the cities 311 were inundated with calls. The television and cable news was finally catching hold of the story. Regular programming was being interrupted with breaking news from the UN. The Ambassador from China collapsed on the UN floor. When the paramedics arrived and attempted to resuscitate him, the Ambassador rose and attacked them biting through one of the EMT's throats. There was pandemonium everywhere.

11

In Washington, the President sat behind his desk in the oval office, staffers rushing in and out with files and reports. "How bad is it, can we spin it?" he asked the Chairman of the Joint Chiefs. The Chairman shook his head in disgust, turned and walked out.

The Mayor's office was being barraged with reports of violence, a wave of sickness from hospitals and urgent care facilities city-wide, fires, and rioting in the streets. The Mayor had few options open to him. His first action was to enact the emergency alert system; he then called Albany to ask for National Guard support. He then spoke with the Port Authority and had them close off the city until order could be restored.

On New York 1 news, they were showing the same footage over and over: near Central Park, a wide-angle shot of a large group numbering around one hundred people spasmodically walking, shuffling towards the camera, the angle begins to narrow, and you can see bloody carnage among the shambling group; the audio picking up haunting groans from a few of them. It seems to spread quickly amongst the group.

The closer they get to the camera the more apparent it gets that these people are not what they seem. A SWAT Bus pulls up near the camera crew, and out flows a team decked out in riot gear. They quickly assemble themselves into a line to repel the crowd. The siren's howling does little to mask the cacophony of haunting moans. Fear is etched upon the visage of the reporter in front of the camera, but to her credit (or stupidity), she holds her ground as the mass closes the distance. You can hear more sirens coming closer, but the reporter holds firm giving her play by play of the "riot."

When the leading edge of the group gets within melee range, the riot team, behind their poly carbonate shields, begins to batter the monsters with batons and mace with little effect. In seconds, the team is swarmed and swallowed. The reporter is frozen with fear as the first monster reaches for her. The camera drops to the ground as the cameraman's flight response kicks in. The picture rotates ninety degrees, and just as it stops shaking from the impact you can see the reporter's fate is the same as the SWAT team. The screams begin and stop quite suddenly. Then the segment is repeated, all the while the voice of the anchorman is reporting that violence like this is to be found all over the city.

Halfway through the second period, the Islanders lead the Rangers by a score of four to one. Avery, the all too controversial Ranger, cleared the puck from the Rangers zone resulting in an icing call, the players skate around and come back to the Rangers end of the ice and get set for a face off; the puck is dropped, and the players scramble to gain control…and then there is a loud crash as the Zamboni breaks through the boards, steering onto the ice. The driver screaming and searching behind him, as blood sprays from his missing forearm. The players scramble to get out of the way of the big ice resurfacing vehicle, as it rips the goal right off its mooring pegs. One of the quicker thinking players paced the vehicle, he then leaped onboard to try to bring the out of control vehicle to a stop before anyone else got hurt. The driver slumped over and fell to the ice where his escaping blood stopped spurting and more or less puddled. The Linesman skated over to the fallen man in an attempt to render first aid, suspecting that it was already too late. At the same time, a group of the walking dead made their way out onto the ice. Their movement on firm ground was less than graceful, on ice it was almost comical, was it not for the signs of carnage that they each possessed; some with gaping wounds on their faces and necks, others dragging behind them their own entrails leaving a gory streak in contrast to the white ice of the rink.

There were screams from many of the spectators, others stared in disbelief. One of the Islanders noticed a zombie tearing meat from the Zamboni drivers missing appendage with its mouth; the player skated at full speed towards the offending monster and cross checked it at throat level. The monster flew into the boards with a resounding crash, dropping the limb as it fell to the ice. Immediately, it attempted to rise, to no avail as it could gain no purchase. It lacked the necessary dexterity to regain its feet, so it merely crawled in the direction of its antagonist. The player enraged at what he was witnessed to, slashed at the creatures head with his stick, striking it repeatedly until the skull fractured causing enough brain damage to halt the creature. A linesman in a terrified and desperate attempt to evade the carnage skated into the outstretched talon like hands of a zombie while his attention was on others that were behind him. Thankfully, the exquisite pain he experienced was short-lived as more zombies tore him asunder. Other players joined in the action. They were no longer opponents; they were stick wielding warriors on skates. They clearly had the advantage on this terrain, and they used it to their advantage.

Panic began to spread like flood waters amongst the fans; they began to stampede the exits, many falling and being trampled under the feet of those behind them. They did not know that there were many more of the zombies trying to get in from the very egresses they sought. They were met by frightful teeth and tearing claw like hands, seeking to rend and tear their fragile bodies. The mass exodus was stopped; countless people were crushed between those fleeing from both directions. Kyle and Patrick shoved and shouldered their way downward towards the ice, figuring to escape by the tunnels the teams use to get to their dressing rooms. They were joined by a few others of like mind but precious few joined them in their escape.

Several of the players, emboldened by the ease with which they slaughtered the zombies on the ice, climbed the glass and sought to stem the tide of the zombies now flooding into the arena, they knew that with their equipment on and with the sticks that they carried, they could withstand a lot and could perchance save the lives of many of their frightened fans. However, the advantage they had on the ice was muted by being on firm ground wearing their skates, but those too could be used as weapons, so long as they were careful.

Fans parted before the rescuing players like the Red Sea before Moses. The hockey sticks gave the players an edge in combat with their undead foes, keeping them at a safer distance and not allowing the creatures to get a hold of them. That is until the sticks began to break, after all they were not designed to withstand this type of abuse, but the players were holding out fairly well buying much-needed time for the spectators and fans, but the holding action was only that, a holding action. It would be short lived unless there were rescuers coming from without.

Kyle dropped over the edge into the tunnel and waited to be joined by his son. Patrick looked at the players and saw first one then another fall to the zombies attack. He turned away after seeing one of his heroes fall beneath a horde of the ravenous creatures, dropped his stick down to his father and climbed over the rail to drop beside his dad.

Kyle, the outdoors man of the family, had been taking his sons hunting and camping their whole lives; he was used to stalking his prey, being stalked was a bit different but the same rules applied. Move with caution, avoid any unnecessary noise, and keep your eyes moving. Peripheral vision was far more sensitive to noticing movement than looking straight ahead. He had been an eagle scout as had his two brothers and the sons. Kyle learned the skills he needed from his own father, who was far more than just your run-of-the-mill scoutmaster; he had been in the *Special Forces* during the Korean War; he used scouting to make peace with his own soul. Thus, all three of the brothers went on *to* become eagle scouts, creating the family tradition. Here in the city, Kyle felt at a loss. Patrick, on the other hand, wanted to be a US Navy SEAL since childhood; he had made it through *BUDs** well enough but sustained a badly broken leg halfway through SeAL training. He had a natural instinct for close quarter combat, as well as urban fighting.

Pat took the lead, and Kyle followed at an interval. The others in their group just ran by seeking to put as much distance between them and the monsters as possible. They obviously were not thinking that there could be more of those creatures down here. Kyle and Patrick made their way slowly and steadily. They got to the relative safety of the Islander dressing room, they then barricaded the door, and sought telephone contact with the outside world: specifically, his brothers and the families.

12

On Long Island, Katie's cell phone rings. She answers the call without looking at the number on the caller ID; it is a call from her sister like friend Laura. Laura says, "Put on the Television right now!" the stress level in her voice was off of the charts.

"What channel, and why?" Katie asks in reply. She reaches down for the remote control and turns on the TV. Laura's voice was shaking so badly that it would require too much concentration to understand, but three seconds later she knew. The broadcast that had been shown on NY1 was now being broadcast on every channel, with a headline banner that reads "New York isolated, is it another nine-eleven?" She tells Laura she'll call her back. She then presses the speed dial for her Husband Duncan's cell phone, and waits impatiently for an answer. It rang once, then twice, then three times. She was about to disconnect and redial when she heard her husband's voice, and she suddenly released her breath, breath that she wasn't even aware that she was holding. "Are you alright?" she asked, nearly yelling into the phone.

"Of course, I am fine. What's the matter Honeybaby?" he replied.

"Turn on the TV to NY1... New York City is under some sort of attack or something; its cut off; the bridges and tunnels are closed no one in or out, there are riots, don't you know?"

"Slow down babe... what are you talking about... we don't have TV down here... what exactly is going on?" The calm of her husband's voice reassured her enough so that she could relate what she had been seeing on the television. He now knew what was tickling his subconscious, giving him that ominous feeling earlier, that still had yet to disappear. He asked his wife to hold on for a second and told Peter to pull up the news on the internet. "Listen Pete, my wife said there has been some sort of attack on the city. We should have the fucking TV, but look, pull up the net. We should be able to get some information on what's going on."

Peter did as he was asked. "Listen Honey, I am safe here, don't you worry. I am going to call my brothers; I am supposed to meet up with them three blocks from here after work. Let me make sure they are safe. Maybe I can get them here to me, where we can figure out how to get home. I will call you back in a few minutes, don't worry...I love you honey baby... don't worry. I will call you back."

He disconnected the call just as Greg came back into the engine room. Pete was just pulling up his home page and was seeing for the first time what was going on outside, "Holy Shit!"... It's amazing how much those two words can embody. The streaming video showed scenes from all over the city, of the anarchy and mayhem that gripped the city.

The phone rang again. This time the ringer told it was from an in house line. Leneau answered. It was from security at the central station directing us to switch our radios to channel two; there has been a state of emergency declared, and all buildings were being locked down. Duncan hit the speed dial for Liam's cell. Liam was his kid brother. He had always been protective of him; thankfully, he picked up on the first ring. He was already at Molly Wee's behind locked doors, and was safe, for the moment, with a few other patrons. They had the TVs on, so he was more aware of what was going on than his brother. "Liam do you think you can get over here. It's only three blocks. I can meet you in 'A' lobby, and then we can figure out how to hook up with Kyle and Pat?" There was a pause of maybe three seconds, "What's wrong Liam? What has happened to Kyle and Patrick?" There was another pause. He knew the call hadn't been dropped as he could hear the television in the background.

"They were at the Garden... I spoke with Kyle a while ago. I've been trying to call him, and it keeps going to voice mail. There was an attack at the Garden. Duncan there are Hummers racing by going to the Garden...Err...Penn maybe... they might be caught up in it."

Duncan processed that information for a second or two. "Liam..." no response, "Liam!" he said more forcefully into the phone, "Yeah, I am still here." Duncan released his breath, "Can you get to FIT safely?"

"I think so, the mob has passed by here, and I don't see anyone approaching, yeah… I think I can make it."

"Listen to me little brother, listen carefully… in ten minutes, I want you to run as fast as you can to get here. Stay away from anyone; tie a cloth over your mouth and nose; get here as fast as you can, I will be waiting for you inside the lobby doors. I will let you in, and then we can worry about the rest of it. Just get here! Be careful little brother, remember 10 minutes."

"Will do" was Liam's reply. Duncan was glad to hear steel in his brother's response; he hung up the phone.

While Duncan was talking to his brother; Greg sat down heavily in his chair. He looked like a shadow of his normal self. "I was going to go home but with everything going on here…," said Greg to Leneau, who replied, "Man you don't look well, you look pale, and you're sweating like a pig. Go take some Advil or something." Greg normally stood around six foot and was in pretty good shape for a forty-five year old guy, now to look at him, you would not think him the same person.

Making an attempt at levity, Pete said, "Hey, there isn't any light duty here without a doctor's note. You gotta do your own rounds; I'm not doing them for you" This banter had been going on since Peter had injured his shoulder on the job and had been given the watch for almost three weeks. The Joke missed the mark, and Greg stood to go on his rounds, albeit a might shakily.

"Go lay down in the back, rounds are suspended. We are on standby due to the emergency declared," said Leneau. Greg smiled weakly and headed for the lower locker room to lie down for a while.

Seeing Duncan no longer on the phone Pete, asked him if he needed a hand, you know maybe to watch his back. Duncan gladly accepted the offer of assistance. He grabbed two respirator masks, donning one and tossing the other to Pete. He then put on his welding jacket and gauntlets, and grabbed a ball-peen hammer. Pete did the same. Duncan looked at his watch. He had seven minutes to get to the door to meet his brother, absent mindedly on his way he grabbed a fiberglass handled floor scraper leaning against the railing. As he rushed up the stairs, remembering he promised his wife, he would call her back, he dislodged the mask and called her as they made their way through the basement levels of the buildings to the 'A' lobby. "Honey, Liam is a couple blocks away and coming to me here. We are not sure what Kyle and Patrick's conditions are, but when we get through to them; we will figure out how to get home. I will keep in touch, but I have to go now. Liam should be here any second, and I have to unlock the doors to let him in." She said she loved him, and to be sure he called her back. He agreed and then cut the call. Replacing the mask, he went up the stairs to the lobby and waited at the door for his brother. He didn't have anything to say to his partner; he didn't have to. He just took comfort in knowing that someone he trusted was there to back him up.

Katie stood there motionless, holding the phone in her hand, staring at it as if by will alone she could make it ring with her husband on the line. She heard Sean's car pull up, she could tell by the throaty sound of the exhaust of his vintage cougar, a car she didn't like her son having. Duncan had bought the car from their neighbor two years ago, and he and Sean had rebuilt the motor and restored the car, not to stock, but you couldn't tell that from the outside.

Sean had been at practice; his traveling hockey team was in the playoffs. Sean had already secured his athletic scholarship to Duke, and scouts from the NHL were sniffing around the boy. Sean rushed into the house, "The coach called practice early. The police came by and told everyone to get home, a curfew was being declared." She wondered how he didn't hear the news on the radio, but then she remembered he would have had his iPod playing through his stereo.

He noticed his mother standing there, looking down at the phone in her hand. Then he saw the news on the plasma hanging over the fireplace. "Mom what is it? Is dad alright?" he asked anxiously, his voice rising a bit with his nervousness. To look at him, you would scarcely believe he was only seventeen years old and still in high school; he had a powerful build, standing a hair under six foot three and weighing two-forty. He had his father's strong jaw and nose, but had the soulful eyes of his mother.

"Dad is OK. He is with Uncle Liam. They are at the college, and they are trying to make contact with your uncle Kyle and your cousin Pat."

Sean knew they had gone to the Islander game. He was green with envy; he couldn't go because of practice. The calmness of her words didn't jive with her body language. "What is going on mom? The cops said that there were attacks going on, even out here on the Island. They said to go home, lock the doors, and don't let anybody in. They said to button up everything, close the curtains and shut all unnecessary lights. What is going on?"

"I'm not sure Sean; I only just heard about it myself a little while ago, Auntie Laura called and told me something was up and to turn on the TV. Then I called and spoke to your dad, and then you came in." Together they closed the blinds, turned out the lights, and sat down on the couch transfixed by the news on the screen, her knuckles white from holding onto the phone so tightly.

Katie was not prone to panic; she was a "doer," always cool under pressure. She also knew that when the pressure built you were better off being busy, keeping your hands and mind occupied. She told her son to get his sisters together. When all three came into the living room, Katie gave them all tasks to do. The girls started to complain, but one look from Katie was all it took to silence them. She informed them that there was a crisis happening, and they had to be ready in case anything serious happened. She told Kristen first to clean the bathtubs, then to fill them up to the top with water. She had Kaitlyn go down and inventory the pantry and put together the camping gear. Sean, she had check that the windows around the house were all locked, then to go out the back door and make sure the gates were closed and secured. She busied herself in the Kitchen making preparations in case the power failed.

As busy as she kept herself, she couldn't stop wondering why Duncan hadn't called back yet. The phone rang only half a ring before she answered it, "Duncan?" She heard tears from the other end of the connection; it was her sister in law Pamela. She had seen the news about Madison Square Garden and was beside herself with worry over her child and husband. "Pam, I am sure they are alright. Duncan and Liam are right nearby; they will bring the home safe and sound, mark my words." She put as much conviction into her words as she could. "I just got off the phone with my Dad" said Pam, "he is still tightly plugged in with the police, even though he retired 1five years ago." There was a sound of a stifled sob, "His sources tell him that the news isn't telling us everything. He says that it's not some terrorist thing; He says that the riots and attacks are really Zombies, as in the walking dead. I believe him; watch the television footage closely." More sobs come over the line. Katie empathized with her, and wanted to cry herself.

She didn't know what to make of this new development, but her eyes went to the TV. There on the screen, plain as the day, she could see the torn bodies walking along, bodies that could not be alive. Bodies with limbs that had been torn off and other wounds that should have resulted in death, yet they continued to walk, to chase after the living. She could not believe she hadn't noticed it before; her mind was attempting to disbelieve it even now. Reality was too much. This can't happen, but slowly she began to accept the truth.

Pam said she had call waiting from a 212 number. Katie said she'd hang on. A minute later Pam flashed back, "They Are Safe!" the wave of relief washing through her and over the phone line was near ebullient. "They are in the Islanders dressing room. I will call you back!" She didn't wait for Katie's reply. She just clicked back to her missing family. Who could blame her, Katie thought? Now if only her own husband would call...

Nine minutes and fifty seconds after Liam spoke with his brother, he was preparing to make the run for his life. The bartender and other patrons had tried to talk him out of going, but there was no shaking his resolve. They told him if he left, he couldn't come back. Still he insisted on going. With a bandana tied, bank robber style, over his face, he stood waiting for the bartender to open the door, while one of the patrons stood close by wielding a baseball bat, ready for one of those freaks to try to get in. four...three...two...one, the door opened and he was out, running for all he was worth.

He was relatively calm, all things considered; running was one of the things he was good at. He ran marathons; a three block sprint was nothing. The street was somewhat clear, only a few shambelers on the sidewalks. He chose to run in the street. He was thinking he was home free until he saw a mass of stumbling bodies coming around the corner of Twenty-eigth street. He mentally reached down inside for everything he had. Putting the proverbial pedal to the metal, he ran all out steering subtly to the opposing side of the street. Subconsciously, his mind was doing the math on whether he would clear the group or not. He poured it on; the moans ripped right through him, awakening the same primal fear that forced the first humans to seek out the mastery of fire. Passing within inches of their reaching appendages and gnashing teeth, he made it passed and the distance opened. Rounding the final corner a little wide is what saved his life. Had he taken that last corner sharper, he would have run smack into a knot of the ghouls; as it was, they turned to follow the meal that had run past them. Another pack of zombies were homing in on the groans close at hand. Timing was going to be everything. He raced towards the sculpture and took the few steps to the left in two strides, knowing full well that if his brother wasn't at the door, he was certainly going to die.

Inside the vestibule, Duncan saw the groups' gathering. He hoped his brother would make it in time. The window of opportunity was closing rapidly. His peripheral vision picked up quick movement. He knew it was his brother. He turned the key on the crash bar and hefted the long-handled scraper, like it were a medieval pole arm, and burst through the door swinging. Pete remained inside to be sure they could get back in and to guard against any of them getting in while Duncan got his brother.

The group near the door turned towards the street; their attention was drawn by the morsel running towards them. They didn't know what hit them. The engineer burst through the door and began swinging the scrapper like a man possessed. The thing's steel edge cut some and battered others, opening enough space for his brother's passage. Hearing his brother make the door, he turned and raced inside past the waiting Peter, who secured the door quickly. Seeing his brother safe was a balm for his flagging spirit. "Come with us, I don't know how long the glass will hold. Let's get behind some steel. Liam followed Duncan and Pete away from the doors to the left, down the stairs to the basement level, and through a set of doors.

13

Making a right they ran down the hallway, and through more doors. A few twists and turns, another couple of doors and they were in 'D' building's basement; by the engine room door. Duncan unlocked this door, and then they were through descending the stairs to the engine room. Liam's breathing was hard and beleaguered. He could feel his blood pumping in his ears drowning out most other sound, so he didn't catch the names of his brother's co-workers who were down in the engine room as well.

Duncan pulled his brother over to the water fountain next to the sink; Liam drank greedily from it. Duncan's fellow engineers had liberated a plasma screen TV off a wall by the seminar rooms while Duncan was retrieving his brother, a couple of clever splices of coaxial cable later, and they were no longer cut off from the outside world.

Liam realized that his wife was not losing her mind. On the contrary, the horror story she had relayed to him had proven true. "Dunk… can I call Mom and Dad? I need to talk to Erin."

"Go ahead Liam, I'm going to call Katie from my cell; Dial nine for an outside line."

The engineers were all shocked at what was happening; the whole city was. Peter called his wife; they were separated but were trying to reconcile, Leneau and Henry both sought out semi-private places to call their loved ones, While Don monitored the news and the web; George made his way up to the stairs and took the elevator up to the roof. During times of duress and stress, George suffered from claustrophobia, and with the dead rising, this qualified as both.

Duncan found himself in the fire pump room at the base of the stairs and from there he called his wife. "Honeybaby… we are alright. I've got

Liam with me, and he is speaking to Erin right now. Is Sean home yet? We stole a TV, so we have access to the news, and it looks like it is beginning to happen on the Island too."

Katie set her husband's mind at ease. She told him that all three kids were safe and at home and how Sean's coach called practice early on account of the curfew.

"The police are saying we should remain inside... lock the doors and windows..."

"Sounds like a reasonable course of action, we just got called up as the HAZWOPER* team (HAZardous Waste /Operations /Emergency Response). Since that is the basis for any emergency contingency from the Feds on down. Anyhow, the FDNY contacted us and asked us to be in a holding pattern. The school is essentially in lock down, so we are safe here. I am going to try calling Pam, to see if she has heard from Kyle. Liam is scared beyond belief, and with what I saw when I let him in..."

Katie cut in, "I was on the phone with Pam before, and she said that she was on the other line with Kyle, and she'd call me back. She said they were safe, and that they were locked in the Islander dressing room."

Relief replaced the concern and fear Duncan had for his brother and nephew. "Do me a favor Honeybaby, send Kyle a text and have him call me on my cell. We need to figure out how to link up and get home. For now have Kaitlyn put that new computer of hers to work setting up some sort of chat link thing, maybe video chat or something. We all have these freakin smart phones, should be able to use them for this. Tell her to try Skype If we can set up a chat room or something at least we won't keep having to play tag. Furthermore, Babe, get the kids together and start the hurricane drill."

"Way ahead of you, husband of mine. I have both bathtubs full. We are inventorying the pantry, and we have the camping gear together. You should be as proud of these kids as I am. They are doing great, better than I am actually" her voice told of the strain she was under.

Duncan knew she was doing everything she could, and he needed to reassure her. "Baby doll you are awesome. We will get through this; everyone is safe. Let me go for now I have to dig my phone charger out, I want to make sure it's full, in case we lose power or anything. I love you, Babydoll, and I am proud of all of you." And with that he hung up, and began making preparations to get going.

As he turned to exit the fire pump room, he noticed two fire axes on the wall. He took them down, and with a smile, he walked back into the main engine room. He entered the control room just as Liam was hanging up with Erin. "Liam, come over here and help me gather up some gear. I want to have us prepared to go as soon as we can. Pam has been in touch with Kyle. They are safe behind locked doors in the Garden." They made their way over to Duncan's tool locker. He unlocked it and handed Liam a medium sized duffel bag. "Here, take these" he tossed his kid brother a couple of pairs of heavy gloves, a respirator, and a pair of safety goggles. He continued to rummage through his tools, most of which would be useless as survival gear. He grabbed his "wrecking bar" figuring that if he needed to break any locks or to spread the doors on a train, it may come in handy. He saw Geoff Dunn's locker next to his. Geoff had quit two weeks earlier, so he used the "wrecking bar" and popped the lock. From within he grabbed welding jacket and gauntlets, along with another radio and additional PPE* (personal protective equipment) He looked down at Liam's feet, "those shoes have gotta go bro" take a look in the locker room and see if you can find a pair of boots that will fit you, I'll write a check to whomever they belong to. While you're at it see if you can find better pants, those dress slacks will tear too easy"

Liam hesitated. Turning to his brother he asked, "Do you have a plan or something?"

Duncan's reply was curt and to the point, "Just do what I tell you, and after we hear from Kyle, then yes I might just have a plan. Now go!" he said rather forcefully, more forcefully than the situation warranted, but he wanted to establish, here and now, the fact that he was in command and that there was no point in questioning things. He was more than a little concerned, should this not be settled now, if there were hesitation later that they might not make it back to their families; that was a thought he didn't even want to entertain.

Apparently, Katie got through to Kyle, because an unfamiliar 212 number came through on Duncan's cell. He answered and recognized his older brother's voice immediately, even though it was being spoken just above a whisper. "Dunk... it's me and Pat... do you know what's going on?"

"Yeah Kyle, I know. Are you and Pat safe? What is your situation... is there a way for you two to get out of there?" Kyle's reply was lacking encouragement, but he said, for the moment, he and his son were safe, although they could hear the moans and groans of the zombies outside in the hallway. He told Duncan everything that he had witnessed during the attack. Duncan took it all in, "Okay sit tight; I am going to try to contact a buddy of mine who is an Engineer at the garden. Maybe he can figure a way out for you two that will keep you out of harm's way so that we can meet up. Text me if your situation changes, I'll get back to you."

Kyle and Patrick could not do much other than wait, so they began ransacking the locker room. Pat found a knapsack and began to fill it up with memorabilia. When Kyle stopped him saying, "In all likelihoods we are going to need to travel light, or we will get rescued and well how do you plan to explain all the shit you're swiping?" Pat felt a little silly, when he dumped the bag's contents on the floor, he noticed a bobble head doll of John Tavares in the pile. He stooped and picked that up and put it back in. Kyle, on the other hand, located the team's medical supplies; breaking into them was simple using his Leatherman, he had no idea what all the drugs were for, but he figured they could come in handy later. They cobbled together some semblance of "armor" by using some of the extraneous team gear and extra pads. They filled a few water bottles and settled into wait for Duncan to get back with them.

14

Jacob MacGregor walked over to his safe, with practiced ease spun the dial, right, left, right, turned the handle and opened the door. From within he pulled out the satchel that contained his Smith & Wesson .357 along with the box that held the cleaning solvents, oil, rags and such. It had been more than a decade since he had fired the weapon, but he kept it cleaned and oiled. He looked on the shelf and saw that he had plenty of boxes of ammunition. He had checked the gun cabinet in the hallway before coming into his "study," aka guest room. He was sure of the condition of his deer rifle and 12 gauge, as well as the number of rounds he had for each.

After cleaning his pistol, he set it down on a bench towel and retrieved his shoulder holster. He struggled to get it on with no success, took it off again and adjusted the buckles and straps. "Damn, I didn't realize how much weight I've gained since I had this on last" he said aloud to himself.

Like everyone else in the world he had all of his TVs on tuned to the varying news channels. He had his computer online monitoring news there too. He was aware of what was going on. He knew that his boys were in harm's way, but he had faith in them, and he believed with every ounce of his being that he would know if anything bad had befallen them. Three nights ago, he received a call from his youngest saying that his wife would be coming up to spend some time with them, as they didn't get to see them that often, his son said he would be joining her a day or so later, Jacob noted the strain in his son's voice, and asked him what was going on so Liam told him about the stresses she had been under and about the straw that broke the camel's back. Granted it had been close to fifty years since he left the Special Forces, but he had seen plenty of PTSDs* (Post-Traumatic Stress Disorders), they just didn't call it that back then. It was shell shock. His whole team had had it to one degree or another; that was why he had gone into scouting. Back in the mid 60's, he had fallen asleep on the couch one Saturday afternoon, his wife was out and he had just planned to rest his eyes. Marie came home from her father's house,(a prominent pediatrician) where she worked as a nurse/ receptionist. She knew Jacob was sleeping, so she tried to tip toe in. Jacob was on his feet, poised to attack and moving for a strike before his eyes were even open, her scream of fear was what brought him to his senses. Yes he sure knew a thing or two about PTSD. So when his daughter in law arrived, he watched for the signs. She was displaying compulsive behaviors; her moods seemed almost manic, unfamiliar noises had her jumping out of her skin. His wife Marie noticed these things too. They gave her some time and space, and then they just asked her about it. They aren't the type who subscribe to subterfuge, preferring the direct approach. Sure she was stressed out, that was clearly evident, but she presented everything clearly and coherently, and it had the ring of truth to it, so Jacob accepted it as truth, as unlikely as it was to be. He believed her, so it was no surprise that when he started to watch the news, he saw things for what they were even before the talking heads caught on. Now he was beefing up the defenses of his home.

They had bought this house and the surrounding lands a few years ago after they retired, the property abutted state lands and was on the Hudson River. The house had needed a lot of work, but Jacob had the skill set to whip it into shape, and it kept him busy as he made the adjustment into retirement.

Marie liked the area and when Jacob told her his plans of turning it into a family compound, so that the kids and grand kids would spend more time with them, she was sold. The property itself was a little less than ten acres in total, on a sheer hillside overlooking the Hudson. There was a stairway that descends the face to a moorage that can handle four vessels. There was barbwire fencing on three sides of the property cleverly concealed by the trees and shrubbery, although at the mouth of the drive, there was a gate resembling wood, made from a resin composite of some sort. From the front of the dwelling, it appeared to be cross between a modest cape and a ranch, with plenty of round river rock on the face and chimney. It's single story sat atop the crest of a hill that promised spectacular views of the river below. From the river, however you could see that most of the building was actually built into the hill itself. It boasted large windows, and the yard was terraced from the hill giving the effect of an amphitheater. On the upper level of the property, he expanded the garage and put in a backup generator system that ran on the same fuel oil as his furnace from a shared ten thousand-gallon tank. For cooking he had two large LP gas bottles. Several cords of wood were stacked neatly up top and down below.

The other out buildings, were fixed up as guest cottages, each of his children had their own. Plus within the house proper there were another three guest rooms 4 if you count the study. He had plenty of supplies in his garage to secure the windows in the front of the house and on its sides. The big windows in the back would not be much of a problem as they were thick tempered glass; the type of glass that you could hit with a sledge hammer and still not break. They were supposed to be the most energy efficient.

He loaded his Magnum, secured two-speed loaders into their pockets, then moved up the stairs and into the hallway where his gun cabinet sat, there he loaded his deer rifle and finally, the shotgun. He removed the choke and loaded it with deer slugs. If he had to fire it, there would be one hell of a kick, but whatever he hit would go down. He replaced the rifle after removing the trigger lock, something he never would have done before, and still wouldn't do if any of his younger grandchildren were in residence. Checking his holster once more with his right hand, he then picked up the shotgun in his left, and grabbed his keys in his right, he went out of the front door with one of his German Sheppards, a five-year-old male named Max. He turned and locked the door behind himself.

It is amazing how fast his Spec War training returned to him, noise discipline, granted that applied to hunting but this was different. He was moving as he was instructed by the sadists who ran the E&E*(escape and evasion) school: keep low to the ground, move, stop, listen, smell, and repeat. The grounds were lit bright as the day by the sodium lights he'd installed so keeping to the shadows was impossible. He trusted the dog's senses, and it was displaying normal behavior. He didn't find anything amiss. The sounds of nature were as they should be.

Within the house, Marie and her daughter in law were in the kitchen, Erin holding her phone waiting for Liam's call. He had sent her a text saying he was meeting up with his brothers and would come up afterwards or maybe in the morning. She was more than a little upset as she was expecting him this afternoon, but she understood, and then the news started to come in She was beside herself with worry; it was after nine and still no call, so she sent him a text asking him to call. Marie shared her concern, after all Liam was her baby, but she hadn't embraced the idea that there were zombies walking around and attacking people in mid-town Manhattan. There had to be some other, more rational, explanation. She was still worried, but there had to be something less 'supernatural' going on.

The waiting was beginning to wear on them both. Marie opened a bottle of white zinfandel and poured a glass for each of them. She wasn't looking to flee from stress into a bottle; On the contrary, she intended to use it as a mild sedative, just to take the edge down.

Jacob made a tour of the property, checking the barbed wire that surrounded it on its three sides. He made mental notes on areas that he would address in daylight, with the help of someone keeping lookout. He completed his circuit and ended at his garage, where he unlocked the door and loaded a few sheets of plywood on the back of the trailer that he had hooked up to his little John Deer lawn tractor. He threw in some tools and fasteners and quickly returned to his front door to unload. Then and only then did he remove his keys and unlock said door and bring his supplies inside. Discipline kept him alive during his time behind enemy lines in Korea; he hoped the same would hold true here for not only him but his charges as well. He had to think about them that way, rather than as his family. If he had to act or make tactical choices, if he thought of them as his family, then he might falter or hesitate, and then he would lose them all, so they became his charges, nothing more.

After shoring up the defenses as much as he could for now, he began coming up with other ideas and plans to keep them safe. It would be easy enough to electrify the barbed wire, and with a little effort, he could even re-enforce his gate. "Better to sweat now than to bleed later" he thought absently. "Wow, how many of those old sayings are going to pop into my head" Just because they are old, doesn't make them any less true; it's like clichés, cliches are clichés because they are true. They are seeds of wisdom passed down from generation to generation purely because they are valid and true. He hoped that his next thought would not be cliché?: "The only easy day was yesterday." He sighed and resumed drawing up plans.

Erin finally received a call from Liam. He informed her of the situation, and that they were safe. He did his best to assuage her concerns and fears. It didn't work, but he tried none the less. She had yelled at him for not coming when he should have. He endured her tirade; she was whimpering by the time they were through. Liam told them that Duncan was making preparations for escape. He had some ideas on how to avoid confrontations, and they were trying to contact Kyle and Pat to see if they could perhaps rescue them, that is if they were safe and indeed able to be rescued. They were under no illusions; things looked bleak. They would remain hopeful, but they had to face the possibilities. They decided that they would keep trying to make contact throughout the night, and if there was no success by six AM, they would make good their escape alone. Pam and Katie also got through to their in-laws. Jacob took their situational reports, and was relieved to hear that his son and grandson were safe, at least, for the moment. Being as he was so far removed from their area, he didn't offer any additional suggestions, but he would remain in the loop and offer counsel when it made sense.

After disconnecting with his brother, he scrolled through the contacts in his phone until he found the one he was looking for. He pressed the talk button, said a silent prayer, and listened as the phone began to ring.

15

David Bennett was sitting on the porch of his bay house, drinking an ice-cold beer. His boat was fueled. The rods were on board, plenty of bait and the other provisions for a day of fishing were in the fridge waiting to be transferred to the cooler in the morning. His bay house was on the end of a pier eight feet above the water at high tide. This was his retreat. Sure it had electricity and hot water, but no TV, no computer, and no land line phone. He felt his cell vibrate and debated not answering it but seeing the number of his buddy, he pressed the talk button.

"Dunk... what can I do you for?" he asked in a jovial tone that hinted he was on his third or fourth beer. "Dave where are you?" Duncan asked in an urgent tone "Have you seen the news or heard from anybody?"

The tone in Duncan's voice sobered him up immediately. "I'm out at the bay house. I'm going fishing in the morning. Dunk, what's wrong? What's going on?" Duncan filled him in and stressed over and over that this was not a joke. He told David about how his brother and nephew were trapped in the visitor's locker room in the garden. He asked him if there was any way to get to them or at least for them to escape to the street. David believed him because Duncan was not that good of a liar or actor, and the desperation in his voice proved it to him beyond any doubt.

Dave is one of the Local thirty engineers who run the chillers for the ice at the garden; they also maintain the sprinkler systems and other ancillary equipment. Dave knew just where his friend's family members were, even better, he knew how to get them out of there. Duncan told Dave that the Island wasn't safe, he told him that he was having both his, and his brother's wives and kids head down to his boat and to cast off and drop anchor a mile or so off shore and wait to be contacted. Then they were going to sail up the Hudson to the family compound to ride this crisis out.

"You know the East Marina in Pt. Lookout? You know where the Loop Parkway ends? Well, that is where they are going to be. Hook up with them. There is safety in numbers. My other nephew lives in Long Beach but he is in the Coast Guard. He might have been called to emergency action, but he should be able to help you guys out. His mother will know how to reach him, and she's gonna be on my boat."

"All right Dunk, I am going to cast off now; I'll cruise through the night and be at the Marina when they get there. I'll look after them till you get there buddy. Good luck, and God Bless. Be safe man." They ended the call.

Duncan looked over the notes he made of the route Kyle and Pat would have to take; timing will be everything; he thought. Before he contacted his brother, he figured he would call his wife, let her know what he was planning, and give her the last instructions on what to do, in case things went badly. He dialed his wife; she picked up on the first ring. He began telling her what he had planned. She just wanted him to come home; the stress was getting her worked up. "Katie, listen carefully. I want you to get a hold of Pam and Kevin, Auntie Laura, get together enough supplies for at least a week and head to the boat. Then cast off and head out about a mile off shore, drop anchor and wait for us."

"But what about the police and the curfew? I am not particularly comfortable sailing at night."

"Don't worry about that, Sean has been sailing with me since he was little. Kevin is in the Coast Guard for Christ's sake. You know how to sail. You know the systems on the boat well enough, hell you negotiated the Fire Island inlet just last week. The boat sails like a dream you won't have any problems." Her breathing relaxed a little bit, and he knew that she was feeling a little more confident. "When we get to the Island, we are going to make our way back past the house to hopefully grab a few more things. I need you to leave the portable marine VHF on the table, plug it in so I have the charger and know it's fully charged. When we have everyone and everything, we will make our way to Pt. Lookout, and we will radio you to rendezvous. Kevin can drop the dingy and come get us. It will be simple Honeybaby; we will be together soon. I love you… now let me talk to the kids."

Each of his children took up the phone in turn; he offered Kristen some comfort and reassurance, at 12 years of age she still believed in the invincibility of Dad. Kaitlyn said she had it worked out that she could do the video chats and in fact, has already set it up with Grandpa. She had also found blogs popping up all over from other survivors. She was more than a little shaken up by what she was learning, he thought it best to tell her how proud he was of her and that what she was doing, she did better than anyone else. He also gave her the responsibility of the dog. She liked that job, for years she has been trying to become first in the dog's heart. Much to her dismay, the dog truly was man's best friend. Last on the line was his eldest, his son Sean, "Son, I've got a lot to tell you and damned little time to do it. You are the toughest and most capable person I know. You have made me prouder than I ever had a right to be. With that being said, I have no choice but to pile onto your shoulders more responsibility than you should ever have to bear at seventeen. Your uncle Liam and I are going to rescue Uncle Kyle and your cousin Pat. Shhh now, let me finish. It is not without danger or risk, but we have come up with a solid plan. Sean, I have to save my brothers. You wouldn't leave your sisters behind if you could save them, right? Well, we have a plan that should minimize exposure and risk, and if we pull it off then Kyle will be able to get us home to you guys. Now here's the rub son, if you guys don't hear from us within twenty-four hours, then you have to sail up to Grandma and Grandpa's house. Your mother won't want to leave, so you are going to have to make her, Sean you have to take care of them. I know it's not fair but what choice do we have? While I am out of touch look over what Kaitlyn has found on the web, learn everything you can. I'll be with you guys before you know it, but be careful son; I am counting on you."

There was silence on the phone until Sean finally responded, "Dad… I love you; I will do as you say if I have to but don't you FUKING MAKE ME! YOU HEAR ME!" Duncan was taken aback by the swear word and by the strength behind the words. He laughed and Sean joined him. The look of concern that was on his mother's visage was priceless, she had never heard her son curse like that and with anger, but then she heard the laughter and knew it for what it was, an ice breaker. "I love you Dad. Come back soon and bring my Uncles and cousin with you." Duncan told him he loved him too, and he would bring everyone back safely. Katie came back on the line; she didn't ask about the exchange. She knew that this was his way of saying good-bye, just in case. She determined within herself that she would not make it any harder on him; he had enough on his plate, so she just said she loved him and would talk to him later.

6

Approximately, seven hundred and fifty miles away in Atlanta, Duncan's brother in law, Jerry Sixkiller, was kicking back reading this month's issue or *'Wired'* magazine. He worked as a subcontractor for the CDC* doing IT work. He just got home after fourteen hours straight. The CDC has something big that they are working on, this much is certain. They are burning through hardware at an alarming rate. He was hired to do some additional networking and assimilate some of the old systems into the new systems they just put online. There were three enormous data centers that he was working on. He figured this was at least job security for the next two years while each phase of the project came online.

Carrie, Duncan's sister, slipped behind his lounger unnoticed and began rubbing his neck. His head tilted forward to give her greater ease to rub away the tension that found its home there. Carrie and Jerry met on facebook and found out they lived near to each other; they met for coffee after a month of chatting and fell hopelessly in love. Carrie was a forty something divorcé, with two grown boys. Her ex left her when the boys were still very young, so she had gotten used to being on her own. Being a mom was more important than having a social life, when the boys grew up she didn't know what to do. Then she met Jerry; it was his last name that she found so interesting. When she asked him about it, she found out that he was Lakota Sioux, they started dating and the next thing they both knew, they were married. The boys took a shine to him right away: he made their mother happy, and he didn't try to pull the step dad thing, which would have been a little absurd since the twins were almost twenty when they got married, that was almost three years ago.

The boys didn't have much use for their biological father, a six foot-three Swede; whose ethics and morals were wanting. They got his looks and height, and that's about all. He was a deadbeat and never paid any child support. That was why they had joined the guard, they both had dreams of college, and that seemed the only way they would get there. Six months prior, John got transferred to Atlanta, so the family packed up and followed. They moved into a gated housing complex near Jerry's job at the CDC. Several of their neighbors worked there too, in fact, two-thirds of the community did. Carrie had had more than a few fights with her parents as the boys were growing up fast due to the substandard educational system of South Carolina, at least that is what Jacob and Marie felt. "They are calling the Civil War the war of Northern Aggression for Christ's sake" was usually found in the conversations, which was why they were not as close as they used to be.

Carrie was still putting the house in order and figured she would start looking for work in a month or two. Given the economy of the area, she suspected that might be a pipe dream but Jerry made a comfortable living, so there wasn't a sense of urgency there. She got on good with her neighbors; she had tea with one or another several times a week. So it wasn't surprising when their neighbor Millie called. Carrie stopped rubbing Jerry's neck to answer the phone, resulting in Jerry moaning his disappointment. Carrie smiled a promise to continue after the call, and he was appeased. "Hey Millie, what's up?" Carrie said still smiling at her husband.

"Jack says that we should start packing, 'cause something devastating is coming our way, and he's not sure if anything can be done to stop it at this point, it's global." Carrie's blood turned to ice immediately. Jack is a high level scientist there who works on potential pandemic viruses. "The Center is going to billet us, you guys should see if you can get in too." Carrie very nearly dropped the receiver; Jack wasn't the nervous type. "He says he can't tell me anything about it, it's classified, but he seems scared Carrie, so I am packing up now. We will be relocating into the Center in the morning. Have Jerry call and see about you guys. Listen I've a lot to do before then. I just wanted to give you guys the heads up. Good luck, I will talk with you soon I hope." Carrie mumbled her good-bye and told Jerry what she said. The phone rang again a minute later, this time it was for both Keith and Christopher. Their Guard unit was being activated. They both had to report to the base immediately. Carrie was now very afraid. Jerry got on his end right away. He cajoled space for he and Carrie; the boys weren't going to be around so it prevented a difficult choice. They would pack only the essentials and would go to the Center in the morning.

John Roberts was taking a break from researching his next article by watching Star Trek on DVD, when he heard a loud, banging knock on the door of his Park Slope apartment. He yelled, "Who is banging there?" as he got up to see who was at the door. He made sure the chain on the door was in place before releasing the dead bolt and opening the door.

Standing outside of his doorway was a sight few have seen outside of a movie, but John knew it wasn't good. Standing there was a man in a hermetically sealed suit, the mechanical sounding voice asked him to identify himself and made it known that he was from the CDC. Upon confirming John's identity, he asked for John to accompany him to a vehicle that was waiting outside.

John was a little scared but being a journalist. He was also curious as hell. So he snatched up his bag with his laptop and stuff, and followed the CDC man to the street below. As he closed and locked the door behind him, he noticed he was being flanked by two other men attired the same way, although one held a gun while the other was holding what looked like a dog catcher's loop and stick. His mind was racing, what could be going on he wondered? Why did they want him? He was just a journalist, not a scientist. He reported on what scientists did, their discoveries, their theories. At best his talent was writing, being able to put the words of those scientists into context for his readers. They sure weren't telling him anything; he supposed he would have to wait until they got to wherever they were taking him.

On the street, an unmarked RV pulled up at the curb in front of the group. When it stopped, the door opened with a hiss, the sound of an airlock. The CDC man who had spoken boarded the vehicle first. While John watched, one of the others placed a large zip tie about John's wrists securing them and indicated that he too should board. There was no point in resisting. Maybe they had made a mistake, but the potential scoop was worth it. He climbed aboard eagerly.

Duncan called Kyle at the number to the dressing room. Pat answered, "Uncle Duncan?"

"Yeah, Pat… it's me. How are you holding up bud?" he asked his nephew solicitously."

There was a brief pause, "About as well as can be expected" Patrick's voice took on a more *'military'* bearing.

"How is your Dad? Are either of you hurt?"

"No sir, we are both fine. When shit started to come loose we made for our escape away from those things."

"Let me talk to your Dad. Better yet, does that phone have a speaker phone?" Pat didn't answer, just pushed the button.

Kyle spoke to his brother, "I'm not so sure speaker phone is such a good idea right now Dunk. The hall is quiet now, but just a little while ago we were listening to those moans and groans, I can't even begin to tell you how freakin scary those sounds are, especially after seeing those things eating folks."

"I'll talk quietly but I want you both to hear what I have to say. Do you guys see an air register in the ceiling above a doorway?"

"Yep"

"Now remove the ceiling tiles around it… let me know when you've done it."

Pat grabbed up his hockey stick and began knocking them out, figuring neatness counted for nothing here, speed however would be a plus. "All clear Uncle Dunk"

"Good... now do you see the duct work connecting that register to the big steel looking box; that is a mixing box. Don't worry about what it does, think of it as your starting point. The ceiling has lots of Kindorff and pipe hangers all the way. They will be able to support your weight. Even the duct work will hold you, and it will just be noisier. This duct run goes straight to an Air Handling Unit. You will be coming in on the supply side of the unit. When you get to the unit it is in a secondary mechanical room, when you get there, the door should be shut, don't worry it should be locked from the outside; you are dropping in on the inside. Are you clear on it so far?"

"We've got it go on."

"Now you should see some two inch insulated pipe that is painted light blue, coming out from the unit. It penetrates the wall to the left side of the door; it's a fire wall... it goes all the way to the lid, so you can't stay in the ceiling here. You are going to go through that door into a corridor that goes east-west. You still with me?"

"East West got it, continue..."

"Look up, the light blue pipe tees and continues through the next wall, follow the tee left. You will be going east. Be careful bro, you are going to be exposed for a little while; it can't be helped... Dave said that this hallway gets very little traffic but it isn't far from where the Zamboni is kept, so there might be some of those creatures down there. Now do you have anything you can shove into the space between a door and a jam?"

Kyle replied, " I've my Leatherman, that should fit."

"Good, now you are going to come to a tee in the hall. Go to the left and continue down the hall to the third door on the right. The knob is broken, so you are going to have to pry it out. The guys have been using a screwdriver on it for years. Anyhow go through that door; it will lead you to a ladder that hill get you to a catwalk keep following that until you see a ladder going down to the next lower level. When you get there, go to the left again. Keep on the lookout for some eighteen inch insulated pipe; it is colored yellow, that is low pressure steam. Follow those lines. It will take you to a steam tunnel, there will be a bunch of steam lines and it will be hot as hell, then you'll know you're in the right place. That steam tunnel connects to a Con Ed vault that will give you access to the street on Eighth Avenue, near Thirty-first street, directly across from the Post Office. Call me when you are secure in the vault. There are tons of 'em over there so you will need to call before you pop out onto the street. Now read it back to me." Kyle read him back the notes on the directions and told him he would call him when he got there. Best guesstimates were that it would take them the better part of thity minutes to get there barring any unforeseen circumstances.

The adrenaline rush left them with a crash. Pat and Kyle figured they would climb up to the mixing box; there they would try to nap/ rest up for six hours. Duncan said he would call the dressing room in 6 hours then it would be all out, that would give them all time enough to rest up and make whatever preparations they needed. "Listen brother" said Duncan while there was still time "No matter what happens,…"

Kyle interrupted "save it bro, we ain't dead yet. Just call us when you want us to go."

"You're on, six hours. I'll call and God willing we will see each other within an hour after that. Now get up into the ceiling. I will call your wife and tell her you both will be fine." Duncan looked at the receiver a moment longer before he hung it up, wondering if he would ever see his brother again.

As Duncan walked back into the control room, he saw Pete and Leneau huddled next to the computer monitor. "Any news on what's happening?"

Pete's eyes never left the screen, he said two words, tow words that chilled him to his core. What Peter said was, "It's global." He spoke it in a somber tone devoid of all emotion. Video from Russia, China, France, and from several states here in America flashed on the screen in snip its. "There are hundreds of videos popping up on YouTube. The TV is saying that everyone should remain indoors. The violence is escalating everywhere man, the whole city is under quarantine."

Suddenly the buzzer and strobes of the fire system went off as the fire panel went into general alarm. Don levered his morbidly obese body out of the chair and looked at the panel. "It's a pull station in Alumni Hall fourth-floor hallway. It's an evacuation! Do we respond?" No one knew what to do. Suddenly they all realized that Henry was over there minding the chillers and he wasn't hearing the constant radio chatter from security; he was still on channel one. He didn't know what was going on or the danger he was in.

"Engine room to Unit nine! Henry come in!" Leneau called over the radio, after switching it back to the normal frequency. There was no reply. "Engine room to unit nine Henry come in! Its Leneau, don't come down stairs Henry! Do you hear me ... respond!!!"

"Yeah this is Unit nine Henry...I'm enroute to the fourth floor who is heading to the panel in the basement?" in the background you could hear the chime of the elevator as it marked its descent from the 1nine[th] floor.

"Henry! Don't go, this is an emergency, you are in DANGER!" Leneau shouted. Listening for a response, Leneau heard Henry start to speak, the chime of the car stopping at a floor, and the distinct sound of the doors opening; whatever Henry was saying was cut off with the transmission.

As the doors were opening, Henry was asking for clarification of the last transmission. The arm of a tall transvestite shot into the gap between the opening doors. Henry's short stature was all that saved him from being grabbed in this first attempt, but as the doors opened all the way, the he/she creature made a second grab.

Henry shoved the body backwards as it's nails raked his face. The creature rebounded off the wall. Fortune smiled on Henry for the moment as one of the transvestite zombie's impossibly high heel snapped causing it to fall like a tree by a lumberjack.

Henry, who had served as an infantryman in Viet Nam, didn't want to be trapped in the elevator. He jumped over the sprawled out zombie and raced down the hallway to the left making for the stairs. As he was running, he heard screams from several of the dorm rooms that he passed. There were a couple of rooms with their doors ajar; He made the bad decision to look into one as he was passing. What he saw would haunt him the rest of his life, short as it would be, for the scratches on his face allowed the infection access to his body; he saw two creatures eating and tearing at the body of one of the students, arterial blood was spraying the walls and floors. He was sprayed by some of it as he passed.

He went through the stairwell door and onto the landing. There he stopped deciding which way to go. "Up or down" he thought. Chancing a look down, he saw there were other creatures in the stairwell below him. Decision made, he started to race up the stairs, and with fear being a powerful motivator, he made it up to the twelfth-floor before his lung threatening to burst forced him to slow down. Breathlessly he tried to respond to the radio that had been calling to him the whole time, "what…the hell…is … happen…ing?"

"Henry, are you safe? The whole world has gone to shit, it's anarchy everywhere, get behind locked doors," Leneau said over the radio.

Henry wanted to ask for details but thought better of it as he was out of breath. He replied only "copy" as he redoubled his efforts to climb the stairs. He finally made it to the nineteenth floor after stepping over a puddle of blood that was leaking out from under the school's president's door on eighteen.

He heard the moans from below as he fumbled with his keys. Its haunting effect so unnerved him that his fingers were as nimble as if they were encased in ice. He wasn't sure if the creatures were following him up the stairs or if others from other floors were just coming into the stairwell, either way was bad. Finally finding the correct key, he opened the door to relative safety. Once inside, he started piling up the president's wrought iron deck furniture in front of the doors at both ends of the hall. Getting his wind back, he finally called the engine room from his cell phone and found out what was going on.

The radio traffic was nonstop, so the engineers decided to have the base station on security's frequency and the handhelds back on frequency one. George still on the roof of 'D' building, was watching the carnage on the street six floors below. From his vantage he could see buildings aflame down the block and across the street on Seventh Ave. He realized that this wasn't the safest place, but having the openness of the sky above him outweighed caution. He couldn't tear his eyes away from the shambling hordes on the ground. He would see a person chased out from a building only to be engulfed by another group, he would hear screams, and then they would mercifully end.

This was happening more and more often. The creatures did not appear to be working together, it was almost as if each was acting on its own and drawn to the moans of the others, or to the screams and cries of victims. The creatures would stop eating their victims soon after the screams stopped, almost as if they were feeding not on the flesh and blood of their victims, but upon their "life".

George, being the youngest of the engineers at twenty-seven years of age, did not fail to notice how like "Dawn of the Dead" this was. If he had known the last name of the first victim, the irony would have knocked him over. Others around the globe were drawing the same conclusions. Zombies were supposed to be relegated to movies and bad dreams; they definitely weren't supposed to be a reality, walking around Manhattan.

He heard screams coming from across the street on the roof of Nagler Hall; squinting he tried to find the source. There it was, there was a student running around on the roof, trying to get away from her pursuers. She had no place to escape, and she was trapped. Suddenly she threw herself off of the roof. She landed on the sidewalk with a wet sounding slap-thud; the zombies followed suit not wanting their prey to escape. However, where she remained still and lifeless, the zombies that had fallen began moving again. Some would be unable to walk having splintered their legs upon landing; others regained their feet and shuffled off down the street. George couldn't take any more, so he went back inside and grabbed the elevator to the basement level.

When George got down to the engine room, he saw that more people had joined their ranks. There were several guys from the maintenance department among them now. Some of the guys were just sitting there 'broken,' others were glued to the TV and the web. Duncan's brother Liam and Pete were talking quietly off by themselves near chiller three. Duncan was moving to join them carrying a couple bags. He noticed a pile of other supplies near the trio. He figured they were planning something, so he went over to join them.

"Hey George" Duncan said inviting him to join the discussion. "My brother and I are leaving, so is Pete. Don is on the fence but Leneau, Greg, and the maintenance guys are staying and Henry is trapped up atop of Alumni. They think help is going to come." He shakes his head "Believe me no help is coming for a long time if ever. I would not be surprised if the government decides to Bomb Manhattan off the map. This is huge, it's all over the world..., want to come with us? We are going to take one of the transport vans; Miguel already gave us the keys.

It's parked in the loading bay by the cafeteria. We are gonna drive down by the Garden on Eighth Avenue and rescue my other brother and nephew, then we are gonna figure out what to do next. But in my opinion, sitting here waiting is a death sentence. I have an idea on how to get back to Long Island but we need my brother to do it, you in?"

George had tried and tried to call his family but couldn't get through. He didn't know if they were alive or dead but they lived in Astoria, and that was on the way. "Yeah, count me in. I agree staying here is just waiting to die. When do we leave?"

Duncan looked to his brother and Pete then back to George, "In about four and a half hours, so gather your gear and then get some rest, all of you, we don't know when we will get to rest again so take it while you can. I am going to talk to Don and see if he will come on board. Meet back here in four hours."

They started to get up to go when George stopped them saying, "While I was up on the roof, I had a thought… now don't slap me but…well does this seem at all like Dawn of the Dead to any of you?" They all exchanged glances that said yep we were thinking the same thing but were just too embarrassed by the idea to voice it. George continued his thought, "Look in all those type of movies, be it radiation causing the dead to rise, some bio-weapon accident or some experiment gone horribly wrong…at least in all the movies I can think of with the exception of the Omega Man, they all had certain things in common. Number one, the only way to kill them was destroy the brain and number two, if you were bitten or scratched by one you're going to become one."

Greater unease settled upon the group, they all turned as one to look towards the locker room where Greg was sleeping. "Greg didn't look too good when he came back from the infirmary, he said he wasn't feeling very well…" there was no need to say what they all were thinking. "Look we will just have to keep an eye on him. We can't do something just because Hollywood movies say we should."

They were still looking at the door when Duncan said, "But to be on the safe side let's move our gear to the 'B' switch gear room via 'C' pump room. We can use the steam tunnels to keep us out of the hallways. Once we get there, we can check the halls and if the coast is clear move on down into "B." Hell we could go all the way to 'A' building, but if we have to move then we only have the choice of backtracking and I don't really like having only one option." They all agreed and Duncan went into the control room to bring up the Greg situation, while the other three began moving the gear.

17

The vehicle that John Roberts entered was sort of a mobile lab/ command center, much higher tech than what they had used in Siberia. It was nothing short of amazing. Between the sheer awesomeness of computer power and the labs analysis capabilities, it had its own hermetic clean room. It was into that room he was ushered, the door was sealed behind him. Looking out of the windshield was the only way to tell that the vehicle was indeed in motion.

The man he had spoken with earlier had now removed his Bio-Hazard suit and was wearing scrubs. "Mr. Roberts, have you any idea why you are... a guest of the CDC?"

John dismissed the first flippant answer that came to mind, instead he merely said in a calm voice, "I was hoping you would tell me."

"Judging by the fact that you aren't trying to eat us, I believe that the precautions we have taken here are largely unnecessary...however, better safe than sorry. You recently returned from Siberia, yes?" John Roberts nodded his answer. "Have you spoken with Dr. Romero since your return?"

"No I have not, does this," he waved his bound hands in a sweeping motion "have to do with his work? ... He has been working on particle physics and wireless energy transference, what has any of that have to do with the CDC and the riots here about?"

His question wasn't answered, another however was offered. "Have you been in contact with anyone who was with you over in Siberia?"

John was beginning to get irritated, "I sent an e-mail to Dr. Romero containing the finished article that I had written; I sent a couple others to a couple of the Russian scientists I had met while over there ... what is going on? ... You obviously want something from me, and I am happy to cooperate but how about you share some information with me rather than pulling the interrogation routine?" This came out a little harsher than he intended, which in retrospect might not have been a bad thing.

"Mr. Roberts, I am not at liberty to discuss the current situation with you, but I can assure you that answering my questions is in the interest of the health, perhaps the very survival of mankind. And no I am not being melodramatic. Would you mind disclosing everything that you were privy to over there, what you witnessed, anything that you can think of. Something happened over there that has caused my bosses to be extremely scared and we need to know about it."

John saw his angle now, and with the same roguish smile that had worked so often in the bars with the ladies, he replied, "Sure, so long as I get an exclusive on what's got the CDC running scared."

The man in the scrubs looked worn out "Fine."

John fished his cell phone out and used it as a voice recorder, "Your name please?"

The beaten man said, "Dr. Alex Hampton of the CDC, now will you be so kind?"

John told him everything he could remember. "My notes and laptop are in my bag."

"When we get to MacArthur we will see if we can do something about your hands."

John looked shocked, "MacArthur? As in airport? Where are you taking me?"

"I would have thought that obvious, we are going to Atlanta, to the CDC."

John swallowed hard, his throat suddenly dry. "How big is this thing?"

he stammered.

"Pandemic" was the one word reply. The mobile command center pulled into the airport and onto the tarmac next to the waiting plane.

18

A flurry of activity was going on at Duncan's home. Katie was making arrangements with her sister in law and Aunt Laura, and the kids were packing up the minivan with all the supplies to put out to sea. All this activity was a welcome distraction for her. Her sister in law would arrive in less than an hour. Pam said that her son, Kevin, would get down to the boat early and start getting things ready for their arrival. "The van is all packed mom; any word from dad and Uncle Liam yet?" asked Sean.

"Not yet, but they will call, don't worry," she only wished she could abide by her own advice.

Dawn was still a couple of hours away; Katie went out into the backyard to be alone, with the exception of Aloha, the family dog. She needed the solitude but was not about to sacrifice all semblance of safety. She looked about the yard and the memories flooded her mind; she focused on the swing set that Duncan had built for Sean when he was three. She remembered how she thought the slide was too high and steep. She smiled and could almost hear the squeal of delight as Duncan brought Sean out to see it; she also remembered the tears Kaitlyn shed when a baby bird fell out of a nest that birds had built in the rafters of the little house on top of the platform. The basketball hoop was rusted. Absently she wondered why they even had it in the yard, no one ever really played it. Sure Kaitlyn played in the church league for one season when she was age ten. Katie was aware that they were going to move to a dream house but this was different, this was fleeing from their home for safety… she fought back tears, swallowed the lump in her throat, and then she cleared her head and concentrated on the circumstances at hand. She walked over to the shed to be sure that it was locked. Aloha started to growl, a low throaty growl full of warning and the threat of attack. Katie knew what it was that had Aloha's hair up. She made a bee-line for the backdoor. She was pretty sure it couldn't get into the yard but she didn't want to chance it, nor did she want to draw the things attention. She eased open the backdoor and when she was in, she whispered for the dog to come. Aloha was only waiting for her to gain safety; he turned and sped towards the door. She was part of his pack, he was going to protect her, but his senses told him that there was a large predator about, larger than he could deal with, so back into the house he ran. Katie's sudden return from outback, along with the dog's behavior, had everyone silent as church mice.

They huddled in silence, very nearly holding their breath, listening to the soft scrape of its tread, then the rattle of empty Diet Coke cans as it knocked over the recycling can. Kaitlyn and Kristen were petrified and on the verge of tears. The whole family knelt together, held each other's hands, and prayed to God for deliverance. It was then that they heard the moan, it nearly pushed them over the edge into hysteria, but the moan was moving away from their house. It was getting softer and softer, until they could no longer hear it. Aloha showed visible signs of relaxed alertness, and as a group they let out a collective sigh. Ten minutes later, Pam showed up.

As a group it was decided to take both of their vans, just in case. So after a few minutes of transferring some items they all got into the vans and left... Katie wondering if they would ever see this house again. They had decided that they would be less likely to happen upon trouble if they took the back way through Hewlett and East Rockaway to Oceanside, but once there, it wouldn't make a difference as it was pretty much taking a parkway or traversing the Long Beach Bridge. The vans moved quietly down the roads at a healthy clip; they kept about a fifteen foot interval between the vans. Katie decided she wasn't going to hear anything important on the radio, and with the tension from their recent visitor, she pushed the button for the CD player and turned up the volume as U2's Beautiful Day came on. Katie was struck by the irony of the songs message.

19

Duncan pushed open the door to the control room, hopelessness was the flavor in the air and the overall mood. Leneau had his feet up on the desk in the corner reading a text on his phone, Don was back in his chair surrounded by the guys from maintenance looking at the latest news on the TV. It seems as though some folks from the Society of Creative Anachronism thought that by donning their chainmail shirts and wielding their swords, they were going to take on the zombie horde in Central Park. They only succeeded in feeding the horde and ultimately joining it. Greg was still in the back locker room sleeping.

"Leneau, you busy?" Duncan really wasn't sure how to broach this subject.

"Sure, what's up?" He stood and walked towards Duncan. Seeing that Duncan wasn't coming further into the room, and recognizing the look of discomfort on his face, together they exited the room and walked over by the dormant chiller.

"Look, we are going to be leaving soon…and I know you are staying, but I have a bad feeling… Listen we were talking and well it was George who put voice to some of what we were all thinking. Does this feel sort of like Dawn of the Dead to you? Or any other zombie movie for that matter? You have seen the news footage. Leneau, just be careful ok… Keep an eye out for a change in Greg." Leneau looked at him with a sense of detachment, which was better than he expected. He figured it would already have been dismissed but Leneau was listening. "I'm not saying anything for sure, but the thing is that the thing all of those movies have in common is that if you get bit then you become one. Look at all those people out there, something changed them. You saw how bad Greg looked when he came down from the infirmary. He had gotten bitten. Why would he have been so pale and clammy?"

Leneau took in a deep breath; Duncan figured here it comes… "Dunk, you might be able to get home, so go. Me on the other hand, there is no way for me to get back to Jersey. I was worrying about something, I just didn't know what it was till you started talking. We'll keep an eye on Greg." Together they headed back to the control room.

"Don we are going to be leaving soon; we've got a pretty good plan to get back to the Island. You coming or not?" Don was vacillating, he was on the fence, but seemed to be leaning towards trying escape. The radio base station screamed out 'C' lobby has been breached!!! C lobby has been breached!!!" The moans in the background came to the foreground, along with more screams from more victims. That sealed it for Don, he was in. With a salute to Leneau and the rest, they turned and headed towards the steam tunnel.

Duncan was starting to regret asking Don to come along almost immediately. Don, who under normal circumstances was annoying at best with his constant complaining and his laziness, was infinitely worse under these conditions, added to that the immensity of his bulk made traversing these cramped tunnels just short of impossible. He made it over the first of the obstacles, a knee wall access onto a low ceilinged, dimly lit walkway. He complained the entire time, it seemed he never even stopped for a breath between words. "This is crazy man… I mean it, this is no good. We are never gonna get out of here. We should just dig in like ticks. This is just fucking crazy."

Upon exiting the far end of the tunnel into 'C' pump room Duncan stood and stretched his back, then moved towards his brother and Pete who were near the door to the hallway. Don's complaints preceded him out of the tunnel by at least thirty seconds, and were loud enough to be heard over the din of the pumps and compressor that are always running or cycling. "Don shut the fuck up man, you want to get us killed?" shouted Pete albeit in a whisper. Mercifully Don complied, granted at least for the present, but to Duncan the reprieve, however short in duration, was a god-send.

Liam had his ear to the door, attempting to hear anything in the hall, which was an exercise in futility with the noise from the equipment within the room. They quickly decided not to silence the equipment fearing that it may draw attention to where they were hiding. Cautiously, Liam took the knob in hand and prepared to open the door a crack; Duncan lowered his bags and took up his ice chopper in both hands and steeped opposite his brother to a better vantage point to strike if need be.

Liam nodded a count of three then turned the knob. Nothing cam bursting in through the door, so he opened it just enough to see a slice of the hallway without. Not seeing anything, he chanced increasing his field of view a little more. Still they seemed safe. Emboldened by these minor successes he chanced sticking his head out to scan the hallway. Satisfied that there were no creeping monsters within view they exited their temporary haven.

George was first; being the youngest and most agile; wearing a knapsack and with the master sergeant key in hand, he crept up to the double doors that separated 'C' building from 'B'. He was followed by Pete, Liam, Duncan and lastly by Don. George peered through the small window in the door. He saw no signs of disturbance, although the field of view was limited by the way the hallway jinks left. So they proceeded in silence, with all the caution they could to the stairwell doors, there George flattened himself against the wall, crouched so that his head as it came around the corner would not be at the expected normal height, and took a look.

Here too the coast was clear, he could see down the hallway to the 'B' switchgear room and beyond to the doors that would lead to 'A' building. The fluorescent lights cast an institutional glare on the stark white walls of the hallway, which was devoid of color save for the splash of red on the floor where a puddle of fresh blood gathered at the base of the doors that they would have to eventually pass through, and a bloody handprint on that same door. The upside was that there was nobody in the hall, the downside was that the room they were headed for was much closer to the blood than they were comfortable with.

They had come too far and this was the only way out-the safest way out. They rolled the dice, and raced down the hall. George had the door open impossibly fast and they were in with the door locked behind them without a pause. Don looked to the others and said, " You know we are trapped in here. Why did I leave the engine room to follow you guys on this fool's errand?" As if in answer to his question the radio broke silence, sounding as if someone had fallen and the transmit button were stuck. You could hear screams and groans fighting for dominance, you could hear Leneau pleading with Greg to stay back followed by more screams, some of pain some of terror. Then nothing as silence returned.

20

"Mr. President, you have to speak to the people… they need to know that there is someone at the helm. We need to have you in front of the cameras sir" exclaimed the President's chief of staff.

"We have no idea what is happening; I don't have anything prepared"

"Sir… It is expected of you sir!" the chief of staff interjected.

"Very well, but you of all people know how the numbers go south when I speak off the cuff" This sent the COS (chief of staff) nearly into hysteria "Numbers? Sir the world is in chaos. You have a meltdown both metaphoric and literal in the Middle East; you have China rattling her saber over the UN incident, NYC is all but lost in violence and riots. Christ alive half of the city is in flames…Moscow has gone silent! And you are worried about how your approval numbers might suffer if you don't have a teleprompter? Good Lord man, you are the President of the United States, so act like it Sir!!" The tone in the COS's voice left no doubt that he was spelling that last word 'cur!'. "Fine, we will do it from here, in the oval office, No active press; I will just speak to the people. Get one of our speech writers in here to whip up something *"for the people"*. One of the lesser white house staffers scurried off to make it so, while others came and went with files. The President turned back to the COS, "With that done, I don't appreciate the way you have been speaking to me" not bothering to veil his implied threat.

"Sir if you want my resignation, you've got it after America is safe again. Is that soon enough for you, because I can go now!" venom practically dripping from his lips as he spoke.

"Woe, slow down son, I just don't want to be spoken to that way. As you said, I am the President lest you forget."

What the COS thought was, "Would that weren't the case", what he said however was, "Will that be all sir?" not waiting for an answer, he turned on his heel and left. One of the staffers brought a report from the CDC to the President along with reports from the DOD command center and the Secretary of State. The Department Of Defense command center was continuing to monitor the satellite imagery from the Middle East, in addition to all the other strategically significant places. The Secretary of State was informing him that things were deteriorating with China, however she suspected this was just more maneuvering on their part regarding trade and our national debt. The President's eye took in the note from the SOS and laid everything else down as more files were placed on top of them by the steady flow of staffers. He wanted to settle things down with China fast; his policies depended on their continued financial support. He was ever mindful of his upcoming re-election campaign.

In a conference room elsewhere in the capital, the Vice President was meeting with some of the cabinet members and senior military advisors, with the Senate Majority leader and the Speaker for the House conferencing in over the phone. The VP received the same intelligence that the President did, the main difference however was that the VP read through it all.

The preliminary report from the CDC had disturbed him greatly. It referenced that data sent to them from hospitals in New York that had them looking at something they had never seen before. Furthermore, it drew possible connections to the outbreaks of violence in other cities and states, as well as requests for assistance from foreign nations in Europe and Asia, whom had forwarded similar data to them. The VP also had seen the satellite images from over the Middle East. He had seen the massive movement of people moving through the region; analysts had concluded that they were refugees as there were no signs of material among them. He didn't know how these things were related, but he was sure they were.

"The Governors of both New York and New Jersey have activated the Guard in response to the unrest in their states." The VP wasn't sure who had spoken, but he was aware of this fact. "I have here some alarming information from the CDC that suggests something truly nasty is on the horizon; they feel that this could possibly be the big one. You all know the CDC is always talking about possible Pandemics, especially around budget time, but this time it looks like the real deal, which is why we are all here." He passed along copies of the report to those who were present, all marked confidential, and summarized it for the benefit of those who were there via teleconference.

The Secretary of Defense was the first to speak, "Activation of all the Reserves and having the Military work in tandem with local law enforcement and FEMA is the only option. Declare martial law!" The VP was not at all comfortable with where this conversation was going, the word coupe came to mind. "Sir we have to act in the interest of the country first. The President seems more concerned with how he will be viewed in the history books. If we fail to act, and decisively, there won't be anyone left to write the books, period, and the end of the story."

The Vice President had his face in his hands. Moving his fingers to his temples, he began to massage the ache that was developing. With a sigh he said to those present, "Depending on what more the CDC learns, I will go to see the man and try to urge him to action one last time. If not, we will talk to the Justice Department and see how we go about transferring powers." The others got up and left without further words; leaving the Vice President with his thoughts and his aching head.

21

Time was running out, they were going to have to move again soon. Duncan looked at his watch, hoping his brother and nephew were safe in their ceiling, and called the phone in the dressing room to signal them to go. They waited another 1five minutes to give his brother and nephew the time that was estimated to get to their *"escape hatch"*.

"Alright guys, we are almost there; just a final push through 'A' basement to the freight elevator and into the kitchens to the loading dock. Get your weapons ready." He stood up and put on his backpack, put his welding gauntlets back on, and picked up his ice chopper. Liam and Pete did the same grabbing their fire axes. George and Don made themselves ready by wielding a pair of aluminum pipe wrenches each. Duncan gave the count and when he said "Go", they were out the door going left through the blood stained double doors over the puddle of blood.

On the other side of the door, just to the right near Binsky's book store, was Eric, chewing on the carcass of M-fifty-five John. John had been eviscerated, his intestines spewed forth from the abdominal cavity. Eric's security uniform was soaked in blood, and with him, enjoying their feast, was Collin who was normally found in the CC-fifteen computer center. Collin was sucking the marrow out of M-five-five's femur. The two zombies looked at the new arrivals and began to moan as they rose to seek fresh meat to ingest. Don vomited immediately adding another smell to the stench of John's body's final act of voiding his bowels. It mixed with the smell of blood and the scent of the beginning decay of the zombies permeated the air. Melee was joined as Duncan thrust the blade of his chopper through the bridge of Eric's nose, sheering the top part of his head away, while Pete closed so that he could swing his axe without fear of striking one of his companions. The Zombie's call was answered by two others, students by the look of them, who must have come from the corridor by the escalators.

Neither Don nor George realized their plight as the zombies approached from their rear. An agonizing burn was felt by Don from his neck as one of the new zombies tore away a chunk of trapezius muscle. He screamed as he turned to fend off the assault; that scream and Georges reflexes saved George from the same fate. George spun with the agility of a dancer, and smashed first one and then the other of his wrenches into the head of his would be killer. The zombie collapsed as would a puppet whose strings had just been severed. George turned from his fallen foe and began to beat upon the creature tearing at Don. Duncan yelled to George to come on and leave Don where he was, there was nothing they could do for him anyway, but while life was left in him his screams might draw other zombies away from them. Don heard this command and turned his gaze upon Duncan. The look of betrayal was replaced by one whose message was clear, that Duncan was a filthy individual and that he would burn in hell for abandoning him to this fate.

The four survivors raced down the corridor to the waiting freight elevator. As they closed the doors and the cage they could still hear Don's agony in his screams. As the button was pushed for the first floor, the companions spread out in preparation for another engagement. To their relief their caution was unnecessary as the kitchen was empty. They could hear zombies out in the cafeteria but there was no access to their locale from the other side of the counters.

They made their way through the maze of kitchen equipment and boxes, finally making the relative safety of the loading dock and the College's transport van. Duncan jumped down and produced the keys while the others stood guard by the doors. As he opened the door, he hit the lock button so that his companions could get in; thanking God that the steel overhead door was down.

Once inside of the van, Duncan told Liam that he was going to have to hit the open button and get back into the van as fast as he could as there were likely to be zombies on the other side of the door.

Duncan started the van and inched it closer to the overhead door, Liam got out leaving the door ajar and pressed the button, the door's motor engaged as Liam slammed his door shut and locked the doors.

The overhead door groaned its protest, but slowly climbed in its tracks. Sure enough they could see the legs of more than twenty zombies on the other side. As they turned around to face the opening door. Duncan watched the doors slow progress. As it crept upwards inch by inch, time seemed at a standstill. The door had yet to open high enough to allow the van to escape, when the zombies started to flood into the loading bay. They began to pound upon the van, trying to smash their way in. Fortunately they had yet to start pounding upon the van's windows as the zombie's lack of pain response may have allowed one of them to shatter the glass and gain access.

The door cleared the mark painted on the wall that let the drivers know when the door had opened high enough for the van to proceed. Duncan floored the gas pedal and took his foot off of the break, having the van in gear already. Zombies bounced off of the hood and fell before the van while others were crushed under the tires as they sped off making a right on Eighth Avenue.

What they saw through the windshield threatened to extinguish all of their hopes; for what they saw was hundreds of the walking dead on the streets, and copious amounts of blood rushing along the gutters and into the sewers. There were corpses on the sidewalk here and there that were from the suicidal plunges of those on the upper floors of some of these buildings who in despair took back control by ending their lives on their own terms. They got the van moving around five0 mph and plowed through the assembled hordes racing for the garden. They knew that their timing was off; they were going to have to keep driving around the block until they received the text from Kyle.

This strategy had a benefit however, the zombies en masse began to follow the van. It was Pete who noticed; they were not sure how they were going to get their new passengers into the van, with all the zombies milling about. Duncan decided to slow the van down enough to keep the zombies following, and like the pied piper he led them on, teasing them to follow. Slowing to little more than five miles per hour, he led them down Eighth Avenue, occasionally veering to the left or right to avoid the rare abandoned vehicle left in the street.

The headlights were now misaligned from the collisions with the undead; he kept the slow pace egging on the horde. At Chevy's the famous burger joint he made a right onto Forty-Second street. Dawn was still almost an hour off and although the sky had grown somewhat lighter, on Forty-Second it seemed as bright as day. It was eerie, there were almost no zombies to be found here. Under the bright lights of this most famous of blocks, visibility was great. Passing Madame Tussaud's, and the Chase building with its massive moving ad space comprised of hundreds of monitors, he led them onward. He turned left on third and drove by Smith & Wollensky's, where just days before he had dined with his family.

He had to speed up to crash through another group of shambling denizens. He was a little worried that he might damage the radiator or some other crucial part of the van with the constant crashing through zombies. Then again, if he did puncture the radiator he would still be able to push the van enough to get back to Penn. When he got the text from Kyle he sped back to the appointed location.

****

Kyle heard the ring of the phone then he shook his son awake. "Time to move Pat." They started to move along the duct work, following the directions discussed earlier with Duncan. The speed with which they traveled was reduced by their make shift armor and the gear they dragged with them. Kyle thought of the fable about the "Hare and the Tortoise", it seemed like a fitting analogy, one that he hoped would come to fruition. Slow and steady, they moved through the ceiling, following the duct work, slow and steady; they finally reached the AHU* (air handling unit). Pat broke through the drop ceiling with the butt of his stick. Looking around, it was exactly as described.

It was a small ancillary mechanical room, and better still, an *empty* small ancillary mechanical room. Kyle and Pat locked wrists and Pat was silently lowered to the ground below. Pat then assisted his father down minimizing any noise so as not to attract attention. Kyle easily located the two inch pipes he was told to find, and sure enough they penetrated the wall to the left of the door that Pat was listening at. He couldn't tell what he was hearing, he thought it sounded mechanical, but he wasn't sure. Truth be told, they had no other options. Kyle stood to the opening side of the door jamb with his hokey stick ready, he had already put the helmet on and fastened the chin strap, gloves were on, all the pads and gear made movement a little awkwardly, but the protection they offered allowed them a modicum of hope about surviving an encounter. They both drew in deep breaths. Then Pat opened the door.

As the door swung outward it slammed into what had been a mechanic, judging from the remains of the uniform and the tool belt. The body was torn apart and was missing its head entirely, as well as large pieces of muscle. There was gore throughout the small hallway. Not being prepared for such a sight, the two men stopped in their tracks. Pat felt his gorge begin to rise as his stomach wanted to void itself of its meager contents. A distant groan snapped them out of this surreal nightmare.

Kyle tapped Pat's shoulder and motioned for him to continue. Escape was the only option, so they moved onward towards their goal. Fortunately, they were moving away from the groan. Unfortunately, there were more groans joining in chorus. They quickly moved through the corridor; which was a lot longer than they had envisioned from the description. They felt awfully exposed.

Finally the corridor ended at the tee they were looking for. Pat made a right and started down; however the third door wasn't there. Kyle realized their error and as they turned to retrace their steps back the way they came, the hair on the back of both of their necks rose. They weren't alone in these halls.

They looked at one another; Kyle noted the look of determination on his son's countenance and took pride and courage from it. They made no battle cry, better to preserve any element of surprise, they just charged the tee.

Kyle started his chopping swing even before rounding the corner. He was rewarded with the feel of his stick making meaty contact with one of the flesh eaters, knocking it into the wall where it caromed off into another as it fell. The force of the strike had broken the creature's neck and it moved no more. The now still form was obstructing the path of the three others behind it, having fallen and becoming tangled in the feet of the next zombie in line.

The two men knew they had to destroy these creatures quickly before their location was compromised. Pat and Kyle attacked, slashing and chopping away with adrenalin assisted swings of their weapons. The zombies fell before them in short order; their clear plastic face shields were speckled with blood, their sticks dripped with gore.

When this skirmish was over, they quickly made their way to the door they had been expecting to find. Kyle removed his glove to locate his Leatherman, his efforts hampered by the make shift armor. He finally extracted the vital tool, opened the file attachment and slid it between the door and the jamb. He had applied just enough leverage to pry the door open when they heard the shuffle of a zombie's gait. Through the door they went, closing it fast behind them. Kyle wished just then that he had been clearer of mind when they found the ravaged body of that mechanic. If he had picked up those tools he could have pinned the door in place. Instead they just had to hope that the zombies couldn't get through, or at least were delayed enough so that they could make their way to freedom.

They were now standing on a grate-like platform that was perhaps five foot by five foot and directly opposite them was a set of steeply ascending stairs. "This must be the ladder, up you go son, and I'm right behind you. Keep your eyes peeled for those eighteen inch insulated pipes." Action was Pat's response; he climbed the 'ladder' using one hand for balance and keeping his head on a swivel. Kyle, true to his word was right behind his son. If Pat stopped short Kyle could legitimately been called a brown-nose. The stairs brought them up about eighteen feet through a cut-out in the catwalk that had been directly above them. If they hadn't had other things on their minds, like survival, then they would have been impressed, having only seen the public side of the famous arena previously.

They moved through the space and listened for everything. Four Large yellow insulated pipes came up through a penetration in the catwalk making a ninety degree turn and running parallel to the walk. They followed these pipes. They found an actual ladder going down. The steel ladder was bolted into the wall and had a cage around it to prevent one from falling backwards. "I'll go first, then you drop the sticks down to me on the bottom then you climb down after, okay?" Kyle told his son.

"Dad let me go first…"

"No son, this way if I slip, I won't fall on you." His reasoning made sense. His son nodded and accepted the stick from his father. There wasn't much light down below, so Kyle put his faith in God and began his descent. Twenty-five rungs later, Kyle was surprised by the fatigue he felt in his arms. He called up to his son and caught first one stick then the other. He stepped back away from the opening and Pat dropped down the bag which landed with a metallic clank. Kyle put his back to the wall and looked alternately left and right, scanning for anymore danger. When Pat joined him, looking fresher than he had a right to, Kyle snarled at him thinking it wasn't that long ago that he wouldn't have felt as winded as he did now. They continued to follow the pipes.

The temperature in this area had climbed significantly; they had to be getting close. More pipes joined with the ones they had been following, some yellow and some orange, some of different diameters with gauges sticking out of the insulation. They followed along to the house steam station and, thank God, the entrance to the Steam tunnel. They were just about free. Through the tunnel they went, and when they got to the door that was the entrance to the ConEd vault, they nearly panicked because they saw a robust chain and heavy lock on the door. Their emotions ran the gamut, from despair, to anguish, to disbelief, and finally to rage. Pat began looking about for something to try and pry it open with.

Kyle took a closer look at the chain and started laughing. Not some idle chuckle, but a gut wrenching guffaw that had Pat turning to look and see if his father had cracked under the pressure. When he got closer to his father, he saw that in his father's hand was one end of the heavy chain. He was threading it back out of the doors handle. Pat looked questioningly at his dad. Kyle pointed to a masonry nail that was off to the side of the door. "The chain was just hanging on a nail head," he chuckled some more and opened the door. "Text uncle Dunk… let him know we got here and in one piece."

Pat did as he was told. They took a few minutes to relax and loosen up their muscles as the constant tension and the exertion had caused various muscle groups to settle into a dull burn. "Hey this could be the start of a new fitness regiment… Run away from zombies and get six pack abs" said Kyle. They both laughed, not at the joke really, more just to relieve some more of the tension.

The chirp of an incoming text message startled them both; Pat nearly dropped the phone. "Uncle Dunk says there is a change in plans." Another chirp "He says he has lead most of the zombies on a WGC*…"

Rise Fall Rise Again: A New York Zombie Encounter

Kyle was stumped "A what?"

"Oh a wild goose chase, he says he will be screeching up in a few minutes. Be ready." They put their helmets and gloves back on and positioned themselves to pop the access hatch to the street.

22

Duncan and company were nearing Penn via Seventh Avenue; they saw several HumVes parked on the sidewalk and in the street. He hoped that was a good sign; that maybe the military was on the scene. Navigating the slalom course would have been easier had his windshield not been streaked with so much grime and gore. Duncan said, "The last fat one splattered big time. It must have eaten more than his buddies, because the contents of his guts are all over the hood and windshield."

As they got back to Eighth and Thirty-first he noticed the moving sign above that entrance to Penn Station, warning that there were no trains, that NYC was under quarantine, and everyone should return to their homes, get off the street and await assistance. That got him to thinking about how in a city of six million or so people at least seventy-five percent of them had to still be alive, hiding within their residences. He wondered if they would receive help and rescue in time. He would have been horrified to know how many would die from this plague. There were just too many vectors to spread this, how many were already doomed, becoming what they feared?

In the window of the psychic advisor on the third floor of one of the buildings near there, Duncan saw the jerky movements of one of the ghouls. He slammed on the breaks and his tires skidded, for he had almost over shot the hatch. The van was still screeching to a stop when he saw his brother push up and out of the hole. Were the situation less dire, he might have laughed. Seeing his brother and nephew in their makeshift armor was damn funny, especially how it made them almost waddle.

George had the side door open before either Duncan or Liam had theirs. He stepped down scanning the street for any threats, when a nearly skeletal hand shot out from under the van and tore through the tough cotton of his work pants. It appeared that they had been dragging that fat one underneath the van for awhile and it was hungry. George jumped away from the thing and shouted a warning to his companions who each jumped from the van out of any possible reach. The creature was trying to drag itself free and was beginning to let out its accursed moan. With its head exposed, it was an easy target for George and his wrench. The head exploded like a pumpkin vandalized by teens on Halloween. George could feel the blood soaking his sock, he could even feel the burn from the wound. The others hadn't seen his torn leg. Maybe he wasn't infected; maybe he wouldn't become a ghoul. His attempts at self delusion were futile, he knew what he was going to become, just as he knew what he was going to have to ask his friends to do.

They gathered together quickly; Duncan had already explained to the guys in the van what was going to happen. He took a few precious seconds to go over it with Kyle, to make sure that they were in agreement. He established that Kyle was in command and he would be leading them through the railroad tunnels back to Long Island.

 Having worked twenty years for the railroad, he knew the protocols for emergencies; he knew the contingency plans. No one balked, they were ready to proceed, and none too soon because off in the distance the moaning could be heard. They looked around quickly and could see a few of the stragglers moving in their direction, although those monsters hadn't yet seemed to have noticed the party of escapees. They formed up into a wedge like formation with Duncan and his ice chopper at the point, Liam and Peter flanking him with their axes, Kyle was in between them and behind Duncan, (so that he could better direct them where to go) and Pat and George closed up the rear. They passed out the additional equipment and supplies and redistributed the packs. They moved as one for the entrance.

They were sure that they would have to fight their way to freedom, and they were equally aware that they might not all make it through. Hell, none of them might, but with wills of iron and the determination of gods, they closed upon the doors which opened before them as they were acknowledged by the door's electric eye. Once inside, the doors closed again. They considered tying the doors off so more zombies couldn't get in, but they rejected that idea in case they needed to beat a hasty retreat. They moved slowly and cautiously towards the escalators; they stayed to the right, opting for the stairs not wanting to be slowed down should they need to turn back. From their limited vantage point, they could see lots of debris and discarded bags from the panic that had spread through the people down here when the attacks had begun. Evidence abounded showing signs of conflict. There was a lot of blood and gore around, smears of it from where bleeding bodies were dragged across the floor. It wasn't the bright red of the freshly spilled, no, and it was more that dirty brownish rust color of dried blood.

They crept onward and downward, more and more was becoming visible. Halfway down they could clearly see the Amtrak Police counter. There were a few bodies on the ground near it, but they didn't appear to be moving. Behind that was one of the numerous Hudson News that could be found throughout the station; this particular Hudson News' crime gate was down, but the store looked as though it had been hit by looters before they were able to seal it off. They heard the pleasant sounding female voice of the recording warning that "the police used dogs to detect specific things on a person or in their baggage, and you should never attempt to pet one of them." Other than the recording, it was silent down there. When they reached the bottom, Kyle told them that they needed to get one level down to the LIRR tunnels.

They came upon the body of a soldier in a seated position leaning against the booth. He had been cradling his bitten arm in his undamaged one. There was a small bullet hole in the center of his forehead. As they got closer they could see that although his rifle was missing he still had useful gear on him, so they rummaged the dead man's pockets and pack. They came away with a gas mask, three smoke grenades, three frag grenades, and an H&K nine mm pistol with five full extra mags in addition to the one in the gun. They were fortunate enough to also find that the poor fellow had night vision goggles too, along with other more mundane supplies.

Peter noticed movement off to the left, turning he saw one of the creeping monsters. This one was moving pretty quickly and with far less Jerky movements; it had to be an older zombie, for the pathogen had far greater control over this one's body. Were it not for the gaping hole where its throat should have been, it could almost have passed for a living being by its movement -almost being the operative word. Be it luck, karma, or good fortune was with them, the fact was that this one had no voice box. It couldn't attract others to them with its moan. It had quickly closed the distance; it was now only a few feet away. Its teeth were gnashing, slimy and viscous drool coming from its mouth, even its hands seemed to be oozing. It was reaching out with both hands ready to grab whomever it could. Duncan repeated the move he had used in the engagement near the bookstore: a swift thrust with his chopper's blade directed at the bridge of the nose. The flesh split and the steel blade caused cartilage and bone to part before it as it traveled through the brain and case, sheering off the top half of the thing's head. With nothing controlling it anymore, the body fell to the floor unceremoniously. They decided after finding the night vision goggles that it might not be a bad idea to forage around a little, so long as the coast was relatively clear.

Moving in unison was proving to be a difficult task, so they opted to loosen the formation. They kept relative position, but with a bit more space between them. They passed the various shops in the concourse; they hardly seemed to notice the remains of the devoured, only registering the potential threat that each posed looking for signs of reanimation. The constant sight of ravaged flesh and all of the blood somehow desensitized them to the carnage. In the window of a store that sold stockings, the display had an arch of leg shaped cutouts wearing thigh-high stockings of every hue and design from sultry fishnets to cute rainbows, inside, they could see people hiding behind the sales counter.

Dispassionately, they continued on.

There was nothing that could be done to save or even to help those folks cowering behind the locked door; they were paralyzed by fear, so much so that no amount of entreaty would get them to unlock the door. They saw firsthand more numerous, better equipped and trained military personnel torn asunder. They certainly weren't going to open up for six guys carrying a hodge-podge of tools and sporting equipment. Secondly, despite the first aid almost all of them were dead already, showing signs of multiple bites and scratches. They were most likely all infected, even if one wasn't... well he would be dinner when the others changed.

They continued past following the circular hallway that would eventually lead them back to where they had started; they came upon "the little Big Horn" of Penn Station. Before them was the scene of the last stand. A squad of military men in a circle fought to the last. Like Custer before them, their cause was lost, and they were overran. Sadly, in all likelihoods they would soon be joining the ranks of the zombies. Their training worked against them. They had all been conditioned in basic training to shoot center mast, to aim for the torso, shots there would have no effect on the walking dead. When forced to resort to melee. They were taught to use pressure points, and strikes to pain centers. This would not even slow any of the creatures they had fought. Zombie combat is counterintuitive; their physiology is such that things that would cripple a normal man, stopping him dead in his tracks, are not even felt by the zombie. These brave men never stood a chance.

All of this, the companions noted from the back side of the escalator. They could see from their vantage point that there were lots of movements outside the doors on the upper level, but they didn't see any nearby. However, they had only a limited view. They decided to go for it, a quick snatch and grab, hopefully without any zombies noticing and sounding like the dinner bell. George and Pat volunteered; Duncan figured he would go too, and then Liam said he would go. No one wanted to be left behind, that cinched it, they would all go and pilfer anything they could grab quickly before heading back the way they came so that they could drop down to the lower level.

Kyle gave the count, "One…Two… Thr" pop pop pop! The sound of a three-round burst from the AR1five*. Then another, and another after that. There were others fighting down here. Thankfully, Kyle didn't complete the word three because a large numbered group that had been out of sight heard the staccato of gunfire, their moans began, and they shuffled off looking for more meat to consume.

"Should we grab the gear and follow. Try to help them stem the tide?" asked Pat hopefully. He felt as though he was shirking his responsibility, being active duty and trained in combat.

His father's look answered the question, and Pat seemed to deflate just a little. "Look Pat…" his words tried to soften the sting "we have the rest of the families counting on us. Its family first Pat… it has to be." He put his hand on his son's shoulder and squeezed. "Come on let's move before some come back." The group rushed forward to the fallen warriors and began to grab their loot; Pat, however, grabbed a K-Bar and in a solemn, near reverent way began moving about the corpses of his brothers-in-arms, and thrust the blade into their ocular cavities.

Pete looked as though he was going to say something, but a look from Kyle told him that this was something Pat needed to do. It made sense. It was sound military doctrine to deprive the enemy of resources, but that wasn't why he was doing it. He knew that they would not want to return from the dead, and moreover, he hoped that were their roles reversed they would have done the same for him.

Liam found a comms unit and was picking it up, but Pat informed him that the unit was toast. They were collecting the guns and ammo. Some they discarded as they were visibly jammed, and others that had been used in a manner other than how the designers intended, as clubs, when the guns had run dry, and they didn't have time to reload. The stocks of those weapons were a gruesome reminder of what had happened here before they arrived. They would have to travel light, so they would sort their booty in a safer or at least more easily defended area and leave the rest behind for other survivors.

They dragged their haul into the Club Acela lounge and shut the door behind them. There they went through all the equipment, what they had brought with them and what they had just acquired. They ended up with six functional AR fifteens, four forty-five caliber Colts, four H&K nine mils, night-vision gear for each of them as well as gas masks, a canteen for each of them, three flares each, and a dozen more frag grenades. As for ammunition, they had reloaded all the empty magazines that they could find resulting in a grand total of thirty-six for the ARs and four for each of the handguns. They emptied the remainder of the loose rounds into one of the packs to be sorted later. Pat made certain that each rifle was locked and loaded, with the fire select switch on single fire; ammo was going to be at a premium, so he didn't want them burning through clips. He gave instructions on how to eject spent mags and how to charge the weapon on a reload. He figured he would have time to teach them everything else if they survived and escaped.

 Kyle was duly impressed with the professionalism which his son gave the instructions and said so. The praise was not lost on Pat; it seems you never get too old for taking pride in pleasing one's parent. They were all scared, but there comes a point, when you can't get any more scared, that you just become numb to it. You either push through or you freeze up into inactivity like those folks in the stocking store. They were all scared, but they were functional. George was looking as if he might slip past the point where action was still possible. Duncan went over to him to try and talk him back off of the proverbial ledge.

"Dunk, I'm done... I came this far to help you guys, and I'll help you down into the tunnels..." he trailed off.

Duncan was lost, "what do you mean you're done? We are all getting out of here; my brother will get us through…"

George interrupted and showed his torn calf. Three furrows spiraled down his calf from behind his knee where that zombie had grabbed him. The wounds, although no longer bleeding, looked angry and inflamed, yellow pus was coming from the greenish scabs like mucus. The veins in his leg were dark almost black and very close to the surface. Sorrow etched Duncan's features; he was at a loss for words. He knew what this meant; George did too, "Dunk when we get you through, I want you guys to take my gear and go. You're going to need it where you're going; but you've gotta promise me one thing; you've gotta put a bullet in my brain. I'm Catholic, and it would be a sin if I offed myself, so you have to promise me you will do it." There was finality in his words, resignation. Duncan agreed.

The others had observed the exchange and each one in turn expressed their condolences, their heartfelt gratitude for the help he had given and respect for the decision he was making. "I ain't dead yet boys. There's still a chance we will ALL be the main course, so don't look so glum." His feeble attempt at levity was appreciated by the rest. They each shouldered their gear. Keeping their melee weapons at the ready, they quietly exited their temporary refuge and made their way to the stairs to the lower level.

23

The plane on which John found himself didn't have the same laboratory *'feel'* as had the mobile command center, quite the opposite actually. It was a Gulf Stream private job, very well appointed, trez chic by most standards, with leather seats and phones at each of them, along with power sources for the gamete of electronic devices that the business traveler needs. John found the *'normalcy'* of it all comforting.

Before they let him out of the clean room, he was asked to disrobe for a full inspection of his entire body as well as having to submit a blood sample and have his temperature recorded. His hosts were leaving nothing up to chance. He now found himself in a comfortable chair cruising at thirty-thousand feet with his hands free. He was no longer under the scrutiny of what one could only refer to as his guard with the gun who looked as though he would be quite content to have shot him earlier. Dr. Hampton was in the seat opposite him reading through various files on his computer.

A call came through on the phone at the doctor's seat. After a brief exchange, the doctor pushed a button that transferred the call to speaker, "Go ahead he is sitting with me," said the doctor, to the as of yet anonymous person on the other end of the call.

"Mr. Roberts, I want to thank you for your cooperation on such short notice. I am Dr. Manis, the director of the CDC virology division in Atlanta." John didn't respond. The silence hung in the air for an uncomfortable few seconds. Dr . Manis continued, "Reports are coming in from all across the country, and around the world, mostly, however, from New York City. Were they not coming from credible sources, these reports would be chalked up to someone's idea of a bad joke. The dead are rising! However, some concrete data came in from the Russian Academy of Science. Now, as you know, something happened after you separated from Dr. Romero and left Siberia. We have received access to all his e-mails and files. Coupled with the information you have already given us, we have a fairly complete picture of what he was working on along with some shocking information that was forwarded to him from a hematologist at the Russian Academy of Science in Moscow. That e-mail and the subsequent slides and data he sent have given us the first glimpses into this plague that is attacking the world." John was taking copious notes on the conversation as it unfolded. "What few in the world know, is that our enemy is not the *'walking dead,'* but in reality, a parasite and a retrovirus that work symbiotically. We have a working hypothesis on how it mutated, but we have yet to identify its entire gnome and to be quite frank with you Mr. Roberts; we have never seen anything behave like this anywhere in nature, or in a lab, for that matter. Preliminary computer modeling is extremely pessimistic to say the least."

Those words sank in swiftly. John was not here on a scoop. He was here because the CDC was grabbing at straws and were hoping he might remember something else that might help them save humanity. "I am not really sure how I can help, but rest assured Doctor. I will do anything you ask of me."

"You will have unprecedented access to information here. We want you to do what you do best; write. Your work will be linked on our website, and we would like you to author a blog, or you can even use one you already have, or that of a colleague. The point is we want people to have a reliable source of information, survival tips, anything, but what we want is to give you the current information for you to pass along. The public is going to need hope. This has the potential to be more dire than the bubonic plague and the black death, hell all of histories pandemics rolled into one, let's say biblical in proportion. Now we have PR people, but you have public credibility due to your publication in Discover. Plus you have the added feature of having been there where this happened and survived. Will you give the world hope Mr. Roberts?"

The whole speech was like a bad TV movie, *"just win one for the gipper,"* but the sentiment was true, and he could see himself being of help in this regard. "Sure, like I said, anything I can do." The pilot's voice came over the cabin speakers saying they would be on the ground in fifteen minutes; they were on final approach and had priority clearance to land.

John was suddenly nervous. He hadn't been nervous since the first article, he submitted to Discover that landed him his career and even that paled by comparison. He had committed because he knew it needed to be done. He just wasn't sure that he was up to the task, but he damn well was sure that he was going to give it his all. A small area of his thought, the mercenary side of his brain, thought that if man survives, then this might make his resume. When the plane taxied to a stop, he grabbed his gear and followed his host as they disembarked.

It was a relatively short ride by HumVes to the CDC. John wasn't sure what to expect; he wouldn't have been surprised to have arrived at some sort of military base with fences and constatina wire. What he found however, was what looked somewhat like an office park. Sure there are check points and hard points, there are gates and fences, but it doesn't look like an impregnable fortress. There was a sizeable military presence: sandbagged gun emplacements, armored personnel carriers, tanks and more. Military men were erecting more fencing in concentric circles around the compound. The preparations were not lost on John, who noticed right away that they were expecting to be under siege. It didn't take a degree in higher math to know that this facility didn't have the resources to handle mass refugees, if they could even safely screen for the infected who had yet to succumb. So in the pit of his stomach he understood that the gun emplacements were more to fend off the survivors then to fight the apocalyptic hordes.

24

An innocuous container ship steams towards New York from Beijing. The manifests indicate that the cargo onboard is of the innocent variety, products that would fill the shelves at regional Wal-Mart stores. That could not be farther from the truth. Inside these ordinary looking shipping containers, a horrifying transformation is taking place. The cargo of this ship was human in origin. Hapless people who had gambled their lives on a better future in the United States. Their escape from China was orchestrated by nefarious human traffickers, who accept as payment a contract of servitude for a number of years. That is of course, if you don't have twenty thousand dollars. These people would be lucky to earn that sum in a life time.

Their accommodations on this journey were cramped, and the food provided inadequate. The sanitary measures were anything but. Yet these people would endure all of these hardships for the chance to live better lives free of oppression. It was a chance to carve out a life for themselves and their families. Sadly, this dream would never come to fruition.

When they were herded into the steel boxes, no one knew that among some of the hopeful were people infected with this new plague. They were in the earliest stages of the disease; none yet showed the symptoms. Families fought hard to stay together as the human cattle were shoved in and the doors were secured behind them. This ship would carry twenty such containers with no less than fifty souls in each, sometimes even more were crammed in.

The crew of the ship were paid to turn a blind eye. Some of the more altruistic of them would slip more food in and during the dark would occasionally open the doors and allow the passengers out into the fresh sea air. This rarely happened; there were strict rules that were enforced by the smugglers. Offenders paid dearly, yet on occasion the *"cargo"* was checked upon, and medical treatment was provided on a limited basis. After all if the cargo died in transport, there was no way to recoup the fee.

The first of the victims to change had seemed ill and listless, a small woman of middle years. She had been an academian in her old life, but had drawn the unwanted attention of the Government. She was a physicist who had returned from Russia recently. She and her family were spread amongst the containers. Their possessions, few that there were, traveled with them. Before they were loaded and the ship left port in the dark of the night, the would-be cargo, were huddled in a warehouse to await the next step of the journey, the loading into the containers. The fleas and bedbugs jumped hungrily from person to person. It would be safe to say that there were infected in every container.

The metamorphosis worked at differing rates in different people. When she took ill, she found her way into a corner and suffered in a stoic fashion. She was apart from everyone she knew. Nobody took notice as she expired. When she reanimated however, the screams of terror and pain drew sympathetic crew members. It also drew the smugglers who adamantly prevented the doors from being opened. She tore wounds into many; she had bitten and mauled many more. One of her fellow passengers attempted to subdue her but broke her neck in the process. The calls for help finally convinced the smugglers to investigate and render what minor aid they were prepared to grant.

Only three had died in that box, but many were injured. Those three bodies were thrown overboard. The more serious wounds were bound. The rest were cleaned haphazardly, and the doors were shut again. The sickness spread rapidly. In all of the human containers, the infection had predictable effects. Off of the coast of Long Island the traffickers decided to cut their losses. They began having the containers dumped overboard. To them, it was a bad business deal; they had no compassion.

The people in the containers had already disappeared... it didn't matter if they drowned.

This was too much for the ship's crew, money or not they would not send a thousand people to drown on the ocean floor. The doors were thrown open on container after container, but instead of the meek passengers out came a host of zombies two hundred strong. The ones in other containers were busy devouring those few living inside. The two hundred scoured the ship. All souls were lost, and the ship foundered. Those 200 that had been on deck were washed overboard, taken by the sea.

25

The two vans were in constant communication via cell phones on speaker, they weren't so much as talking as they were, taking comfort in the ambient sounds of life in each of the vehicles. Katie was in the lead van with Auntie Laura and the girls, while Sean road in the other van with Aunt Pam whose white knuckles threatened to snap the steering wheel if she wasn't careful. Dawn was just approaching, and the grey light did not help visibility, but rather it hindered it substantially, couple that with a low ground, fog lent more to the imagination than any of them really wanted. It was downright spooky, Katie keeping her own council wondered if it were better to fear the unknown, huddled in the dark with your loved ones, rather than to have those fears proven in the light of day.

Seeing the images of these things on the television gave one a sense of detachment, allowed a measure of disbelief to remain; the fear was there alright just compartmentalized. Driving, here and now, if they see something there is no way to deny the existence, no measure of self-delusion would work. "Kaitlyn and Kristen, I want you to hunker down get down to the floor." She would spare her youngsters any horrid sights. "How come ma?" Neither of them wanted to miss anything, just the morbid curiosity of any adolescent. Katie just told them to do it; they weren't happy but they did it. Auntie Laura was a little slow on the uptake as her questioning look was searching for some danger that prompted the instructions. Sean listening from the second van smiled. He caught on right away.

They were just passing their old parish; the one Katie had belonged to before she and Duncan were married. She took comfort in the architecture; more akin to Greek Orthodox in design, a flood of memories came on. They made the turn, and the doors came into view. Katie almost slammed on the breaks. She was horrified by the scene there. She could see the ruin that was entryway, the signs of violence evident even in the poor visibility. The defiled body of the Pastor lay there torn and broken upon the stairs. Tears filled her eyes, and a single sob slipped beyond her control. It wasn't much but enough to clue her children that she had seen something that threatened to break her tattered spirit. Curiosity had the girls careening their necks to hopefully catch a glimpse. Katie caught their attempt and told them to get back down a little more forcefully. "Come on Pam let's speed up I want to get out of here" with that being said she accelerated a bit leaving the sight of the ruined church behind.

The vans made the turn *onto* East Rockaway Road; a fairly busy residential road normally; although normal wouldn't be coming back around anytime soon if ever, with curves that if you weren't paying attention could spell disaster. The vans passed the academy and a few higher-end homes that make up this part of town; so far, they had no sign of life or undead for that matter; Katie muttered a quiet prayer for it to stay that way. It, however, did not.

As they pulled out of another curve, they saw in front of them a Black Range Rover in the middle of an intersection, with its hazards on and the driver-side door ajar. They slowed marginally as they passed. The image of the scene became indelibly imprinted within Katie's brain; as they passed she could see the imprint of where the car had smashed into a pedestrian just off center on the hood to the right. Laying in the road about twenty feet away was a body being devoured by several of the creatures, the body, presumably the driver had hit one of them at a frightening speed, she stopped to investigate thinking that she had killed someone, she had hit them so hard, when she got to what she was sure to be dead, the thing must have grabbed her and started to feast, the others in the area must have responded to the screams of the victim or to the moans of the Ghoul. Even the affluent neighborhood of Hewlett Harbor was victim to this scourge. The zombies had heard the approaching vehicles and gained their feet, quicker than the drivers would have expected and began to move in their direction with a slightly stiff legged trot, rather than the uncoordinated gate that was shown in so many of Hollywood's depictions. The vans sped away. One of the zombies had actually gotten close enough to Pam's van to grab *onto the* passenger side mirror. The vans mass and speed cast the creature to the ground in a roll, but it was enough to quicken Pam's pulse as her grip on the wheel got even tighter. "That was close," said Sean to his aunt, although his mother heard it over the open line. "Yeah it was… Katie let's pick up the pace huh? We aren't running into any traffic so let's get a move on." Katie couldn't agree more and answered by bringing the speedometer up to five mph, only slowing when they came to intersections, and then only enough so that they could avert a crash if there were any other cars.

They made it through East Rockaway without further incident, when they got into Oceanside, and made the turn *onto* Lawson Blvd. they chanced a bit more speed. In years gone by this stretch of the road was often the scene of late-night drag races. On both sides of the road, they saw the industrial buildings that zoning permitted here, a mile and a half away up atop the hill, they saw a conflagration. Several vehicles were a blaze effectively blocking the way. Katie and Pam had no choice but to detour around then the heard the unmistakable sound of an air horn in three short blasts, they slowed and continued forward more slowly, then they could see off, in the distance, a figure step in front of the blaze and begin waving a large white flag emblazoned with a big red lobster in its center. Clearly, they were being told that this way was safe, and that they could make it around sans detour; so up the hill they went.

When they got there, they could see skeletal remains within the blaze, as the figure with the flag; a fireman in full gear, including his SCBA (self contained breathing apparatus) strolled up to Katie's van and knocked on her window. They were at a choke point/ checkpoint. The fireman took off his mask and smiled while gesturing for her to roll down the window. Katie opened her window a scant inch; the fireman appreciated her caution and told her so. "Has anyone in either of your vehicles come into contact with any violent people? Has anyone been injured? So much as even a scratch?" "No we are all right. We are just trying to get to Pt. Lookout and our boat." He shined a light within the van and saw their supplies, as well as the two children on the floor in the second row of seats. "Ma'm would you mind pulling over and each of you getting out. We aren't letting anyone with any wounds past this point?" This was not a question. She could see the Long Beach Fire Department insignia on his heavy fire coat. In response to her delay she saw several similarly attired men step out of concealment brandishing weapons. If these men had bad intentions, there was nothing any of them could do, but her gut said they were on the up and up. "Sure, where do you want us to pull over?" The fireman seemed to relax a little, he apparently didn't like the idea of having to strong-arm people, but he had a job to do and was damn well going to do it. He had family in town and wasn't going to let this spread there if he could help it. Little did he know that it was already there and more was coming from the direction no one was watching, from the sea.

They climbed back into their vans after stepping out and having lights shined on their extremities. This procedure was done with as much courtesy and deference as possible under the circumstances. They drove *onto the* next checkpoint and then to the third just before the Long Beach Bridge, which was in the up position when they were cleared by the guards the bridge operator was called on the radio, the horns were sounded and the draw bridge began to close. No sooner had they cleared the other side when the horns sounded again, and the bridge again was raised.

There was plenty of activity here in Long Beach, especially when you considered it was just past dawn; the town had responded very quickly to the news in NYC. They had managed to come up with an action plan and implemented it with amazing speed. Just the sight of people moving about was very reassuring, the town had mobilized, the entire police and fire forces of all the little towns and communities that made-up Long Beach banded together, There were pickups and SUVs being loaded with supplies from the supermarket from there headed to unload in the High

119

School Gymnasium. Various contractors were plying their trades to better security and defense capabilities throughout the town, the police and the auxiliary were working with the fire department at all accesses to the island; they were spread a bit thin, given all the bridges, but they were effective.

The family's vans made the left turn *onto* Lido Blvd, and they all felt significantly safer. They continued on, passing homes on the left and accesses to the beaches, both public and private on the right. The water tower came into view. They knew they only had a short distance farther to go. Here too the Loop Parkway Bridge was raised, a comforting sight actually, and just beyond the ramp was the entrance to their marina. It seemed as if the entire membership of the Long Beach Yacht Club was here making preparations to get under way and put out to sea. Katie mused, "Maybe Duncan was right?" she said aloud to no one, in particular, and then they pulled into their parking spots.

Kevin looked like he had just stepped off the set of some Hollywood surfer movie, with his toned body and well muscled physique, along with his tan: the kind of tan that most people don't achieve until late June or perhaps early July. Kevin's was from a life spent out of door and on boats whenever possible. He and his brother looked very much alike. They were both well-built and well proportioned with strong features, and both had their fathers dirty blonde hair, and the arresting deep-blue eyes of their mother; although Kevin was a few inches shorter than his brother. Their personalities, however, were nearly diametrically opposite; where Pat was austere and serious, Kevin bordered on clownish; satire was Kevin's existence.

When the vans parked Pam and Katie saw that Kevin was talking to a man who looked somewhat familiar to Katie over by the bulkhead. Pam ran over to her son. She needed to hold him in her arms and prove to herself that he was there, safe and sound. Kevin was speaking with David Bennett, one of his uncle's friends, the likely savior of his dad and brother.

His mother's arrival was a trifle embarrassing as she wordlessly engulfed him in a bear hug. It was difficult to disengage from her embrace, but he eventually managed and introduced her to Dave. "Mom, this is David Bennett. He's the one who gave Dad and Pat their escape directions." She threw her arms around the man whom she had never met before and hugged him tightly, all the while saying how thankful she was to him. It was now Dave's turn to be embarrassed. "No thanks are necessary, truly; I can't believe what is happening, if Duncan hadn't called me, I would be oblivious, have you guys heard from them recently?" asked Dave hopefully. The happiness drained from her face, and he knew the answer before she even spoke. "No we haven't heard from them in a while, but we expect to hear from them soon... I imagine they are a little too busy trying to stay alive than to be calling us" she chuckled in an attempt to put a brave face on her emotions. "I am sure that's just the case... your husband is a good man. I've met him a couple of times with Duncan, and from what Kevin has been saying about his brother, I imagine they are just fine. Dunk and them will get out of the city rest assured." She looked for deception in his face and words but found only conviction. He truly believed what he was saying. She warmed to him again. "Yep they will be fine; those McGregor's are a crafty and resourceful bunch" she laughed, in earnest, this time.

The rest of the family had made their way over to join in the conversation. Sean and Kevin started to unload the vans; they appropriated a pair of shopping carts and started to haul the gear down the dock to the waiting sailboat. Maryanne, the Commodore of the Yacht Club came over to the group to say hello to Katie, telling her that they were all going to go off shore a ways and make sort of a flotilla, and that their vessel was welcome. Dave's fishing boat was tied up next to the Persistence. It was dwarfed by the sailboat. There were two fifty-five gallon drums on board that were marked property of the US Coast Guard concealed under a tarp. Maryanne raised an eyebrow as she noted the drums. Dave looked a little sheepish, "Kevin there helped me get some extra cruising fuel. Hell mine can't be the only boat in the flotilla running on gasoline" She looked to him and smiled. She too liked him right away. So did Aunt Laura, who keenly felt how alone she was, her divorce was finalized 18 months ago, and although she has dated a few different men since then, she didn't have a significant other in her life, and with all the chaos and danger, it was even more apparent than usual.

They finished unloading Katie's van and moved *on to* Pam's, which was by far more interesting as hers had her husband's guns and ammo. The large plastic cases that held the rifles were very distinct as were the ammunition boxes. The other people on the Warf took notice. A couple of enthusiasts came over to see what sort of firepower was in the cases. Kevin having grown-up hunting with his dad and brother was proud to fill them in on the details, " Well the first case has two Remington three-oh-eight Hi powers fitted with Zeiss seven and a half to twenty power, by fifty milimeter scopes, that big one over there is a Browning three-three-eight Lapua Magnum A-Bolt action fitted with the same glass on low mounts" one of the enthusiasts whistled in admiration. Kevin continued, " We've got two Mossberg Double slide twelve-gauges in that case with deer slug barrels separate, and in the satchel here we have matched Sig Sauer nine mils in black and my dad's pride and joy a Dan Wesson .three-five-seven with all three barrels" Kevin's chest was swollen with pride as he was speaking. Sean listened intently. He had shot these guns with his uncle, but his mom wouldn't let his own dad have any, so he was always envious of his cousins.

They finally finished loading the boat. As they put everything away in the holds and storage spaces, they realized there was very little extra space. Sure the boat was big and could accommodate everybody and Aloha, but it would be tight. They inflated the dingy and lashed it to the foredeck; I double-checked the rigging and furling gear. The boat was ship shape; they were just waiting for the "grownups" to finish talking so that they could get underway.

Finally, all the "captains" got together to plot the course, suddenly disaster horns were blaring. Everyone started looking at each other dumbly, frozen where they stood. Their false sense of security was now shattered like so much broken glass, there were zombies coming out of the surf and *onto* *the* beaches. The sand hampered their already uncoordinated gate so the progress they made was slow, but the sheer number of them was astounding. Panic gripped the people who had thought themselves safe in this little hamlet.

The family made for the boat, Maryanne shouted orders to a few other captains, someone said that a container ship that was being used in a human trafficking ring apparently had some infected passengers within, and that set off a chain reaction, these that are washing up here have got to be from that ship. Dave jumped into his boat; the throaty rumble of his twin Mercs was impressive, plumes of exhaust smoke tainted with that oil smell filled the air. Kevin untied Dave's bow line and tossed it to him. He began back away from the dock so that when he was clear, he could exit the marina. The other boats were similarly making ready to get under way. Once Katie and the rest were aboard, they too cast off; just as they saw two shambelers enter the parking lot about fifty yards away.

Kevin estimated that the zombies might get close enough to do harm before everyone would be able to clear the docks and get into the bay, quickly he went down through the companion way, to grab and load one of the three-oh-eights. With the safety still on, he then slung the rifle and went top side again. He laid down on the deck below the boom and assumed a prone shooting position; his arm looped snuggly through the strap, with a perfect cheek weld to the stock. He relaxed. His breathing was measured. He took careful aim on the forehead of the leading zombie through his optics, the rise and fall caused by the water became a predictable pattern. When he was confident in his timing, he shut his eyes and opened them when he believed he would have a clear sight picture in his scope. Sure enough the cross hairs were centered on the approaching creature's head. Slowly, he tightened his finger on the trigger as he completely exhaled his last breath; the trigger broke, and the rifle kicked into his shoulder. Across the parking lot, the head of the zombie blew apart and the now decapitated corpse fell in a heap to the ground. He allowed himself a moment's satisfaction, and then repeated the whole process again with the following zombie; who came on without notice of the fate his predecessor met with? Cheers immediately went up, those on the boats still at the docks breathed a little easier; eventually, an orderly exit from the marina was made.

The scene looked as if it was the start of some regatta or other; with boats tacking and jibing until everyone was in position; S.V. Persistence cutting through the swells like a hot knife through warm butter. It made the channel and followed the markers out of the inlet; the swells becoming slightly more substantial as they made the Atlantic Ocean. The rest of the boats followed to the same relative position, on the same baring, ultimately dropping anchor a mile off shore.

26

The Vice President asked the President for a private meeting. When the door to the oval office was closed by a departing secret service agent, they were seated across the desk from one another. "Shoot, I have a meeting with the Hill in thirty minutes." The President said as he looked at his Omega.

"Mr. President, have you read the latest Intel briefings and the preliminary report from the CDC? We have ourselves a real shit storm here." He waited several seconds for some sort of response from the President; he was disappointed.

"Listen we have a lot on our plates just now. I don't have time to worry about what the CDC is saying just now, it's sure to be the budget justification show, now what I am really concerned with is China's posturing."

"You had better make time!" interrupted the VP, "We have major uprisings happening all over the country, there is something happening all around the world and the CDC thinks it's all connected. You are aware that NYC is up in flames right now right? What are we doing about it? You have to demonstrate to your fellow Americans that this administration is up to the task." The VP could see that his words were falling upon deaf ears. "Am I free to act on your behalf regarding the domestic crisis?"

"Tell you what, give your recommendations into the hands of my COS, and I'll review them and give 'em my chop… anything else I'm running behind?"

It didn't matter what his reply was going to be he was summarily dismissed. The VP stood and smoothed his slacks; was about to say something then figured why waste his breath. He turned and left. He didn't like what he knew he was going to have to do, but for the country's survival, possibly for the world's survival he was going to be forced to take steps.

When he arrived back at his office, he put in a call to the Attorney General and another to the Chief Justice of the Supreme Court. He also contacted the Senate Majority Leader and the Speaker for the House. He bade them all to meet with him at his residence, aware as he was of the unorthodox request. He laid the cards on the table and told them each that the President was failing in his oath of office and that the United States survival and possibly the survival of mankind was in jeopardy, and that he has information from the CDC that clearly shows this. They all agreed to an informal and non-binding meeting at the Naval Observatory Residence.

27

The Club Acela lounge was quite comfortably appointed, there were even plenty of snacks for the guys to nibble upon and a Keurig coffee service. They were safe, for the moment, unless of course, the zombies had a membership card and could swipe it in the reader, and then they still would have to be able to unblock the door and untie its bonds, yes they were relatively safe and took a few minutes to rest and rejuvenate.

George was looking through the door towards the New Jersey Transit waiting area; he was watching a group of zombies stumbling around in there. They appeared to have absolutely no cognitive abilities. They were unable to circumvent even the simplest of obstacles; they were tangled in a section of portable nylon station barriers. George had already gotten the commitment from Duncan to prevent him from returning from the dead, seeing this made it all the more important of a promise; he noticed a larger group coming from by the GNC store coming towards where he, and the rest were hiding. He quietly alerted Kyle and Duncan then continued his watch. Duncan and Kyle came right away to see if they were going to need to revise their fragile plans. The group milled about in a confused manner. They were joined by another group from the lower level, and they headed off past TGI Fridays and KFC; the zombies were moving with purpose and away from them.

Duncan said softly to his brother that they were probably headed to find another pocket of survivors and that now was the time to move. Kyle was in agreement so the word was passed and they collected their gear.

They had already divided up George's gear at his insistence. They gave the zombies a thirty count before they left their hidey hole. They moved as quickly and as silently as they could keeping as low as they could move; it was about fifty feet to the Amtrak police desk and from there it was another forty feet to the first set of stairs, but they opted for the next stairs as those were closer to the tunnel they would have to enter and since they were fairly confident that there were not any zombies hiding around here the same could not be said for below. They continued their approach moving with all the care that they could muster.

Slowly, they began their descent, step, step, step, pause, slow agonizing progress, but they could see from their vantage that there was a terrifying scene below them. There must have been a confrontation between the military and the zombies, there were bodies torn apart everywhere; to the point where the remains were hardly recognizable as having been human beings.

The men continued, unaffected by the scene. This was their only hope of getting home. They all had their guns within easy reach but were prepared to meet conflict with their melee weapons first figuring that the loud reports from the firearms and rifles would have more of the zombies falling upon them. The columns and kiosks below could have hidden an army of zombies if they had the intelligence to avail themselves of the cover. Pete took one side and Liam the other; George was looking behind them towards the Amtrak tracks, the lack of the normal ambient noises that everyone was so used to was disturbing in that subconscious sort of way. However, it did allow them to hear the slurping sound as marrow was being sucked from a bone.

The creature was not in sight, the sound suggested that it was coming from somewhere near the Starbuck's at the "T" with the concourse. If there was one, there were likely to be many; hand signals were used to pull everyone to the right side of center as the passed tracks fifteen and sixteen and approaching track seventeen. They were all tense, figuring that one or more of those things were going to spring at them any second, maybe from one of the track stairwells they were passing. Moaning was starting to be heard, perhaps from the stairs that lead to the subway system.

First it was only a couple, then others joined in, and then still more, this was a very large group; the companions looked at each other, knowing that if they didn't go for it now, all was lost. George thrust his rifle into Liam's hands, he then he pulled his nine millimeter and carefully stalked off.

He retraced their steps to over by the stairs he crossed to the other side and as noisily as possible, yelling at the top of his lungs he sprinted passed his friends acknowledging them with a look and then he was passed. The large group took the bait; the companions had a small window of opportunity where the sounds that they would make dropping down into the tunnels would be overtaken by the noise of the horde.

They went for it, down they went one two three four five there were trains on each of the tracks, no doors were open, and they were blocking the platform access to the tunnels. Large amounts of blood and body parts were strewn about haphazardly. The stillness of the air compounded the smell of the blood, shit, and gore. You could nearly taste it all; the air was vile.

George was running for all he was worth. He was going to buy the guys all the time he could. He knew he had fifteen rounds, so he would fire fourteen at the zombies' heads, and he would end his own with the last, surely God would understand and forgive this. He was running towards the sculpture down by McDonald's, others had heard him and were flooding from there too. He ran passed the ticket counters and turned left; he ran up the stairs by the LIRR waiting/ rest area taking the steps two and sometimes three at a time.

George had gone about as far as he could. He was surrounded on all sides now, so he stopped mid way, he took aim at the head of the closest one; this one happened body to be a fifty-ish woman in pajamas with no visible wounds, he aimed and squeezed. The gun kicked in his hand. He was rewarded with the sight of a small entrance wound between her eyes; the body collapsed as if whatever was powering it were suddenly shut. The next was barista from Starbuck's; George noticed with sick fascination that her left forearm had been stripped of flesh and mussel, so that only bone and a little sinew remained; he aimed and shot her too. Then they were coming too fast for him to pick out the details about them. He dropped another eight in quick succession that made ten; he would take out another two and then turn the gun upon himself. He miss judged the speed of one of the closer ones; it managed to grab a hold of him with talon like hands ruining his shot on the next.

They were on him now; he felt the pressure of their bites but thankfully, the pain was diminished; whether from adrenaline or from the work of the virus that was already changing him, it didn't matter, he had one thought remaining; get control of the gun and put it into his mouth and pull the trigger. The horde had him and they were pulling him apart. He struggled for all he was worth; finally, he was able to free his gun hand. His last words were, "God forgive me" then he put the barrel into his mouth and fired.

****

Duncan and Pat were covering Kyle and the rest with their assault rifles. Kyle was busy looking for his railroad key; the key that would allow him to open the doors on the train blocking their way. All of the trains that they could see were blocking access to the tracks towards Long Island; all of them had lighted signs that read "No Passengers." If Kyle could locate his key, he could get them inside and be able to shut and seal the door behind them, if not they could always use the emergency access by breaking a little plastic panel and using the little red handle enclosed, if they pumped that handle it would open the doors, but then they could be followed. Caution had won out; Kyle located his key; cursing himself for not having had it ready at the start. He inserted the key and turned; to his, and everyone's relief the door sprung open. Pat loosed a three-round burst at a group of shambelers that had found them.

Kyle cursed again loudly as they all dashed into the train car. The door shut, and they began to move through the car heading to the end so that they could escape onto the tracks. Zombies were slamming against the train windows trying in vain to get at the fleeing men.

Kyle suspected it would only be a matter of time before the zombies battered their way through the glass or knocked in an escape window. He only wished that Pat hadn't fired, but what's done is done. They exited the train from the front where the driver sits, Kyle locked the partition *to* maybe halt any following or at least to slow them some. Once he had joined them outside of the train, he then tied off the dog legs on the door.

Kyle, Duncan, and Pete secured their Night-vision goggles, adjusted their straps, and then powered them up. Pat was using a helmet that had a flip down monocular type, as was Liam the device took a little getting used to for Liam, but Pat was familiar with it and was more comfortable with its use than the type being used by his father and uncle. They had George's helmet and monocular setup tied to one of the bags; it would serve as a spare in case Mr. Murphy of the Laws fame showed up and wreaked havoc on them.

As they began their way down the tunnel, Kyle noticed that there was a movement in the old "tower," not the uncoordinated movement of the undead, rather that of people in hiding. The old tower now served as a location for several backup computer systems, in the early five0s when that whole area was open to the air, before they built the whole garden complex it had served a more prestigious purpose but now… well now it was a place where there were living breathing people were hiding out. They figured it warranted checking out; Kyle was sure it would be railroad guys who escaped and figured it was a good place to hide.

Kyle's hunch was right, inside the structure were three guys and a dead body whose head had been smashed to a pulp; given that the corpse had a bite mark, and the other three were undamaged told that these guys had a clue at least or had drawn the same conclusions as Duncan and the rest.

Felix, Eddie and Harold were all track maintainers; they hadn't been able to get back in time to hop the last shuttle car that took all the rest of the uninfected crews to safety before Manhattan was sealed off. They didn't have any supplies with them, and their flashlights were running low on battery life. They asked if they could join with the companions as they made their escape.

Duncan was concerned that this could jeopardize their chances, but Kyle assured him that they would be of great assistance. Duncan had put Kyle in command, so what Kyle said went, so he conceded to their coming with them. However, he adamantly rejected giving any of their gear over to these new guys, and that included George's gear. Kyle thought he was being irrational but Duncan was fixed in his position.

Now that the party had grown, and they started to get going... Duncan realized that their flashlights could give them away so he dug out a FLIR* hand held monocular (Forward Looking Infer Red) and gave them George's helmet and night optics, the last guy would have to try to keep up while using his flashlight sparingly and from the very back of the group. Harold took a piece of electric tape and closed off the light from his Mini Mag Light so that no light shined, he then took a razor knife and put a slit in the tape that allowed him to see adequately but could be scarce been seen from more than four feet away. Thus prepared, they started upon their sojourn that would lead them back to their families.

All the signal indicators along the way were red, so even had they been able to disengage a train car, the railroad's interlock safety systems would not allow any train to operate other than to sit there with minimal electrical. This made it exponentially safer to be walking the tracks, sure they still had to worry about the walking dead, but at least they didn't have to worry about the third rail, or anyone stealing a train and running them down. Their only fears were of getting lost and or of running into another horde down there. So far, the only other creatures any of them had seen were rats, large sewer rats, but those typically fled from the human's approach.

The night-vision technology was great, but it took a lot of getting used to, thus keeping the party's progress agonizingly slow.

The utter darkness of these tunnels was akin to the images conjured within the mind when one ponders the abyss; it made everyone uneasy. Man's natural environment is within the light. It is his fear of the dark which prompted early man's mastery of fire. Every sound was amplified. Every stumble exaggerated. Nervous chatter overtook any hope of maintaining noise discipline. Pat gave up after the fifth attempt to enforce that protocol. The darkness altered their perception of time. They had been walking for a mere twenty minutes, and yet it seemed to the dispirited men as if they were trudging along for closer to six or seven hours.

By Kyle's reckoning; and confirmed by the track maintainers, they could hope to emerge from the tunnels within two hours or so, given their current speed. The echoes within the tunnel brought their worst fears to fruition; they heard that familiar and disturbing sound, the moans of their pursuers, and the call of the zombie. They were at least getting better accustomed to their enhanced vision, thus allowing them to increase their pace. An eerie series of squeaks were closing on the group, as thousands upon thousands of sewer rats raced down the tunnel towards the men; apparently, sewer rats avoid zombies even more than they avoid men, as the river of rodents flowed past them. This added further disquiet to the beleaguered men, in that each step they took ended with a squeal of pain as rats were crushed under foot, the tunnel was carpeted with fur.

The moans were getting closer. Duncan chanced a look back towards their pursuers. He could see a pack numbering at least forty of the things and they were moving with the more stable gate of the older zombies, and they were less than a hundred fifty yards away.

It was decision time; they could run and hope that they could make it to the end of the tunnel and find some means of escape, all the while praying for deliverance from this and any additional hordes, or... they could engage this group with their guns from a distance and hope that there aren't any reinforcements around in these tunnels.

If they chose to battle they had to be sure that they kept good fire discipline, as they had a limited amount of ammunition. They chose the latter; it was decided that Pat, Duncan, Liam, and Kyle would create a firing line and take them out with aimed shots from a distance. They had the most experience shooting since they were all raised by Jacob, who had taught them how to shoot and to hunt, fish, and camp.

Duncan and Kyle both kneeled, Pat, who was not squeamish regarding the rats, assumed a prone position, while Liam would shoot from a standing position. Duncan and Liam would start on the left side, Kyle and Pat on the right each alternating firing.

They would work from the edges towards the center. The synchronization of their shooting was impressive. The interval between shots was extremely short just long enough to shoot and acquire another target. It sounded to the others standing behind them as if it were just one long burst of machine-gun fire, sort of "spray and pray" this could not be farther from the truth.

After each report, a creature went down, then another, then another, then another after that. The strobe light effect of the muzzle flashes gave the whole ordeal a sort of film noir feel. The zombies continued to press them, closing the distance, even as their ranks were thinned by the marksmanship of the quartet. Bodies fell and were trampled by those that followed. The ravenous creatures took no notice of their fallen brethren. They didn't slow their press as they ground the fallen under their march, their sole goal was sustenance, to rend, and to ingest their prey. The cacophony of gunfire was deafening.

The horde had closed the distance to less than fifty yards as their numbers dwindled. Duncan had underestimated their numbers, easily fifty of them had been dispatched and there remained around twenty more. Their line would hold; the last of the creatures fell not ten feet from their position; the smell of cordite filled the air, thankfully eclipsing the smell of the dead.

Duncan stood bumping into Pete, who had come closer with his axe in hand; ready to engage in close quarters combat had they not dropped the last, before they got too close. Pat and Kyle regained their feet; Duncan was dismayed by the fact that the other three hadn't closed ranks, on the contrary, they had drifted perhaps twenty yards farther down the tunnel, add to that, they had taken Peter's gear with them; Peter had dropped his pack so that if it came to it; he wouldn't have had his mobility impeded.

As the brothers and Pete caught up to them, Pete reached for his gear, Felix, who had been holding it appeared reluctant to return it, in that he was still holding onto it three seconds after Peter had his hand on it. There was a tense moment, but ultimately Felix let go of the bag, a moment after that he realized that three AR fifteen were pointed in his general direction; no one was aiming or sending threatening signals, but it was obvious that what had transpired was not to the liking of the others.

Harold looked ashamed, "You guys are hard-core..." he said in an awed tone "Man, I mean, you guys just stood there shooting away as they came at you... I mean, Man, I was almost about to run away, and I was behind you... Fuck, you guys are tough." He was sincere, but it did little to alter Duncan's thoughts; as far as Duncan was concerned, these three just became "Red Shirts" of the Star Trek fame, disposable.

The four changed the magazines in their weapons and were preparing to get back at it when, in the distance, Liam thought that he heard another moan. No one else seemed to hear it but they all got moving again anyway. The tunnel was bending to the left, as they got past the apex of the arc, in the distance, they could see the illumination from work lights in jars attached to nineteen-hundred boxes on the conduit. The walls had recesses in them so that folks could press into them to avoid getting squashed by trains, some of these had doors in them; Pat's curiosity had gotten him so as they passed he checked the knobs; they were locked.

They were getting closer to the lights and could make out a raised platform; where various equipment that was used down here, was stored. They climbed up onto the platform to take a short breather taking comfort from the pitiful light. Liam hardened his ears, straining to hear. Felix's pants; which had been tan in color before were now black from the knees down, and the black looked like it was moving. "Ugh!!! Fucking cover in fleas, as the others looked at each other, they could see that they were only marginally in better condition. "Must have been from all those fucking rats." On the platform there was an old diesel generator and some Gerry cans of fuel for it. Kyle splashed some of the Diesel onto his legs and the fleas jumped off. The others followed his example, example. Pete the opportunity to break open one of the gang boxes; that he found on the platform, with a little help from the wrecking bar. Inside of the box he found some tools and power cords; nothing that they needed.

Felix was talking to Kyle in somewhat hushed tones over by the generator. "Look we were just a little panicked...you got to let it slide" Felix was saying to Kyle, whose face was the embodiment of accusation. Felix continued unfazed to plead their case "If you had given over that extra rifle to one of us maybe we would have dusting those dead heads with you" he said in an accusational tone. That did it; Kyle had had enough, "You three can go off on your own! But you aren't leaving with any gear, we have LOANED you! How long do you think you can last before you get eaten?" Kyle bellowed. Felix was visibly cowed by the force behind Kyle's words. He sat down and wiped at his clammy yet sweaty forehead; he wasn't feeling too well and over the past couple hours, he was feeling worse and worse.

Pat was watching his father intently. He also watched the other two men who had joined their group. He was looking for any action that would let him take them out. He was all about team work, shared responsibilities and shared goals; these guys weren't part of the team, and to Pat's way of thinking if you aren't on the team, then you are against the team and that made you a liability. They too were watching, were overtly being placid. They didn't want to be left behind, or worse, sent off on their own sans any support or supplies.

"Look, we have only another forty-minutes or so to go before we are in Queens and out of these tunnels, can we stick it out with you guys?" As he said this,he included everyone.

To Kyle's surprise, Duncan was the first to answer, "Sure… and why don't you guys walk point; we'll guard against pursuit." There was something that his brothers picked up on that was missed by the rest; it sent shivers down both of their spines. They knew their brother well and knew that these three were in some serious danger if they didn't watch themselves. Duncan had declared them cannon fodder with his spoken and unspoken words.

After leaving the platform, the track maintainers moved ahead 30 yards, then the others followed. "We can't trust those fuckers!" said Duncan to his older brother. Peter agreed; they proved unreliable. "At least if they are in front of us, we will have some notice if they stumble into a horde, and well if they were behind us… well you saw how that turned out." Kyle was brooding as he listened to the conversation without offering comment.

The anger that each of them felt, helped to combat their natural fear of this dark environment. Pat moved ahead a ways drawing closer to the lead group, moving silently he was able to get close enough to overhear anything they were saying. Eavesdropping may not be polite etiquette in most circles, but it could be a great source of intelligence. "Look we need them a hell of a lot more than they need us; besides they didn't have to take us along... we owe them our lives" said the tallest of the three, Harold, Pat thought.

"It s every man for himself... well you know what I mean, we watch out for each other, we always have... these guys, we don't know them, why should we risk our lives for strangers..." that was definitely Felix; Pat recognized the belligerent manner of speaking. "I just wish we could get a hold of a couple of guns, hell even pistols, I feel naked walking here." Felix continued. One of them stopped and held up a hand grabbing the others' attention, the rest followed suit.

Did you hear something?" Pat made a hand gesture back to his family that signaled caution.

Pat stood stone still and concentrated on hearing, trying to discern any noises; Duncan and the rest caught up to Pat's position. They were tensed and prepared for battle. Kyle looked to his son and shrugged the question, "What gives?"

Pat pointed to his ear and cupped it, pantomiming listening; Kyle nodded his reply. They all were standing there listening; each second seemed to go on for hours. First Pat and then Liam heard it, a dragging sound accompanied by a sound that was akin to pea-sized gravel in a cardboard box. Their technologically enhanced vision didn't help them find the source of the sounds.

What they could see was two of their travel mates, the ones with optics panning left and right searching the oppressive darkness for something. The sound was intermittent; you would hear the noises, then they would cease and then the sounds would disappear; almost as if the sounds were figments of over stressed imagination.

Spurred on by the fear of the unknown, the trio crept forward hoping to identify the sounds. Everyone's nerves were frayed; Felix seemed to be having trouble concentrating, still the silence was unbroken, "There it goes again... what is that?" the nervousness evident in his voice. They edged a little closer. Again, they heard the noise, but it now sounded more mechanical. The two groups came together to investigate.

It turned out to be a combination two things, the first being an old defective track switch failing to make and trying again and a cardboard box containing of all things a cat toy; some sort of pompom on a spring, that when the pneumatics of the switch tried to move it made the dragging sound, and then it would shift the box causing the spring to drum on the box. Collectively, they all sighed their relief; this last scare sapped the last of Felix's reserves, he sat himself down and was short of breath, they couldn't see the pallor change, since the night-vision gear washes out all colors.

Duncan voiced what they all suspected, "I think he's got the disease"... he grabbed the ball-peen hammer out of his belt, preparing to crush his skull. He thought this a kindness; Felix's friends, on the other hand, did not.

"What the fuck do you think you're doing? He ain't been bit..." shouted Harold. Eddie was riding the fence; he had his doubts too, but Felix, and he worked in the same gang for eleven years. They had been to the Christenings of each other's kids. They had drunk many a beer together, and eaten a herd worth of barbecue together over the years; loyalty demanded he stop the mercy killing.

There was a puzzled expression on Felix's features, like he couldn't comprehend what was happening. He strained to put together the words he wanted to speak, finally he said, "I be ok... just need some rest...can make it into work..." he paused and looked annoyed at himself "I mean home... err... out of the dark" the lack of cohesion in his words convinced Duncan's group. It might have even convinced Eddie, had not Harold bent down to help Felix up and bodily move him away from the others.

"He will be ok; he just has low blood sugar…" The excuse was plausible but doubtful; Duncan wanted to press the issue. "Look we either end his suffering and likely save ourselves in the process, or we leave him to be eaten and come back from the dead and come after us, that is if he isn't already infected and changing as we speak."

Harold wasn't giving in. He shoved Felix behind him to protect him, "Eddie this is Felix, you know he is hypoglycemic!" Eddie knew this was true, but he had seen Felix at his worst and it never impaired his cognitive skills to any real degree, no, he felt that Duncan was right.

The point was made moot when Pete moved with the speed of a hunting cat, and buried the point of his fire axe in Felix's skull. Harold spun on him to attack, just as all the guns came up and were pointed at the two men. Pat spoke to them both, "His suffering is done, let's get going or do you two want to join him?" he said this in a way that left little doubt that he would prefer the latter choice.

You could cut the tension in the air with a variety of cutlery; to say that the situation was tense would be to greatly understate the gravity of the moment. Eddie understood why Pete had done it; he even agreed that it was necessary; he was just surprised by the ease with which he had carried out the execution.

"Do you want me out on point again?" he asked as a means of conveying his decision. Harold shot him a fierce look; his face shouted his thought even louder than his voice possibly could have, "Judas." Harold adjusted Felix's limbs in a manner to suggest quiet repose, the tapped him on the shoulder by way of saying farewell, he then grabbed the FLIR and stormed away without a word. They may be traveling in the same direction but they were not together. Eddie wanted to make a mends, but Harold clearly wouldn't have been receptive to any overtures. He just hoped that they would survive long enough to get passed it. With the world the way it was now, with this plague taking humanity to the gallows at spear point Harold was one of the few people Eddie was likely to have left. All he could do was hope, may be it would be enough.

They were getting close to the end of the tunnel. You could smell the air was fresher, cleaner, and with each step that increased. Soon they would see light at the end of the tunnel; both literally and figuratively. Eddie had folded in with Duncan and company. He wasn't accepted wholly, but he was not treated with overt suspicion either. Harold's rage was still white hot; he stood apart from the group, and if looks could kill, well the zombies would be disappointed.

The team gathered for a quick strategy session, "We don't know what we are going to find at the end, we might be arrested and thrown into quarantine, or they might shoot first and ask questions never, or there maybe no one there at all." said Duncan to the collected group.

Pete chimed in, "Or there could be a nation of zombies out there waiting for us" …"Ever the eternal optimist" thought Kyle.

"Be that as it may, the point is we have to expect the worst…; Kyle do you have any suggestions on how to get out without discovery?"

Kyle thought about that for a minute and was about to speak when he was interrupted by, surprisingly enough Harold.

"Just up ahead we are going to come to an access door to a set of side tunnels. We use the pretty often doing our jobs, but there is a ladder that leads out of the top of the tunnel complex. It t not be guarded." The idea made sense; Eddie was glad that Harold offered the idea. He d that maybe he was getting over the way Felix was killed, he doubted it bit, as they say, "hope springs eternal" "That seems like the best idea and was better than the one I was going to suggest, I was going to say we should move into the light singing the Star-Spangled Banner our hands over our heads" Everyone chuckled over that Harold included.

"Let's get going, remember noise discipline, there could be more zombies around, and we are violating a quarantine zone so anyone seeing or hearing us doesn't have to treat us well" This was a sobering thought. Everyone was sure that once they escaped, they would be safe or at least as safe as they could be considering the zombie plague, but the thought of being shot by the military or some other agency hadn't occurred to them.

They resumed their interval positions and continued moving through the darkness; knowing that they were almost free of the gloom that had been weighing so heavily upon them. According to Harold, they had another seventy five yards or so around a slight bend to their access portal.

The hairs on the back of Pat's neck stood straight up. He panned left and right searching for something; intuition has kept many a warrior alive in the past and right now Pat's intuition was screaming at him that they all were in grave danger, he immediately used the hand signals for danger, they hugged to the inside of the bend and prepared for a hasty ambush.

Peter gave Eddie a nine mil and two spare clips. Eddie nodded his gratitude and held the gun in a two-handed grip like you would see on any cops show on television, squatted and arms out in front. They listened to the silence, nothing, no sounds of footfalls, and no sounds of shuffling or dragging, just silence. Tensed muscles were beginning to burn, tremors in the gripping of the guns, still they waited in the silence.

They were close enough to the end of the tunnel system to feel motion in the air. That of the minutest of breezes, and on that breeze was the smell of death and decay. They waited another ten minutes and still no sign of anything.

Harold and Eddie wanted to push onward. Pat shook his head; he knew something was just around the bend; but they couldn't just sit there waiting any longer. They had to keep moving. Eddie emboldened by the gun in his hand moved to the point followed by Harold and then the rest of them, with Liam bringing up the rear. Collectively, their heart rates were racing. Beads of sweat trickled down, stinging eyes, pulses thundering in their ears; slowly, they crept along, moving as silently as wraiths.

They couldn't go very far; they could see, in the distance, edging towards them a host of creatures and the portal was almost halfway between the two groups. There was no longer a choice; they made a break for it, running as best they could, a few seconds later the moans went out from the zombies, and they charged after their meals.

Eddie reached the passage first and started shooting at the lead zombies. Harold made the door and was through it-like shit through a goose.

Pat fired bursts as he ran; the door was shutting. Duncan through his entire weight behind his shoulder and into the steel door, Harold was thrown into the wall by the door.

Duncan pulled his pistol with his right hand, and with his left he grabbed a handful of Harold's hair and dragged him to his feet, Harold grimaced in pain and Duncan shoved the barrel of his pistol into Harold's mouth, knocking the front teeth in. Harold was backing up as Duncan kept shoving him hair in hand and gun in mouth, he slammed up against the wall, white-hot rage and murderous intent in his eyes.

There was the staccato popping of the rifles, and then they were all in this small corridor. They Sealed the door behind them throwing the deadbolts mere seconds before the dead began pounding on the door. When Duncan heard Liam's shout clear, he squeezed the trigger, the report was deafening and the mass of brain matter and blood that slapped against the wall to run down in rivulets.

"What he Fuck Dunk!!!?" said Peter'

Eddie seeing the gore turned away and answered for him, "Harold went through the door and was gonna lock us out here with those..." he trailed off pointing at the door; he was spent emotionally and physically.

"Fucking piece of shit" exclaimed Kyle as he kicked the offending body.

143

Duncan still appeared as a man possessed turned to Eddie still with the gun in his hand, and in the most disturbing voice, a controlled and soft voice that did not match the glare in his eyes, he said, "Lead the way please, I have a family that needs me."

Eddie sprang into action. He lead them through a short tunnel and to a ladder that went up to a "manhole" up to top. He pushed up, and the cover lifted. A little struggle freed it so it could be shouldered aside, he climbed out, turning this way and that with his pistol leading the way, he didn't see anyone or anything so out he went into the daylight... the rest climbed up and out, colors abounded, the grass surrounding the opening was greener than any of the men could remember having seen a grass look like in their entire lives; and it was still wet with morning dew. They each took in huge lungs full of clean sweet air. The grip that the darkness had upon their spirits was broken by the delight they had in being in the sunlight. Never mind that they still had to get back to Long Island and their families, they were just happy to be out of the darkness.

Kyle, Duncan, and Liam crept off towards the precipice where the tunnel began, while the other three relaxed on the grass, their position atop gave them a good field of vision by which they could see if anything was headed their way. Kyle and Duncan got down on hands and knees as they neared the edge they belly crawled the rest of the way; they wanted to see, not be seen, so this seemed prudent. Liam stayed far enough back from the edge so as not to be seen from below.

As they inched closer to the edge, they could hear activity below; they were not encouraged by the sounds. What they heard was the sounds of a diesel truck engine, that of a ladder fire truck, there were also the sounds of pounding on metal and the shatter of glass, they could also hear the sound of water gushing from hoses that were not controlled by anyone, as the whipped around bouncing and slapping as the water pressure escaped the nozzle.

When they got to the edge and looked down they saw that there had indeed been a holding action here to prevent escape from the infected. The sight itself was grief strickening. It was clear what had happened; Firemen supporting guardsmen were tasked with controlling this possible escape point; they employed the use of fire hoses to keep anything from escaping.

There were fire trucks and military transport vehicles on the tracks below; now all that was to be seen was a charnel house scene of slaughter. They could see bodies of zombies bloated in the sun. Abdominal cavities ripped open spilling their intestines about like ribbons, limbs separated from bodies, other bodies cut in half by gunfire. Then there were the torn bodies of the defenders; who were obviously over run, the protection offered by heavy fire coats worn by the FDNY was ineffectual, as their shredded bodies testified?

There were still too many zombies walking around and eating of the fallen to count. Duncan and Kyle had seen enough, and they carefully backed away from the edge before they got to their feet and high-tailed it back to the others to relay what they had seen. "We've got to beat feet and in a hurry, there're a hundred or so of those creatures down there feasting on those poor sons of bitches who were trying to stem the tide. So let's get out of here fast besides we all want to get back to our families, I know mine are safe but you guys..." he looks to Pete and Eddie "Have you guys heard from yours?"

Pete's estrangement from his wife had her relocate to Fla., But he had been trying to reconcile recently, and she was supposed to be moving back to NY. He couldn't recall seeing Pete talk to her, but he was here. He has become family, so he would be coming along with him. Eddie didn't have anyone to check on, but he was welcome to join them. One or two more would make it a tight fit on the boat but Duncan's conscience wouldn't allow any other alternative.

They made their way to the concrete buttresses and climbed down away from the track area and away from the horde. They eventually got to street level, everyone watching their area of coverage responsibility; they were looking for a vehicle that they could use to get back to the Island.

They were made their way up fifty third Ave. trying to keep as low a profile as possible. They heard gun shots and screams off, in the distance, there were sirens and alarms wailing away; the area, industrial by zoning, urban blight by opinion, was not exactly teeming with activity, but there was enough so that the travelers moved from cover to cover, quickly and quietly, all the while searching for a vehicle. They continued on fifty third until they came to eleventh street where they made a right hoping by getting away from the industrial area they might have better luck finding a vehicle.

Panic had hit this area pretty early on in the crisis; signs of looting were everywhere, as were signs of battle. You could hear zombies moaning in the distance; they sounded interested in others farther away, much to the relief of the group. They moved onto Jackson Ave. they could see that some of the apartment houses had been fortified. There was plenty of evidence to suggest other survivors, pockets of them, many of them would last for a few weeks, where others would fall within two maybe three days. At the corner of Jackson and Court Sq. there was a deli that had been barricaded well and it was obvious that we were being watched from within and not by mindless zombies but predators of human design. The guys continued on, not wanting any more trouble than they absolutely needed to get into. They had walked pretty damn far, when they finally laid eyes onto a Honda Odyssey, and as fortune had it, there weren't any changed, former people in it either; the last three vehicles that they found still had occupants inside just lacking the cognitive skills to manipulate the door handle to get out and to eat..

Liam whom had always had a passion for tinkering with cars managed to break in and hot wire the car in relative short order, they had better than half a tank, so fuel wouldn't be a problem right away. They had made good their escape from NYC, now they were looking forward to reuniting with their families.

146

28

Dr. Manis was finishing his latest report so that he could send it to Washington. His ever-present voice recorder clutched in his left hand, he sat up as he heard a knock on his door. "Dr. Manis, the man you asked for, a Mr. Sixkiller is here to see you." said one of the admin types whose names he never bothered learning as they changed so often.

"Send him in please..." he paused searching for the name, giving up with a sigh, "Thank you" and in walked the technician who took the position n front of the doctor's desk, he was obviously ill at ease.

"Mr.Sxkiller, may I call you Jerry?" Jerry nodded his ascent "I can't begin to tell you how crucial those data centers are now..." his voice was starting to show his anxiousness and his displeasure, so he took a breath held it for a fraction of a second and regained his composure "You have been given a mountainous task, of that we are aware. You were originally given a deadline of eight months, and I know you have been working at a heroic fevered pace, but we need those centers online yesterday. Is there anything we can do to help you? Perhaps we could second some of our IT people to assist you with this undertaking?"

Jerry was relieved that it was an offer of assistance. He's all too aware of the fact that he and his wife's safety hinged upon this man's good graces. "How many extra hands will that give me sir? If I have eight additional people I am sure we can give you the majority of you the functionality side of ten days maybe even a week if I work around the clock only taking cat naps every ten hours or so…and these other folks can work in shifts…"

 Dr. Manis knew that the IT department had their own problems that they were undertaking, but he felt he could get John maybe six people. Jerry was content with that

"Doctor. I want to thank you again for making room for my wife and me in here…" He was clearly uncomfortable with his eyes cast towards his shoes, shifting his weight to his left foot then his right. "…um Doctor, is there any truth to the rumors?"

Now it was Dr. Manis' turn to be uncomfortable " Well that would depend on the rumors, what I can tell you is that we are working very hard to combat something that is very deadly, and affecting the entire globe."

Jerry went for the direct approach seeing as how the doctor seemed hesitant to answer his query directly, "Is there a zombie apocalypse brewing?" The doctor very nearly choked.

"Jerry, what we have is a pandemic that some are saying is a zombie plague, what it is actually is parasite with a viral component, true the hosts are similar to what Hollywood has represented as zombies, but as a scientist, would be remiss to call it that… but that makes it all the more important for you to get us completely up and running as fast as you possibly can."

Jerry's shock at hearing the news was obvious, but he shook it off quickly, "I will do the best I can as fast as I can, and thanks again doctor. Let me get back to it" and with that John saw himself out of the office and headed back to work.

Carrie was in the cafeteria drinking a chai tea latte, when John Roberts came in. She was wearing a set of borrowed scrubs, she had volunteered to assist in the cafeteria since so many more people were on campus, and the shifts were tripled in size. Many of the civilians volunteered to help out, often it was just to keep busy rather than to have too much time to worry on their hands. For others it was to earn their keep and to show their appreciation at being housed within the compound.

John grabbed a cup of coffee and came over to where Carrie was sitting and asked if he could join her. They were quartered in the same area, and Carrie had seen him around several times but had never been introduced.

"Sure, sit." Said Carrie as she indicated with her hand for him to sit across from her, "I'm Carrie Sixkiller, we are staying just down the hall from you, and you are?" her voice raised a little to pronounce the question.

John sat and offered his hand, "I am John Roberts, I write for Discover Magazine, and now I am doing some Blogging and other things for the CDC helping to get the truth out on this thing" by the time he was finished introducing himself he went from appearing warm and engaging to having a haunted look on his countenance.

Carrie really had no idea at all what exactly was going on, all she knew was what she had gotten from Millie in that phone call, and she had yet to find her here on campus to try and glean more information from her, so after hearing what John was doing for the CDC she figured maybe she could find out what was going on for real.

"Are you at liberty to discuss what is actually going on?" she asked hopefully. "Well they want me to publish a blog, and they told me it wasn't going to be censored... so I guess yes I am." They spent the next sixty minutes talking about everything that John had learned to date about what was happening, when he excused himself saying that he had an appointment to go over some of the new data they had uncovered. "Well John why don't you stop by our quarters later, I'd love for you to meet my husband, they have him real busy but he should be home for a little while around eight or so."

"I will try to, see you later Carrie, thanks for the chat." He waved his goodbye and headed back out the door.

John Roberts met with Dr. Hampton in the grandstands of the surgical theater, there were several other people here watching the dissection of one of the specimens. The operating theater itself was a clean room, so the doctor below was in a bio hazard suit complete with air hoses that hung from the ceiling that connected to the suit, and on the table in front of him was the body of one of the(until recently) reanimated creatures.

It was a standard post mortem being performed. A full selection of tissue and fluid samples were collected, and through each and every step and stage the doctor was recording all of his findings while cameras recorded it in its entirety from multiple angles. All of which was displayed on monitors for the spectators to view in greater detail.

John was amazed by how different the body that had been alive less than 2 days prior, had undergone such a radical change. Even with the naked eye he could see the "chains" of the grown secondary nervous system. When the 'ME' opened the cranium to remove and weigh the brain, he was significantly shocked by what he had found, much of the brain had been eaten away with many similarities to the brains of those with Creutzfeldt-Jakob disease or like a bovine brain savaged by mad cow disease.

The brain weighed less than one third its normal healthy weight. Only the brain stem seemed un-withered, in fact that area seems to have grown to some degree. The samples were tested and looked at as they were collected, the product of that research could be seen on additional monitors in the area. John didn't know which he should be looking at more, the whole thing was so alien to him and he was being overloaded with information.

Dr. Hampton was studying the findings intently and he shared his thoughts with John, as well as explaining the things John didn't quite follow. "So you are saying that the gist of the matter is that this "toxoplasmosa gondii" parasite has mutated and uses a retrovirus that creates all the havoc, and that the retro virus itself not only creates these chains but it can also alter the stem cells and grow the parasite from nothing?"

John wanted to be sure of what Dr. Hampton was saying. "That is what we suspect is happening but in all honesty we have never seen anything behave like this before. No one has ever even hypothesized anything like this could have ever happened in Nature or in a laboratory for that matter."

"Okay, now what can be done about it, obviously this mutation and virus are super contagious, is there any antibiotic that can touch this thing?" John asked of the doctor. "Well we are mapping the viral component's gnome and doing the same for the toxoplasmosa gondii mutation as we compare it to what we know of its original form. We at least have a jump start thanks to those e-mails that were sent to Dr. Romero from those folks over in Russia. "Is there anything I can post on the blog that would help people not infected to stay that way... apart from not being bitten?"

The doctor thought for a few moments, "Well so far we know it is not an airborne vector, we also know that it is blood to blood, so that means any wounds, sores, or abrasions of any kind should be covered at all times, protect mucus membranes and eyes, obviously you cannot ingest any contaminated substances, most of which are common sense procedures, but apart from that I can't think of anything really beyond that but with each passing hour we learn more and more."

"Well thanks doc, we'll talk again later, I'm going to do a couple of posts on the blog site and see what else I can find out online." John exited and headed back towards his living quarters.

Carrie was sitting in the common area that served as a lounge for the residents, in her lap was a paperback novel about a 19th century detective in NYC by Caleb Carr, but for the past twenty minutes she hadn't even turned a page as she was lost in her own thoughts. She was worried about her sons and the rest of her family in New York. She knew that her sons were okay as they had left her a voice-mail while she was working her shift, but that doesn't prevent a mother from worrying. What was plaguing her thoughts most was the rest of her family, even though she had a somewhat strained relationship with her parents, she hadn't heard from them since she called them on the way here.

She knew that attempting to read was an exercise in futility, so she decided to call and see if they were all right. Even though she had resigned herself to calling she hadn't budged, it was as if she were frozen where she sat. The little voice inside of her was saying, "What if something bad has happened to your brothers? What if they all fell victim to whatever is going on?" That little voice of doubt had plagued her for years.

She was the type of person that needed to be needed for validation. Even the slightest criticism could shatter her and send her into an abyss of self doubt and depression that could last for weeks. It was far worse when her ex was in the picture, but it was still a problem that she fought to overcome daily.

Her internal struggle was a stalemate, so when John Roberts came into the lounge he had to call to her three times before she responded. "Sorry, I was lost in thought" she said feebly. "Think nothing of it, seems to be going around these days" he said encouragingly. After a moment of an uncomfortable pause he asked, "So what are you reading?"

He reached out and pointed towards the ignored book. "Oh, I really don't know, it was just left here so I picked it up to give my mind a break." He sat down across from him and pulled out his laptop and cords and began the erroneous task of plugging things in and booting it up.

"I'm going to be posting an update on my blog later; right now I was going to do a little web surfing to get an idea about what's happening that the media isn't reporting. Thank god for bloggers, now they may not be the most scientifically accurate people in the world but at least you get info that is cutting edge and uncensored. Since this whole thing started happening blogs have been popping up everywhere." This was just the sort of thing that could help her fight off her looming funk.

"Is there anything I can do to help you, I've got some time, my husband is working all the time trying to get the new data centers online so I can be your assistant..." she just realized that he might not need or want her help and she had just invited herself in.

"That would be amazing" he said to her relief. She quickly stood and fetched her laptop, glad to have something to do that would keep her mind occupied, and when she returned they got down to some serious searching. She made certain that John's blog was added to her bookmarks so that she could show it to her husband later. They sat there in the lounge working for the next four hours, they hardly spoke to one another yet they both were taking comfort in the others presence, a shared camaraderie.

"Wow, you are right my last search yielded fifteen thousand hits on survivor blogs alone. It's amazing how many of them are talking about two e-books in particular, one by Roger Ma and the other by Max Brooks, both are zombie combat manuals, they were written as science fiction novels but people are saying that they should be classified as technical manuals or at very least as self help. Amazon books website went down for several hours because so many people were trying to download it, but Barnes and Nobel's has been picking up the slack"

John immediately picked up on her enthusiasm and smile inwardly, he noted the titles and immediately downloaded them both, Carrie had already done so.

"I am famished; do you want to grab a bite?" John asked innocently.

153

"No, I think I will wait for my husband and eat with him later" she replied.

John realized that his overtures could be misconstrued so he quickly stammered, "Well thanks for all your help; I am around so anytime you want to help me dig feel free."

She relaxed a little bit and said, "Sure, we can hit it hard again later after you eat..." she looked at her watch and was surprised by the time "... or in the morning rather" she chuckled and he joined in her mirth.

"Okay the morning then... hey Carrie when your husband gets back why don't you two come by my room, I would love to meet him and if we are going to be spending time together I think he should meet me too."

She smiled and was grateful for the suggestion. "We will if only for a short while, he is likely to be exhausted." He finished packing up his gear and set off in search of something to eat.

29

The Vice President was pacing back and forth while waiting for the others to arrive. Finally he sat down on the overstuffed sofa in his private office, pulled out a vanilla tipped cigar from the humidor, clipped its end and lit it, drawing a lung full of the smoke. He blew out a plume of smoke and then drew another in, this time he attempted to blow smoke rings. It was something he did since his college days years ago. Whenever he was stressed to the gills he would blow smoke rings to help settle his nerves while he collected his thoughts, it had become somewhat of a ritual that few knew about, and those that did never commented about.

All of his expected guests arrived at the appointed time excepting the chief justice who arrived 15 minutes late. The staff had laid out refreshments of finger sandwiches and a coffee service. There was also a wet bar on which sat crystal decanters of spirits with matching tumblers. The Attorney General, Congressman and the Senator were talking about the infrastructure, and what would happen if there weren't anyone able to man and maintain the power grid and other utilities. "As for the National Power Grid… there are enough redundancies and automation to allow it to continue for about 2 months before we start to see or feel any degradation, the water and gas that can go for about 6 months before that starts to crap out, but we should be able to protect those enough to keep them running. I am not sure how long the internet will remain viable, I have been told about 6 months but it will degrade rapidly after 4 months, but again I cannot stress enough that I really do not know how accurate that statement is. Again I must stress this is worst case scenario talk here, no one able to do any maintenance on any of the equipment anywhere in the nation, and I really don't think it will get that bad or at least I hope things don't get that bad."

When they had made themselves comfortable the staff was dismissed so that they could get to the reason that they were all here. Copies of the latest intelligence reports were neatly stacked along with the most up to the minute findings of the CDC and the discouraging computer modeling of the pandemic that was ravaging the nation and the world.

Each of the five men, aware how this meeting could be perceived. However, each knew that something drastic needed to be done for the good of all. The packets were handed to each of them and the VP sat down and opened his own copies to the areas that he had highlighted earlier.

"Gentlemen, thank you for coming, I appreciate the delicacy of the situation and need for discretion so if you would all be so kind as to take a few minutes to familiarize yourselves with the information in your hands, so that we can figure out just what needs to be done." The chief justice was the only one who was not up to speed on the whole, he busied himself with catching up to the rest. His job had cultivated certain talents for absorbing vast quantities of information and assimilating it rapidly, 20 minutes later he felt he had the broad strokes of the situation.

"Justice…" began the Vice President. " Make it Anthony, this is informal and well if we all follow the protocol we will never get anywhere" said the Chief Justice of the Supreme Court. "Very well, Anthony, is there a legal precedent that allows for ousting a sitting President short of Impeachment, or at least for transference of his powers, maybe due to mental health." Said the VP, his body language saying that he was reluctant to go down this path, but that he felt there clearly was no other choice. The assembly each noted this, and that little insight made them all feel more at ease, and less like this was a conspiracy or a coup. Anthony was deliberating on the subject while the others conversed as to the necessity of pursuing this course of action. A voice entered the conversation from a source that no one expected, from but when the initial shock wore off they agreed that that would certainly be more expedient. The Chief Justice concurred that any other rout would take far too long and that mankind didn't have that to spare.

Now that it had been said, they were all in unchartered waters. These were all honorable men who had chosen a life serving the citizenry of the country they loved; they were not murderers, yet they really had little option but to form their little cabal and plot the assassination of a sitting President in order to save their country and God willing the rest of the world.

"It really is an easy solution… with all of the turmoil in the world and with the contagious nature of this plague, no one would suspect foul play." The others agreed in principal, but they all needed to distance themselves in order to maintain plausible deniability. They were all in agreement, so they left the VP alone with the secret service man who would be the one with the dirty hands in this

30

The flotilla was still at anchor, other boats who had heard broadcasts via VHF had joined them, even a coastguard cutter steamed up to check on them and offer some supplemental supplies.

Kaitlyn was below decks at the navigational /communications station on the web. She was reading blog after blog trying to learn everything that she could. She served as the entire flotilla's communications hub, sharing the information she was gathering with all the rest. Kevin was talking to a couple of his fellow "puddle jumpers" about the container ship that had foundered. The survivors were in custody aboard another cutter who had picked them up. The cutter's skipper gave Kevin a TAD (temporary additional duty assignment) to serve as a liaison for the flotilla and allowed him to remain aboard with his family.

New news was brought to the captains telling them of an incident off of the coast of Somalia. "It seems that a refugee ship, a ferryboat that had been converted to rescue refugees was attacked by pirates. The pirates, however, had bitten off more than they could chew. It seems that there were a few infected among the refugees, who had later expired and reanimated when the ship was far out to sea. The infection had spread like wild fire aboard the ship, so when the pirates thought that they had won the lottery by taking the ship with greater ease than they had expected, they themselves became the meal ticket or meal rather." The Coast Guard captain paused for effect. "The moral of this story is don't let anyone board your vessels without having them wait for two days… you can toss them a line and send whatever supplies you want but don't go near them for at least two days, if any of them is infected you will know by, then." That parting bit of caution was appreciated since boaters more often than not tend to help first and think about their own safety later.

The adrenaline had long since worn off of the group, the mood was somber and threatened to become one of despair. Many of the boaters had family and friends still on land, and cell reception was dodgy at best this far off of shore, so the decision was reached by majority consensus that they would move to within half of a mile of shore so that they could use their cell phones to check on those left behind. At a depth of less than fifty feet no one was in danger of running aground, and it seemed less scary for those who were in their little motor boats who usually spent their time in the bays.

The watch schedule that had been established earlier was now doubled, half a mile is not that far for folks to swim, especially if they are desperate, and the captains had taken the Coast Guard skippers advice to heart. All the boat captains agreed. The safety of the flotilla was paramount and superseded any individuals wants or needs. Anyone was welcome to leave the flotilla, but if they wanted to rejoin, there would be a three-day waiting period when they returned.

Most of the boats were not well provisioned, and fresh potable water was going to be an issue for them. The Persistence had a reverse osmosis system as did a couple of the other yachts, even so, there had to be rationing. Some of the boats were fishing boats and so their skippers through their lines into help feed the group. Spare tarps and other gear were shared to build shelter on some of those that had no accommodations.

They tied off to each other to make moving from boat to boat a little easier. It was a communal atmosphere, those who had gotten bad news or worse no news about their loved ones left behind commiserated, while those who were relieved to learn that theirs were safe offered their condolences and offers of whatever help they needed.

Katie was taking a nap in hers and Duncan's stateroom. Kristen was helping out with a couple of the younger kids who were part of the flotilla; they were really scared and Kristen was very mature for her age, so she became sort of a big sister to them, and was teaching them how to make friendship bracelets from colored string she had. Laura was spending time with Duncan's friend Dave on his boat. She was listening to everything he had to say as if it was the most important words ever offered, she giggled often and all in all, was acting like a schoolgirl with a crush. Dave was happy for the attentive audience and welcomed the company. He also appreciated Laura's looks. She had somehow managed to apply a complete makeup job even under these conditions, not that she needed much, she was pretty enough without any but still she managed to. Sean was at the helm listening to the VHF and monitoring the equipment suite and was absently rubbing Aloha's belly with his foot while the dog snoozed away at his feet.

Katie's cell rang, and Sean picked it up expecting it to be his dad. He wasn't disappointed as he read the caller ID. "Hey, Dad." He answered.

"Hi on, how are you guys doing, you are all on the boat I trust. Did you have any problems getting there?"

"No Dad, we made it fine. It t a little dicey a couple of times, but we came through with flying colors. How are Uncle Liam and Kyle? How's Pat? Where and when should we meet you?" "

"I'm not sure yet son, what are you tired of being in command already?" Duncan said with a laugh.

Sean's cheeks reddened a bit, "it's not that, it's just, well… we just miss you is all. Mom been keeping a brave face for us bus, we can tell she has been worried sick about you. Let me get Kevin over here to take over the helm, I will go get mom, is taking a nap"

"Kev, come over and spell me for a minute my Dad is on the phone, I want to wake up mom for him."

The kids heard that their father was on the phone, and they rushed over too. Sean passed the phone to Kristen first because she got there a half second before Kaitlyn did, and went down to tell his mother. Kristen took the phone, "Hi Daddy, are you okay? When are you going to be back?" she asked into the phone.

"We're fine sweet pea, and we will be with you guys in a few couple of hours hopefully." Duncan was really choked up all of a sudden, the voice of his littlest hit him hard. He allowed himself to think about how worried his wife and children would be with him gone; he many other things to worry about just staying alive and rescuing his brothers. He realized to himself but now hearing the worry in his little girl's voice he felt that he had been very selfish, he still had to do what he did, but should have thought more on the effects it had on his family. Well he would spend a long time making it up to them.

"Sean put me in the boson's chair and sent me up to the top of the mast, I was terrified at first, but then I got cool with it, and it was like really cool."

"Why did he send you up there?" Duncan asked getting a little irritated with his eldest.

"Oh, Kaitlyn and I were fighting… and we… well, I started it, and Mom was trying to get some sleep, so Sean told me I was due for a time out, and well, I said who did he think he was, and he was like, well I am the acting captain, and I said well there aint any corners to make me stand in, and he was like I got a place for you, and so I ended up in the chair atop the mast." It was all Duncan could do to keep from bursting out in laughter. He had to give his son credit for taking on the roll he had given him, but Jeez Louise the top of the mast; he laughed to himself.

Next up was Kaitlyn, "Hi Dad, I've been doing what you asked me to do and I've learned a lot and well, I am the communications officer for the flotilla" she said with extreme pride, she knew she was doing a grownups job and doing it better than anyone else would be able to do. She knew without a doubt that she had earned the respect of the captains even begrudgingly, but she did earn it, and she wanted her dad to know it.

Duncan's first thought was to be impressed; his second was tinged with a little sadness because she sounded so much older than she was, and he realized that she was not going to be able to just be a kid again. She continued to tell him about what she was doing and about the other captains and how much they were relying upon her information in their planning. She also filled him in on the preparations Grandpa had made and that they were doing okay and how they wanted him to call when he could. Duncan said he would and that he was extremely proud of her and the job she was doing, which of course had her beaming with pride.

 It was then that Katie got to the phone; Kaitlyn was a little disappointed about having to give up the phone but not too much. "Hey you" she said to her missing husband.

"Hey Honeybaby, we made it to queens, and we just stole a van and are on our way."

She wasn't even fazed by what he said. "We are sticking with the plan of grabbing more supplies and heading to join up with you guys. Is there anything, in particular, at we need to look for and grab?" Being the consummate wise ass that she was her reply was, "A dozen roses would be nice" and then she laughed. He was almost sorry he had asked, almost, but to hear that magical laughter made it worthwhile. "

"No seriously what supplies are we short of?"

She gave him a short list, most of which were more creature comforts than absolute essentials. She had left them behind because she wasn't sure how of how much e they had for storage aboard. "... oh and grab a few of Kristen's stuffed animals, there are a couple of little kids here, it would go a long way towards making them feel normal again; it Kristen's idea. Dunk you have no idea how great our kids are handling it all; they all so grown-up all of a sudden."

"Yeah, I was just thinking that when I was talking to Kaitlyn. Listen my battery is almost dead, am going to go for now I'll grab my charger and call you later, call my parents and let them know we are all right, we will be seeing them in a couple of days."

"I miss you sweetheart." She said sweetly.

"Me you too, Honeybaby. Talk with you soon." He disconnected.

Pam had been talking to Kyle and Pat all the while. It was like the weight of the world had been lifted off of the shoulders of these two women. They had grown very close during this trial, shared adversity and all. Before they liked each other well enough, Katie was just closer with Erin of her two sisters in law, now there was a new freshly grown bond with Pam, and it was mutual and genuine. Feeling more in control now they called the kid's together and prepared lunch, it seems that they all rediscovered their appetites.

31

Carrie sent an E-mail out to the whole family figuring that, that was a safe way to get an idea of their situations. She got a reply within five minutes from her niece Kaitlyn, who gave her a complete 'sit rep' (situational report) on the entire family. Carrie corresponded back about where she was and how she, and her husband were safe inside the CDC compound and how she was working with John Roberts's blogging about the CDC findings. She provided Kaitlyn with the site address along with numerous other URLs and website addresses that she had discovered had good information to share. Carrie received a longer list in reply. Kaitlyn told her she had been doing this research for a couple of days now, hence the size of the list.

Carrie was relieved to be hearing all of this. All of her fears were groundless, well maybe not all of her fears, just the ones about her family. Her husband stumbled through the door to their rooms after putting in fourteen straight hours, dragging his tail…he looked worn out, the normal luster in his eyes that she found so compelling was replaced by the glassiness of fatigue. She had so much to tell him, but she could see that he needed to decompress, so she grabbed a Dr. Pepper and cracked it open for him. "Rough go of it darling?" "You could say that twice and still not have the half of it" he was attempting levity, but it came out as pure exhaustion.

"I've got so much to tell you and there is someone I really want you to meet because I am going to be working with him a lot on something really important, and well, I want you to be comfortable with it."

The long hours were beginning to take their toll upon him. He irritably responded, "Look I am interested, it's just, I am all used up. I trust you so don't worry about it, as for meeting him and what not, can it wait till I get up I need to get some rack time, and maybe four hours then I got to go back to work?"

She was clearly disappointed, but he didn't even notice as his eyes were already at half mast. He moved to the bed that they shared and removed his work shoes, laid down and was asleep within minutes. Carrie grabbed her laptop and went out into the lounge and got back to the research she had started earlier.

32

The Capital had become a "police state" the likes of which had only been seen in films about the Third Reich. There was a curfew in place, a military presence throughout the city, vehicles and pedestrians were stopped at check points. The only thing missing was a guy in a Gestapo uniform saying, "Papers, vit out zem you vill be shot!" Point in fact the use of deadly force was authorized for any violation of the orders.

Most of the citizenry left the urban area anyway in hopes of fleeing beyond the reach of coming doom. There were very few who braved the streets, and those were people in search of additional supplies for their larders, so that if a siege began, in earnest, they could last a few more days. There hadn't been many reports of reanimation in the metro area but there were a few, and as time passed the frequency of such reports grew in geometric proportions.

The President felt that he would be perceived as less "presidential" were he to leave the oval office, so he stayed at 1600 Pennsylvania Avenue, and insisted that the VP move to a secure location along with much of the cabinet.

Much of the staff had failed to report for work, who could blame them. That is not to say that security had become lax, quite to the contrary, in fact, the added military presence was notable. Due to all the commotion, the Presidents security detail was shifted around a bit, however if things continued to degenerate the President would be evacuated aboard Air Force One.

It was therefore, child's play for Aaron, the secret service agent who was assisting the Vice President to smuggle in a small vial of contaminated plasma. He was intimately involved in the security planning sessions and routine goings on since he had been reassigned to the President's detail. He was on duty, stationed just outside the oval office. Fortune smiled upon the agent in that since so much of the staff was absent, he volunteered to bring the President and the Ambassador from China a tea service along with some food while they met in private to discuss the UN incident.

It went unnoticed as he slipped the tiny vial from concealment in his watchband and emptied its contents onto the cutlery on the tray. He then wiped the utensils dry with a linen napkin emblazoned with the presidential seal.

His mission was nearly complete; he carried the tray to the door and knocked before entering. His conviction that he was serving the needs of his country fortified his resolve, he gave no outward sign that there was anything to suspect. Boldly, strode through the door and set the tray down, neither the President nor the Ambassador even acknowledged his existence, he was dismissed. He mechanically turned upon his heel and left.

His conscience was clear, he did what needed to be done. He shut the door behind him and resumed his post.

The single-celled organisms began their replication the moment that they were ingested. In a matter of hours the signs of infection would be obvious.

Within the privacy of the agent's thoughts, he prayed that it would happen quickly, far too much time had already elapsed, and the country could ill afford any additional delays.

An hour later reports of a sizable horde was headed towards DC from Baltimore, and another coming from near Richmond, within the City itself. There was more unrest as the plague spread. "Get the President airborne!" yelled the section chief, the commotion was executed in good order with magnificent discipline. The evacuation was underway, The President, now onboard the Marine Helicopter was beginning to show the first symptoms of illness. Had he deemed to read the CDC reports he might have known the transformation occurring within his body, but since he did not, he was ignorant of the danger, he posed to those tasked with his care and security. He was rushed off of the chopper and hurried onto Air Force One and within minutes, he was climbing into the sky, along with his minions and those brave souls who guarded him.

33

Liam tried to avoid the residential area as he weaved his way through the streets of Queens. This was a harder task than it would seem. More than once they had to double back and take alternative routes, finding roadways blocked and impassable. Gunfire could be heard from every direction, knots of survivors battled in defense of their homes and neighborhoods. The bodies of victims left half eaten were a commonplace sight. Groups of the shambling denizens stalked towards these heroes. Many creatures fell to withering gunfire, but many more took their places.

The men continued to drive. They could do nothing to stave off the inevitable outcomes; their positions were unsustainable, barely defensible, and the houses were just too close together. The defenders could only hold for a short while before their positions were overrun. Some of the apartment buildings were a little better off. At least they had erected barricades and boarded up their lower-level windows. Some guards could be seen on various fire escapes shooting into the hungry crowds below. What they had going for them, was that the walkup building's stairwells were natural choke points, and easily defended by few numbers. It would not matter. The ravenous crowd would only grow in number, and the other parasites, namely fleas and bedbugs would prey upon them soon if not already within their fortress.

Duncan and the rest preserved their meager supplies so as to defend their own; they had a plan and were going to stick with it. Their need for speed balanced against their need for caution, speed tipped the scale. They abandoned their avoidance of main thoroughfares and jumped onto the highway. It was nearly noon. The unseasonably warm temperatures combined with the stillness of the air and the high humidity, made them pray for a downpour of cleansing rain, to wash away the gore and blood that seemed to be everywhere.

They exited off of the Van Wyck onto the Belt Parkway. Sadly, they saw precious few other vehicles driving on the roadways. Many cars were just abandoned on the roads. Others were wrecked in collisions, still others were burned out or burning, and the ever-present zombies smashing windows and pounding upon hoods. The expected sounds of aircraft from the nearby JFK International airport, the blaring horns of traffic were absent, replaced by groans of the undead and occasionally by the blare of car alarms. As they drove passed Green Acers Mall, they couldn't fail to notice how few cars were in the parking lots, they noted a huge assemblage of the undead outside of Target pounding on the doors trying to get in, a hopeful sign that there were survivors within.

Pat pulled out his cell and called directory assistance, not expecting an answer but the automated system responded, "what city and state please?"

"Valley Stream New York" Pat answered.

"What listing?"

"Umm…Target…"

After providing him with the number it connected him at no additional charge. The phone rang and rang then finally someone answered, "Hello?" in a timid and stressed out voice.

Pat let them that there were other survivors and to keep the faith. Help would eventually get there. He told them that they should be careful of anyone who had been bitten or even scratched.

The voice on the other end said that they knew about that the hard way when a couple of the people who came in just ahead of pursuing monsters expired and rose again attacking those that had helped them escape. There had been seventy-five people then now there were only forty-eight souls remaining. The voice rambled on and on as if Pat's voice was the only thing that he could hold on to. The voice belonged to a guy named Thomas who had only been working there for three weeks. Thomas said that they had more than enough supplies and they had buttoned up the store real well, they could hold out indefinitely.

Pat said "He was glad to hear it" and he promised to be in touch again soon.

Thomas was crestfallen, Pat reassured him saying that his battery was failing, but when he got to safety, he would send help. The promise seemed to help Thomas somewhat. They said their farewells and exchanged well wishes, and finally disconnected the call.

Pat said, "I'm sure that there are a lot of people holding up in places like that, we should try and find them, you know just call places that we think of."

Kyle looked to his son, not wanting to trample his idealism, his compassion, as it was a quality that could be crushed under these sorts of circumstances. "Maybe we can do something for them but let's worry about getting back to mom and the rest first okay?"

Pat smiled at his dad's indulgence, recognizing it for what it was, "Sure thing dad."

As they neared Duncan's house, they drove around a few blocks to scout the area out. There were few visible indicators that things were not as they should be. Even though this was a generally quiet neighborhood, one could always expect to see at least some amount of traffic or at least a person walking a dog, perhaps a mother with a child in a stroller. Now there was no activity, nothing, not so much as a squirrel frolicking about.

They turned the corner of Sandalwood and Gibson Blvd. coming to the final leg of the circuit. They heard a burglar alarm wailing away accompanied by the groans of the reanimated. The groans were not as numerous as some of the hordes that they had thus far been able to avoid.

There were nine of the creatures congregated around the house whose alarm was still sounding its siren call. Only nine, they could take them out in just a few seconds, and the noise would be marginal given the wailing of the alarm system. The benefits to such action were obvious. They would have more time to collect the supplies they intended to collect from Duncan's home.

They stopped the van down the block from the group of zombies, as a group they filed out of the vehicle with assault rifles at the ready, Pete remained in the van, ready to fly in and pull the guys out if things went badly. They crept up the block using what cover they could. Duncan realized as that got closer, that the house in question belonged to Petra and Yuri, a very nice couple with three young children who had moved here from Poland before their first child was born six years ago.

Duncan had a sinking feeling in the pit of his stomach. As they drew closer any and all doubt was removed pertaining to the owners of the house. On the small patch of lawn out front were the remains of Yuri; it appeared that he had been torn asunder. His arms had been ripped off of his torso. Duncan imagined the force required to accomplish that feat because Yuri had had the physique of a man who had spent his entire life as a laborer. He had had a little extra around the middle, from consumption of a few beers after working hard all day, but the rest of him was toned and muscular. One leg was removed from the hip, the other below the knee. The abdomen was ripped open, and the intestines had spilled out onto the once green grass, their bluish-white color in stark contrast to the blood-soaked lawn.

Duncan didn't even notice the fiends chewing away at the meat on the severed limbs, what commanded his full attention, the way you can't look away from a train wreck, was seeing Petra's body being feasted upon by her three-year-old daughter Olga. Olga had been the cutest little girl when she was alive, precocious didn't even scratch the surface describing her. Michelangelo's depiction of cherubs in the Sistine chapel could have been inspired by her face that is before it was torn. Now the child's blonde locks were matted with dried blood and her fiendish mouth with exposed bloody baby teeth that were encrusted with tissue and gore.

Duncan figured that Petra and Olga had been out walking in the neighborhood as was their custom. They must have been set upon by one or more fiends. One of the monsters must have gotten a hold of Olga, and maybe that is when her face was torn. He assumed that they had made good their escape but were followed back to their house, the zombies must have laid siege. Things must have gotten desperate in side, maybe Olga's health was failing, and she needed medical attention because Yuri must have come out and engaged the creatures. Olga had probably turned by then and attacked her mother. Petra obviously would not have been over powered by the toddler, but as a mother she probably couldn't bring herself to strike her child.

There were no signs of the two other children, but it was likely that they too had met with a gruesome end inside of the house. Duncan's firing team used the Cadillac parked in the neighbor's drive way for cover, at this range they could not possibly miss their targets. Pat nodded a count of three, at which time the five of them popped up from their concealment and opened fire upon the ghouls. The Bullets found their marks, as heads blew apart. Duncan didn't know who shot the child, but he offered a silent thank you for being spared that task. The whole exchange was over in just a few seconds; they crossed to the doorway and entered the house figuring that there could be a few more hiding inside, Kyle and Liam went in with Pat, since the layout of this house was exactly the same as Duncan's, they had no problem navigating. Duncan remained outside on guard with Eddie. He knew if he had gone in he would never sleep again, because there could only be one of two things discovered in there, the first being finding the shredded bodies of the other two children or to find that they had changed into ghouls as well, and then he would have to destroy them too. This knowledge alone would cause him to lose countless nights of sleep in the future, but to see it or worse have to do something about it, no it was better that his brothers and nephews took care of this business. They didn't know them. Moments later, two rifle bursts confirmed his fear and his brothers exited a few seconds after that.

The team back tracked to the van and pulled around the corner and into Duncan's driveway. They left the van running as they got out of the van and went up the steps to the front door. Duncan produced his key and was unlocking the door when two bullets came through his door scant inches away from his face, Pat's reflexes were amazing, he spun and fired his rifle, two three round burst with incredibly tight groupings back through the door. His marksmanship was rewarded with a scream. Duncan yelled through the door, "Who the fuck are you in my house!!!" He kicked the door and went in with his rifle leading the way. There was a trail of blood running from the door around the wall with the fireplace and into the kitchen. Duncan followed the trail, eyes scanning all possible threat directions, when he rounded the kitchen, he saw a man sitting on the floor leaning against the white cabinets with his hands pressing in on the wounds to his stomach where Pat's rounds had taken him. His pistol was on the floor so Duncan quickly kicked it out of reach.

Behind Duncan were the stairs that lead to the basement, Duncan could hear the cry of an infant and the whispered hush of the mother trying to stop the babe from crying too loud and giving away their location. Duncan never took his gun of the wounded man, but he stepped back and called downstairs, "May as well come up. Your man is hurt and needs help."

He turned to the wounded man lowering his gun as he did. "Look we only came back to grab a few things left behind... you are welcome to the house and anything left behind after we leave. In the shed out back are plenty of tools and hardware for you to seal up the front door, the combination is nine-seven-three-eight."

The man on the floor smiled and said tiredly, "Thanks", he apologized for shooting at them explaining that he was only trying to protect his girlfriend and their child.

They had been running and running and just needed a place to crash for a while. Duncan didn't care he was only here to grab a couple of things.

The others were inside and raided the fridge for cold Diet Cokes. Duncan grabbed the radio and charger that Katie had left out for him. He went into the bedroom closet and opened the safe, from inside, he grabbed the family passports and the flash drive that had digital images of his and Katie's wedding photos. They filled a duffle bag with a few light-weight jackets, some extra socks and a few other sundry items and several of Kristen's stuffed animals. Before he turned and left he tossed his key towards the kitchen door.

"Lock up after you leave" and out the door they went, climbing back into the van. Seconds later they were gone. The ole thing had a surreal feel to it mused Duncan as they raced down sunrise highway. Ignoring red lights, perhaps the only benefit to a zombie apocalypse, and since they were in a stolen van they didn't even have to worry about the red-light cameras that were recently installed at various intersections in the area.

The roads weren't exactly clear but the vehicles were stopped and abandoned, for the most part. The towns and villages in this part of Long Island were close together. Lynbrook passed in all of thirty seconds, but they had to slow down in Rockville Centre due to an overturned semi lying on its side across the median blocking two of the three lanes. It was clear that panic had hit this area to devastating effects. There were bodies strewn about as if some giant child through a temper tantrum and threw her broken toys about with abandon. Most of these bodies suffered trauma of one sort or another, yet most of the heads were undamaged suggesting that they were killed by fellow citizens and not devoured by ravenous undead creatures. Not to say that there weren't any signs of zombies about, there was plenty of evidence supporting that, it was just the mania that had taken hold was the result of fear, that much was certain.

Park Avenue in Rockville Centre had been somewhat of a destination spot before the dead started rising, with all the restaurants and bars providing nightlife and lots of shops and stores for patrons during the day, now it was dead, devoid of all the hustle and bustle of commerce. The only activity was that of undead creatures wandering around trying to sniff out survivors to feast upon. They continued to drive past. The brothers had grown up in this affluent community, as an incorporated village it had its own fire and police departments, its own power and water. It boasted good schools with an excellent athletic department. It was a safe and homey town. Now many of the stores and shops had broken windows, some were burned out shells.

The bar where Duncan used his older brothers ID to get into when he was only 16 was just up ahead. Stinger's Pub was a great place to drink and chase skirts Duncan remembered. He could see the river rock façade but the double glass doors were torn from their hinges and lying on the sidewalk, there was plenty of broken glass on the ground as well, in passing he chanced a look within and saw the swaying uncoordinated movements of undead inside. Kyle pointed out that even before this plague you would see people staggering around in there. His attempt at levity fell flat as Duncan was thinking that yet another place where he had only fond memories would never be that anymore.

They passed the vacant movie theater, it had gone out of business due to the newer multiplex theater that had opened up on park, it had struggled for a decade and then gave up the ghost and up went the space for rent signs, the building had remained empty for a couple of years

Patrick who was riding shotgun now noticed that someone on a roof top was waving an enormous American flag trying to get their attention. As the van got closer they realized that the man dressed in Hunter's cammies was standing on the roof of the Long Island Outdoorsman.

There were sand bags piled high, if it were an Army Surplus store it would have looked more natural but inside were lots of guns and plenty of ammo.

Patrick used his cell to call the number on the signage; the fellow on the roof stopped waving the flag and answered the phone. "Outdoorsman… can I help you?" came the voice over the phone.

"Is that you on the roof waving the flag?" Patrick replied.

"Sure is, you guys are the first folks I've seen in hours… how are you guys fitted for fire power?… why don't you guys stop in for coffee… we are going a bit stir crazy in here and would like to hear what's going on. We can make it worth your while."

"How many are you in there?" asked Pat.

"Just me the wife and our son and daughter" replied the voice on the phone.

"How do we get in?"

"Just pull up to the sandbags and climb over, we won't shoot" he chuckled good naturedly.

Pat looked to the rest. Kyle said, "We could use a few more guns and as much ammo as we can get so let's go for it" everyone else was in agreement.

"Just give me a couple minutes to get down before you come over. I have to tell my daughter we are expecting desirable guests and not to shoot you guys."

Three minutes later everyone with the exception of Pete and Eddie had climbed over the barricade.

Peter and Eddie had elected to stay with the van in case they needed a speedy get away. As they climbed down the back side of the barricade they were greeted by two enormous red Dobermans. They seemed friendly enough but there was also a hint of restrained danger about them too. "Baron! Stonewall!... Splatz!" the two dogs immediately dropped to the ground, then the first one got up and sauntered back happily towards the voice that had given the command.

The camo clad gentleman walked up to them with an outstretched hand and a smile, in his other hand was a loaded handgun but with his trigger finger outside of the guard. "I am Mike Anderson, come in get comfortable..." with a practiced eye he gave a slight nod to the hardware that Duncan and the rest carried.

Duncan shook the offered hand, "Duncan MacGregor...and this is my nephew Pat" as he pointed out the others in succession "and my brothers Kyle and Liam" Duncan set his rifle down as did the others. Mike's smile broadened and he relaxed some holstering his own firearm. Pat walked over and shook Mike's hand next and walked over to introduce himself to Mike's son Walter, a broad shouldered kid with impossibly large biceps that were threatening to burst the seams of his red and gold "Uncle Sam's Misguided Children" tee shirt that had the Marine Corps logo under the words.

Liam and Kyle offered their hands as well. "Those are some nice guns you boys are toting, I'm guessing that they are military issue am I right?" Duncan smiled; he couldn't help but like the guy right away. Mike introduced his wife Samantha and his daughter Lauren. Samantha offered them coffee and lunch, "We have got plenty of MREs" (Meals Ready to Eat)

Mike was starved for news, his cable went out thirty-six hours back and the radio was just giving the same emergency broadcast telling people to remain indoors and that help would be coming soon, blah, blah, blah.

Duncan shared with him the details of their escape from Manhattan and about their families on his boat. Kyle filled him in on what he and Pat witnessed at the Garden. Liam told what his wife had seen at the Hospital, and what had been on the news when last they had seen it. Pat had collected the guns and brought them over to a work bench so that he and Walter could clean them. Mike listened intently soaking it all up like a sponge. He used "body English" during the high drama parts, and was visibly saddened at the loss of George. "You boys had a rough go of it. Man alive…" shaking his head

"We have had it easy here, when the first news hit I packed everybody up and we came to the store, figuring there would be looters all over the place and since I live closest I told my brother I'd get down here right away… see it's his store, I just work here. Anyway, me and my brother Richie are big into doing reenactments, we do the Civil War, and WWII, and we were supposed to be doing a world war two one this weekend that's how we have all of these sandbags here. Even my son caught the bug"

The three brothers looked over at Pat and Walter over at the bench. Walter came out from behind the counter on one natural leg and a prosthetic below the knee on his other. Mike saw them notice and said simply, "An IED in Afghanistan four years ago"

Walter called over his shoulder, "Yeah I even use a wood and leather peg leg for the Civil War ones."

Mike continued, "You see Richie came into a lot of money from a law suit some years back, and as kids we grew up near Lake George. We were fishing and hunting all of our lives. I sometimes think he bought this place just to give me a job that I would love. Anyways we got here and things weren't too bad yet but I figured it would get bad and quick so I started stacking the sand bags just by the windows, we still had cable then and we were seeing all the reports and well I called my brother and told him I was going to barricade everything so I went back out and continued stacking and then I heard that moan… you know what I am talking about and well then I saw my first couple of those things and they were coming straight for me. So I pulled out my nineteen-eleven and I told them to back off... they just kept coming so I drilled the first one center mast and the thing staggered back but didn't go down so I shot it again still the thing came on so I put one between its eyes and boom lights out, the second one was maybe seven feet away by now so I drilled it through its open mouth and it fell too. Wally and me finished the barricade and came in. The cable went out perhaps an hour later so we lost internet and the TV."

"We've seen a few more but they don't seem to be able to figure out how to get in so they just pass us by after a few minutes." Samantha came over and refreshed his coffee. "So I called my brother again, his buddy owns a bus service out on the Island and well they are over at his shop welding up one of his coaches with some armor then they are gonna come this way and pick us up and some inventory then we are heading for the hills." Duncan told him where his father's compound was and said if they wanted they could head up there. Mike said his thanks but that they were gonna head further south maybe towards Kentucky... but Duncan made sure to give him his radio frequencies and his sat phone number.

"So boys the store is going out of business so... you are going to need ammo for those ARs and some other gear. "Wally come on let's get these guys sorted out" Lauren was pretty shy and stayed off to the side watching Pat, her eyes never left him. Wally grabbed a case of twelve gauge shells and put it up on the counter and then went in back for more ammo for the ARs. Pat could feel Wally's sister's eyes upon him and it was starting to make him uncomfortable.

When Wally came back carrying a wooden crate Pat went to help figuring maybe he could get out from under her gaze by being closer to her brother. Wally seemed to notice Pat's discomfort but didn't make any mention of it and with a small smirk just kept on putting together supplies.

That tactic didn't work either, she would just move to where she could see him. He was really beginning to get the freaked out. Duncan and Mike were going through some camping gear while Liam and Kyle were over with Samantha gathering a selection of MREs. Duncan's phone began to ring, he looked at the ID and saw Pete's number. "What's up?"

Peter's voice sounded stressed, "We've got company you guys better hurry up. There is a huge mob forming and headed this way. More than we have seen clustered together, and these are moving faster than most of them."

Duncan called to his brothers, "We've gotta move, Now!" "Pete pull up front and pop the side door we are gonna toss over supplies"

Liam climbed to the top of the fortification, Kyle stood at the bottom while Duncan started tossing boxes to Kyle and up they went. Pat grabbed the guns while Mike and Walter brought the crates of ammo over. It took only a couple of minutes to get what gear they could fit into the van, they might have been able to fit more if they had had the time to pack it all properly but the throng was getting closer, they had only a few minutes left before they would be surrounded.

Duncan took Liam's place up top while Kyle climbed up and over, Pat was about to climb the sand bags when Lauren grabbed him and turned his face to her and planted a kiss on his lips, she pulled away and said, "Be careful sweetheart" and ran to the bag room with tears streaming down her cheeks. Pat was stunned for a moment.

Mike joined Duncan on top and began shooting his own custom three-oh-eight semi. Each time he pulled the trigger a zombie collapsed.

When he was empty he dropped the gun down to Wally who handed him up a replacement gun already locked and loaded. Duncan jumped down and yelled up, "Thanks man keep safe" and with that the automatic closer took over and slowly began to shut. The speed was agonizingly slow but there was no manual override. The van pulled away

181

before the door had shut completely but the loud reports of the high caliber rifles could be heard in the cabin from several blocks away. Then the shooting just stopped. "I hope that means that they just buttoned themselves back up in there...I mean I hope we didn't just get them killed" said Liam.

They all shared the sentiments. Eddie was lovingly caressing a Remington 12 gauge with a folding stock like it was his date on prom night. Pat was still processing Lauren's kiss and parting remarks. Kyle was quick to explain as best he could. "Son, she had been under a huge amount of stress. She probably didn't think she was gonna survive, and that she was never going to meet Mr. Right before she died. Then out of nowhere you pop in a young and handsome "warrior" type, she was probably a shy girl by nature, and she probably had a whole fantasy relationship with you in her head while we were there. She fell in love with the fantasy you and when you were about to leave it stopped being a fantasy and well you know the rest." Pat hoped that she would be all right, and in his heart of hearts he hoped that someday their paths would cross again. That kiss had gotten her under his skin.

Jacob was following the news feeds on his computer. He noted that the dead were making fast work reducing the population of Croton and Peekskill, two towns that weren't that far away. He was worried that they might get here before his sons, and if that happened he wasn't all that sure he could hold his possession. He had managed to reinforce his fence and electrify the wire; all the windows were boarded up and secured. The place was as secure as he could manage in the time he had. He with the help of Erin and Marie managed to string together a low tech alarm system consisting of a trip line of fishing line run through lawn spikes and gardening stakes along the perimeter that ran back to the house and through 1/6" holes that were tied off to empty cans and a cowbell. All he could do was wait and hope.

He wished that they would call. He was in touch with his daughters in law through Kaitlyn and he knew Carrie was safe in the CDC, but he was terribly worried about his sons even though he wouldn't admit it. Not even to himself. Marie and Erin were nearly frantic with worry, Jacob was doing his best to assuage their fears, but his attempts lacked his full conviction so they had little effect. He felt a little like a caged animal himself. He had reverted to his warrior self in many ways, most ways actually, but he had changed… maybe it was the birth of his first grandchild that did it, be that as it may he could erupt with deadly force still but he could no longer divorce himself from his emotions as he had during his times in the teams.

His watch began to beep it's alarm, shaking him from his ruminations, it was time for his perimeter patrol. He checked his pistol, more out of discipline than any concerns, and then he grabbed his shotgun. Max, the German shepherd knew what that meant and was waiting for him at the door.

"Erin, Marie, it is time for me to make my rounds. One of you lock the door behind us, you know the signals for when we return. If you hear shooting do not open the door unless I give you the signal all right?" Erin was not in any condition to do any of this, but Jacob included her anyway to try and keep her in the game.

Marie, who was made of hardier stock, came to the door and kissed her husband, "Yes dear, we know the routine… three, two, three got it" she smiled indulgently putting on a brave face. He opened the door and Max went out first followed by Jacob. He waited to hear the locks slide home before he stepped off the step and began his patrol.

Erin had heard from Liam off and on so with the rational side of her brain she knew he was all right, but state of the world right now was anything but rational. Her emotions were getting the better of her. She was even having bouts of vomiting. She found herself weeping at the drop of a hat, the stress of it all was becoming too much for her. She picked up her phone and texted Liam again just so that he could let her know he was still okay.

34

Air Force One leveled off at cruising altitude. The service men onboard were attending to their individual responsibilities with the precision of a Swiss watch. The communications suite on this plane alone rivaled that of any other developed country in the world. The signal was displayed, indicating that it was safe to move about the cabin. The first lady and their children got up from their seats and moved to the living quarters, still a bit flustered from the evacuation. The two daughters were blissfully ignorant of the events transpiring around the globe. They were among the few in the world who still possessed the innocence of childhood. The Presidents security team, always vigilant, had noted the symptoms of illness on the man. Having been up to date on all the information concerning the current crisis, the CDC info included, they kept a wary eye upon the President. He went to his office onboard to gain a few minutes of solitude. The ambassador, showing no ill effects was made comfortable and the flight crew busied themselves with the business of flying this behemoth of a plane. Refreshments were offered, and the status quo was established.

Aaron found himself with the rest of his detail, seated in their area talking amongst themselves. The subject was how badly this President was handling things. These men were not glory hounds, nor were they just hired muscle. They were intelligent men with a deep love of their country; Patriots all. They like Aaron, truly believed that the country hung in the balance and if steps were not taken, and soon, the United States could crumble and millions upon millions of people would suffer and die horrific deaths.

Not willing to admit his treason, even though he felt morally justified, he listened. The other SSAs (Secret Service Agents) seemed kindred spirits in their indictments and admonishments of the President. As secret service agents, they are supposed to be apolitical, that, however, does not mean that they cannot have opinions on matters of state. Each of these men had families and friends who would likely die if they were not already dead because of the Presidents inaction. Aaron gazed out of the window at one of their fighter escorts, an F-fifteen Eagle. The pilot noticed Aaron's gaze and gave him a thumbs up before adding speed and disappearing from Aaron's view.

 The conversation that he had been monitoring was progressing, right to where he wanted it to go. "Has anyone else noticed how pale he has gotten. I mean his skin looks sallow and waxy. His forehead looked sweat slickened… I don't know but do you think he could be infected? Should we have the flight medical officer check him out?"

 The other members of the security detail shared that concern as well. The agent in charge or AIC, joined the collected agents. After overhearing the gist of the conversation and said, "Whatever your personal feelings about the man behind the desk…" he looked into the face of each of the assembled men, "leave them at home. You all have jobs to do and taking part of a sewing circle is not in the job description."

"But sir… (spelled sir as he had the respect of his men) if the President is infected…" Aaron was cut off before he could complete his thought.

"We have jobs to do. I will watch the man, and if he shows any symptoms, then I will bring in the flight physician… good enough?" The tone of the statement left no one doubting that he wasn't asking for their approval or consent.

The President was mopping his brow while at the same time trying to suppress the chills that had recently over taken him. He was having trouble staying focused on things. He hit a button on the phone built into the desk and ordered some coffee. He wanted it brewed strong. Moments later a crew member brought in the beverage and asked if there was anything else that he required, receiving no reply the crew member left.

Colonel Franklin, who had the job of guarding the *'nuclear football,'* the satchel that could put all of the United States Weapons into action, knocked on the door seeking to speak with the President. "Sir, we have just been informed that DC has gone black sir. The Pentagon is under siege. Our forces are holding and moral is high, but they have a pessimistic opinion on how long it will take to clear the enemy sir."

"Jim, have you seen the reports from the CDC? What is going on? Is it really this bad?" asked the President. They were simple enough questions, but the Colonel was troubled by them.

"Sir, am I to understand you have not reviewed the CDC materials?" asked the Colonel a bit incredulously.

The president was unresponsive. He asked the question again and still no reaction from the commander in chief, "Sir!" The President returned from la la land.

"Jim, what is going on, how did we get here? Where is the Chinese ambassador?" The colonel knew for certain that the president was not in complete control of his faculties. The AIC tapped on the door, "Excuse me sir, sir; Colonel Franklin may I have a moment?" The Colonel turned and exited. When the door was closed the most powerful man in the world became lost in his thoughts again only now he was wondering how he was going to get the answers to his biology test. He had regressed in mind back to high school.

The AIC and the Colonel shared their observations and went in search of the chief medical officer to consult.

The first Lady sought out her husband after getting her daughters settled. She didn't bother knocking. It was a wife's prerogative to see her husband whenever she wanted. Her handlers had striven hard to sculpt her into a first lady who was not hated by the populous. On the campaign trail, she had made numerous gaffs, that had many concerned that she would cost them the white house. They worked diligently to revamp her image. The end result was downright astounding. She was not adored by the citizenry but her approval ratings far exceeded that of her husband's. The worst of her habits, they were ineffectual at curbing, that of her feeling, she could go anywhere she felt whenever she felt. In her mind when they elected her husband; they had also elected her after all two heads were better than one.

She had prided herself on her influence on policy decisions that they had put forth. Never mind that the vast majority of Americans believed these same policies to be destroying the country. When the AIC attempted to bar her access from her husband, she whirled on him and began to berate him as if he were some insolent child. The agent was used to her tirades and just let it roll off of his back. "Ma'am the President is indisposed, and I really think you should return to your children." Just then the flight medical officer showed up and slipped past the two of them. The first lady knew something was wrong and with all of her one hundred and thirty five pounds, pushed passed the burly agent obstructing her way.

The Chinese ambassador showed no symptoms what so ever, he just drifted off into sleep, at least as far as anyone knew. Had anyone bothered to check, they would have seen that his vitals were nonexistent. People went back and forth, going about their responsibilities without giving a single thought to the dignitary. The tag team of organism and virus were working at a fevered pace and were very near to being able to reanimate the ambassador.

The doctor was putting a blood pressure cuff around the President's arm and positioning his stethoscope when the first lady entered. "What's wrong with him?" she asked. The doctor began squeezing the bulb and answered, "I have only just gotten here…" His thoughts were far from complimentary. "If you would please give me a few moments to examine him." As he indicated that she should leave the room he continued plying his art. She was having none of it. She finally looked at her husband and noticed that his complexion was pale and sallow, and that he was bathed in sweat.

"What is wrong with my husband?" she put such emphasis on that last word as if it meant she was entitled to know and that the doctor was withholding the information to spite her. The doctor ignored her and continued examining his patient. This won him the enmity of the first lady who was not used to not getting treated with the deference she felt she deserved.

He employed a temporal thermometer and received a reading of one hundred and six degrees. With a swiftness born from expertise, he inserted a hep-lock into the vein on the back of the president's left hand and secured it with surgical tape and then started a bag of IV broad-spectrum antibiotics and a bag of saline fluids.

The President was slipping in and out of coherent thoughts, when he looked up and finally noticed his wife. "Hey good look-in, why don't you come over here and give me a kiss… I am the President you know" She thought he was being playful. In reality, however, he didn't know who she was, and he was just trying to get some action.

She went to his side and bent to kiss him. The kiss seemed at first to be chaste but then proceeded to get more passionate. It broke suddenly as she drew back in pain. "What the F…" as her hand went to her ruined lip, blood escaping her hand from where she had been bitten.

The doctor had had enough. "Get her ass out of here! Now!" he bellowed with authority. The AIC was pleased to do as he was told. The President was smiling; you could see he was reveling in the taste of his wife's blood. He started to laugh and attempted to rise. The doctor shoved him unceremoniously back into his seat. "Mr. President, we have to get into bed" as he crushed a couple of instant cold packs in an effort to get the fever down.

Rise Fall Rise Again: A New York Zombie Encounter

The communications officer was in contact with the VP and the cabinet in their bunker on speaker phone, informing them of what was going on aboard Air Force One. It was assumed that with the President incapacitated that he would take the reins. "With the President infected…" (no one seemed to notice the slip, that it was never said that he was infected.) "I'd better be sworn in right away. This time of crisis requires swift action, and the people need to know that there is a steady hand at the helm."

"Yes Mr. President was the reply." The President up in the air had yet to even expire, the coups had succeeded, and no one was the wiser.

The medical facilities on Air Force One rivaled any ER in the country, apart from the cramped space. Blood was drawn and was being scrutinized under scopes. There was no longer any doubt. The President contracted the infection. The doctor had restrained the "former" President to the table and then started antivirals in addition to the antibiotics. Time would tell if this course would yield any hope, but the doctor was pessimistic.

The sound of gunfire erupted from the cabin. The corpse of the Chinese ambassador rose from his seat, after a moment's struggle with the lap belt saved one of the flight crews from a rending bite. The security detail was quick to respond. Low velocity rounds were fired from two guns. The first agent fired center mass the second, however, had gone for a double tap to the head. Blossoms of crimson blood dotted first the lower left portion of the abdomen and second, the sternum; the third round tore through the muscle and bone of the right shoulder, severing the appendage. The kinetic energy of that third round was not entirely spent. The round had continued its course and entered the arm of Aaron, just as the pressure from the two rounds fired at the creatures head caused the cranium to explode showering the area with brain matter and bone fragments. The threat was removed, within a matter of a few seconds the deck was secure.

189

Aaron knew that the wound was fatal even though nothing vital had been hit. He knew instantly that the bullet in passing through the creature had picked up at least minute amounts of its blood and tissue before it had entered his arm where it lodged. There was no doubt he was infected now. The irony was not lost on him, the fact that he had in essence, murdered this once man. He was now infected by his own treachery. He removed his own weapon and checked to be sure he had low velocity rounds in the magazine. He put the muzzle of the weapon under his jaw behind his chin and squeezed the trigger. More brain and bone were added to the mix.

With all the excitement and commotion, the injury to the first lady's mouth was forgotten. She had been escorted back to her children, where she had to tell them that their daddy was very ill. The children wept, and she did her best to console them while humming a comforting tune, the way that mothers throughout history calmed children across the millennia. The hours passed slowly as the plane circled aloft. Finally, the children drifted off into fitful sleep, having cried themselves into exhaustion. The first lady laid with her children, mentally spent, exhaustion leeching her energy reserves. Her body ached, and her nose was runny; she fought against slumber. A battle that she lost, and her children would pay the price for. Her last thoughts were of her husband, sure that they would wake her if things changed with his condition.

The doctor was fighting a losing battle. He had given up hope that the antibiotics and anti-virals would yield results, so he introduced potassium iodine into the cocktail as a hail mary attempt. As time passed, he racked his brain. He drew another blood sample and looked at it under the scope. He could hardly believe his eyes; he double checked the results. The infection was not reversed, far from it. Its progress was, however, slowed. He immediately went to the comms center and contacted the CDC to report what he had found. Returning to his patient he watched and recorded. It took three more hours before the President finally expired, and a mere 6 minutes after his death before it reanimated. The bonds restraining it held it fast to the table. They now had another specimen in custody to research in hopes of finding some way to save mankind.

The moral onboard had fallen into the abyss. The business continued, but the mood was somber.

Screams of pain and horror erupted from the family's quarters. Agents burst through the door to see what had been the first lady savaging one of her daughters. The other one was already dead, eviscerated by the very mother who hours prior consoled her. The First Zombie's teeth were tearing away at the scalp of her daughter while her talon like fingers, were shredding the soft skin of her cheeks. The screams of pain and fear were deafening. The child could not comprehend the betrayal that she felt as yet unrealized. The agents were paralyzed by the sight. When the zombie turned and lunged for the new source of food two shots rang out from behind. The AIC stepped forward as he safed his weapon. "She was a fucking bitch anyway." He said as he stepped into the room past the two agents who were only now aware of just how close they had come to being eaten. When the AIC saw the children, one dead the other about to join her sister, he un-safed his weapon and put a bullet into each of their small heads. Visions of shooting children would haunt him the rest of his days.

36

The now President was in heated debate with his cabinet on what should be done first. He knew, with certainty, that he would need ask for several resignations but now was not the time.

"I want to be in touch with the people at Google right now" he said to the assemblage. The arguing continued but many of the people there stopped their bickering and looked at him with that RCA dog look of confusion. The former Vice President explained, "Google Earth… if we allow them to have real time satellite imagery we can save millions of people worldwide."

This touched off a whole new series of arguments. The loudest opponents being the military advisors. They were saying that this would compromise National Security not to mention the safety of military and law enforcement personnel. "You are not seeing the forest for the trees…what good is any of that if everyone on the globe is a fucking zombie!" The President dropped the "F" bomb to shock everyone into silence. He miscalculated, not by much, he was known his entire political career for his colorful language among other similarly related gaffs of speech but he did succeed in grabbing their attention with common sense. This in his case was not all that common.

"Next I want the military redeployed concentrating on our infrastructure, most notably on the power grid, water supplies, and communications." He still had everyone's attention "If we can't preserve those, society will degenerate too rapidly to restore. We will pull back and try to set up safe zones, and try to find where people have survived, and help them where ever we can, but by keeping the lights on and the water flowing the survivors stand a better chance of holding out till we can get them the aid that they need." He had received tremendous support on this. Even the military men had no argument for this logical approach.

He had been President for less than an hour and all ready he had done more for America than his predecessor had in two and a half years. His staff was busy setting up a press conference that would be carried live on every channel as well as streamed on the web on hundreds if not thousands of sites and feeds. He was inundated with intelligence reports from all over the globe. He too received the hopeful news that came from Air Force One, this tidbit of knowledge warmed the cockles of his heart knowing that he was in part responsible for the discovery due to his participation albeit remotely in his predecessor's demise. When he had been tapped as the Vice Presidential candidate, he knew he and his running mate had many ideological differences, hell they had been rivals for the Democratic Presidential nomination, but when he was tapped he put those differences aside. Now that he WAS President he hoped to repair the damage his partner had done. "All that in due time" he thought to himself. He began combing through the reports with fervor.

37

Pat had very little room in the back of the van to work on his brain storm idea of fashioning IEDs from some of the supplies garnered from the Long Island Outdoorsman. He figured he could make something like a cross between a Molotov cocktail and a napalm grenade using an accelerant and a sticky substance, like gasoline and dish soap. He just needed to come up with a simple yet reliable ignition solution and a delivery vessel.

Peter was driving towards the Meadowbrook Parkway. He had to slow the speed of the van due to all of the abandoned vehicles. He did not have a good feeling about things, judging from the chaos that had taken hold around the area he was not sure that they would be able to make it to Long Beach anytime soon. He voiced his concerns to Duncan. "Look we have made it this far, whatever we face we will just have to overcome it." Pete thought he heard desperation in Duncan's voice but he was alive because of Duncan, so he opted not to judge his friend.

Little did Pete know that Duncan's thoughts echoed Pete's concerns. He had only recently thought about the drawbridges. Those could stop them in their tracks but quick. All of the guns in the vehicle had been reloaded, the other supplies had been broken down and consolidated for easier transport just in case they had to abandon the van. They still had far too much to carry if they had to make a go of it on foot, but all in all the supplies served as a balm to his nerves and a buoy to his flagging spirit.

Pete brought the vehicle to a stop about three miles before the bridge. The road way was blocked with empty and not so empty cars, trucks, vans, and vehicles of every sort as far as the eye could see. Add to that was the horde of nightmarish proportion milling about. The unlucky survivors trapped in those vehicles had no avenue of escape. Any who had firearms had likely ended their own suffering but those who didn't…

well no one wanted to imagine the sheer terror that they had to be experiencing, knowing that they soon would be torn apart and eaten by this ungodly host of zombies.

The zombies were too far away to take notice of the van's arrival. Pete executed a quick three point turn and raced the wrong way on the parkway back in the direction from which he had come. "Any ideas, I am fresh out" he said to all in the van. "Chances are all the bridges are going to be the same, so how do we hook up with the rest?"

It was Eddie who jarred Duncan's brain into action when he said, "Did you guys arrange for an alternative rally point?" "That's it…Eddie if you didn't have three days worth of beard growth I could kiss you, hell I just might anyway. Liam hand me the portable VHF." Liam looked back at his brother a little confused. "The walkie talkie looking thing we grabbed at my house" Embarrassed by his brain cramp Liam handed the device over.

Duncan turned the knob to power on the unit, checked the channel to be sure he would be on the correct frequency and then depressed the transmit button, "Loop parkway bridge operator, Loop Parkway bridge operator, this is the Captain of sailing vessel Persistence, come in please."

There was no response.

He tried again, "Loop Parkway bridge, Loop Parkway bridge, this is the captain of sailing vessel Persistence, come in please." Again there was no answer. He tried a third time, expecting the same results as the two previous attempts. This time however he was rewarded with an answer to his hail.

A frazzled voice broke the static, " This is the Loop Parkway bridge operator, the bridge is open, but I don't see your vessel captain, over"

Duncan was glad to hear the man's voice. "Bridge operator, we are not aboard our vessel… are any of the area bridges down and able to allow access to long beach? Over."

The voice responded, "Negative captain… all bridges are up or secured in an effort to prevent contamination. To no avail it seems, they came right out of the surf…" Duncan was disappointed to hear this but he wasn't surprised by the news. "Bridge, how are you set as for security and provisions?"

The quick reply told volumes, the man was feeling alone and beaten. Fear was etched into every word he uttered, but he was there and countless people owed his their thanks for stemming the tide of death that surely would have made short work of the beach communities. "I'm buttoned up in here pretty good, still have power but well I ate my lunch six hours ago so apart from a couple of granola bars food is pretty scarce. I have a couple cans of Dr. Pepper…(laughter) not much but hell, I can't exactly make a run to 7 eleven."

"Bridge, listen, do you have any line to lower yourself down if I can arrange for a vessel to be below you?" There was a long pause.

"No line but if you can get a boat down there I will drop into the drink and be fished out." Hope and strength infused in the words of the bridge operator.

"Okay, I will be back in touch, keep the faith my man. If I can get in touch with my people you shouldn't have much more to wait than an hour or two at most." Duncan said to the besieged man.

The mood in the van was a somber one. The constant fear and struggle to get this far had sapped much of their strength. Duncan seemed to be the only one not functioning on auto pilot. They had all heard that the bridges were not an option, there for they believed that all was lost. Duncan however still thinking clearly said, "Guys why the long pusses? It doesn't matter if we get to Long Beach, boats can go anywhere on the water. We will just call and arrange for a rendezvous elsewhere, no big deal."

The men looked at each other like morons, "duh…yep" they were all a little embarrassed for slipping into despair. Sure the usual excuses were still valid. It had been a busy and exhausting battle to get to where they were. Duncan called his buddy Dave from his cell. Dave answered on the third ring, Duncan could hear Laura in the background telling him that the phone call better be life and death because she wanted him now, maybe not later. Duncan smiled, Dave came on the line a second later.

"Dunk… where the hell are you guys?" Duncan answered, "It's been a little hairy bro, looks like we are going to need to change plans a little, we are cut off from Long Beach, and all the bridges are up."

 Dave told him that he knew that was the case, and gave him a run down on what was what from his end. "Dave that boat of yours… how shallow of a draft does it have?" Dave chuckled. "Dunk it's a fishing boat not a schooner, she will float in eighteen inches of water."

Duncan was grinning as this last element of his plan fell into place. " Listen pal, I need for you to run Reynold's channel and be somewhere near Oceanside or East Rockaway. I am thinking by Bay Park golf course to meet up with us and haul our asses and the supplies we grabbed back out to safety. I am sure if you don't have charts for the area someone in the flotilla will."

"Sure man, how long till you get there?" Duncan looked at his watch.

"I figure we can be over there in forty-five minutes or so but let's call it an hour and a half to be safe, you should be able to get there in about an hour. Call me from the bay by the course, you should be able to pull right alongside the bulkhead, we will drive the van right out to there and make the transfer ten minutes tops…"

"Ten minutes?... how much gear did you guys find?"

Duncan told him about the Long Island Outdoorsman and the haul they liberated.

"All right bud, I will clear the decks and be there as fast as I can."

Duncan told him not to worry and to keep to the schedule and that he would see him in an hour and a half, plus or minus. They said their goodbyes and disconnected.

Laura heard enough of the one sided conversation to realize that it was indeed life or death. Even though if it hadn't had been she still would have intended to share his bunk. She helped him stow gear and transfer the extraneous stuff, hers included, to the Persistence so he could take his leave.

When he was ready to go he met with the Captains Council, as they were now calling themselves, and told them of the plan. With their approval he was underway ten minutes later. The twin Mercs carving deep wakes as the bow planed skyward. An hour, he laughed he figured he could make in damn near half that time. Dusk was approaching so he eased off of the throttles a bit and turned on his running lights out of habit.

38

Television stations all over the globe were going dark or replaced with words on the screen that read "We are experiencing technical difficulties, please stand by" in a variety of languages. Cellular technology was overloaded so large areas in Europe and Asia were no longer covered.

In Australia there were reports of the dead rising. All throughout Africa zombies were plaguing the living. The nations in Africa were slow to react to this new threat. Plagues and disease were commonplace in this area of the world. The rate at which the spread of this infection was happening was unprecedented.

It seems that the only place in the world where there have been no reports of zombies was Japan. That was likely due to the fact that after that horrible earth quake and subsequent Nuclear Meltdown, no one had wanted to travel there. Now that the world was collapsing the Japanese Government closed its borders to one and all. This was made abundantly clear when two commercial airliners were shot down for violating Japanese airspace.

Wild fires were burning out of control in California incinerating thousands upon thousands of acres, touched off accidentally by a collective trying to defend their community. A smallish horde of zombies laid siege at the gated community. The residents behind the walls shot many of the creatures. Being concerned with leaving the bodies where they fell, fearing that the bodies might attract more unwanted guests, they figured that they could douse the zombies with gas and burn them up. They hadn't figured that the ones not dead for a second time would walk around until they turned to ash. By the time they realized their mistake the fires had spread too much for them to get control of. Their community perished first among the flames that threatened thousands more.

People in the flood plains surrounding the Missouri and Mississippi rivers were moving to high ground as fast as they could. Dams and levees were breached hoping to wash the undead downriver or out to sea. Produce would be scarce in the foreseeable future as countless farms and fields were now under water, and the dead keep coming. Livestock was washed away along with those not fast enough to escape the torrents of water. Panic was the flavor of the day. New Orleans had not fully recovered from the effects of Katrina, and now the city was underwater again.

The dead not easily deterred sought out any of the living to devour. The only warning many people had been the scent of fetid decay approaching on shambling legs. The armies of the dead are swelling with more and more zombies as victims fall and rise again joining the ranks of their murderers.

Elsewhere, communities chose to follow the example set by Jonestown. Whole towns gathered in school auditoriums and gymnasiums, and drank poisoned Kool-Aid. Better a peaceful death than to be torn apart and devoured. The children in these communities trusted their elders. They went off to their afterlife without any knowledge. The parents followed their children.

The CDC and it's counterparts around the world were working tirelessly to understand and defend against the growing apocalypse, began to see cooperation between nations on a scale never before seen. Relief efforts were thwarted due to too much demand on resources, but the sharing of information on an unprecedented level gave one hope that humanity might just survive, that is if they caught a few good breaks.

Dr. Manis and his team were following their new leads with fervor. Outside of the fence lines refugees were massing, a tent city popped up almost overnight. By the third day nearly twenty percent of the population of Atlanta was camped outside the fence and more were coming all the time.

Rise Fall Rise Again: A New York Zombie Encounter

The soldiers tasked with guarding the fence were loath to do what they knew they must. There was a mass of undead coming their direction and the civilians outside would storm the gates, as soon as they found out. It was the duty of those men on the guns to prevent any breach. Their machine guns stood at the ready to unleash wholesale death when the bullets flew. There was talk about letting the refugees or at least their children past the first fence line, but that was quickly dismissed in that there would be no means of being sure that none of them were infected. Grimly, the soldiers stood their posts and waited for the inevitable to start.

The whomp, whomp, whomp, of helicopter rotors churning the air as a flight of gunships moved against the approaching horde. Vainly, trying to buy time for the refugees, as they fired rockets into the mass of zombies to devastating effect. Sadly it didn't even slow the progress of the fiends. The sad fact is that the weapons that the military could bring to bear rely on shock and awe to halt the enemy. Zombies cared not at all about moral or their own safety. They were driven by the most primal of desires, and they sought only to eat. They were unable to fathom even the simplest of ideas, they could not be awed much less shocked by any actions the military took.

In the tent city people gathered at the feet of "preachers" who were saying, "that the rapture was at hand and that God would smite wicked and the ungodly. What more proof do you need than seeing the dead walking and eating upon the children of God."

The fear was palpable, as people crushed up against one another trying vainly to get away from the approaching horde. The Guards in the observation posts could see from their elevated position the wave of panic radiated out from the edge where first contact with the horde would take place. The putrid smell of decaying flesh preceded the horde by twenty minutes.

The smell alone was enough to spark off the powder keg that was the tent city. The fence line was supported by bulwarks of sand and earth. People were crushed to death against the line. As the crushing mass grew, the bodies began to pile up, and the zombies had yet to take their first bites.

The soldiers were transfixed by the sight. The command was given to open fire as the bodies began to pile up and threatened to create a ramp for the zombies to march over and gain access inside the outermost perimeter. The whirr of electrical motors engaged, rotating the barrels of the gun emplacements followed a second later by the buzz saw sound as a wall of lead was spewed forth from the modern day Gatling guns. Whomp went the mortars as the delivered white phosphorous death, burning the living, the dead, and the undead alike. Mercifully, the soldiers could not hear the screams and cries over the cacophony of noise made by the weaponry. Mothers and fathers did their best to shield their children, some even through their children over the fence to relative safety before they were cut down, many in half, by the relentless machine gun fire. The soldiers were supposed to eliminate any that got inside the first fence line, but that was too far beyond the moral compass of most. So for a while at least those children cried and sobbed as they watched their families shredded by bullets or by undead monsters. The CDC was under siege.

From inside the safety of the walls, the sounds of battle could be heard. From the rattle of the machine guns to the initial whomp of the mortars followed a few seconds later by the inevitable explosion as the mortar rounds detonated. Mercifully, the dorm areas were on the other side from where the battle was taking place. People with nothing to keep them busy collected in the lounge areas. Many produced bottles of booze and set at emptying them with vigor down their gullets. Others massed with friends and co-workers to cry and some to pray. All the assembled thankful that they were in here and not out there watching it all unfold.

Moments before the first detonation Carrie finished reading an e-mail from her sons, both of whom were now stationed at an energy hub to help guard the fragile national power grid. She was relieved to learn that they were safe and that they weren't near any major cities and that there had been very few reports of zombies in their area of deployment. It had been hard for her to even come here without her sons, a mother's instincts to protect their offspring and all, but they were men and soldiers now. They had to report and she and her husband came here. That didn't stop her from worrying. The e-mail helped assuage her trepidation, however. That all changed with sound of distant gunfire and the explosion of the mortar shells.

Jerry was on his way back to his and Carrie's quarters when the battle got underway. He raced through the halls as soon as he heard the machine guns. He collided with an unfortunate person who had the bad luck to step into his path, which resulted in said person going sprawling. Jerry didn't even stop to see if the fellow was all right. He burst through the doors to the "Dormitory" wing with enough force to require a maintenance person to adjust the hinges later. When he got to their room he found that she was not there so to the lounge he went in search of his wife. In the rational part of his mind he knew she was safe, but his emotions needed verification. When he found her a wave of relief flooded him, followed quickly by a momentary flash of annoyance at her not having been in their shared quarters, which he just as quickly swished away.

Carrie looked up just as Jerry entered. She could read the concern on his face like it were printed in neon. She pushed her laptop to the side and rushed to meet him half way. He folded her into his arms and buried his face into her silky blonde hair.

"Carrie, sweetheart, when I heard the guns I got so worried… I have left you alone so much since we have been here…"

She shut him up with a kiss. "Jerry you have been working your ass off to help save us all… don't worry about not spending time with me."

"But..."

She kissed him again and he relaxed markedly.

John Roberts watched the interplay of the Sixkillers from a distance with envy. Not that he had any aspirations with Carrie, he just didn't have anyone to worry over or have worry about him. When he saw that the intimate moment was passed he made his way over to the couple to introduce himself to Jerry.

"Umm... Carrie is this a good time?" he said with his hand thrust out to shake. Carrie turned partway around to see John and then turned to her husband and said, "Babe this is John Roberts, the guy I was telling you about." Jerry smiled warmly, he didn't remember much of the conversation but had a vague memory of her mentioning some guy she wanted him to meet.

"Hi, pleased to meet you. I am Jerry Sixkiller." As he took John's hand and shook it. John got a good feeling about Jerry right away by his handshake. Firm, but no macho squeeze, easy smile...a good feeling.

"I am John Roberts,...sorry if I have been usurping too much of your wife's time but she has been a colossal help to me with the blog the CDC has me writing." Another mortar detonated and they all jumped a bit.

"Hey John why don't you come to our room and we can talk a while... unless you have more pressing things...?" said Jerry.

"Sounds great I think the conversation would be a welcome distraction from the sounds of battle" They adjourned to the Sixkiller's quarters.

Two hours and thirty seven minutes later the first wave of battle ended.

39

Jacob was sitting in front of his computer reading the news on his home page. "Google earth along with the assistance of the Military and several other countries around the globe was now going real time" This was a little misleading in that it would have some lag time... three to seven minutes in major metro areas, and for many outlying rural areas there would be no streaming of satellite video at all. For Jacob however this was not a problem. His compound was close enough to NYC that he could stream with little delay.

He clicked on the link and located his area and zoomed in three-quarters of the way figuring this was a good compromise of detail and distance. He would be able to see any approaching hordes, although if there were only a few or a small group, he wouldn't be able to see them. He moused over towards Croton and saw a huge horde numbering around one thousand by his estimation judging by the area that was covered. The good news was that they did not seem to be moving his direction. He wanted to keep an eye on the area, so he moved the screen back putting his compound off center due to the Hudson River.

"Erin... would you come in here please." He called to his daughter in law.

A minute later she nervously entered the room. "Hey Dad, what's up?" she asked trying to sound better. She knew that she was clinically depressed, she was also aware that there were things she could do for herself to make things somewhat better. She was putting forth the effort. Jacob noticed this and was relieved that she was shaking off the worst of the PTSD.

"Google earth now has live feeds from the satellite, I want you to keep an eye on things while I make my next set of rounds" She shook off the hollow look of despair and eyed Jacob with a level expression.

"Sure Dad... can do" she knew that those words would brighten her father in law's spirits. He was a can do sort of guy. He stood up and offered her his chair. She sat and familiarized herself with his computer.

"Oh... and I dug out these walkie talkies that we had for the kids. They have a decent range and are water proof. They even have headsets. He took one of the units and put it on, handing her the other. She did the same. They tested the radios before he turned to leave. "Hell these radios are a hundred times better than the ones I used in Korea" he mused as he headed for the door and his waiting German Sheppard.

Marie was at the door, the routine having been established. She kissed her husband and locked the door behind him.

"Dad can you hear me?" came Erin's voice over his headset.

"Copy' he replied 'I read you five by five."

Erin was puzzled, "what does that mean?" Jacob sighed, "Loud and clear Erin"

"Just checking is all... Dad... come back safe."

"Will do."

He stepped off of the porch preceded by Max. The dog moved up the path about twenty-five feet when a deep throaty growl emanated from the dog, and the hair on its back stood straight up sharp as a razor. The dog's posture was menacing as it lowered its haunches ready to spring if need be. Whatever Max smelled was outside of his own olfactory limits. It was also likely to be outside of his perimeter. Jacob switched the safety off of his gun. The failing sunlight of dusk provided the worst visibility conditions.

"Erin... have Marie turn on the outside lights" he whispered into the mic of his headset.

"Got it." Seven long seconds later the yard was lit up bright as noon by the sodium lamps. Max's growl became even more pronounced and menacing. It was outside the gate, whatever it was.

Jacob didn't investigate further; he knew what was there as the first hint of smell reached his nose. He didn't want to attract its attention, so he moved off to check the sides of his perimeter. He listened for the sound of movement through the fallen leaves and underbrush. He cautiously stepped over his alarm trip wire and moved towards the barbed wire. He inched closer, his shotgun at the ready.

"Erin can you zoom in on the property, tell me if you can see any by the gate and how many?"

"K" was here reply a few seconds later, "looks like three and they are milling around across the road" "thanks" Jacob moved up the path to near the gate.

When he was fortifying he had left a six-foot ladder at the gate for just this sort of circumstance. He inspected the gate silently to be sure that the poles he had driven down were solidly against the gate. The tension was what it should have been. He did not want to chance any movement that could knock him off of the ladder when he climbed it. Not only could he be injured from the fall, but he could accidentally shoot himself, or worse one of his charges.

Jacob climbed the ladder and looked over the gate. Erin was right there were three of them and they were thirty feet away across the gravel road. He brought the gun to his shoulder, wrapping the sling. He got a good check weld and sighted down the barrel. "This is gonna hurt" he thought to himself as he remembered that the gun was loaded with slugs. He thought about switching to his pistol. He could make the shots but better to use the right weapon. The pistol was his fall back. He took careful aim at the closest zombie and began applying pressure to the trigger. The shotgun roared and kicked ferociously, as the muzzle flashed the head of the zombie just disappeared in splatter of blood and brains. The second and third zombies turned in Jacobs's direction; their slow uncoordinated movements posed no difficulties for Jacob as he re-acquired and blew the head off number two, and the devastation created as the deer slug impacted with the skull was surreal. The sound of the slug tearing through Jacob's neighbor's mailbox was punctuated by the peppering said mailbox took as pieces of ruined skull and flying teeth followed their trajectory. Zombie number three had now located the source of meat it sought and it ambled towards Jacob at the speed one would expect from Otis the Mayberry town drunk as he staggered past Barney and Andy looking to sleep it off in his cell. A third terrific explosion as the shotgun fired for the final time. With no more visible threats and no sounds to suggest any, Jacob climbed back down his ladder massaging his pulverized shoulder. "Next time definitely the deer rifle."

Max padded up to Jacob's side and together they finished the rounds of the property and re-entered the house.

40

"Head west on sunrise, then before the Louis Koch sign make the left onto Foxhurst Road…" Duncan said to Peter, who looked as if he were on a leisurely Sunday drive. "Pete did you hear me? What's got into you… are you okay?" Pete glanced in Duncan's direction.

"No probs brother, Sunrise west, Foxhurst got it."

"What about the rest of it I need to know are you cracking up?" Duncan asked in complete sincerity.

"Dude relax, I am fine, it's just that we are finally going to be safe… it's almost over… well you know what I mean"

Freeport was becoming more active with the dead growing more numerous by the minute. What had once been men, women, and children, were now fiends seeking to devour their one-time fellows.

Within the Best Buy shopping center, a small group of survivors were fighting a losing battle. They had managed to secure the door to the yogurt shop that they had been hiding in. There they had spent the past thirty-six hours not daring to open the doors lest the few zombies that had been in the lot should smell them and renew their assault. The horde's numbers grew and grew. They had no weapons with which to use to defend themselves, so they cowered in the store. They were desperate; their time for flight had passed them by. There were others trapped similarly in the electronic store, although they did not have the food and drink that were to be had in the yogurt shop.

Neither group knew about the other. The situation in Best Buy was even more desperate than that of their fellow shopping center survivors. For something had drawn the attention the horde, which now was massing at the doors pounding away to get in. The doors were holding but it was only a matter of time, as more and more zombies crushed up against the doors. The constant pounding and pressure would fatigue the metal and eventually the doors would give. The haunting moans could be heard from three blocks distant. With each moan the emotional strain built among the survivors, their mental reserves were almost depleted.

The yogurt survivors figured that they might be able to escape while the horde was engaged with their assault on the doors five stores away.

They made their run for it. They over estimated their preparedness, thirty-six hours of crouching behind a counter had seized muscle groups and reduced their flight speed to little more than a trot, barely able to out distance a zombie. The zombies had the advantage of not knowing fatigue or pain, they would never tire, they would chase until they flaked away like so much dust. The group had made it fifteen feet out of the door before they were spotted by some of the horde. The fetid putrescence was causing the group to retch slowing them even further. This was the scene that Duncan and crew came upon.

Panic had taken over the group fell apart. As they began to separate the zombies followed. The ratio did not change. However, their survival rate plummeted to nonexistence. Each of the survivors was taken down in rapid succession. One after the other, after the other, 'until finally the last was brought down by the mob that pursued him. The screams of anguish passed through the rolled-up windows of the van. Other zombies north of the High way were drawn to the screams. The area was teeming with the undead denizens.

Peters experience crashing through groups of zombies as they had when they fled the school told him that this van with its plastic front end would succumb quickly to that type of abuse. He did the only thing he could. He attempted a bootlegger's turn to escape. The suspension of the van was not designed to accommodate such maneuvers and screamed its protest. Kyle and Liam thankful for the Odyssey's windows, not many vans sliding doors had widows that could go down into the doors. This afforded them the ability to fire their weapons and if necessary they could raise the windows again to afford themselves of the meager protection that they offered. When the vehicle was broadside to the monsters the Brothers opened fire. Pete was able to keep the van from rolling, then through the car into reverse backing into, and then over a few of the closer creatures before he put it back in drive and completed his turn.

With the gas pedal floored he zipped across the median and into the train station's parking lot. The zombies followed only much slower. The driving was hazardous, between the parked and abandoned vehicles, the speed with which he was navigating was tempting fate, and hell double dog daring fate was more like it or so thought Duncan.

"Cross back over when you can and take any side street you can... I'll figure out how to get us there..."

Pete sped on through Oceanside to the border with Rockville Centre. They were very near The Long Island Sportsman again. Thankfully, they could turn down Kensington before they could find out if they had cost that family their lives. Duncan knew this area fairly well, his scout troop met weekly not far from here. In fact, several of his troop mates had lived on this very block. He fed Peter directions, and they made their way through. Duncan's apprehension about the narrow side streets proved to be unwarranted, when the road was blocked Peter just drove up on the sidewalk and lawns until he passed the obstacle by.

"Okay now make a right onto Lincoln just up ahead, then make the left at the church..."

Peter no longer had on the look of the leisurely driver. He had been reminded that they weren't safe until they were. He continued to follow the directions that Duncan was giving.

They were traveling up Rockaway Avenue at a healthy clip when Duncan shouted, "slow down...there is a pile up ahead, we are going to have to make the turn on Pearl Street."

211

So far, when they had come upon the pile ups and major accidents, there were zombies about in plentiful numbers.

"Turn here…right damn it Right!" Pete screeched the brakes, so much for anti lock brakes he thought absently. The noise of the screeching tires drew a few zombies like moths to the proverbial flame. These they ignored, choosing to conserve their finite ammunition, as they sped away leaving them behind.

They made the left turn onto Ocean Avenue. They were now in East Rockaway, and maybe five minutes away from their destination. Duncan was wondering why he had yet to hear from Dave when he looked at his phone and realized he had yet to plug in the charger. His phone was flat line.

"Shit … shit, shit, shit!"

"What's the matter?" Exclaimed Pete as the rest searched out their prospective windows for some unseen threat.

"My phone is dead… Dave is probably out there and been trying to call….shit"

Duncan began to rummage around in his pockets looking for the charger. He finally located it and plugged it into the cigarette lighter (which of course was not a cigarette lighter, no newer cars had those anymore it was a twelve-volt accessory port or some such nonsense) he was rewarded with a friendly musical sound as the phone booted up. This seemed to take forever. Here they were not five minutes from their rendezvous and they were sitting there idling waiting on his 'effing' phone. When at last the display indicated he now had service, he saw that he had a voice-mail. He checked to see who had left the message. He was sure it was Dave but sought the confirmation anyway. He didn't bother to listen to the message but instead hit send. The phone dialed Dave's number. He picked up on the first ring.

"Dude,… what's with not answering your phone? I've been sitting here scared shitless waiting on your ass… I almost turned around and left." Dave ranted.

"Hell man, we had to make a few detours… wait we aren't over do yet, in fact, we are right on time…," said Duncan, exasperation creeping into his voice. The stress had him frayed at the edges. "Dave, is the course clear so far as you can tell?"

"Looks pretty clear to me" he replied. "Okay cruise into the bulkhead we will be there in three minutes."

Dave said he would be there with bells on. Duncan replied, "You might want to rephrase that some zombies might get confused and think you meant dinner bell" The attempt at levity fell flat. The cord pulled out of the socket, and the phone went dead again. Eddie, however, was quick thinking enough to have scribbled down the number just in case. He immediately produced his own phone and dialed it.

"Hello?" Duncan took the phone from Eddie nodding his thanks. "Dave, me again… my phone crapped out" The van passed the empty booth at the park entrance bouncing over the speed bumps. Duncan's sore head had impacted with the roof of the vehicle as he noticed the sign declaring a five miles per hour limit. The van's shocks protested the treatment, but they sped up the cart path and onto the course.

If the green's keeper were still among the living, he would have been pissed, instead he was just hungry, as he limped after the van on a leg that showed more bone than muscle, still holding onto the rake that he used daily on his job and that he likely used for defense before he died. The implement's teeth showed signs of combat; some flesh was still to be found stuck to the implement. Pete brought the car to stop, scant inches from the bulkhead.

"Could you get any closer?" said Liam sarcastically. With rescue within reach, their irritability began to surface. Pete to his credit did not rise to the bait but instead moved the car to allow them more room to unload. Pat climbed onto the roof of the van to cover them with his gun.

The throaty sound of Dave's boat's approach roused the few ghouls in the area. Dave tossed a line to Kyle, who looped it off to the bulkhead's piling. Liam caught the stern line and did the same. The distinct sound of the AR-15's fire was heard from the van's roof, as Pat protected them. Eddie jumped off the edge into Dave's boat as Liam, Kyle and Duncan began tossing the supplies downward to them. Pete grabbed up one of the deer rifles with a scope attached, leaned on the hood and sent a 7.62 millimeter metal jacketed round down range decapitating the green's keeper one hundred yards away. Pat shooting iron sights dropped two more of the creatures at greater distances. The gun fire was drawing more attention to them, but they had time. At the distances that the creatures had to travel made them easy targets.

"Okay boys, time to go" shouted Dave.

Pat and Pete climbed down into the boat that was now sitting lower in the water due to all the gear they loaded on board. There was precious little clear deck space. Duncan was wiped so he made his way to the bow birth and sprawled on the bunk, asleep inside of three minutes. Fatigue was grabbing at all of them. Each found their own little niches and followed Dunk's example. Dave was at the helm with his throttles at their stops carving deep furrows in the water churning up seaweed and froth in his wake as he sped for the inlet at maximum speed.

41

Dave called ahead and let Carrie and the rest know that he had the guys and a shitload of supplies. This news made everyone ecstatic. When his boat approached the flotilla he was greeted with cheers and the braying of air horns. Carrie was looking through binoculars looking for her husband. She couldn't see him or any of them other than Dave and feared the worst. It was like a cold hand had reached into her chest and seized her heart. She shook away most of the fear, dismissing it, but a tiny portion of it would not allow itself to be dismissed. It stayed with her as a looming threat.

Dave pulled alongside of the Persistence and tossed lines to Sean and Kevin who made fast the lines to the portside cleats. Carrie almost fell into the water as she tried to get aboard without timing the swells. She caught herself, regained her balance and climbed aboard. Dave pointed to the birth and she practically flew through the companion way.

First Pat and then Kyle jumped across to Pam's waiting arms enfolding them both into hugs that threatened to force all the air out of their lungs. Laura was waiting for the reunions of the families not wanting to intrude, while Sean kept Kaitlyn and Kristen on board telling them that mom and Dad needed a few minutes alone. This didn't sit well with either of them, they were pining for their Dad, but they none the less stayed where they were.

Duncan's exhaustion was so complete that he slept through all the air horn blasts. He felt Katie's hands on his shoulders and woke with a start reaching for anything to use as a weapon. Katie drew back in fear with tears in her eyes. It took him several long seconds to realize where he was and that Katie's hands didn't belong to some creature trying to eviscerate him. As the confusion fled from his eyes and recognition dawned Katie slapped him hard across the face, her fear being replaced by anger, the loving reunion she had pictured in her mind shattered by his reaction to her touch. He was a lot quicker on the uptake now, as she drew back her hand for another slap he sat forward quickly grabbing her wrist and pulled her into his arms crushing her lips with his own. She gave into his hug and kiss. The tears that cascaded this time from both of their eyes were not of fear or disappointment but rather that of love and happiness.

Eddie and Pete being strangers to the rest sat on Dave's stern feeling awkward. Liam came to their rescue, being at least loosely affiliated, though truth be told he didn't know most of the assembly that made up the flotilla. He introduced them around. They were greeted warmly, as family even. After countless handshakes and introductions, both of their heads were practically spinning. Each of them knew they would not remember the names but they felt welcome and safe, that was a start.

Duncan and Katie came out through the companion way. Kristen and Kaitlyn couldn't wait any longer and launched themselves at their dad knocking him back onto the canvas covered cargo. More tears of joy were shed by all of them. Sean held himself aloof, wanting to run to his dad but held fast by his *"manly pride"* Duncan saved him from himself by reaching out an arm indicating a hug. This time it was Sean who knocked his dad back down onto the cargo crushing several of the cardboard boxes containing the rations. The children were all talking over each other, asking this and that and telling him how much each had missed him and how worried they had all been. Duncan soaked it all in, he figured he would sit down with each of them one at a time and go through the past few days with each of them. His flagging spirit had been rejuvenated. Surrounded by those he loved most in the world he was happy.

The captains waited what they considered an adequate amount of time before making their presence known. In reality they should have waited at least a few hours to allow the families to revel in their reunion, but many of them were mourning loses and the joy of this family was lost on them. Liam, Eddie and Pete pulled back the canvas revealing their haul.

Maryanne was dutifully impressed but as commodore she wanted to get down to the business of inventorying and dispersing the supplies. Liam stepped between her and the *"booty"*.

"Just what in the hell do you think you are doing?" Maryanne was taken aback. "This is our stuff, we fought for it! We brought it back! We will decide what we are willing to share! You will not requisition or whatever the Fuck you think you are doing!" Liam was all swollen up like a prized cock waiting for a fight.

Pete and Eddie had his back and he had their allegiance. No one was going to lay a hand on the cargo until Duncan said so. Maryanne looked to Katie to intercede. Katie in turn looked to Duncan.

"Maryanne... we have been through a lot just let us get our bearings...okay? There is plenty to go around but my boys do have a point."

Maryanne looked as though she was going to protest but then thought better of it, "You are right, I am sorry. Whatever you decide to share will be greatly appreciated."

She turned to Dave and engaged him in some idle conversation. Katie took the opportunity to fill Duncan in on the needs of some of the smaller craft, focusing on shelter food and the likes.

Duncan called to Maryanne, "Well lets at least divvy up the necessities, we have got tents, sleeping bags and tarps for shelters. Food isn't a problem yet is it? Can the rest wait till morning?" Maryanne smiled glad that things had turned back to a more congenial, communal environment.

As the survival gear was passed out, the calls of thank you and the smiles on the faces of those who had nothing were enough to melt steel. When Duncan handed Kristen her stuffed animals for her to give to the needful children, she beamed with happiness. These toys that had sat for so long without her notice would change the lives of these kids who had lost everything. Duncan was so proud of his daughter he couldn't even begin to express it, so he settled on just hugging the stuffing out of her.

Kaitlyn had returned to her "duties" when the commodore came over. For the preceding few hours before her dad got back she had been in contact with many survivors back on shore. There was a coordinated effort to eradicate the threat that had assaulted the beach communities. They had suffered far more losses than they had expected, but some semblance of order was being restored. Each community was organizing house by house searches. When zombies were located they were put down like rabid dogs and the bodies were transported to the high school to be incinerated. The community roles were being updated around the clock. Kaitlyn knew how many of the people in the flotilla were waiting for news, any news, for good or ill. She tied her best to find out for them.

Duncan sought Kaitlyn out next. He stepped down the ladder into the salon of the boat. As much space as the boat possessed, it was not so large that he didn't see his daughter right off. "Princess?" he called.

Secretly she hated when he called her that, she was no longer a child, but she endured it knowing that he had no idea that it bothered her and she hoped he would stop on his own. This time hearing it wasn't so bad, it harkened back to when she was a child... before the dead began to walk.

"Hey Daddy." He walked over to her.

"Are you busy honey?" She got up and hugged him guiding him over to one of the cushioned chairs so that they could sit together. "I just wanted to tell you how proud I am of what you have been doing."

She beamed under his approval. Wanting more she was eager to show him everything she had found and to demonstrate the video conferencing she had set up. "You know dad, I want to show you how we talk to Grandpa, this satellite internet is so fast… it blows away cable internet."

The excitement showed in her eyes. "I have been learning as I go but I've got things wired for sound. I linked my laptop to the system and well I surf the web while I do the things people ask me to do. Dad it is horrible what has been happening… and its going on everywhere…"

 Duncan looked at his daughter in a new light. Gone was his little princess, replaced by a growing woman. Capable and strong. She was adapting to the shitstorm that the world was descending into. She was becoming the woman he always hoped she would be. He only wished that it hadn't happened this way. He missed the little girl he remembered from just a few short days ago, but he was overjoyed at the woman she has become. It was difficult to reconcile the two. He took in a deep breath, exhaled, and felt better.

She went on and on while he was lost in thought; not that part of his mind hadn't registered everything she said, he heard all about the blogs she had found. About the people in the flotilla who had lost all of their families. It was just that he was picturing her in pigtails screeching with delight as he pushed her in a swing at the park when she was five. As his mind returned to the present he cued in on his sister's name.

"Wait … what about Katie?" he asked. "Like I said, we have been in communication daily, sometimes two or three times a day."

"Where is she?"

She sighed exasperatedly, "Weren't you listening?... She's in the CDC in Atlanta and the boys are in Nebraska or somewhere. Their guard unit got activated. They are guarding a power plant or something.

Suddenly he was racked with guilt. He hadn't even thought about his sister or nephews since this whole mess happened. True he didn't have a lot of time for it, but it was the fact that she had been gone for so long that she just wasn't on his mind. He had worried about his parents and his brothers, but they were here in the same danger he and his family were. She had moved far away, sure they talked but infrequently. He was relieved to know that she and her new husband were safe, and that his nephews were too from what anybody knew.

"All right kiddo, show me what you got" as he stood and walked over to the Navigation / Communications station. Kaitlyn squealed with delight mirroring the sound in his memory of the swing.

Kaitlyn worked her magic and a few minutes later Duncan's father and sister's images were on the screen. Tears leaked from the corners of his eyes. His sister looked like she had aged ten years yet his father seemed younger, as if this catastrophe had somehow rejuvenated him and restored him twenty years. They all got caught up. Forty-five minutes passed before Duncan knew it.

"Listen Dad we will get under way tomorrow. I can't leave these people in a lurch, how many more can you place handle?" he asked.

"Son,… we will just make do hell if they are living on their boats there they can tie up at my docks. We may just have to tighten our belts a little sooner. We will make do, anyone that comes with you will be welcomed."

Duncan turned to his daughter whose face showed her pride in her accomplishment. "Honey, go get your Uncle Liam and tell him that Aunt Erin wants to talk to him. She quickly left the salon for the deck.

"Dad I think maybe we should conserve as much fuel as we can so it could take a few days to get to you… or do you think we should go under power?" Jacob paused before answering. He wanted them here as fast as they could but he had to acknowledge the point about the fuel.

"Use them both sail where you can but use your motor when the wind isn't working for you." Just the Liam came down the ladder. "I'll talk to you tomorrow dad let's let Liam and Erin catch up, talk to you soon Katie, stay safe sis"

"you too Dunk" said his sister.

He gave Liam his chair. "Come on Kaitlyn let's go find your brother" as they left Liam to talk to his wife.

Topside, Duncan found Sean at the helm. Katie was onboard Dave's boat chatting with Laura. A charter fishing boat had either joined or had returned to the flotilla while he had been talking with his father below. Either way Eddie was on that vessel drinking a beer. Kristen was off taking care of the little ones. "Honey" he said to Kaitlyn, "Can you give me some time alone with your brother?"

"Sure dad I'll go hang out with Pat and Kev" and off she went. He remembered the first time he had taken her sailing. He smiled she didn't get seasick anymore.

"Seaney Roo" he called to his son, knowing full well it would irritate the crap out of him. But he had called his son that from the day of his birth and wasn't about to stop now.

"Hey Dad... you settling in okay?"

The question struck something in Duncan. "Does he know how hard a time we had getting back, and that the stress had taken a lot out of me?" he thought.

"Well it has been a rough go, but being back with you guys makes it easier... I should be back to normal in a day or two, I think."

Sean reached into the cooler by his feet and grabbed a coke for him and a can of Bud for his dad. "Sorry I don't have any of your Harps up here on ice. We keep that in the stores below." He said with a smile as he handed his dad a beer.

"You know if you want one son, I won't tell your mom" as he motioned with his beer.

"No worries dad, mom already said I could have one now and then if I wanted... something to do with the end of the world and all" They both laughed at that. Duncan could see Katie saying that.

"We set up a tent on Dave's boat on his deck for Uncle Kyle and crew. Auntie Laura has installed herself in Dave's cabin already. I think your friend Eddie has found himself space on the SuperHawke" as he indicated the charter boat where Eddie was drinking his beer. "Pete can bunk in with me if he wants, but the couches in the salon are very comfortable." Sean sipped from his coke and then continued, "It would have been pretty crowded if the SuperHawke hadn't joined us yesterday. We were going to quarantine it but it had been out to sea before the whole thing went down so no one on board even knew anything about it. So we figured it was safe to let 'em join up. Besides the have additional resources."

Duncan was again awed by how fast his kids had grown up. They weren't the kids he thought they were, this crisis matured them fast.

"So how bad was it dad? Can you tell me about it?" he asked with sincerity. Again Duncan wasn't sure if Sean was incredibly insightful or what but it was almost if he were trying to give his dad an improvised therapy session. Like a doctor dealing with someone suffering battle fatigue.

"It wasn't easy that's for sure..." and he proceeded to tell Sean the whole story from when he got to work his last day till they got back. Three beers and four cokes later he finished his tale and looked at the clock on the instrument panel. "Wow its late, I think I am going to turn in. We are going to head up the river tomorrow, God willing we will see Grandma and Grandpa in a couple of days. Wake me when it's my turn on watch." "Don't worry dad you aren't even in the schedule yet. I've got a couple hours till I am relieved but I will see you in the morning."

Duncan Stood up, stretched and yawned. "Katie" he called over to Dave's boat. "Honeybaby... I am ready to turn in... are you coming?" She popped her head out of the cabin.

"I'm coming sweetie" She made her way over to their boat. Sean gave his mom a hand up. As she stepped on board she tussled his hair and followed Duncan below.

"Night mom" called Sean.

They made their way to the aft cabin and shut the door. Katie dimmed the lights as Duncan sat on the bed, not feeling anywhere near as tired as he was before he saw his bride in the white tee shirt sans bra. The ocean breeze having aroused her nipples, which in turn aroused something in Duncan's pants.

They undressed slowly for each other. And came together under the sheets. The danger of the past days awakened their passion. Their love life had always been great, amazing by anyone's standard really, but this night was even more than they had known in decades. Somehow they managed to keep it quiet and after they had exhausted each other the slept free of the nightmares of life.

Peter joined Sean in the cockpit for the remainder of his watch. They chatted the time away. Kevin came aboard to relieve Sean, but Peter volunteered to assume his watch saying that he had to earn his keep and that maybe Kevin would want to re-join his family and catch up with his brother. Kevin didn't have to be asked twice and said his thanks and joined his brother. He heard the distinct sound of bottles being popped open and soft murmuring voices.

The sky was clear, all of the stars were out in the glorious brilliance. The caress of the swells as they passed the boats by on their way to shore had a soothing effect. Most of the flotilla had gone to their racks. The chill of the ocean air had Pete donning a fleece an hour into his watch. Sean had left his IPod connected to the stereo since there was no music being broadcast on any stations. He popped a couple Dramamines to ward off sea sickness. Pete was not much of a boat guy, but he had to admit this vessel was heads and shoulders above any he had been on prior. He hadn't gotten sick or queasy yet, but thought, "Why tempt fate".

Standing a watch can be torturous when you are already tired. It was fortunate for Pete that he had already grabbed a snooze earlier. He figured he would try to call his wife again, he had already left her sixteen voice-mails. He truly believed that she was alive and safe, he felt that somehow he would know if it had been otherwise. He let the phone ring and ring until the greeting came as it switched over to voice-mail, he was preparing to leave yet another message when it told him that the mailbox was full. Disappointed he plugged his charger back in and scanned the waters towards the shore for danger.

Hours earlier Kevin had received a communiqué from the Coast Guard skipper whom had issued his TAD. The Skipper told him that they would be sinking that foundering container vessel. To be alert for any fuel on the water surface and the occasional zombie floating on by. The flotilla hadn't seen either on the surface. What they hadn't known and couldn't have known was the number of zombies that had been in those containers on her decks. As the ship took on water and sank below the surface those very containers dropped to the ocean floor, and with them nearly one-thousand zombies. Being as many of the body cavities were ripped and torn and the short time that they were dead hadn't allowed for enough of the decomposition process to generate the gases to bring the bodies back to the surface. The army of zombies marched along the ocean floor in search of land and prey.

Peter's watch was drawing to a close, it was three-forty five in the morning. He was looking forward to crashing out, but he didn't want to disturb Duncan's family inside the boat with his horrific snoring. That was one of the multitudes of issues between him and his wife. He felt that she was making mountains out of molehills. She felt that he should at least try the damn C-Pap machine that his doctor suggested for his sleep apnea. She had been right as he discovered a few months ago when they started to reconcile and he finally gave in on this issue. But he didn't have his machine, it was still in his apartment on Staten Island. He wasn't enamored with the idea of sleeping in an improvised hammock, but it would hardly be considerate to impose on his host's family so he would make do. He spied the inflatable dingy that was lashed to the foredeck. "Turn it over and re-lash it, put my sleeping bag inside, bingo, I know where I'll be sleeping" he thought or maybe even said aloud he wasn't quite sure.

Dave came out of his cabin to relieve the watch, waved to Pete, who of course waved back. He sat down and fell right back asleep. In the old days he would have received a severe lashing, were he caught asleep on watch. Pete was busy setting things up for his own sleep. He tripped on the anchor chain and nearly fell into the drink while he struggled to flip the inflatable boat over. Finally getting things as he wanted, he got inside his bag and lay down to shut his eyes. He felt something digging into his kidneys, so he felt around and came up with a waterproof pouch that contained a flare gun and flares. He laid it down next to him and tried to get some sleep.

The ocean floor, devoid of light, the current moving up the continental shelf sending waves towards the shore is what was guiding, pushing the army of the dead towards Long Beach and the sleeping communities on it. There is no way to know if the undead sensed the pressure change as the water above their heads grew more shallow. They relentlessly continued moving, each step bringing them more shallow, closer to the food source they sought. The sandy bottom was barren, no marine life was evident as the swath of death trudged onward. One of the hosts stumbled tripping over the Galvanized anchor on the floor securing one of the vessels above. It began pulling itself up the chain and rope of the rode, steadily ascending to the surface. Other zombies encountered other anchors and likewise climbed in search of prey. The vessels above had no clue about the predators below them. The few members of the watch, at least those who were still awake, were looking for danger coming from the shore. It never occurred to them that death might come from below.

The first creature broke the surface at the bow of the Persistence, soundlessly. The creature no longer breathed, and water had filled the lungs so there was no telling moan. The creatures lacked coordination but the water made it easy for them to ascend. It reached the top and began to pull itself up onto the deck drawn onward by the sound of Peter's snores.

Peter woke to the searing pain of his thigh being ravaged. The creature had gained purchase and found its victim, it's maw of savage teeth tearing into the muscles of his leg. Its grip, vice like, not that it was any stronger than when it was alive, it was just that the pressure was constant, unhampered by fatigue or pain. Peter yelled the alarm, an instant later the watches flicked on their handheld spotlights and four million candles worth of light pierced the darkness sweeping the area for danger. Dave woke to the sound of Peter's shout, snapping up *onto* his feet. This saved his life, for a pruney hand reached over the rail to grab at him, another zombie had climbed the stern anchor rode.

Shots rang out followed by splashes as zombies fell back into the water. Pandemonium ensued as people who were only moments before asleep were now doing battle with zombies. Peter was finally able to overpower the creature that was assaulting him. The creature had been a girl of perhaps eighteen when she died although it was hard to tell given the water logged state. The lacerations on his leg were bleeding profusely collecting in the bottom of the rubber boat but in the struggle he had pushed her away and attempted to crab backwards away from her. His hand came onto the flare gun that he had found earlier and had never replaced into the waterproof bag. Instinctively he grabbed it and leveled it at her ruined face as she was rising and squeezed the trigger. The flare ignited as it flew out of the short barrel melting its way in through her eye. The soaked flesh steamed and burned at the intense heat from the phosphorous. The body pitched overboard and returned to the depths. The flickering red light still burning away revealed to the horror of all that countless creatures were passing below.

Duncan had come instantly awake, his slumber interrupted by Pete's shout. He grabbed his AR- fifteen and stepped from his cabin. He could see through the companion way as two of hells minions struggled to drag their rotting corpses over the rail onto his boat. Two shots sent the creatures back into the sea from which they had climbed. Dave's movement almost cost him his life, for Duncan caught the movement in his periphery bringing his barrel into line prepared to dispatch yet another denizen. Dave's eyes wide with fear yelled out just as Duncan was squeezing the trigger, luck would have it his gun had jammed. Body temperature fluid ran down Dave's leg from his brush with death.

Pete seeing more zombies climbing knew instantly the necessary solution. He needed to cut the anchor line. The pain from his leg making it difficult for him to open his pocket knife, grit and determination won out as he sawed back and forth cutting the fibers of the line. "CUT THE ANCHORLINES!!!" he shouted above the din. He was losing a lot of blood he was afraid he would swoon and maybe fall into the infested water. The rope finally parted the chain at its end dragged the cut line into the deep. Dave quickly turned to the stern line and untied it from the cleat and just let the line go, he had felt a tugging vibration while he untied it that told him the next "dinner guests" were not far from the surface.

The Super Hawke was in trouble, it's enormous anchor lines were heavy chain all the way attached to a winch so cutting the anchors quickly was not an option. Several of the ghouls had gained her decks trying to get at the people onboard. There was a valiant attempt of Eddie to defend against three of the fiends who were trying to get at one of Kristen's little friends. He wielded the fishing gaff like a shaolin monk, well maybe that was a mild exaggeration, but seeing him swing that long staff with the barbed stainless hook on its end was impressive none the less. Kevin and Patrick responded quickly and with efficiency, producing two of the recently acquired ARs, wherever they saw the ghouls they dispatched them, sometimes with a short burst to sever the anchor line in addition. Katie huddled below with her two daughters. Pam joined her sons in the stern of Dave's boat firing on of the H&K nine millimeters. Her boys seem to have forgotten that she had grown up shooting guns under her dad and brothers tutelage, them both being policemen. She was pretty good with that pistol.

The skirmish seemed to be winding down as the last of the anchors were cut away save for those of the Super Hawke whose were being raised as the winches labored under the combined weight of anchors, chain, and zombies. Those that had made it to the deck were cleared away, but before they could do that the zombies had caused some casualties.

Each of these injured knew the score and were resigned to their fates. They themselves suggested a hangman's knot and a final drop, in order to preserve the community's limited supplies. No one wanted to return as one of those things.

Pete knew he was done for too, but he fastened a tourniquet around his leg above the bite very early on. He called to Dunk. He needed to have a heart to heart with him, his brother from another mother. Duncan didn't need to see the wound or the blood soaked jeans that Peter was wearing. He knew from the moment he heard the scream that had awakened him that Peter's fate was sealed. That much pain heard in his voice as he got the warning out, saving perhaps all of the remainder of the flotilla. Duncan knew right away that his friend, no, brother would not be long in this world. Peter was sitting in that damn inflatable boat although he now had control of the blood loss. He still didn't want to make matters any worse. Duncan responded to Peter's hail, His eyes were almost moist maybe a little glassy even as he carefully moved up the port side of his boat. In the background motors were heard springing to life through out. The fleet being without anchors, they used their motors to keep relative positions.

Duncan called to his brothers, "Liam, Kyle, get over here as soon as you can."

Not waiting for their answers he continued making his way to Pete. He saw his friend sitting in the Inflatable, barely noticeable sobs causing his shoulders to bob imperceptibly. Duncan's heart sank to the oceans depth. He made overt noises to let Pete know that he was approaching, to give him a chance to put on whatever brave face he needed to. Duncan was putting his best face on too, although he knew he was failing miserably. His mind was racing, "how do you look into the face of your friend, your brother from another mother, at a time like this without bawling like a child?" he asked of himself.

"Hey, bro…" he said in a somber tone. Peter looked up at his friend, there was no fear in his eyes, and he actually looked at peace.

"Don't look so glum mi amigo, it isn't that bad." Duncan tried a weak smile and failed again. "I'm not sure I would have wanted to live in a post apocalyptic world anyhow… I haven't been able to get a hold of Miriam anyhow, not much point without her."

A crack appeared in his veneer of calm as he choked back a sob. "Dunk, promise me one thing…"

"Anything Bro, you know that." Duncan replied.

"You have to find out if Miriam is still alive… I'm telling you I just know in my heart she's still out there somewhere, when you do take care of her for me."

Duncan wanted to give Pete the peace of mind he sought. "Sure pal, I'll see that she is looked after…"

"Dunk I don't want her just looked after… you have to promise me you will take care of her, make certain she wants for nothing…" tears began to run in tiny rivulets down his face.

Duncan looked into Peter's eyes and with complete sincerity said, "As if she were my own wife."

Liam and Kyle showed up within seconds of each other. Even though they hadn't known Pete as long as Duncan, there was still a sense of kinship. Peter was still breathing and talking yet they mourned his loss as if he were their brother.

"The tough question…"Duncan said to Pete "How long do you want to wait?" he didn't elaborate, there was no need.

Pete looked to the three of them, a roguish twinkle in his eye, "Surprise me boys…" and with that he laughed. The three of them joined in although it was forced and unnatural.

He looked to Kyle and Liam, "Let's make it sooner rath…" The report of Duncan's side arm finished the sentence for him.

The three of them were riddled with grief. They did what they could for Peter's mortal remains; they cleaned his body up to the best of their abilities then wrapped it in a blanket. Then they wrapped the body and blanket in chain, the family gathered at the stern of the boat. There were no words to be spoken, the pain was too fresh. Ultimately they bowed their heads in silence and with as much reverence as they could muster the consigned Peter's body to the deep.

Kristen noticed that Peter's phone was still plugged in and sitting in the cup holder on the helm console, and there was a light flashing, indicating a message. "Dad… your friend's phone…" she handed her father the phone. Duncan looked down at the phone in his hand. He felt awkward, as if he was invading Pete's privacy, but Peter couldn't mind anymore. After a moment of inner turmoil he finally pushed the power button and the screen came to life.

There was a voice-mail waiting. Duncan didn't want to play the message; his gut told him who it would be from. He had made the promise to Pete, so he pushed the button, tears started to roll even before he heard

Miriam's voice. "Amore, I got your messages… I am safe… I made it to the Marine base, in the mad dash I left my phone behind, I am so sorry that I worried you. Someone reprogrammed an old phone for me so call me when you get this message. I love you and miss you… call me. I have to go for now, I love you." Press nine to save this message or press seven to delete this message" the mechanical voice said. He shut the phone, he would call her later when he figured out what to say to the wife of his friend that he just buried at sea.

Elsewhere in the flotilla, similar scenes were playing out. Peter's body would not be alone in the deep, he would be joined by the others who had shared his fate.

Dawn was still a couple hours away. They would begin their sojourn in the light of day. Perhaps it would seem less ominous in the light of the sun. Sleep was no longer an option, so each and every person in the flotilla began making preparations to get under way

42

The second, third, and fourth wave of the siege on the CDC went much the same as the first, save for the civilians. Mortar rounds and gunfire, followed by teams in biohazard suits retrieving samples, and the remains being incinerated. The samples processed and tested. The new avenues of research yielded mixed results, those that showed promise were followed up on, and the others were cold storage bound.

Carrie called her father at home.

"Daddy, we have been under lock down it seems forever. I have never been so scared in my entire life."

Jacob replied, "These are scary times, I wish I had words of consolation to offer you but frankly I am scared too... your brothers will be here in a couple of days... as much as I would want you here with us you are safer there than we can hope to be... So do you have any further information to share?"

Carrie told him about the research on the anti-radiation meds and the effect that was documented on the former president, and about the "combat manual". They talked for a while which had a comforting effect on both of them. She lamented on not knowing where her sons were, he commiserated. Marie took over the conversation and for the first time in a long time they shared closeness.

When the conversation finally ended over an hour had passed. Jacob wanted to see if he could apply any of the Intel he had gained and began to skim the e-book manual. Sure it was a work of fiction but it was prophetic too boot. He cued his printer even as he read the words on the screen. Better to have a hard copy or two just in case he thought being the pragmatist that he was.

Another phone call came in. When the he looked at the caller ID he was hoping it would be another of his fledglings but it turned out to be one of his neighbors checking in and offering for them to join them as they were heading north. Jacob declined the offer, saying that his sons were enroute and that they were gonna ride out the storm here where they at least had some defenses in place rather than foraying into the unknown. He hadn't intended to call the neighbor's judgment into question but that's how it came off. After the conversation paused for an uncomfortable amount of time they said their goodbyes and mercifully terminated the connection.

Marie asked why he hadn't offered them solace here. His reply was rooted in logic, "We have a finite amount of supplies and we don't yet know how many are coming with the boys." Her look spoke volumes, "They are our neighbors, ring them back and at least offer, we can use their help as much as they can use ours." She was not questioning his judgment nor was she making demands, the subtext of the exchange was easily several paragraphs in length but there was more upside than down so he conceded and returned the call.

"Arthur, hi it's Jacob, no we haven't changed our minds but we would like to offer you and yours to come into our compound..." he itemized the defenses he had employed and commented on Google Earth. The conversation was pretty one-sided but in the end Arthur his wife and their two teenage boys accepted the offer. Jacob opened up the gate and they drove in their suburban which was packed to the gills with all the supplies they could find, along with a bunch of sentimental crap as Jacob eyed the cache'.

Arthur was an attorney, soft around the middle with a growing bald spot up top. He was half Jacob's age but was in far worse physical condition. His boys however had the benefit of youth and the energy that accompanies it and the physiques of boys more at home on a lacrosse field than shut ins who only played video games. Jacob was glad now that Marie had changed his mind. "Sometimes it's good to have fresh eyes to help avert bad decisions" he said to his wife by way of acknowledging her wisdom.

Jacob gave them lessons in firearms safety, and familiarized them with the weapons he had here. Arthur didn't own any guns, Pauline his wife would not have one in her home. Now she was a bonefide second amendment sister. She took the lessons too right along side of her boys, and proved to be a better than average shot, although the .357 had too much recoil for her.

The boys, Thomas and Aaron, named after Jefferson and Burr... who said attorneys didn't have a sense of humor or a sadistic streak... were "Irish twins" born 10 months apart, were near the same age as Sean, Duncan's eldest. Right away they were enamored with Jacob who was a man of action as they saw it. If this ruffled Arthur's feathers no one could tell. Jacob was glad to share the rounds with them. Not that he let them take them on their own or even together, he would take one and then the other with him.

Pauline had a great effect on Erin, whom had already battled back from the worst of the PTSD. They spent hours getting to know one another, and before long had become fast friends. Arthur didn't have much to offer apart from support staff, which he did without complaint and to be honest with good humor. He knew his limitations and filled in the position where he could best. He monitored the computer and tried to dig up any and all the information he could. He had incredible recall, honed by the years of law school where he worked on the law review and later in his practice as a litigator, and was able to convey any information he garnered in a simple straight forward manner that Jacob appreciated. They would all earn their keep Jacob was relieved to note.

Jacob, Aaron and both dogs Max and Skeela where getting ready to do rounds when Arthur told them that he was tracking a fairly sizable group of "critters" as he put it. Referring to the 80's movie about space aliens that ate everything and everyone. Jacob went into the office to put his own eyes on it for tactical purposes. Sure enough there was a group of thirty to forty moving up off the main roadway onto the gravel "private road"...(which only meant that the county was not responsible to plow it) Jacob decided to put off the patrol and monitor the situation from within. He didn't want to attract their attention and end up being under siege. He checked the breakers to be certain that the fence was electrified, and that the alarm trip wires were as they should be. "Going to have to make a run into town for some additional supplies now that I have some help "he said out loud although he had intended it to be an internal monologue.

"What was that ?" Asked Arthur.

"Oh just thinking out loud" replied Jacob "After this group moves along I was thinking that now that we have more manpower we might take a ride to the hardware store and pick up some additional goodies. I couldn't do that before and leave Marie and my Daughter here alone. Not to mention the folly of going off alone but now someone could be waiting in the truck with the motor running if there is any sign of trouble."

To Jacobs surprise Arthur volunteered saying that he was the obvious choice to drive since the he wasn't much help in the home defense department. Jacob had to agree but wanted to take one of the boys too. He wasn't overly concerned about the compound being overrun while he was out, but with the extra set of hands his time exposed would be halfed and that would also allow them to grab things that one-man alone might not be able to get.

"Okay two hours after this horde moves along we will go." Everyone was in agreement. The women of the house were not enthusiastic about the venture but recognized the wisdom of it so with a little trepidation gave their unasked for ascent.

43

The sun broke the horizon, rapidly replacing the predawn gloom chancing away the darkness that had the oppressive characteristics of gravity and had permeated the thoughts of all in the flotilla. The sky took on a reddish glow, a bad omen for mariners from time immemorial, "Red sky at night... Sailors delight, Red sky in morning...Sailors take warning" was the old adage. The omen could not portend anything worse than they were living through in these apocalyptic times, a squall might even be welcome as it would give them something normal to work against and through, yes this might be a welcome distraction from the reality of the Zombie Days.

The Captains gathered aboard the Persistence in order to go over the final arrangements, course, frequencies, contingency plans. Since the flotilla was comprised of vessels of varying design and methods of propulsion it was decided that the slowest of the boats would set the pace. It was argued the Super Hawk could be tow the slow movers at a faster rate, but that would compromise her maneuverability. Communication would center on Duncan's vessel with Kaitlyn handling that responsibility. She had been doing a great job so far so there was no reason to change that. It was stressed over and over that there needed to be fairly large spacing between the boats given the need for the sailing vessels to jibe and tack. Eventually, it was all hashed out, and they were ready to get underway.

The Persistence took the lead as she had the best or the navigation and radar technology of the small fleet. They headed south west towards the Rockaway's and the city after rounding the horn so to speak they would then correct north and sail up the Hudson. There was a nine knot wind that made sailing easy and enjoyable, the seas were relatively docile, not glass like you might find sailing the sound but with minor swells that were fun in their own right. Each of the vessels checked in at their appointed times and there was even some friendly banter passed back and forth amongst the boats.

They continued running parallel to the coast as they sailed past at a reasonable ten miles an hour over ground about half a mile off the coast. Most chose to look east out across the Atlantic rather than look upon the Island, for the sky was choked with billowing black clouds of smoke from the burning buildings and homes. The distance muted the sounds of gunfire, reducing them to sound like kids lighting off lady fingers and fire crackers a block or two away. There was nothing any of them could do. Near 1000 of the undead abominations made the shore in the dark of night and fell upon the seaside communities like a biblical plague of locusts. Not a one in the flotilla wanted to be reminded of that devastation.

Duncan was at the helm of his boat, wearing a white captain's hat that his wife had brought back from Venezia Italy the summer before. It was a little cliché' but he truly liked to wear it. He put on his Regatta apparel consisting of Sperry topsider boat sneakers. The soles of the shoes were designed so as not to mar the decks, cargo pocketed shorts in tan, and a white crew neck that had "S.V. Persistence" embroidered on the pocket under a likeness of the vessel... on the shirts back in big red letters was printed, "The floggings will continue until morale improves" and on his face, he sported his Maui Jim's sparing his eyes from the glare of the sun on the water. Feeling the wind in his face and listening to the snap of the wind upon the sails, feeling the motion of the water as his boat knifed through, was almost enough to make him forget the ordeals of the past few days.

Katie came topside to spend some quality time with her spouse, the kids, below decks trying to get some rack time, since their sleep the night before had been interrupted by the attack from below. Well at least Sean and Kristen were in their racks; Kaitlyn fell asleep at the comms station in her chair. It was getting on towards lunch time. Katie watched a pair of seagulls riding the air currents playfully. Liam came out of his stateroom and climbed the stairs to the cockpit bringing Katie back to the here and now. Liam looked as if he had been the victim of a mugging, his clothes were rumpled and tattered, his hair disheveled, in bad need of a shave, but his eyes had a thousand yard stare haunted by what he had seen and been through over the recent days. "Dunk, where are we at?"

Duncan lanced at the chart plotter, "We will be able to see the statue of liberty in another hour or so..." he gave his best guess given the winds and the currents. "We should make Dads in two days give or take a few hours. Why don't you wake Kaitlyn and send her to bed then you can call Erin and have some privacy." Liam nodded and went back below decks.

Katie looked at Duncan and smiled. "Will you ever look at him as anything other than your kid brother?" she asked of her husband.

"What do you mean babe?" his eyes scanning the horizon then back to the displays on the con.

"It's just that well I don't know..." she paused. "Out with it hon, what do you mean? Do you think coddle him or treat him like a kid and not as a grown man?" He seemed a little irritated by the thought. "

"No not at all, it's more like you feel you have to protect him or something..." she said knowing she was reaching for a better turn of phrase to convey her meaning. However, Duncan and she had been together long enough for him to know what she meant even if she couldn't find the right words.

"Hon, he feels like he let his wife down, she may or may not feel that way, but he had thought she went nuts and sent her to mom and dad, staying behind.... then all this shit happens, he nearly gets killed time and again. He still hasn't seen her, sure they have talked but well... Kyle and me; we, our families with us, his wife is still two days away..."

Rise Fall Rise Again: A New York Zombie Encounter

A warning tone sounded, indicating a radar contact well multiple contacts actually, about two miles out. More survivors no doubt. The display showed a small fleet much like their own.

He raised Marianne on the radio and switched to a private channel. "I just picked up another fleet a couple miles distant, do you want to send one of the power boats to investigate?" Duncan asked of the commodore.

"Do you have a bearing? Numbers? Are they underway or are they moored?"

Duncan supplied the requested data.

"Let's take this on the cautious side... we will keep an eye on them but let's not go and get too friendly until we know more."

Duncan agreed with her decision. The Long Beach Flotilla was following the same relative course as the radar contact, slowing their pace by a small amount they were able to hold the same distance and were still making progress. If the radar contact was aware of the Long Beach Boats, they weren't making any attempt to signal them or investigate either. After about an hour Duncan raised the Commodore and suggested that Dave shoot over with a wipe board giving our radio frequencies and contact info, approach slowly stay far enough away to keep safe ... show the board and then come back this way we can talk to them and find out what is what." Marianne liked the idea and gave it her chop. A few Minutes later Davis Mercs were leaving deep wakes as he sped towards the other group of boats.

With the spray coming over the bow as the boat cut through the water at highest possible speed, it was almost fun being out on the water, almost.... were it not for the fact that the dead was walking everywhere you looked, and that they were trying to eat anyone not dead already it would be fun thought Dave. With so few boaters out here on the water there were no wakes to cut across or jump. The sun was shining, a gentle breeze, and gulls riding the air currents or lazily floating on the water; this could be normal....,but it wasn't. As Dave drew closer to the other boats, he began to feel awfully exposed, as if there were a high-powered rifle scope trained on him this very minute. Dave hoped that the white flag he had been fluttering would grant him safe conduct. When he got within one hundred yards or so of the group, he cut his throttles to next to nothing and grabbed the wipe board with the contact information on it. He was close enough that he could make out people moving about on the boats. He didn't see any guns, but he didn't feel any safer, still onward he moved at a snail's pace. The closer he drew the more animated the folks on the boats appeared. When he got to fifty yards, he dropped it into neutral and bobbed along on the water. He held the wipe board over his head in both hands hoping that his intensions were clear enough. His hopes were answered when a bullhorn assisted voice acknowledged him.

"I take it; you want to chat?" came the mechanically distorted voice.

Dave's head bobbed up and down in an exaggerated affirmation.

"Don't come any closer.... but it seems that you already know not to. Okay we have your radio frequencies. We will call you in a few minutes... for now let's keep the distances we have. Glad we aren't the only ones had the good sense to make it out onto the water."

Dave wasn't sure, but something did not feel right. He wiped the board clean, took out a dry erase marker and wrote that he was heading back to the flotilla. When he finished writing he held it up and was acknowledged again. He put his boat back in gear and pushed his throttles to their stops and sped back to his people.

When he got back to the flotilla, he pulled up to Persistence and tossed a line to Sean to tie off and came aboard. A few of the captains were already aboard and in the saloon. It was standing room only. They were already talking to the other group, and everything seemed to be going smoothly. Dave couldn't shake the feeling that something was wrong, and he said as much to Duncan and Marianne. "We are going to be really careful Dave don't worry."

Duncan suggested that they maybe meet up at Liberty Island figuring that there most likely would not be any infected there, and that they might be able to find some useful gear and supplies, and if all went well it would be a place for everyone to stretch their legs on dry land.

Duncan looked to Marianne and said, "You, me and maybe one or two more can go ashore on the dingy. They could land on the other side; we would be covered by guns on our boats, and we can get to know these folks... what do you say?" Marianne couldn't find any fault with the plan and agreed. Duncan took the mic and proposed the idea to the leader of the other group. Arrangements were made, and then they got under way.

Lady Liberty loomed before the flotilla, standing sentinel over the harbor. Her oxidized patina an even green, never suggesting the rich copper of which she is made. The grounds of her island are well maintained and open. No sign of people living or dead. This close to the statue, one could not help but be awed by it as it stood there on its brick base holding her torch aloft with her book in arm. She said give me your tired, your poor, your huddled masses... these words described to a "t" the long beach flotilla. It almost seemed like divine providence had brought them here. The island itself had quite a few other structures and a wooded area behind her, the ferry terminal where millions of tourists had landed to visit the colossus of New York's harbor. The National Park Service maintained the island exquisitely. Both groups opted to land on the long "t" dock rather than make landfall near the ferry terminal. On the dock, no one could sneak up on anyone.

Duncan, Marianne, Patrick and Dave went over in Dave's fishing boat rather than the inflatable, just in case they needed to get out of there fast. The other boat tied up opposite them with four occupants on board, albeit less well armed. Kevin and Sean were looking through rifle scopes keeping their cross hairs on top of the approaching people from the other boat.

Marianne and the rest climbed onto the dock as the other boat was tying up. Up close you could see the haunted expression on their faces. "Greetings... how are you guys doing?... We are from the Long Beach Yacht club." Said Marianne in an attempt to break the ice.

The leader of the strangers was a retired police officer and at his hip was his old service revolver, a nickel plated-thirty eight. His three compatriots were themselves unarmed. "If you guys are planning to raid us...." as he noted the arms that Duncan and the others had "... you guys don't have to fire a shot. We don't have much, just leave us alone in peace."

Duncan looked puzzled. "We have no intension of taking anything from you... we were thinking of how we could help each other." He said with complete sincerity. "

"That's what the other guys said before they hijacked two of the bigger boats and kidnapped all the girls between ages twelve and forty..." One of the other strangers interrupted saying that his two daughters and his wife were taken as he broke into tears.

"Those bastards took away ten of our family, just bound their hands and held their guns on them... my twins are only thirteen..."exclaimed in his grief.

"When his happen?" asked Dave clearly disturbed by these events. Duncan's own rage seethed below the surface.

"About seven hours ago. They had guns, was nothing we could do to stop them, but they didn't care, they shot three of us anyway.... some sort of object lesson..."he trailed off sinking into further depths of despair.

"How many of them were there, what was their heading do you know where they were going?" It was clear that Duncan, Patrick and Dave, were considering a rescue attempt if it was possible.

Marianne interjected, "have any of you been bitten of injured by any of the Zombies?"

"No, well there were but they aren't with us anymore," said the retired cop as he tapped his pistol at his hip. "I Used the last of my bullets putting them down that was a few hours before those pirates took our people." Marianne looked at the faces of these people, and her heart went out to them.

"Would you excuse us for a minute?" she said stepping away with Duncan and Dave, Patrick remained clearly he felt he needed to help these people.

She looked at Duncan and Dave...look this is a good place to hold up I think we should get everyone over here and share our supplies with them. This Island is defensible, what are your thoughts?"

Duncan replied, "I agree... but remember my families are going to continue upriver to my father's compound. We knew this would only go so far, but you guys could do far worse for a place to ride this out from."

Marianne looked disappointed, true she knew Duncan's ultimate plans, but she was hoping he would change his mind. "

"I know Duncan, you know you might just want to come back with your folks..." she left the statement open ended, and Duncan sort of nodded as if to say you never know. With that said, he reached into his pocket and pulled out his portable VHF and contacted the flotilla and told them to come ashore they would decide what to do next when everyone was here.

They returned to the others, "You might want to bring your people in off the boats..." indicating that their flotilla was coming ashore.

"We are going to want to make shore this Island is as deserted as it appears to be... then we will figure out the rest..."

They signaled back to their folks that help was at hand... the relief on the other side of the radio transmission was obvious. She then made introductions...

"Now what information do you have on the folks who took your people?"

44

They made a tour of the Island in relative short order, as expected there was nothing out of the ordinary. The whole of it was abandoned. They broke into the lobby of the museum, this would provide shelter and security should it become necessary. The losses that both parties had taken were written in bold letters on the faces of the collected. Duncan spoke with his wife about going on the rescue mission.

Katie was adamantly opposed to his going, "Why are you risking your life for strangers?" she asked on the verge of tears.

"Honey, what if they had taken you and the girls? You know what is likely happening to them. Being in the hands of those animals."

Reluctantly she had to concede, the human race was fighting for survival but humanity was even in a more tenuous position.

Kyle and Patrick, having had a similar discussion with Pamela, were gathered with a few others who had taken up this cause for a planning session. Kevin and Sean felt left out until it was made clear that with the majority of the firepower going off to rescue... they were to be the best and last line of defense for everyone here on the Island. They weren't easily appeased but it made sense and it would mollify their mothers.

It was learned that the "pirates" had taken up on the little island with the lighthouse west south west of Rikers Island on the East River. They numbered eight men with pistol gripped twelve gauges and pistols. There could possibly be more of them on the Island but it didn't seem likely.

The problem was that the lighthouse itself was as stout as a fortress, and the sounds of motors would be heard from a distance. Patrick took the lead during the planning session.

"What we need to do is sail a boat nearby and then insert a small group via Uncle Dunk's inflatable dingy paddling and keeping low as possible. Then after the fire team gets on land then we use IED's launched from the sail boat into the boats they have. When those explode that should create enough of a distraction to take down the bad guys and rescue the women."

Duncan asked the obvious question, "what IEDs and launch them how?" Patrick was expecting the question and had come up with a clever solution to the problem.

"Remember the grenades we had liberated with the weapons?" his uncle nodded "Well we launch those from a water balloon sling shot... however we tie fishing line around the spoons with enough lead so that they travel real far before the spoons pop and the five second time delay kicks in."

 Patrick looked rather pleased with himself and an amused grin came over the faces of the assembled. "We should only need to use two or three of the grenades but the fire team should carry a few of the smokes and a couple of the flash bangs too. Launch them after you see my blue flash in a two -two pattern"

The boat chosen to tow the dingy was John Stein's MacGregor 26, being a trailer sailer it could sail silent but when things hit the fan it's sixty horse engine could get them anywhere quickly ... hell they could use the engines most of the way and switch to sailing two miles out to prevent from being heard coming. There was some discussion about whether or not they should destroy the boats at all and that maybe the landing party could sneak onto land and just take the guys out. Patrick over ruled them on this.

"Look if we had a military unit maybe that would be an option but seeing as we don't, hell I am the only one with any of the sort of training required for an operation like this we are going to do it my way! If when I get there I see another option I will call an audible on the fly and communicate any changes via cell phone and headset, are we clear?"

His military bearing and the fact that three of the landing party were his uncles and a family friend ended any objections. They would set out at midnight so as to arrive and be in position to attack around three am when the "pirates" would be at their most vulnerable.

Everybody was pulling together; they managed to make a relatively comfortable area where each family could have its privacy without compromising their safety. They broke into the concession stand area and were able to forage up lots more in the way of food and beverages. The Island had its own power plant so they were able to enjoy more amenities, add to that the fact that there were flushing toilets made it a whole lot more comfortable for most of the group.

They now numbered more than sixty people or would after they rescued the missing women. The food and supplies would be an issue for that many and quickly, Duncan thought, it was a good thing that his twelve would be making tracks soon. It will be for the best of everybody. He went to his cabin to lie down and get some rest before the nights festivities began. He passed the word that everyone who was involved with the operation should get some sleep.

Much to Duncan's surprise, he was actually able to get a few hours of sleep. It was still several hours before they were to begin their rescue journey, but Duncan knew with certainty that he would be unable to return to sleep so he began putting together the gear that they would need, most of which they had gathered from the dead soldiers in Penn Station. He checked the batteries in their night vision equipment, and then went about cleaning the AR's. He was keeping his hands busy while his mind went over the fact that he and his would be leaving the group soon and he planned on bringing most of the firepower that they had gathered with him. He had no intention of leaving them defenseless but the weapons were his by right and he was not about to give up what he had gathered when his family's safety might depend upon it.

The smell of the cleaning fluid and gun oil was reassuring. After he finished, he stowed everything away. Then he went in search of his wife and children. He didn't think that tonight's mission would be overly dangerous but he wanted to spend time with his family just in case.

Kristen and her minions were playing inside the museum, he stood just inside of the door watching her and her merry band of marauding children as they raced about here and there, seemingly to have forgotten about the horrors that they all had been witness to. Those children were actually smiling and laughing as they played.

"Remarkable" he said to no one in particular but was overheard by one of the parents who was watching them. "They truly are the future... if we can keep them safe." She said at just above a whisper. Duncan didn't recognize her, but that didn't mean anything. She seemed to be lost in her own thoughts as she watched, Duncan felt like he was intruding so he continued on seeking the rest of his kids and wife.

Kaitlyn came storming in as only a teenager can, muttering words under her breath. The only ones Duncan caught were "unfair" and "not a kid anymore." Duncan hurried to catch up with her.

"What's the matter peanut?" The pet name earned him a scornful glare.

"Your wife, my mother...has banished me from the boat until after dinner...and when I asked why? She said I needed to be playing in the sun...playing in the sun... do you believe that? I was listening to the radio and following Aunt Carrie's blog and then she comes in and starts treating me like an six year old!" The level of emotion couched in her words would have been disconcerting in anyone else, but Kaitlyn always had a flare for the dramatic.

"Listen to your old Dad a minute will you sweetheart?... Your Mom just doesn't want you to miss out on your childhood. Before this all went down you were a normal kid doing normal things... since then you have matured to such a degree that your Mom is worried that you will never get back to just being a kid again..." he paused in his dialog to search her eyes and be sure that she was getting his point. "None of us will be able to be who we were before...but there is no reason why you should have to have the responsibilities of a grownup" He immediately regretted his word choice. "Err... you know what I mean." The look in her eyes went from indignation to understanding. She really has grown up over the past week he thought to himself.

"I get what you're saying Dad, I really do, but you've got to understand that I haven't heard from any of my friends other than Katharine in several days... I need to keep busy or I am gonna lose it..."she then lunged in for a hug burying her face in his chest as sobs racked her shoulders. Duncan couldn't do anything other than hug her back and try to comfort her in an inconsolable situation.

When her tears finally abated and she had regained her composure, she looked up at her father and said, "Do you think you could speak to mom for me and sort of get me back on the net... I got to talk to Kat and see if I can find anyone else."

He said that he would and he was pretty sure that Katie would understand and would relent given the reasons she spelled out. "In the mean time kiddo, why don't you find your brother and ask him to show you what he has learned about shooting a pistol... once mom hears that she will be begging you to be back on the net" he laughed and she did too but the chance to shoot a pistol was a strong draw for any kid in a post zombie world, and she raced off to find her brother.

Duncan headed back towards the dock and his boat, as he walked along the bleached wood of the dock he wondered when if ever the wood would be re varnished so as to stand against the weather. The wind was picking up a little and spray from the water moistened his shirt and shorts. The low humidity of the day allowed for quick evaporation cooling him down nicely.

He passed Dave's boat and tried not to notice the rocking and the noises coming from within the cabin. It was none of his business, but man when Laura sets her sights on something she gets it. He quickened his pace and made it to his boat just as the sounds of Laura's orgasm assaulted his ears. He climbed aboard and went below and found Katie reading something on her nook. She looked up and smiled, her eyes were a little red around the edges and a little puffy too. She'd had obviously been crying. He figured he would let her bring up why if she chose to.

He sat down on the loveseat next to her and put his hand on her knee. Her feat were curled underneath her, she put down the e-reader and held his hand in hers. They didn't say anything for a long while just enjoying each other's company seemed right. "How do they get the wood this soft?" she asked making small talk.

He told her they used real fine sand paper and then sprayed the varnish on in many light coats. He then told her about his conversation with Kaitlyn. He could see by her body language that she hadn't realized that she was worried about her friends and that they might very well be among the undead, that thought chilled her to the bone enough that she actually shivered in the middle seventies temperature.

To distract her from those maudlin thoughts he figured he would try a play from Laura's book and let his hands talk for him. She saw it for what it was and followed it with her own efforts. She stood and took his hand guiding him to their cabin where they wouldn't be disturbed.

They reveled in the post coital afterglow, sharing tenderness that is often lost in couples whom were married as long as they were. They talked for a while about nothing and then the moment was past. Their conversation turned to the matters at hand.

"Listen baby doll, while we are out tonight I need for you to start getting our things together, we are going to be leaving the group tomorrow, have Liam start getting the arms together. I am worried that it won't be so easy to get all of our gear back unless we start while everyone has other things on their minds."

She agreed with the idea, being somewhat of a pragmatist herself she was want to be certain that they had everything that they needed to ensure their survival.

The two groups were preparing a barbeque, sort of a community building event. Duncan and his brothers along with their families opted to dine alone on the Persistence, but would join the festivities later. Duncan took the time to go over his concerns and to make plans for how they would depart after the mission. It would make it easier since the "team" going to rescue the captives would be in the majority, part of Duncan's family. Couple that with the fact that they would provide the group with arms and ammunition. There might not be much of a fuss but Duncan wanted to have all his ducks in a row so that there would be nothing that anyone could do to interfere with their plans.

45

Patrick was going over the navigational charts for the night's rescue operation, in the background, the Coast Guard tide and weather advisory could be heard. Occasionally, he would make a note on his pad in response to what he was hearing broadcast on the VHF. Kaitlyn was down in the saloon with him. She was providing him with assistance by calling up Google earth on the net and zooming in on the little island where the victims were being held.

Kaitlyn was eager to assist in whatever way she could. It didn't require an active imagination to envision herself with her mother and sister at the mercy of such villainous rouges. Pat provided her with the coordinates from the charts, which she just plugged in and within seconds, the small island occupied the screen.

Pat pulled up a chair and was looking at the screen trying to discern if they had made any additional fortifications or taken any additional security precautions. So far, he hadn't noticed any, which was good but if there were subtle changes, well that could be very bad indeed. The time lag made the work difficult but not impossible. Pat wish and not for the first time that he had access to the military feeds that streamed live with no delay, but wishes are only that wishes. He scrutinized the screen and watched the 'guards' as they made their rounds.

He asked Kaitlyn if she could overlay the screen with a grid so that he could get scaled data. Kaitlyn was disappointed to have to tell him she couldn't. He really didn't expect that she could he just took a shot in the dark and told her so.

Patrick was pleased to note that these guys were behaving like they didn't expect any trouble or rescue attempt they showed absolutely no discipline. That one fact alone upped the likeliness of the mission's success exponentially.

He continued to watch and make notes for the next two hours, until he was sure of the routines. He assigned monikers to each of the assailants he saw by noting what they wore and by physical appearance. He had yet to see any of the victims. He assumed that they were under guard inside the lighthouse proper.

46

Jacob continued watching the monitor. The horde predictably made its way up the private road. Their mindless shambling evident as there was no cohesion in their movement up the road. Stragglers broke from the larger group to investigate possible prey at some of the other houses along the gravel road. Whether there were residual scents from occupants whom had already fled no one could know. The larger group continued along their path, drawing ever closer to the compound's gate.

The tension in the air could be cut with a knife; it was so thick. Jacob was confident that none of them in the house would crack under the pressure; they all seemed to have their wits about them. They were made of strong stuff indeed.

The monitor showed the horde loitering near the gate as if confused by something. The bodies of the zombies that Jacob had shot down had been disposed of long ago, they must be picking up on some vestige of smell or other tells that there were living people about. There were no moans suggesting that they were certain of the location of the prey. They were just milling about. Some were pushing at the gate but not in the way you would expect if they were laying siege. The light that was hooked into the generator circuit dimmed markedly, showing Jacob that something just took a large jolt from the electrified fence. The compound itself was adequately lit and at maximum zoom on Google earth you could make out enough detail to see if any had breached the fence, but it failed to show exactly where the perimeter was tested.

The bulb dimmed several times in succession suggesting that several of the ghouls had tried to get through. The voltage should have been sufficient to kill a living man, which of course when dealing with the undead would still be enough to put it on its ass. The muscle fibers were not altered by the transformation from living to undead. They would still contract when current was applied, was this enough to prevent them from breaching the barrier remained to be seen. The theory was sound and should prove to be effective, unless there were sufficient numbers to disperse the current enough, but that would require the fiends working together and nothing so far has suggested that they had the capacity to do so.

The boys grabbed the shotgun and deer rifle and made their way to the defensive positions that Jacob had shown them when he briefed them on what to do, if there was a breach. The modifications he made to his initial defenses included slots that would allow the rifles to shoot from with overlapping fields of fire, yet these slits were too small for the zombies to reach through. They were also engineered so that even if a zombie could gain purchase with its fingers, by pulling it would increase the strength of the fortification, and pushing would yield the same result. It was a cunning design, for all intents and purposes, he had built two boxes that were mounted inside and out. These boxes were through bolted into the frame, not only did this allow them to pivot and expand the field of fire, but it added significantly to the structural integrity. The boys left the slits sealed for now and would only open them if the dead made it into the compound.

Something grabbed the attention of the horde. The harrowing sound of a solitary moan could be heard from within the house. Then another and another joined in becoming a haunting chorus that chilled everyone to their marrow. The volume of the horror decreased as the horde began to move on quickly. Jacob figured that they had discovered some prey further up the road. It was unlikely that this group would return having not discovered anything to eat here. Jacob breathed a sigh of relief as the monitor showed the group continue. He zoomed out to follow the denizens with the computer, sure enough about a half-mile away the group had found a house with people inside. The zombies were battering at the doors trying to force their way in. It was only a matter of time before they broke through the meager barriers put in their way.

However, an SUV broke through the door of the attached garage as the survivors their made their escape.

It looked like the zombies efforts were going to be frustrated, as the vehicle ran them down. Perhaps half of the zombies had been mowed down, but each impact robbed speed and inertia from the vehicle. The grill could not absorb all the impacts without damage. It was not long before steam erupted from under the hood, and the vehicle's progress slowed significantly. To make matters worse many of the creatures that had been run down were getting back to their feet and others that had been crushed underneath were crawling and dragging their destroyed legs and lower bodies along. The rest of the horde finally broke through the vehicle glass and gained access to the occupants. It was a feeding frenzy. Even though you could not see clear details, you could see that the occupants were being torn apart.

It was a sobering experience, witnessing how quickly the creatures were able to achieve their goal. Those creatures had been loitering for over an hour outside the compound. They moved up the road and had sacked that house and disabled the car, devouring the occupants in less than twenty minutes. Jacob studied the footage over and over trying to get his mind around their ' *tactics* ' for failure of a better term.

They would wait three hours after the horde had moved on before they would make their supply run. They needed to beef up their security even more if they wanted to avoid the same fate of those folks up the road.

Jacob got a better understanding of the strengths of these creatures by watching and re-watching the footage of the assault. He devised some additional precautions to strengthen their defenses. He made a list of the supplies he was going to need from the hardware store. He didn't want to go to Home Depot or Lowes as he figured that there would likely be lots of those monsters there. He wanted to go to the local Ace Hardware a couple of miles from his home. First of all, it would be less likely to have been looted. Secondly, it was in a far less populous area ergo, there should be fewer if any of the creatures. So he tailored his designs and plans to fit with the supplies, he would be likely to find at his desired store.

They made quick work of removing the seats from the Suburban to make room for the supplies. They used plywood scraps from the earlier fortifications to reinforce the windows along the sides and the back of the vehicle. The glass of the driver and passenger windows remained vulnerable as did the windshield but there wasn't much to be done about that given that they did need to be able to see in order to drive.

The ground clearance of the vehicle made it seem unlikely that they would become high centered and stuck. The tires were off road in design and seemed pretty tough, not likely to be punctured, but they used a few cans of a green tire sealant that would make them almost as good as run-flats. All preparations were made. They were as ready as they were ever going to be. Pistol in holster and shot gun loaded Jacob, Arthur, and Thomas, said good-bye to their loved ones and got into the vehicle. The crunching of the tires on the gravel seemed deafening as it made its way to the gate.

Skeela and Max along with Aaron, were there to re-secure the portal after the truck went through. After pulling out onto the private road they waited until the gate was Sealed and re-secured before they headed toward the direction of the little town two miles distant. If luck was with them, they would be returning in an hour or so with the supplies they needed.

47

The trip up the east river from Liberty Island was disturbing to say the least. There were still many lights burning in the darkness, just not as many as one would expect before the dead reanimated. The smoke from the various fires burning out of control since the FDNY stopped responding and were overwhelmed, hung in the air. The sounds that any New Yorker, even those from the 'burbs' knew and expected were absent, giving the overall feeling one of creepiness at level previously uncharted.

Each of the landing team members checked their equipment and loaded their weapons. The green glow from the light amplification gear added to the disquiet. Pat went over the plan once again leaving nothing unsaid, they were as prepared as they were going to get and getting antsy with 'pre-op' jitters. Pat checked his K-Bar since that was the first weapon he would be employing, the dull non-reflective blade almost invisible in the darkness. Duncan noticed Pat inspecting his blade and followed his example by checking the garrote that Pat had assembled for him. The Garrote is a simple yet brutal weapon that has been used for centuries. Sinew and bone were used in the earliest incarnation of the weapon, Duncan's was made from piano wire strung between two palm length pieces of pipe. It was a weapon that would kill silently and did not require much in the way of training to use. It was an instinctual weapon that drew upon the innate knowledge from our primal natures. Slip the wire around the throat of the victim from behind, pull back while uncrossing your arms.

Duncan's strong arms were more than adequate to the task. Pat had asked his uncle to be his partner on this part of the operation for several reasons. The first being his competence, his uncle had proven to Pat that he could move silently, was alert, and knew enough 'field craft' to accomplish what needed to be done, such as utilizing his peripheral vision to notice movement. The second reason why he wanted his uncle rather than his father was that his uncle was less likely to try and protect him at the expense of his own safety, to his father he would always be his baby boy. Lastly he knew his uncle's moral compass was unwavering. He had no doubt that his uncle would kill the men they were about to stalk, but he knew with equal conviction that his uncle would not take pleasure in it or react from an emotional place of rage.

Kyle completely understood why his son had chosen his uncle rather than himself. He actually approved of the decision. He and his brother had always been close friends as well as brothers. Although he would never admit out loud how much he was relying on his younger brother to see him and his family safely through these ordeals. He was extremely proud of him and duly impressed by his actions and quickness of thought. "Enough sentimentality" he thought to himself as he charged the weapon, then ejected the magazine to add another cartridge and put it back into the gun.

The others too were readying their weapons or lost in their personal ruminations, when the motor/sailor's engines were cut reducing their noise signature, they extinguished their running lights and sailed onward in silence, pretending to be just a hole in the water.

 The final leg of the journey was at hand. They untied the inflatable boat and began paddling while hugging the gunwales of the boat. Their faces, necks, hands, and any other exposed skin had been blackened with grease. Four of the six men had paddles in hand, methodically paddling towards the island and the upcoming conflict, Duncan and Patrick were low and amidships with their ARs locked and loaded while scanning the shore through their night optics. The water gently lapping at the gunwales of their boat as it glided across the water. They were fearful of discovery as the beam of light from the tower stabbed out across the water like an accusing finger and swept over the raft only to plunge them back into darkness and relative safety a moment later as it made its circuit.

They were perhaps fifty yards from shore, sweat stinging their eyes from the exertion of paddling all the way with undersized paddles. Duncan clenched a fist and held his arm forming a ninety degree angle, bicep level with shoulder and forearm standing erect, this was the signal to stop all activity / possible danger. Sure enough the illumination of a flashlight could be seen coming around the structure telling of an approaching sentry. The temptation to hold their collective breath was strong but that could have adverse effects on their vision. They merely stayed where they were breathing normally albeit a tad shallow and watched as they man walked by following his flashlights beam doing a circuit. The sentry never even paused to look out over the water, he walked past quickly, so quick in fact that the noise discipline on the inflatable was almost un-necessary.

The light disappeared behind the structure again. They resumed their efforts painfully as the lactic acid had built up in the muscle groups used for paddling. The current had pushed them back so that they had to cover half again the distance they had achieved before they had sighted the sentry. Their efforts were rewarded as they drew near the island and into the grass that was growing along the edge of the shore. They all got out as quickly and quietly as they could. Duncan and Pat took up 'guard' positions as the others dragged the boat up onto shore and worked to conceal the raft where they secured it. The team moved into their assigned positions quickly.

Pat decided to set the charges himself rather than rely upon the other team getting the correct range with the water balloon slingshot. He was worried that if they overshot the boats that the shrapnel might puncture some of his team. With Duncan and the rest covering him he grabbed some fishing line and a couple of grenades and made his way into the shadows to creep his way to where the pirates had their boats tied up.

The shadows were his friends, he moved through them with a graceful economy of movement that bespeaks of cunning and lethality. Wraith like he moved betwixt the boats carefully placing his charges so that when they exploded it would yield a tremendous fire ball that would draw the attention of anyone in the vicinity. After he set the final charge and ran out the fishing line that would serve to trigger the device, he made his way back to his position. He checked in with the boat crew and signaled his team, as soon as the two sentries showed themselves they would be silently killed and then they would trigger the grenades. He checked his watch, so far everything had gone according to plan. They should be showing up within five minutes or so. Five minutes is an awful long time to wait in an action like this, and there is of course the old adage that states no plan ever survives contact with the enemy. He hoped that would not be the case tonight, his plan was shaky enough as it was he didn't want to have to change it on the fly if that could be avoided.

The tell tale sound of music or what passed for music in the minds of the pirates, it was gangsta rap, could be heard from inside the building briefly as the two sentries left the inner room heading out for their rounds. Duncan caught Pat's eye and gave a brief nod of his head indicating that he too had heard the sounds and was ready for action. They had their backs pressed up against the wall to the sides or the exterior door so as to remain out of sight of the pirates until it was too late.

The door opened and out came the first of the men whom were about to make the trip to hell. He made two steps past the threshold when he noted the blur of motion to his right then felt the bite of the wire against his windpipe instinctively his fingers sought to get between the cutting wire and the unprotected throat. It was a futile action for Duncan's powerful arms were pulling the noose tight. The sentry was not even able to scream his agony, there was no release... not from the pain of the wire slicing its way through, nor from the burning at the lack of air. He was aware of the sensation of wetness on his shirt caused by the flood of blood pouring from the wounds. His vision tunneled then faded to black, an instant later he felt nothing as death claimed him. Duncan continued to exert himself even after the body had gone limp.

The second man had seen his partner get taken from behind and yanked off to the side, he reacted predictably to try and help his comrade. As he was crossing the threshold in pursuit Pat appeared in front of him with is K-Bar already coming down aimed at the indent at the top of his clavicle. The soft flesh there offered no resistance and parted for the sharp blade. It sank into the hilt severing the air supply and with two rocking movements the blade cleaved the heart into three pieces. The man was dead even before Duncan's victim expired. Now it was just lifeless meat wearing an NBA jersey.

Duncan and Pat dragged the corpses away from the doorway and lowered them to the ground. The sounds from the scuffle were minimal, certainly not enough to have been heard inside over the din of the Rap Music. Duncan was surprised to find that the man he killed could have easily been one of his son's or nephew's friends, he was perhaps 18 to 20 years old, white or Hispanic it was hard to tell which. Either way not much more than a kid. What was more important was the fact that they were in some ways worse than the zombies. These were living humans who were preying upon their fellow man. You really couldn't fault a zombie, it was doing what it did without thought or malice, following instinct. These pirates had killed their own kind, had taken by force of arms women and girls for their own lustful purposes. Duncan felt no remorse for having killed his foe. He looked at his nephew and gave a curt nod to let him know he was ready.

Pat called the boat and told them to fire up the engines and pass by as noisily as possible in two minutes hoping to draw out some of the occupants he would detonate the grenades shortly thereafter. He had his fire team split into two groups with overlapping fields of fire splayed out so as to cut down the pirates as the exited the building. He would take the first shot, that first round was the signal to open up on their targets. He hoped to take at least one of them alive so as to learn the layout but that was a secondary priority. Just under two minutes later he heard the throaty sound of the sixty horse power Evenrude power up and started closing on the island. The so called music inside stopped. There were muffled shouts from inside accompanying the screams and cries of the girls within. When Pat heard the sound more clearly he pulled on the monofilament fishing line.

The door to the building opened inward just as the grenades went off, producing the desired effect of a flashy explosion and accompanying fireball. Three of the 'men' cleared the doorway with pistol gripped shotguns leading the way. Pat squeezed his trigger and the pop of his AR signaled fusillade. Pats first shot took the lead man in the patella felling him like a tree, the other two were not as lucky as the rounds from five other weapons ripped into their bodies. The impacts in such close succession making the targets seem to dance like a crack head to some thrashing beat, spasmodic and without rhythm. As they went down two shotgun blasts erupted from inside the doorway in quick succession, the shots tearing up the turf ten yards out in front of the door.

One of the fallen was preventing the door from being able to be closed from inside, as the bloody corpse lay across the threshold half in half out of the doorway. Kyle had the best vantage point to clear the portal, and he wasted no time releasing a three round burst that was rewarded by a scream as at least one or his rounds scored a hit on an occupant. The ARs fell silent again the only sounds were that of the two wounded men crying in their agony and the Evenrude growing faint in the distance.

Richie kept his gun trained on the fellow Pat had dropped with the first shot of the volley, as Ralph and Pat moved towards the doorway from one side and Kyle, Duncan and Dave closed from the other side. When both teams made the safety of the wall to the sides of the doorway Dave dropped to the ground in preparation for looking around the edge, hoping that by having his head at ground level rather than where a man's head should be he might be able to get a quick look inside the door without being shot by a twelve gauge. With two short breaths and a deep third which he held, he executed his maneuver, quickly popping his head past the frame getting a look and then pulling it back. He pulled his nine millimeter and leaned back in hooting two shots into the back of the fourth man inside who was crawling up the stairs to the door at the top, his shotgun abandoned at the bottom of the stairs.

Richie dragged the wounded pirate by his shirt to the doorway and began asking the kid about numbers inside and general layout. Retirement had not dulled his cop interrogation skills. The kid whose knee was destroyed was aware enough to know that if he wanted to survive his only option was cooperating, and even that might not save him, but he gave up the information. At the conclusion of which Ralph rewarded him a crushing blow to the temple with the butt of his weapon splaying him flat. He then knelt across the pirate's throat and produced a buck knife and buried it into the man's heart. Rage unsated in the father's eyes burned brightly.

What they had learned was that there was a store room to the left of the stairs, immediately inside the door was where the generator and drums of fuel were kept. At the top of the climb was a steel door that led to the area where living quarters were, it was a large open circular room with a kitchenette, a bathroom, a couple cots and other furniture. The girls were tied up and along the wall under a set of steel stairs that led up to where the light and equipment to run it were. There were only two more assailants inside, at least that were what they were told, and Richie seemed to think the guy had told the truth. It turns out that the guys remaining were corrections officers who were on the take and supplemented their income by helping inmates get contraband inside of Rikers Island. They took off after the first sign of outbreak among the general population in the prison set off a riot. They had led these six out and provided them with the shotguns and pistols, stole a boat and headed to the light house. They killed the two lighthouse keepers and then were on the lookout for boats that they could waylay.

Pat and Richie discussed the situation. The two inside would likely be using the women as human shields, and without knowing exactly where they were inside... a dynamic entry was out. Their best option was to try and negotiate. The steel door would stop the shotgun blasts most likely so they were not in a fatal funnel at the top of the landing.

Pat's training was woefully inadequate for this type of situation. Richie was the only one who had any applicable experience here. Ralph was out for blood and was likely to get the hostages killed if he were to take charge. Duncan looked to his brother and Dave, shrugged and said he would follow Richie's lead. Kyle and Dave agreed. They climbed the stairs with guns at the ready.

 Richie knocked on the door loudly. "You inside... we are here for the girls... send them out and we will leave. You guys can do what you want after that what do you say?" Silence apart from the whimpering of the hostages was the reply. "Come on guys... you know why we are here, so you know we aren't leaving without our women...we will even leave you with a boat so that you guys can go where you want or stay for that matter... we don't care, we just want our women back?"

The whimpering became fully fledged crying. Ralph was certain that his twins were the source and tried to get to them. Kyle and Duncan had to physically restrain him for he was attempting to charge on in heedless of his own safety and the safety of the hostages. If they were to let him go chances are that not only would he be killed in front of his daughters and wife but likely as not one or more of the hostages would also be wounded if not killed.

"Listen man... you want to save your family... that's why we are here...be smart man" said Pat into Ralph's ear while his dad and uncle held the grief stricken man against the wall.

"They need me! Let me go damn it!" he yelled at his antagonists. "Alice! Amanda! Daddy is here!" The cries from inside the room intensified.

Richie glared at Ralph and whispered through clenched teeth, "Are you trying to get your family killed? You just painted a huge target on them you know?"

Inside the room activity could now be heard. "No... You bastards...they're just little girls" came the voice of Ralph's wife. Ralph went limp when he heard that.

Richie tried again in a calm voice, "This doesn't have to go south guys... we are offering you a way out." Muffled male voices could be heard as the two pirates inside discussed their options inside.

Fifteen minutes ticked by and the stalemate endured. Finally one of the villains shouted through the door, "Open the door slowly and put your weapons on the floor and we will see if there is some way we can end this where we all are happy."

Richie put his assault rifle on the deck although he kept his pistol tucked at the small of his back in his waistband. He then whispered, "They most likely didn't know how many of us are out here" After a few seconds of hushed conversation it was decided that Pat and Duncan would stay outside of the door and the other four would go inside.

Richie reached out for the handle of the door, nervous about being out front but they had little choice. He turned the knob and pushed the door. The door swung slowly open on its hinges, the hydraulic door closer reached its apogee and started to close. In front of them was one of the two pirates huddled behind four naked hostages with duck taped hands and mouths. Signs of violence were apparent on several of the faces in the form of bruises on eyes and one with a swollen blood encrusted nose. The rest of the girls couldn't be seen because of the door but it was assumed that they were in no better shape and the other gunman was probably with them.

Richie stepped over his rifle and into the room with his empty hands visible in front of him he stepped to the right and used his hip to prevent the door from closing. Ralph bent over and laid his weapon on the floor and mimicked Richie's actions although he stepped left. Dave was next, he put his gun down and stepped in between the two with his hands clearly visible. Kyle stepped in behind Dave after adding a captured shot gun on the pile, he was still holding his AR, hoping that it couldn't be seen. He looked at Ralph's profile noticing the clenched jaw and the pulsing of his temporal vein. At least one of his family was helpless naked and abused right in front of him, right before his eyes. Kyle was amazed that he kept it together and didn't lose it at the sight. Inside his own mind Kyle wasn't sure he could have stood there were it his family.

The pirate broke the uneasy silence by saying, "What's to stop me from killing you all where you stand?" He added an exclamation point in the form of pumping a round audibly in the shotgun and pointing the barrel in their general direction. Kyle brought the barrel of his AR up and into line over Dave's left shoulder. His gun was already ready to fire, he didn't need the theatrics displayed by their adversaries. Richie smiled, "You stand more to gain by not killing anyone else."

"He won't shoot! He would hit one of the kiddies!" The pirate punctuated the statement with menacing laugh.

Richie countered quickly stealing away some of the thunder by saying, "Not any of his family and the rest of us already agreed we would rather see ours dead than suffering under you... so go ahead and start shooting see how many survive, but I can guarantee that you two won't..." several uneasy seconds ticked by in this Mexican standoff without either side blinking or moving. Kyle was pretty sure that he could drill a round through the eye of the one behind the girls, but he still wasn't sure where the other guy was.

Pat and Duncan had heard enough, moving silently the retreated back down the stairs, they had to come up with an alternate plan. When they got to the exit, Pat looked around with fresh eyes. A quarter of the way around the tower there was a rope hanging down from a pulley system secured to the rail at the top of the light house. Duncan had the rudiments of a plan at first sight. They could climb to the top and gain access through then light room, and from there they could each pop one of the bad guys. No way were these assholes getting off this island alive.

The thug cracked first. "How do you suggest we handle this... we can't just let you have all the girls and trust you not to start shooting once they are clear? And I am sure you don't want to let us keep hostages with us onto our boat?" Which of course was what they were hoping would happen.

Dave chimed in, "You could take me and Ralph here as hostages, we could go with you and then jump overboard once you guys are speeding off?" sounding hopeful he added "hell you can have our guns too and the extra ammo we got with us...come on you get something out of this and the girls get to go home it's a win win what do you say?" ...."Hell me and Ralph can even carry your gear to the boat come on it's a no brainer. We shouldn't be messin with each other anyway... we got fucking zombies to worry about."

Pat went up the rope first assisted by Duncan from the bottom employing the mechanical advantage of the pulley system. At the top he climbed over the rail, now it was Pat's turn to help his uncle get to the top. Duncan swung his leg over the rail and gained purchase, he finished climbing and crouched by his nephew looking through the glass. The access hatch up there was not even secured slightest of fashion. Inward they crept moving like specters or other ethereal entities, silent with the aura of fury and malice in their hearts. They could hear the words being spoken inside.

Duncan eased open an access panel and had clear LOS (line of sight) of the second goon, he braced his gun and had the man 'painted' it would take nothing but the gentle stroke of his trigger to turn that guys lights out, as if he were in a book depository tracking a presidential motorcade in Dallas. Pat found his sweet spot and had acquired his target they would synchronize their shots to minimize the chance of anyone escaping or anyone else getting hurt.

They could both see that Dave and Ralph were now on their knees a couple of feet from the human shields. Neither Duncan nor Pat liked this turn of events, they would have to act and soon. Pat adjusted his aim and softly counted off, one, two, three... two shots rang out as one. The full metal jacket round that Duncan had let loose traveled at supersonic speed, entering his targets head from slightly above and behind his right ear, blowing through releasing much of its energy to the matter through which it passed. The round upon exiting blew directly through the mandibular joint on the left side of the guys face, taking the guys jaw off in the process and embedded itself deep in the wall behind. It was a particularly gory shot as the head exploded like an overripe melon, and bits and pieces of the guy landed all over, on and around the girls in which he was hiding.

Pat had placed his shot to turn this asshole into a quadriplegic as it smashed into the vertebra at the base of the neck where it joins the back. The guy's fingers lost all control and the pistol gripped shotgun slipped from his nerveless fingers to slip harmlessly to the floor. One of the naked adolescents reached for the shotgun once she saw that he was not dead. Upon acquiring the weapon she felt empowered and wanted nothing more than to seek retribution. She wanted to castrate him with the shotgun, turn the guy into a paralyzed eunuch and justice would be served.

When the shots rang out Richie, Ralph and Dave dove to the sides believing that they had come under fire. Kyle had dropped to his knee, never losing his sight picture. "Clear! Clear!" shouts were from the rafters. The freed prisoners dashed for their clothes that were in the kitchenette. Duncan and Pat descended the stairs into the living area. Everyone averted their eyes so as to allow them to don their clothes. Pat called the boat and told them that everything was under control and that they could come ashore. Ralph swept his family into his arms amongst a multitude of tears.

The presence of Richie and Ralph went a long way towards assuaging the fears of the women. John Stein's boat could be heard coming. Duncan and his people felt out of place, these people needed to be amongst their own so Dave, Pat, Kyle and Duncan busied themselves gathering up all the plundered supplies including the shotguns that the pirates had been using. They began boxing it all up and carrying it all down to the boats.

There was a surprising amount of supplies, apparently the lighthouse was well stocked. It would seem that the men who worked here kept plenty on hand. It was a virtual cornucopia of canned food. Duncan had to admire the choice of location the pirates had made. It would serve as a good place for a small group to ride out the apocalypse, plenty of fuel, sturdy and defensible. Yes he had to give them credit even if they were amoral sociopaths. The food and supplies were loaded and the women got onto the undamaged captured boat. They retrieved Duncan's dingy and tied that to a tow line and made best possible speed back to Liberty Island.

When they arrived it was a tearful reunion. The families reunited with loved ones, withdrew from the masses to revel in the joy of the *lost's* return. The supplies were being offloaded and added to the inventory of supplies in the concession stand area. Dave and Richie were celebrated heroes, and were giving an account of the events albeit with advantages to the eager ears of crowd. Duncan went in search of his family, he wanted to check in and let Katie know he was okay and then he wanted to speak with Liam to see how he had fared while they had been out.

He was ten feet from his boat when Marianne caught up with him. She wanted to confront him, he could see that she was angry and upset. This of course was not unexpected. He was just hoping that it could have waited until after he had kissed his wife and assured his kids that they were all right. He spun around and faced the commodore squarely. His jaw was set, his posture indicated that he was ready for any sort of conflict that she wished to engage in. He didn't think that it would be a physical one but he gambled that by presenting himself in this fashion it might take some of the wind out of her sails. He guessed wrong, there was no wind... she was making use of steam and she had a full head of it.

"Where the hell do you get off trying to take away with you the guns and the ammunition?" she practically screamed into his face. "It's bad enough that by leaving you are taking away most of the resources and communication gear... but you are going to leave us defenseless too! You won't get away with it..." Katie had heard the commotion and came topside and had closed on the two unnoticed. She stepped around her husband and invaded Marianne's personal space and jabbed her right index finger in Marianne's sternum.

"Listen bitch! My husband has just gotten back from risking his life to help these people, just as he has helped every last one of you people! Do you even say thank you? No! You just fucking come at him like he was sneaking off in the night after having robbed the poor box at the local church! Where the Fuck do you get off. Now step back or I am gonna kick the living shit out of you. That title you have is a hollow one and bares no power. We will leave and we will leave with our stuff! You got that! Anything we leave you with is a gift and a display of our good graces!..."

Duncan had to fight very hard to keep the smile off of his face, as he watched and listened to his wife. He always knew she was feisty, hell that was one of the things that had drawn him to her a lifetime ago in that little pub in Bellmore, but he was practically swollen with pride as she dressed this woman up and down. The effect that it had on Marianne was priceless, she was visibly cowed and seemed to have shrunk. Duncan put a restraining hand lightly on his wife's shoulder and said to her in a gentle voice, "Honeybaby, I got this... go back on board and I will join you shortly" then he gave her a peck on the top of her head. He then turned to Marianne and said, "We will be leaving with the tide, we have brought more supplies for the community including several shotguns and shells. We will however be retrieving the guns and equipment that we have loaned you all. Those supplies, were supplies that my family and I brought with us at great peril, and not you or anyone else is going to take them." He had spoken in a calm and collected voice, no signs of anger or threats. It was spoken 'matter of factly' as if you would sooner doubt gravity than his words.

"Listen, I got off on the wrong foot here..."she said by way of apology. "Whatever supplies you can spare we would greatly appreciate." She looked down towards her feet as she said this. "You and your family, your brothers, all of you... if it weren't for you guys we would all be dead, of this I am sure, and well with you guys leaving... well it is going to be unsettling for the community." She turned to go. As she started walking away she stopped and said over her shoulder, "Before you go... I want you to know that you will be welcome here if you want to come back... good luck, I hope you find your family safe and stay in touch." With that said she continued on her way, Duncan turned and made his way onto his boat.

48

The CDC had just forwarded their latest findings, the former vice now President and his advisors were assembled in the *'war room'* the displays and maps showing just how bad the pandemic was. In just shy of three weeks the dead were walking on every continent save for Antarctica. The only country that had not had even a single report of infection was Japan. The President was envious of the fact that Japan's earthquake, Tsunami and Nuclear accident of a few months ago had made tourism to their country non- existent subsequently sparing the nation. They were willing to assist in a limited capacity, but they had closed their borders.

The extreme north and south showed the lightest levels of infection. Ergo the Scandinavian countries and the Australians had the best chances to respond to the global crisis by securing their countries. The leaders of those nations were in contact with the President's team, and they were trying to coordinate plans.

Norway and Finland were going to assist Western Europe by setting up 'safe zones' with quarantine facilities, but those plans would take months if not years to implement.

New Zealand and New Guinea would be clear of the few recorded outbreaks within a couple of days, and the Aussies were going to establish refugee centers there. They offered America their unconditional help showing just how good allies they have always been.

An Air Force colonel was in the process of updating the displays; the latest modeling projected a bleak and desperate future. Already twenty five-percent of the world population has succumbed to the infection or at least been exposed and will ultimately turn within forty-eight hours. It is projected that within sixty days seventy-five-percent will be among the walking dead unless drastic measures are taken worldwide, among some of the proposed measures are firebombing large population areas and cities with infected of thirty-percent or greater.

The Colonel addressed the President, "The CDC has also suggested the wide-spread use of DDT to control and or eliminate some of the vectors. This is a viable option for countries other than the United States. Unfortunately, DDT was banned in the United States thirty plus years ago as a suspected carcinogen even though there was no conclusive data to corroborate these claims.

 DDT's opponents had deep pockets for lobbyists and was very successful in their deaminization campaign. However, it is still produced overseas. I believe that there are three or perhaps four pesticide companies within the States that produce it for export only. I think said companies are foreign owned."

The President stood transfixed by the displays in front of him. He then turned to the Colonel and said, "Seize those facilities, they are vital assets and should be protected at all costs, once we have them secured increase output of DDT to the maximum, maybe we can slow this thing down enough to save ourselves."

 The Colonel exited the room to put the orders into action while the President poured through the rest of the reports and communiqués that were streaming in like flood waters. His sincerest hopes were that he would be able to keep from drowning in the mire and find some way to save his people. His though processes were beginning to change, he was beginning to see the wisdom in less Government interference and regulation. He laughed out loud because he had been a lifelong liberal, and yet he was having a conservative epiphany.

"I just may have to change party affiliation" he thought to himself, and he chuckled again. Thankfully, for him, he was alone in his *war room*, else someone may think he was cracking under the pressure.

He called in some other advisors to garner more information on the infrastructure. He was extremely concerned with the nation's power grids and telecommunications. He could only hope that he had enough manpower to keep everything going. He had to prioritize in the event that he didn't. They got down to the nitty gritty in short order; however, they didn't have enough information on attrition rates.

The Secretary of the Navy reported that Pacific and Atlantic fleets were standing by awaiting orders as they have all been recalled from theater operations and were enroute to American waters.

The Secretary of Agriculture voiced his concerns about farming production ..."We are going to run out of food if we don't take some actions to protect food production..."

The Chairman of the Joint Chiefs was sorting through the pertinent data on strength of arms and the alarming number of AWOL incidents being reported.

Global information was being fed to another of the displays showing radiation blooms from two reactors in France and one in Germany, the satellite information suggests meltdowns, but they were awaiting more information.

"This may be a global crisis, but we have to each tend to our own" said the President in response to some querry or other. More reports and data were flooding in by the minute. The staff was working as hard as they could, and he needed more bodies everywhere. They were on pace for rapid burnout. He needed rest, as did everyone else. He tasked his Secretary of Defense with putting together a shift schedule so that everyone had at least six hours of uninterrupted downtime to recuperate. "If we don't get enough rest, we won't be able to think clearly, and that can only make matters worse" with that said he left the room, he was going to need pharmacological assistance to get through this. When he got into the hallway, he reached inside his jacket pocket and retrieved a cigar, clipped its end and drew in a lung full of smoke and headed to his quarters for rest.

"At the CDC in Atlanta, they have determined that the viral component is indeed airborne, and that its DNA affects the toxoplasmosa, and that it is the symbiotic relationship that causes transformation. They have also ascertained that any bodily fluid carries both the virus and the protozoa. Therefore, any open wound or sore exposed to even the smallest amount results in contamination and infection one hundred percent of the time, likewise, any exposure to membrane tissue like the eyes. Furthermore, they discovered that the nail beds of the zombies secrete contaminated fluids thereby making even a scratch that breaks the skin a death sentence. Ingesting of contaminated matter results in infection eightyfive to ninety percent of the time. It is therefore recommended that proper PPE (Personal Protective Equipment) such as protective eye wear, gloves and masks be worn by anyone and everyone who may come into contact with the infected. The airborne virus alone cannot cause the infection without the protozoa. Anyone who currently carries the toxoplasmosa in its original form should seek medical attention as antipsychotic drugs have been shown to inhibit and in many cases destroy the protozoa. Should the protozoa come into contact with the virus the transformation will occur." Carrie just finished and published her most-recent blog post. There were more survivor blogs popping up all the time, and many of the threads linked straight to her blog as well. She was gratified that she was part of this heroic effort to get the facts out to the world.

Many of these blogs were sharing survival tips, and combat techniques to help minimize infection. Small pockets and communities were popping up all over. Many of these were under siege just like she was here in Atlanta. She hoped and prayed that the Government was going to be able to get these bastions supplies to help them survive the sieges.

In reading these blogs, she noticed that some of these safe havens were in contact with other havens and that those that were in relatively close proximity were helping each other out not bothering to wait for the Governments assistance. It was almost a frontiersman's mentality, just like our fore fathers when they carved their communities out of the wilderness. Another of history's examples would be fiefdom and serfdom of the feudal age.

Carrie composed e-mails to her dad and to Kaitlyn with hyperlinks to the blogs that she felt had the best information to offer. She was exhausted, she had been at it for eighteen hours. After she filtered her e-mails and read the ones from family she signed off and went to bed.

49

Arthur was behind the wheel of the Suburban, his small plump frame looking childlike in such a large truck. His eyes were scanning everywhere at once, his knuckles white as he gripped the wheel in an attempt to draw forth strength from the inanimate object in his grasp. Jacob sat is the passenger seat searching beyond the windshield for any danger as they continued down the road that would lead them to the hardware store. Thomas was in the back sitting on an empty joint compound bucket holding onto the handgrip as if his life depended upon it, which in retrospect it did. The shot gun was tied to the back of Jacob's seat with the safety engaged, it was tied so that a quick tug on the dangling line would free the weapon and it could be brought to bear quickly.

"Okay Arthur the parking lot is just is a couple hundred yards up on the right. Pull in and go around back, I want to circle the place and look, if the coast is clear I want you to drop us off at the front and circle around to the loading dock where the contractors entrance is keep your Bluetooth on, we will be right on the other end of the line."

Arthur nodded his head in the affirmative not trusting his voice not to betray his abject terror of being alone in the truck, a sitting duck. Thomas reached his hand to his father's shoulder and gave a gentle squeeze sharing his own fear tempered with the confidence in youth's immortality. He turned on his directional out of habit and pulled into the lot. There were three other vehicles parked in the lot two of which Jacob knew belonged to Matt and Gus who worked there were parked farthest away from the store, the other probably belonged to a customer was parked in the space near the front door.

The sight of the vehicles gave Jacob a sinking feeling in his guts. If Gus and Matt's cars were here chances were they had unwanted visitors drop in on them. The lights were on in the store, and as they drove up there were other signs that that there had been trouble here. The sliding doors had spider cracks from where buckshot had peppered it and a reddish brown smear could be seen on the ground between the doors that were partway open.

From their vantage point it didn't look particularly fresh but that didn't mean that there weren't any zombies around. As they drove around the store to the left they passed the large propane tank where folks would get their grill tanks filled. The tub filled with water sat undisturbed next to the scale that needed a fresh coat of paint and a wire brushing, and a locked cage that held prefilled tanks for exchange. The fire code required this side of the building to be bricked and windowless so they couldn't see anything inside. They continued their circle and came around the back by the dumpster, there was no evidence here of any trouble, they passed that and slowed their pace as they came abreast of the loading dock. Here to the coast was clear, the corrugated steel door was down suggesting that they had been closing up when whatever happened had gone down. On the east side of the building as they continued around towards the front had windows that let in light to the store but were high enough that Jacob couldn't see into the store to see if there were any inhabitants.

They returned to the front and came to a stop. Arthur turned to Jacob and asked, " Are you sure you need to go in there? Can we just go back to your place?" his voice was pleading with Jacob, the subtext of which was "Do you really need to risk my son's life on this errand?"

Jacob replied as calmly and patiently as he could, "I'll go in first to make sure that there are no zombies inside then you can send Thomas in so we can get what we need. If we don't get these supplies I am not sure how long we can keep those things out if they get passed the perimeter fence. Besides the supplies we are grabbing will provide us with more time to prepare in the event that they do get through the wire."

Thomas interjected, "Look dad, we have guns and we can get out real fast but anything that improves our chances has got to be worth a little risk aint it?" He intentionally murdered grammar in order to get his father off worrying about things that were out of his control by focusing him on correcting his son's speech, which of course he did out of habit much like the use of the directional when they entered the lot.

Jacob eased open the door and shut it softly so that only the faintest click was heard. He drew his three-fifty-seven and walked to the door where he crouched and inspected the bloody smear. As he though the smear had dried, whatever had happened occurred several hours ago at least possibly the evening before. He stepped closer to look at the doors themselves, one of the doors was out of its track which was why it wasn't closing properly. As he had stepped closer the electric eye pick up on his presence and the other door opened completely scaring the bejeezus out of him. He could hear the gear system in the stuck door struggle in its attempt to fulfill its purpose. His nose picked up the smell of death inside but not overwhelmingly thick. He chanced a couple of steps inside.

Jacob was light on his feet, he kept his center of balance low and over the balls of his feet, prepared to move whatever direction he had to in an instant. His pulse rate had increased in direct proportion to the adrenaline that was flooding his veins. His eyes were following the bloody trail of the violence and he found the body of a zombie with a pickaxe embedded in its skull and a gory tunnel through its middle where the shotgun blast had carved through it near the door.

Jacob silently crept through the store moving and listening for any sounds that would tell him he was not alone. As he neared a rack of tools he grabbed a 6lbs. sledge hammer figuring that if he came upon one he could crush it's skull without a loud pistol crack that might attract others. He continued to stalk about the store but he heard nothing, strangely the lack of any sound was not as comforting as it should be. He knew in his heart of hearts that Matt and Gus were in here and dead, he just wasn't sure if they were still walking.

The spacious shelf and rack lined aisles teemed with various products for use in and around the home. Jacob noticed several things that needed to be added to his list for procurement after the store was rid of any lurking denizens.

"So far so good" he whispered and his Bluetooth transmitted his words clearly so that Arthur and Thomas knew what was happening.

He was nearing the end cap of the aisle he was in, about halfway to the counter in the back where local contractors would place their orders in more peaceful days, where he noticed a minwax display was toppled spewing cans of wood stains and polyurethane all over the floor. An apparent struggle had taken place here judging by the disarray. Jacob moved forward slowly, hardening his ears listening for any sounds and hearing nothing save for his own pulse thundering in his ears. He crept closer to the end cap and chanced a look around its end. On the floor he saw several smallish puddles of blood that were partially congealed, fresher than the smear at the front of the store but still not recent.

He crossed over the bisecting aisle continuing towards the back of the store. Ahead and to the left were pallets loaded with sacks of cement and sand. Jacob figured that he could chance a little more speed sacrificing a modicum of his stealth for efficiencies sake. He finally was nearing the back of the store when his nose picked up an increase in the pungency of the stench of death and shit. He slid his dominant right hand up the shaft of the sledge hammer and gripped its butt more firmly in his left, preparing to swing as he rounded the end of the aisle.

What he saw was the body of Matt laying half on a pile of peat moss sacks, his upper body had slipped to the floor. His blue uniform vest stained with what could only have been blood. Matt's left forearm was wrapped with gauze from a first aid kit. The white bandage was wrapped from elbow to wrist and at its center was a dark crimson oval. Jacob noted that the oval was about the same size of a mouth. The body was still, the way a body in death should be. Jacob approached it with

281

caution. What he noticed next was half of its head was missing obliterated by what he presumed to be a shotgun blast.

Jacob lowered the hammer silently to the floor and drew his pistol again. He intended to go behind the counter and investigate further and he knew he wouldn't have the space to swing the hammer effectively in such close quarters. Jacob used his left hand to raise the fold down on the counter so that he could keep his gun in line to his front, and then slipped through to the back. He didn't have to go very far before he noticed the absurdly little feat that Gus had always been ridiculed about, sticking out of the bathroom door. The feet were as motionless as Matt's body. Jacob leaving nothing to chance peered around the open door and saw Gus or most of Gus anyway as the head had been blown apart and was splattered all over. The walls behind where the body lay were covered in a modern art collage of blood, skull fragments, and brain.

Jacob was able to piece together what had gone on here as well as any forensic pathologist from TV. The zombie had come into the store when they were trying to close up. Gus blew a hole straight through the thing and it kept on going, Matt had gotten into a struggle with the thing and had gotten bitten before he was able to destroy the brain with the pickaxe. They bound Matt's wounds and he eventually laid down on the peat moss and expired and then reanimated. He must have been trying to get to his feet and Gus had gotten scratched up but was able to put Matt back down with the blast that took off part of Matt's skull. Gus then must have known he was a goner and went into the bathroom and put the shotgun under his chin and pulled the trigger.

Confident that there were no other zombies in the store he told Thomas to come into the store and had Arthur circle around back to the dock, while he began gathering and piling the supplies that they would need. He jumped on the battery powered pallet jack and moved a pile of pressure treated plywood to the bay so that when they opened the door and began loading that would be the first thing in. When Tomas came in Jacob yelled to him to use another pallet jack to move some stuff to block the doors he had just come through. Thomas sprung into action quick enough to make Jacob's old drill instructor happy. They located a portable generator and some other battery powered tools and added them to the pile of supplies.

Jacob gave Thomas the list of things he wanted gathered and he went over to security section with a basket and began gathering cameras and cables along with the rest of the doodads that he wanted to employ. Before long they had more than they would be able to fit into the Suburban, they would have to make two trips. Jacob thought for a moment and then it was obvious what he had to do. He told Thomas to open the steel roll up door and he ran over to Matt's corpse and rifled through his pant pockets to find the keys to his pickup truck that was still in the lot and then ran to the front door and climbed over the obstacles that Thomas had labored to block the door with.

Jacob looked all around and then sprinted to the truck with keys in his left and Magnum in his right. The truck was ideal as it had a contractors frame in the bed. He jumped into the seat and fired it up. Gravel was spit up by the tires as he sped around the back of the store to the loading dock where he backed the vehicle along side of the Suburban. Fortunately the keys to the little forklift were hanging on the wall next to the door in the back which made loading that much quicker. The noise that was made by the dock door and that made by the fork lift were sufficient to make them even more concerned with speed. That much noise might very well attract the attention of any zombies in the area and they wanted to be long gone before any came along in search of them.

Timing is as they say everything. They had completed loading everything and securing the remaining lumber to the roof when they heard the tell tale moans from the west side of the building. Jacob estimated that they had enough time do one last thing, grabbing a pair of bolt cutters he then jumped into the truck and the two vehicles pulled away headed in the direction of the propane. The pickup made the turn first. Just as Arthur was making his turn he glimpsed the first of the zombies in his side view mirror rounding the back of the store. Jacob had already jumped out of the truck and cut the lock on the cage and was tossing as many tanks as he could fit in the limited space of the bed and a couple more into the cab. He then reached behind the seat and grabbed a road flare. He deftly snapped off the cap and struck the end. Bright magenta flame erupted from the end of the flare. He tossed it under the huge tank. He then jumped back into the cab and the two vehicles pulled away, Arthur was on the road and heading back to the house when the sound of the pickup trucks horn caught his attention, it was then that he noticed that Jacob had stopped at the curb cut of the parking lot and was leaning on the horn.

They had never severed the phone connection. Arthur practically screamed to Jacob, "What the hell are you doing Jake.... let's get the fuck out of here!!!" Jacob sounded as cool as could be, "Patience my friend I just want to give them a little heat" he said cryptically. Jacob was watching as a horde of twenty or more of the shambling monsters approached, he aimed and squeezed off two shots from his magnum at the large white Tylenol shaped tank. The tank ruptured and the flare ignited the escaping pressurized gas. The resulting explosion was awe inspiring. The immensity of the fireball obscured any sight of the zombies caught in the emollition.

The truck caught up with the Suburban and the sped back to the compound. On the way Jacob called the house and had them ready to open the gates when they got there. Once the trucks were safe inside the compound and the gate re-secured, he got out of the truck smiling.

Arthur rolled up on Jacob with seething temper apparent in his face and the tremors of barely controlled rage in his hand, "What was that all about?" he yelled into Jacobs face, spittle flying from his lips with each word. Jacob continued smiling. "Come on that was cool, you have to admit... and besides that makes thirty less left to attack us here." Jacob smiled and walked over to the truck and began unloading. Arthur stood there for a moment longer and had to laugh himself, Jacob was right of course and it was cool to see.

Aaron and Thomas were already unloading the Suburban and Jacob laid out his plans. They got to work on the additional fortifications and installing the cameras and motion detecting spotlights. They worked for several hours before breaking for a meal. The hard work was yielding results and they all felt significantly safer. They worked into the night, as the compound lit up like day by the low sodium lights. They then returned to their labors at first light to repeat the process.

The most substantial changes that were made were the sheering of pipes at sharp angles and the cut at four foot lengths these became punji sticks, that were staked into the ground on the close side off a 4 foot deep trench that the boys and Arthur had dug with the assistance of Jacobs little excavator, along the perimeter inside of the barbwire fencing. The excess dirt from the digging made an excellent bulwark that bristled with the pipe punji sticks effectively creating a sheer six foot wall from the bottom of the trench to the top of the earthen works. The erection of stout barricades to the left and right house sealed off the cliff face. Had zombies breached the perimeter before this they could have wandered off the cliffs to tumble into the back yard below which could have created additional problems. The installation of low light cameras provided detailed views from every angle of the fence line and beyond, they would be able to see any zombies long before they go anywhere near the fence. This allowed them to secure the main generator and preserve their fuel supplies.

This trip had been so successful that they discussed additional forays out of the compound to grab supplies from a pharmacy and to the market to load up on canned goods and other provisions with good shelf lives. Amusingly enough Arthur was all for it, apparently the road trip had given him more confidence as he asked Jacob to teach him about shooting and other such things.

50

Laura and Dave were on his boat with Kyle and his family, idling 50 yards off shore as Duncan was making ready to pull away from the dock. Marianne was holding the bow dock line and prepared to toss it to Katie. Kristen was saying her goodbyes to the children that she had been leading around. Kristen herself was fine but many of those children were crying, one little girl in particular, Alison was clutching one of Kristen's old stuffed animals and waving its arm farewell while sobbing uncontrollably. Many of the others were gathered along the quay to say goodbye to their saviors.

Duncan let two blasts from the boats air horns in farewell and Marianne tossed the line to Katie who caught it like a seasoned sailor and deftly coiled and stowed the line. She then took the opportunity to sprawl out on the dingy that was now re-lashed to its cradle on the bow, hoping to improve her tan since the unseasonably warm weather was holding. Summer was still officially still a couple weeks away but it appeared to have set in early.

Liam was below making sure that the last of the gear and provisions were stowed in the appropriate lockers and hatches. He had personally inventoried everything, from the first can of food to the last bullet and shotgun shell. When he was finished he popped his head into Sean's cabin but Sean was preoccupied with his ear buds and MP3 player blaring as he cleaned the nine millimeter pistol Duncan had given to him as a present the night before. Liam turned and headed for the ladder topside and gave Kaitlin a smile at her usual post as he climbed to the cockpit.

"Dunk how long till we get to Dad's place?" he asked of his brother at the wheel.

Duncan glanced at the chart plotter and the navigational computer.

"About a day and half maybe less I am going to use the autopilot overnight... but I would rather be prudent and sail most of the way to conserve our diesel" he replied.

"We have full tanks and I stowed two additional barrels... we have plenty. Wouldn't we make better time under power the whole way?"

Duncan inhaled a deep calming breath and held it for a second before letting it out.

"Liam, Erin is fine and we will be there soon but using the motors uses allot of fuel... fuel that we don't know when or where we will be able to replace..." he paused for effect and to emphasize his point "We need to keep as much fuel in reserve so that we have it if and when we need it."

Liam flushed with embarrassment, he realized what he was sounding like. "You got a point there bro... can I pop a Corona for you?... sorry no lime though." Duncan smiled and that was all Liam needed to see he disappeared and a second later the unmistakable sounds of beer bottles being popped open was heard. He climbed back into the cockpit and handed his brother his beer.

 "These are finite too but we can only risk drinking them when things are calm so cheers"

 Liam clinked his off his brothers beer and took a deep swig punctuated be a rewarding burp. "Better out than in I always say" said Liam in his best Shrek voice. "So how about teaching me to sail this ship?" he asked.

 "Boat" corrected Duncan habitually. "It may be big but not big enough to be called a ship" he concluded. He then started showing Liam how the various electronics and controls worked.

Most of the fires had burned out and the wind had carried away most of the smoke as the sailed up river along the West side. They had no news about what went on in New Jersey, they didn't have anyone there that they were close to but the assumed it was much the same over there.

They passed the Chelsea Piers and were continuing North, Duncan pointed out one of the buildings he used to work in when they passed thirty-first street. The building was tall enough to be seen from the water as they cruised by. Duncan wondered if any of his co-workers were still alive. There might very well be one of his fellow engineers up on that very rooftop in the chiller plant. He gave a thought to calling the number than reconsidered, if someone answered he would feel bad for not being able to help and if no answered well...

The sky showed signs that rain was coming. Sean came topside to help put the bimini top in place and to zip on the sides enclosing the cockpit with canvas walls that would keep out most of the weather. On Dave's boat similar activities were taking place. The clouds rolled in swiftly and the rain followed fast, Justas they were passing the U.S.S Intrepid floating museum the deluge began. Duncan toggled the switches to furl the Jib and Main sails, the motors hummed as they did as they were designed to do. The rain drops came down in a sheet of water pounding at the deck flowing along in a torrent.

Visibility lessened significantly, Duncan turned on the auto pilot, allowing the boat's radar and sonar systems to take control so that if there were anything floating on the water's surface or just below the boat would steer around it and then correct course and resume heading. Duncan was awed by this technology that he had at his command. He had learned to sail on a smaller bare boned boat that you had to do everything by hand. On that boat he would have had to drop a sea anchor and ride out the storm. This boat was able to keep on going.

Over the VHF Duncan kept Dave appraised of their heading and radar contacts. The pure fact of having another voice over the air was comforting to each of them. Duncan was giving thought to adding another antenna and radio to his boat just so that he could scan other channels for chatter while still keeping communication open on the first, but that would depend upon making another foray onto land, and he wasn't very keen to risk his neck on something so trivial. If the opportunity presented itself while they were engaged in another venture than sure, but only if they were already on land for other things.

The squall was whipping up white caps on the swells, the chop was unusual for this area of the river. Even the sea birds opted to ride out the storm rather than to try and fly in the high gusty winds, which according to Duncan's instruments were gusting around thirty knots. The boats size and displacement made it far more pleasant on board the Persistence than the ride on Dave's fishing boat. The complaints coming over the radio were amusing to say the least. The squall blew itself out after an hour or so but the skies still had that dark steel grey look that hinted at additional confrontations with the weather.

The George Washington Bridge loomed in the distance. The immense steel structure of the suspension bridge was a testimony to man's ability to assert dominion over his environment. At a length of over 4700 feet with the longest span being over 3500 feet it crosses the river joining Manhattan with New Jersey. Millions upon millions of vehicles have crossed this bridge in its history, sadly unless mankind survived this apocalypse it will deteriorate and collapse without the necessary maintenance regiment.

As the boats drew closer to the bridge there appeared to be some activity on the upper deck of the span. Duncan grabbed his binoculars to get a better look and almost immediately wished that he hadn't. A caravan of vehicles had tried to make an escape using the bad weather as cover, the lead vehicle was a huge orange public works truck and it was pushing the abandoned vehicles out of its way clearing the way for the followers. The span was teeming with the walking dead, even with the 40 x magnification of the binoculars Duncan was unable to make out much detail, of which he was thankful. He was unable to see what had stopped the trucks forward progress, it could have been any number of things, it could have become high centered or could have suffered a catastrophic failure in one of the mechanical systems such as the drive train or suspension. It didn't matter, speculation wouldn't save those poor bastards trapped on the bridge. The cars in the back of the convoy tried to reverse their way out but enough of the zombies were behind them effectively cutting off their escape.

Even from this distance the cumulative sound of the moans from the zombies could clearly be heard along with the chatter of small arms fire as the beleaguered convoy tried to fight off the gnashing teeth of their inevitable doom. Another sound was added to the mix. The sound of a pair of helicopters lifting off from Fort Lee on the Jersey side of the bridge as they took to the air. That sound must have lifted the flagging spirits of those in the convoy, for surely rescue was at hand and they would be delivered from the jaws and claws of the zombie plague.

Two Apache helicopters raced along side of the bridge perhaps twenty feet above the height of the deck. The 'birds' slowed to hover even with the convoy. The nose of the lead Apache spewed fire as the minigun unleashed a torrent of bullets that ripped into the crowd of undead and vehicles, raking from left to right. The Bullets continued and then began to rip into the vehicles of the convoy as well. Duncan could hardly believe what he was seeing. The second helicopter let loose with several smallish rockets that raced the short distance and exploded with terrible force and fire. Duncan watched in horror as people in the convoy fled their vehicles in an attempt to escape the bullets, many directly into the reaching arms of zombies. Others were chased by even more zombies, they climbed the barricades and jumped off of the bridge to the waters below. Never mind that on a fall from that height the human body would impact with the water much the same as it would on concrete. The falling bodies were followed by countless mindless zombies who were not about to let food get away.

No one witness to the slaughter could have realized that the pilots were being merciful. They tried to spare their victims the fate of being eaten alive and worse to return as a mindless creature with an insatiable hunger for the flesh of the living.

Duncan and Dave circled on the water down river from the bridge. They waited for the aircraft to return to their base, and for the bodies' human and zombie alike to stop falling from the skies before they resumed their course. They debated calling on the radio informing them of their position and their intension of continuing up river to their destination, after all the military response that they had just witnessed had to have been necessary of justified in some way, but they wouldn't chance it right now.

Duncan asked Kaitlin to see if there was something she could find that would explain why they shot up the bridge like they did. He felt that sooner or later they would need the help of the military or some other Government entity and to have a clear understanding of their current orders would be necessary when that time came.

They crossed the bridge line with as much speed as Duncan's boat was capable of, which was considerable for a sailing vessel although nowhere near the speed to which Dave's boat could travel. They kept the sails furled and remained under power for the rest of the day and through the night. This held two benefits, the first being that the autopilot could be re-engaged and anyone could stand watch and man the helm while the boat did the work, and second it would allow Duncan a chance to get some rest and sort out what to do next. What Duncan had seen haunted him, visions of the helicopters spewing death disturbed him greatly.

In his cabin Duncan took out his cell and called his father to update him on their current position and condition as well as to work through his demons. If there were anyone alive who could help sort through the turmoil inside of him it was his father Jacob.

Jacob answered on the second ring. He was overjoyed to hear from his sons and to learn that they would be united in less than a day, god willing. Duncan caught his father up on all of the 'adventures' that they had had. Jacob listened intently, he would have left those others to fend for themselves but he didn't mention that to his son. His sons held a level of humanity that he had lost decades earlier in Korea, and he felt that that very humanity was in short supply these days and would be needed in abundance when it came time to rebuild the world. Duncan gave him the inventory of supplies that they were bringing with them. much of this information Jacob already had but he understood his son's need to just talk, and sometimes talking about ordinary things helped calm the spirit that suffered disquiet from witnessing horrific events.

Jacob had seen things in his earlier years, but what his sons had just gone through was even worse by his reckoning. He was proud of the men he had raised, the fact that they were all alive and that their families were safe, showed just how competent that they were. He was confident that when they arrived, they would all be able to weather any adversity that came their way. When Duncan sounded more like his confident self, Jacob suggested that he pass off the phone to Liam so that he could speak with his wife.

Duncan found Liam in the saloon watching Pirates of the Caribbean on the DVD. He handed him the phone and retreated back into his cabin to crash. Katie popped her head into let him know that dinner would be in about an hour and to ask if he wanted her to wake him for it. He said he would rather sleep through and grab leftovers when he woke. She smiled and closed the door to let him get the rest that he so badly needed.

51

Carrie wakes from slumber to a soft knocking on the door to her quarters. Whipping the sleep from her eyes, she grabs a light cotton robe from the back of her chair and crosses the floor to answer the door. She looks at the clock and through somewhat blurry eyes she notes the time as being eight o'clock although in truth she doesn't know if that is AM or PM.

"Who is it?" she asks, the question seeming to come from a time when the world was normal and the dead didn't walk let alone try to eat the living. "Mrs. Sixkiller... my name is Eric Ruberg can I come in?" said the voice from outside.

"Just a minute" she said as she surveyed the quarters she shared with her husband, to be sure she wouldn't be embarrassed by a mess. Satisfied that it was relatively in order, she opened the door to find a man in army officer's uniform carrying a black satchel with a sad look in his eyes. He had Captains bars on his shoulder epaulets, his uniforms lapel had the US and directly beneath that on the lower lapel was the Latin cross. The insignia of the chaplain's corps. Of the army. Carrie didn't notice the cross or was oblivious to what this had meant.

"Come in please" as she stepped aside for the man to enter "Can I offer you a cup of coffee?" She turned from the door to the coffee pot that was still warming two thirds of a pot. She crossed the eight steps to the pot and poured two cups not waiting for a reply.

The Chaplin stood in the doorway indecisive, then followed her inside and took the offered cup. "Mrs. Sixkiller I would like to talk with you about..."

"Call me Carrie please" she interrupted. "I am here to talk to you about your sons."

Her coffee cup shattered on the ceramic tiles of the floor, the burning liquid scalded her bare feet yet she seemed not to notice the pain, as she realized what he was and why he was here. The Chaplin moved to offer her his support, he was concerned that she may swoon and collapse. She reeled away from his hands as if he were a leper.

She stumbled away and into a chair, her hands covering her mouth, tears flowing freely down her cheeks in tiny rivulets. The Chaplin, like many others before him who had answered their faiths calling was prepared for her reaction. It was the part of their vocation that they all loathed to do, to inform the next of kin. He had the reverent demeanor and soft spokeness that one would expect. He let the shock and grief run their initial course.

"Wait... you said sons... plural... not son..."a howl of inconsolable grief and pain erupted from the petite woman. Barely distinguishable from the sobs came the words, "not both of them God please" she pleaded with the Lord although it was too late even if it would have helped.

The Chaplin spoke words of comfort and the promise of life everlasting in the company of the Lord. Carrie heard none of it as she sank into the despair. Her sobs abated after a time and the Chaplin continued to minister in her hour of need. He opened the satchel and removed a letter from their company commander. He offered her the letter, she refused to take it insisting that he read it to her. He obliged her.

"Keith and Christopher were a credit to all, and it is with my profound sadness that I write this letter. In the short time that I knew these two men I was proud to serve with them. They each had spoken often about you and your husband often saying how glad they were that you had finally found someone and were able to take time out for yourself and not have to mother them at your own expense any longer."

The Chaplin looked up at her before he continued so as to monitor the effect the letter was having upon her ravaged spirit.

Rise Fall Rise Again: A New York Zombie Encounter

"When our unit was activated we were called to secure a power plant and assist with its continued maintenance and operation, with the nation's power grids being as fragile as they are and with circumstances as desperate as they are it was and continues to be an important job. We arrived on station and found conditions that were relatively easy to secure. There were a few of the infected in the area but we learned how to deal with them pretty quickly and received more definitive orders as command learned more about them. On the third day of our assignment the first wave arrived, we had no idea how tough an assignment this was to be. But we held and a great deal of that was directly because of your sons. They were instrumental in the defense of the facility. The next wave occurred within hours of the first. Your sons demonstrated all that is truly heroic as they fought and protected men who would have otherwise have fallen, even when their own safety was in jeopardy. Ma'm I need to stress just how great of heroes you sons were. The next wave lasted for longer than twenty-four hours, none of us was able to get any rest we were fighting constantly but they helped keep moral and all of alive saying how their mother could fight off these things with only a wooden spoon, and then they told stories about how you tanned their hides with that same spoon and that they figured that would be an effective weapon against these things. Ma'm those stories even if they were embellished kept us alive." Again the Chaplin paused in his reading, he noticed the hint of a smile after he read that last part. He hoped that she was indeed receiving some comfort from these written words. " There is no gentle way to tell you how they fell, all I can do is relate to you what happened and how many of the rest of us owe them our lives, and to promise that I will try to live the remainder of my days in tribute to them. It was the seventh day and still no rest, ammunition was running low, we were expecting resupply anytime... the dead were piling high the piles of the dead were almost to the top of the fence line, Keith proposed toppling the piles outward with poles through the fence, it yielded benefits but unfortunately it was too late as a number of the things toppled over into the compound. While we were fighting to put those down a wall of bodies fell against the fence and broke it down.

Keith and Christopher were covering the retreat. Firing and then leapfrogging, with excellent discipline. I have seen veteran soldiers who have not kept their cool as well. Keith went down first when his ankle was grabbed by one of the creatures that was crawling. Christopher heard his brothers cry and returned to help him, even though he knew it was too late. They died together, Ma'm I am sorry they fell and if I could change places with them I would. The only words of solace I can offer to you is that I made sure that they wouldn't return from the dead personally. You have my deepest sympathy for their and your sacrifice.

Sincerely, Major Jeffery Clayton US army."

The Chaplin folded the letter and put it back into its envelope, and sat in silence watching the grieving mother as she processed the information that told her how she lost both of her sons.

Her tears continued to fall but she was no longer racked with sobs. She made an effort to compose herself, it was halfway successful but the Chaplin took it as a good sign. He again offered comforting words that seemed to have a benign effect. He then stood and offered the sincere condolences and the gratitude of the US Army for her sacrifice and took his leave as he had several other calls to make while here at the CDC. Carrie stood and walked him to the door. When he offered her his hand she again rebuffed his touch but with all the strength she had she thanked him for his time and closed the door.

Six hours and twenty three minutes later maintenance was called about a flood of water coming from under the door to the Sixkiller's quarters. The door was locked and no one answered the knock. The mechanic produced his key ring and used his master key to unlock the door.

The water was coming from a broken sprinkler head. The head had broken when the rod that was holding the pipe let go due to the added weight of Carrie Sixkiller's body weight suspended by a makeshift noose that was made from some of the computer wire her husband had left in their room. When the pipe sagged the wire slid along the length and broke off the head. A medic was immediately called for but all attempts at resuscitation were fruitless.

Her laptop lay open the table on the other side of the room. On its screen was a letter to her husband saying good bye, next to the computer was the letter about her sons. Her note to her husband closed by saying she was joining her sons and that someday god willing they would all be reunited in heaven.

52

Duncan woke somewhat refreshed, he stepped into the head in his cabin and took a moment to splash some cold water on his face. As he looked at himself in the mirror, to his own eyes he seemed to have aged a decade since the dead began rising. He was in dire need of a shave, "Maybe I'll just grow out the beard" he said aloud even though nobody was around to hear it. After draining his bladder he stepped three back into his cabin and donned clean clothes and was prepared to face whatever cataclysms the day was to bring.

He stepped into the saloon and saw that Katie was snuggled up on the couch with a blanket drawn up around her shoulders and over at the comm. station Kaitlyn was grinding her teeth while she slept. The lights were dimmed but offered enough illumination for him to negotiate his way through without fear of barking his shins. He stopped into the galley to make a leftover sandwich and snatched a can of diet coke before he headed to the cockpit.

Sean was on watch, and from the look of his bleary eyes he was due to be relieved soon. "Hey son... how are you doing?" he asked startling his son.

 Sean straightened and snapped to. "I wasn't sleeping ... see look I just made an entry into the log."

Duncan smiled, "relax Sean I know... who is due to relieve you?"

 His smile and calm demeanor defused Sean's defensiveness. "Mom was supposed to relieve me an hour and a half ago but I figured I'd let her sleep a little longer, Kristen was having night terrors and she was up with her for a few hours."

Duncan's smile broadened, he was proud of his children. Sean's consideration regarding his mothers need for sleep was just one in a long list of things that made his pride swell.

"Why don't you get some rack time I will take over from here." He took a look at the chart plotter and was amazed to see that they were within two hours of his father's place.

He took a bite of his sandwich and cracked open his soda. He hadn't realized just how hungry he was as he devoured the rest of his makeshift meal. He picked up the VHF handset and called over to Dave's boat.

His nephew Kevin responded. "Mornin' Uncle Dunk, what's new and exciting?"

Duncan chuckled at his nephew's indefatigable mirth. "Well we are about two hours out from Grandpas place... is your dad rested... who had last watch over there for you guys?"

"Mom was I relieved her almost two hours ago Dad slept through the night... want me to wake him?" Kevin asked.

"Yeah ask him if he would come aboard?"

A couple of minutes later Kevin's voice came back over the air waves, " He said to give him a couple of minutes then I'll pull alongside for him to step over" Duncan said that would be fine.

Duncan popped into the galley and put up a pot of coffee and then knocked on Liam's and Sean's door, Sean answered quickly as he was just about to crawl into the bunk.

"Dad what's up?" Duncan asked him to wake Liam and have him meet him in the cockpit. Sean did as he was asked while Duncan returned to the helm.

Kevin pulled alongside and matched speed, Kyle tossed a line over to Duncan who was waiting to catch it. Duncan snagged it while Kyle stepped aboard and over the life line. Duncan Tossed the line back into

Dave's boat. Kyle looked marginally better than Duncan, but Liam looked the worst of the three brothers, his hairline seemed to be retreating before their very eyes. Kyle couldn't help himself he had to give his 'lil bro' some shit over that. They all shared a laugh although Limas was a little forced.

"So what's the big deal that you got us up at the crack of ass Dunk?" Liam asked petulantly. The smell of the brewing coffee wafted up from below.

"Liam bring up coffee for all of us make mine with a sweet n low and a dash of nonfat, Kyle how do you take it?"

"Regular " said Kyle.

They made themselves comfortable while Liam retrieved the nectar of the Gods. The auto pilot was still engaged so Duncan sat where he could keep an eye on the screens and be able to respond quickly if needed, while Kyle lounged on one of the benches leaving the third bench for Liam.

Liam joined his brothers in the cockpit and they each were enjoying that first sip of coffee in the pre-dawn twilight. The Sun would breach the horizon in 15 minutes and with each passing second the sky grew brighter. Duncan savored his drink for another moment before he began.

"Guys, up until now we have been in pure survival mode, hell I wasn't completely sure we would make it this far or what we would find if we did..." He left that statement hanging in the air with a dramatic pause, "We will be at Dad's place in just about two hours. So now we have got to think about what comes next. Dad has had things pretty well in hand so we should be safe enough to actually think about living not just surviving. We have really been pretty lucky so far, but like Dad says we make our own luck. So what next? Kyle you have any ideas?"

Kyle continued sipping his coffee as he thought about the question. "Well the first thing we have to consider is that we have no idea how long we will be able to enjoy the luxuries of phone service, clean flowing water and such. So we had better get a handle on those sorts of things. We are going to have to do some hunting of game too because trips to the grocery store are I am sad to say a thing of the past or at least will be."

Kyle had just voiced exactly what Duncan was thinking. The gravity of his words were sobering none the less.

"Remember when the movie Red Dawn came out and we used to debate the scenario?... well we had come up with some pretty good ideas back then...granted this isn't exactly the same thing but it is a close enough parable that we can and should follow allot of those ideas" said Duncan.

Liam added a couple of thoughts to the growing equation, "Well we should think about securing as much fuel and other supplies as we can get our hands on. We should also try and find reusable weapons and fishing gear. I am not sure what Dad has on hand but we should make that a priority because there are bound to be other groups of survivors who are thinking the same things, so many of the stores and such are liable to be picked clean already."

"Good then we are all on the same page. Liam what were you thinking as far as fuel goes?" asked Duncan.

"Well the first thought that came to mind was hot-wiring a fuel truck and just driving it to Dad's place. His emergency generator runs on the same fuel oil as his furnace so that seems like the first place to start. Come to think of it... in Mad Max and other similar films, gasoline is another thing that will be in short supply so maybe we grab one of those trucks too. I figure most people are going to try and grab whatever they can from the gas stations we should hit the suppliers" said Liam.

It was a bold and straight forward idea, Duncan was amazed that he hadn't thought of it too. Kyle added his two cents, "While we still have the net we should make sure that we download how to stuff, like bread baking, churning butter, and that sort of crap. I mean look I can hunt and dress a deer, but I don't know squat about how to make flour or yeast... but we should learn how."

"This is great stuff guys let me go down and wake Katie and Kaitlyn so we can get a list going and Kaitlyn can start researching what we need her to research. After we are done Kyle you can go back and get Pam and your boys up to speed."

Duncan got up and almost flew through the companion way and returned a few minutes later with Kaitlyn. "Katie will join us in a couple" Duncan grabbed a wax pencil and some plastic sheets from his chart drawer to make notes.

 Paper doesn't hold up as well on boats. Kaitlyn took the implements and started making notes on all the things Kyle suggested she research.

A few minutes later Katie joined them and added a few other ideas to the growing list, like homeopathic remedies for common ailments, she also suggested that Erin should make a list of things that they would need since she had the medical background, and she should start teaching what she knows to the others.

"In fact we should all cross train, we all have different skill sets so it only makes sense" She then turned to Kaitlyn, "Kaitlyn honey, also see if you can find any other survivor pockets in the neighboring areas."

 She turned back to the men "If there are other communities and groups who are out there maybe we can barter for things and services that we need and help each other out."

The conversation and planning session continued and before Duncan knew it they were rounding the final bend in the river, they were fifteen minutes out. Duncan called his father on the phone and told him where they were. Kyle went back to the other boat to get everyone over there up and ready. It was a flurry of activity on both boats. Everyone was anxious to get there and to get solid land under their feet again.

Jacob was down at the dock waiting for them when they arrived. Liam launched himself onto the dock before the boat had even pulled within the last four feet, he rushed up the long stairway like a man possessed, he needed to have his wife in his arms, and everything else was secondary.

Jacob assisted tying up the vessels and they began unloading the supplies straight away. Kristen and Kaitlyn carried up a couple of the smaller bags and went to see 'Nana'. Arthur, Aaron and Thomas came down and were introduced around by Jacob. They all pitched in and got most of the gear and supplies up to the top in short order.

Brunch was laid out on the table by the time the last of the supplies were brought in and everyone sat down for the meal, they would worry about settling in after. The fare was nothing out of the ordinary but it was the best meal any of them could ever remember having. Jacob recalled a saying that was common among the Special Forces that seemed appropriate, "Life has a flavor that the protected will never know." They all agreed with that sentiment.

While the women cleared the table and set about cleaning up after the meal the men adjourned first to the main living room and then on a tour of the house and compound. Jacob showed them his 'command center' with all of the cameras and monitors. He then briefed them upon the security measures he had taken. They toured the out buildings. With nineteen people and three dogs here now it was going to be cramped to say the least, but they would make do.

Jacob mentioned his idea of digging escape tunnels from inside of the out buildings to the main house. Kyle and Duncan brought up the conversation that they all had on the boat that morning and the plans

that they entailed. Jacob had very little to add, almost all of the bases had been covered. "When do you want to get started? What you guys are suggesting will take several days, and the logistics of pulling it all off are difficult to put it mildly"

Kyle who ordinarily would have assumed the mantel of second in command deferred to Duncan who had been the defacto leader throughout the crisis.

"Well Dunk? What do you think?" Duncan was not all that comfortable with his elevated position in the family hierarchy said, "Well we are going to have to work in teams, we have limited transportation... we have what Liam and Erin's Cherokee, we have your Caddie Dad, that pick up and Arthur... your Suburban right? Dave ... how much gas is left in those drums on your boat?"

"About a hundred gallons or so courtesy of the US Coast Guard" said Dave who was smiling the whole time. Duncan took in the information. "Let's go back inside to your office Dad and look at some maps of the area and figure out where we can steal fuel and gas and whatever other supplies we can get our hands on and then we will figure out who will go on which missions." With that said they all returned to the house.

53

It was decided that the first excursion was going to be two teams of three men hitting two different targets. The first team would consist of Liam, Dave and Kevin. They would be taking the pickup truck and heading over to the Ciotti Brothers Petroleum Wholesalers, about forty-five miles away in the hopes of liberating a tanker truck of gasoline. They opted for gas over fuel oil first because Jacobs's tank at the compound was nearly full so the gas was a higher priority. The second team would consist of Duncan, Patrick and Sean, who would take the Suburban and hit the strip mall 8 miles away where they knew a pharmacy, and a hunting supply were located.

Duncan had some reservations about bringing Sean on this trip. After all, what kind of a father willingly puts his teenage son in harm's way if he has a choice. It was only after Jacob took Duncan aside and explained that Sean was no longer a boy and that if he were not treated as a man, he may question his own value. Which could have two equally bad results, the first being that his confidence be shattered or second he finds away to put himself at even greater risk to prove he is a man and of value. Duncan had to admire his father's wisdom; he could not afford to make mistakes like he almost had.

Both teams would be carrying an arsenal of weapons that would keep them relatively safe, that is unless they came upon hordes of fifty or more zombies, and if there were that many, they would just abandon their quests and high-tail it out of the zone.

Liam grabbed some hand tools from his father's tool box, tools that he would use to break into and then hotwire the tanker, if they located one. These he put into a knapsack along with a few extra magazines for the assault rifle and pistols. Kevin's job was look out / gunner. He was a crack shot and had training on the weapon's platform in the Coast Guard. Dave had driven trucks before and would if the opportunity presented itself learn a little about grand theft auto from Liam while he hot-wired the truck.

They mounted up and were ready to leave, Jacob and the others opened the gates and the pickup took off down the road. They had punched the address into the GPS, thanking God that the technology was still viable and were on their way.

Erin gave Duncan a list of things that were color coded in priority. He looked the list over to familiarize himself with it so that it would take less time in the store when Erin added one more thing if they could find it. She wanted a PDR (Physician's Desk Reference) granted most of the information contained was available online but as a hardcopy backup it would come in handy. They too were ready to go but opted to wait an hour or so since their target was local. Sean busied himself adjusting the tactical holster for his pistol. The soldier whom it had been taken from had considerably more girth than did Sean. After he had gotten it just to his liking, he practiced quick drawing. Jacob shook his head mildly amused at the reminder that he was still a teenager. Now it was their turn to leave. They drove off hoping that they would have a successful trip. Success in this case was measured by getting what they were after and not running into any walking corpses.

Sean showed some outward bravado that was clearly overcompensation for his nervousness. Patrick shared some of his military stories with him to keep his mind off of things. The strip mall was deserted, which they took as a good sign. They pulled into the communal lot and looked around to be on the safe side before they got out of the truck and left the keys in the ignition with the doors left open. The Pharmacy was the bigger priority so that was where they went first.

The sign said 'Durant Chemists', and generally it looked out of place for a strip mall. It harkened back to the old school drug store that had an ice-cream parlor counter and comic book racks. The lights were off and the doors were locked, just as Duncan expected them to be, but here in rural New York, there were no security gates. Duncan employed the wrecking bar he had brought with him to force the door. It looked a lot easier on TV than in actual practice but after a few noisy minutes, they were able to break in. They heard the beeping of an alarm system counting down and regretted not having thought about that first. They miscalculated. They were closer to urbanites than anything else and had just assumed that the country bumpkins didn't use alarms.

The Siren that began to blare was deafening. Duncan and Patrick's assault rifles came up immediately as they scanned for the source of the noise. Patrick spotted it first and let loose a three-round burst that restored the quiet. The Damage was already done, if there were any zombies in the area, the dinner bell was already wrung. They raced into the store and headed for the counter behind which the pharmacist plied his trade. Sean grabbed a basket and went up and down the aisles filling it with bandages, peroxide, alcohol, and other assorted things... all the while keeping an eye out on the door.

"Sean if you see any 'Vic's Vapo Rub' grab all that you find" Shouted Duncan to his son. Pat vaulted the counter and began filling trash bags with boxes of pills, and other medications. He moved with such speed and efficiency that he was back out from behind in under five minutes.

Duncan was loading up on ace bandages and compression braces, and he even found some hinged knee braces. This turned into a smash and grab. They were out of the Pharmacy in less than ten minutes from start to finish and tossing their booty into the Suburban. So far, there were no signs of any zombies in the immediate vicinity but that could change in a moment. His brain said to get out of the area now, but his gut told him they should have enough time to at least check out the doors of the sporting goods store. He vacillated for perhaps a second and then decided to trust his guts.

They drove the truck up to the doors of the sporting goods store hooked a tow chain around the bar on the door and the other end to the bumper, and with a loud squeal followed by a bang the door was torn open and half out from the frame. Duncan attended to the chain while Pat and Sean tore ass into the store. Seconds later they were emerging with arms full of fishing rods and full tackle boxes. They tossed them into the truck and went back in Duncan was keeping watch and more importantly listening for the revealing moans of the creeping dead.

Patrick found the archery section and called Sean to help out. From outside Duncan heard the smashing of the glass as his son and nephew committed their larceny. Duncan heard moans in the distance; he yelled at the boys, " We are going to have company soon so hurry the fuck up Damn it!!!" No sooner had he finished yelling did Sean wheel out a shopping cart overflowing with boxes of shotgun shells and ammo in every caliber and disappeared back inside in a flash. "Sean get back here now I mean it!!! Pat where the hell are you?" Pat came careening around the aisle knocking over a Coleman display. His cart was laden with plastic feathered shafts in boxes a couple of crossbows piled on top of those and three compound bows that stuck out at odd angles. "Sorry Uncle Dunk.... there was a cable that hung me up for a few." Pat started tossing the gear into the truck from the carts.

The moans were closer now, and there was a lot of them. Duncan saw the first group of them stagger around the corner of the building not twenty-five feet away. He took aim and started firing. His opening volley wasn't pretty, but his shots had the desired effect. He burned through the magazine in record speed. He quickly swapped mags and changed the fire selector to three-round burst. Pat too joined the fray. "SEAN WHERE THE F.." he began to yell when a shotgun blast erupted from inside the store. Duncan jumped at the sound and turned to run in and investigate his paternal instincts nearly overriding. A second and third blast followed. "Pat you got this?" Pat gave a nod and dropped three more of the creatures. Duncan turned and entered the store.

54

".... in a quarter mile make a right turn onto Poplar Way your destination will be on the right" said the mechanical voice of the GPS to Dave as they drove the last little bit to the Gas Depot. Liam had the bolt cutters in his hand in case the place had a chain link gate that was locked.

They had passed a group of ten or twelve about five miles back that gave them about an hour and twenty minutes to do their thing and get out of there before that group caught up with them Liam estimated. He guessed the things traveled a mile in twenty minutes, so he figured fifteen minutes into his calculation to be on the safe side.

"You have reached your destination" said the GPS as the neared the fence surrounding the large compound. A number of enormous holding tanks were situated in the center of the compound. Offices were in a building to the left of the gate that had a small staff parking lot that was devoid of any cars, behind the building was the parking field for the delivery trucks and the pumping station where the tanker's various chambers are filled up with whatever grade gasoline that is desired. As it turns out the Ciotti Brothers also deliver home heating oil as well, so they decided to try and grab two trucks rather than one for expedience sake, they had to concede that this wasn't the discrete route, rather it was bold but if successful would be worth it, however it did pose a far greater risk.

Dave pulled the pick up right up to the fence, Kevin and Liam were out in a flash. Kevin held the AR at the ready, his eyes scanning for any signs of trouble, the smell of the air was overwhelmed by the scent of oil and industry. Liam made short work of the gate lock with liberal use of force and the bolt cutters, the ruined lock dropped to the earth with a metallic thud. Looking left and then right, he rolled the gate back on its rack wide enough to allow two trucks to pass through its opening with room to spare. Dave wasted no time and pulled in slow enough for Kevin and

Liam to climb into the bed of the pickup and drove around the building to their goal.

Kevin sought an elevated position from which he could keep look out, the closest of the tanks had an enclosed ladder that went to the top. Slinging the rifle he started climbing, up and up he went. Heights had never bothered him growing up, and it wasn't the height as it were, that was bothering him now. It was the fact that once up top he had nowhere else to go. If the dead massed around the tank he would be stranded. The position did offer the benefit of only having one way to access and the zombies lacked the coordination to negotiate the climb. He figured if all went to hell, Liam and Dave might be able to draw them off and then come back for him.

They had with them three of the walkie talkies that Jacob had liberated from the hardware store. Jacob had figured that there may come a time when cell service was less reliable so he had grabbed several sets of rechargeable radios that could scan over one hundred frequencies. These radios had the benefit of being weather proof and came with an ear piece with boom mic that would serve well in tactical situations such as this. The small units had a relatively impressive range, up to five miles when used in unobstructed environments although the range was greatly reduced in urban areas or when used inside of buildings.

Liam and Dave were quickly able to figure out which type of tanker was which. They had the first truck open and were working on the ignition when they heard Kevin's voice on the radio. "We have a few slow walkers on the north side of the fence, and they don't seem to know that we are here." They were near the south side, but it was good to know where the threats were and it was comforting to know that Kevin had eyes on the entire area.

They quickened their pace, the ignition system on the tanker proved to be easy to bypass, so they opted to get the second tanker prepped before they started the vehicle and alerted they area to their presence with the loud rumble of diesel engines rumbling to life.

They found the fuel oil truck all ready full and waiting for delivery, so they went back to the gas tanker to check the gauges. To their disappointment that one needed to be filled. It took them 1five tense minutes to figure out the pumping station equipment and how to get the gasoline flowing. They moved the truck into position and connected the hoses. They opened the top hatches to prevent vapor lock, which was probably un-necessary but why take chances. The high volume hoses filled each chamber with high test gasoline at a surprisingly swift rate. Of the four chambers they had the first two filled to the brim and were part way through the filling of the third when they heard the shouting of Kevin through their ear pieces.

"We've got company coming our way guys so hurry up!" If his yelling hadn't caught their attention the report of his AR sure did when they heard several bursts of automatic fire rip from the top of the tank nearest them.

The pumping station's equipment was making a terrible amount of noise, so much so that Liam and Dave were oblivious to the moans of the zombies that were closing on their exposed position. "Uncle Liam, on your left, coming around the building... six no seven of them!" shouted his nephew punctuated by another burst of gunfire.

55

Sean was looking down the length of a Mossberg and pumping another round into the chamber. Two zombies were on the floor and four more were trying to clamber over their fallen brethren from the back. Duncan was not in a position where he could safely fire passed his son so he ran towards him to gain a better vantage. Sean's twelve gauge belched fire and led at the additional threats dropping another and another after that. Duncan let his bursts loose now that he was able to shoot and the pile of bodies grew blocking the door.

Sean turned and shoving the cart full of rifles and shotguns in front of him raced for the truck. Pat was dropping them fast but more were coming. They tossed the guns in as fast as they could and then Duncan jumped behind the wheel. The zombies were moving faster than seemed normal and with far more dexterity than Duncan had previously seen. Finally the doors shut, they were all inside. Pat opened the window to keep firing as Duncan peeled away.

There was a group of perhaps thirty loosely assembled and walking towards the truck as it barreled at them. Duncan was confident that the sturdy truck would plow right through the things and not suffer anything more than a few new dents and the need of a washing. Pat could see what his Uncle had in mind so he put his window up quickly. The bodies were obliterated by the massive vehicle. The hood had head shaped dents as the force of the truck impacting on the bodies bending them, the heads bouncing off of the hood in a staccato beat, and then they were through and picking up speed.

Several tense seconds passed with not a word or sound coming from any of them. Finally Duncan said over his shoulder to his son, "Where did the ones in the store come from? Didn't you guys check the store first?" His tone was a tad bit on the harsh side, even he realized that from what his own ears told him. A glance in the mirror confirmed it for him as he saw his son go crimson and look at his feet.

"We took a cursatory look and didn't see or hear anything?" said Pat in defense of his younger cousin. If anyone was to blame it was him as far as he was concerned. He was the one with the tactical experience not his cousin who was still in High school.

Duncan was berating himself internally for not having aborted the sporting goods store all together. Sean raised his head and looked directly into his father's eyes via the mirror and said, "Just when you guys started shooting outside that bunch came through the back door which had been closed. True we didn't check to be sure it was locked, we just assumed it was since the front door was, but we were in a hurry" These were words spoken from a man, not the excuses of a kid. He owned up to his minor error and would learn from it but he was not going to take chastisement when it was not warranted.

Duncan told his son, "Look I would have likely made that same mistake, but when the chips were down you kept your head and did some fine shooting. I am proud of you son. But we will not tell Mom about it right?" The boys in unison replied, "Right!" ten minutes later they were pulling into the compound with the supplies in tow.

56

Liam heard the impact of bullets close by. Dave knew what was happening and turned off the pump and ran to secure the valves and free the truck. They were just about out of time. Liam drew his pistol and squeezed off two rounds into the face of a zombie that had gotten within 7 feet of him. Time seemed to stand still as he saw the furious impact of the nine mm bullets and watched as the bullets transferred their energy to the brain case. In the slowed time he saw with clarity as the head expanded like a balloon inflating, threatening to burst as it must. The thin scalp was stretched beyond its limit, and when it let loose an eruption of gore spread out behind the twice dead creature, time returned to normal.

This group was not the same one that they had seen earlier on their way here, these were locals. Some of them were wearing the oily coveralls that one who worked in the fuel delivery industry would be expected to wear. The corporate logo of the Ciotti Brothers was clearly evident on the back of the zombie Liam had just dispatched. The shuffle of zombie feet stirred dust up from the dirt roadway. Liam backed away from the approaching monsters while sending leaden projectiles in their direction. Five pulls of the trigger resulted in another zombie crumbling to the ground at the feet of its friends. His heal came into contact with the wall of the tank, he could retreat no further, he steadied his grip on his pistol and took careful aim and dropped the next three of the things with four well placed shots. He chanced a look around to the left and right, his heart fell as he took in nine more of the things four on the left and five on the right. Pivoting a little to favor the right he continued to squeeze the trigger. He felt the gun kick three times before the slide locked back due to an empty magazine.

He silently cursed himself for not counting his shots, this mistake nearly cost him his life, were it not for the intervention of his nephew from upon high. The big Diesel rumbled to life and the truck began to move. Liam's first thought was that Dave was taking off, abandoning him to die at the gnashing teeth of the undead. He was ashamed of himself when the truck bowled over six of the things crushing four of them, blocking off the remaining ones and giving him access to the passenger side door.

Kevin's fears had come to fruition, he was cut off. Sure he was safe enough up where he was, he didn't have to fear being eaten. He only had to worry about dehydration, starvation and exposure. He wasn't about to throw in the towel yet though, he stepped closer to the edge and dropped another zombie every time he squeezed. He suspected that neither his uncle or Dave realized his plight, he knew if he said anything magnanimous or self sacrificing that they would compromise their own safety to try and rescue him rather than do the prudent and safe thing of leaving him for the time being and coming back later.

He did a quick inventory of his supplies, he had close to two hundred rounds of ammo for the assault rifle and forty-five for his pistol. He had two bottles of water, one and a half power bars. "Not much in the way grub" he thought to himself. He also had a pair of field glasses in his cargo pocket. "Could be worse though, I won't be up here that long anyhow" he mused. He heard the truck slide into gear and the engines RPMs increase as the truck began to pull away.

He watched as the truck pulled off in the direction of the other tanker, he wasn't surprised to see the majority of the stragglers follow, Liam jumped out of the one cab and race around to the other, climb in and start the rig up. It caught after a few scary moments of grinding before that happiest of sounds, the sound of an engine coming to life. He noticed a couple of targets of opportunity and reduced the hordes number by another four.

The two trucks pulled away, but instead of driving out the gate Dave made a left turn and then Liam made a right. Neither got above third gear as they lead the zombies away on a wild goose chase. The mindless creatures followed doggedly. They were taking the perimeter road along the tank farm, if they stayed on that course they would eventually pass each other on the far side of the property.

Dave noticed where the group was coming from, there was a hole in the fence near the back corner of the tank farm where a homeless enclave was, the make shift shanties and cardboard boxes covered in tarps abounded. The zombie plague must have ripped through there like wildfire, and then they slipped through the hole in the fence and happened upon those few unlucky workers. He watched n his side view mirror as the horde followed stretching behind his truck. It was a horror movie version of 'the pied piper' he couldn't resist his own perverse sense of humor as he began whistling a variation of the seven dwarf theme song 'hi ho hi ho' once he got a hold of himself he radioed Kevin on top of the tank, "You didn't actually think we would leave you did you?" he asked of his nephew.

"It would have been the smart thing to do, you could have lead those things out of the compound and come back for me later" said Kevin in a devil may care tone.

"Nah! your dad would have kicked my ass when we got back if he ever found out" They both laughed at that, knowing it was true.

"Listen bud, Dave is going to swing back for you. You are going to have to climb down on the outside of the ladder enclosure, cause the truck is too tall to do it any other way. He will pull up right next to the ladder, you can step right onto the top of his tanker. While you are up there you can close the lids up there and do your best illegal immigrant

impersonation by climbing into the empty chamber. We are going to leave the pick up behind." Kevin didn't mind the climb, but he was not going to ride all the way back in the chamber off a gas delivery truck, he residual fumes would give him a raging head ache if it didn't kill him first.

"Okay on the first part but I will hold on until we get near the pickup and then I will drop into the bed and then we drive like hell out of here." The revised plan was set into motion as Kevin climbed the protective enclosure with the skill of a monkey. Dave was right on time, he had added some speed and his followers were some distance back.

Fortune smiled on Kevin as he managed to execute the maneuvers without falling. He seemed to step right onto the truck with the grace of a dancer thought Liam.

"Damn both of his kids have that same freakish feline balance as their Dad." he said to himself out loud in the cab, unaware that he had the transmit button depressed and his observation was broadcast. Kevin had heard he comment and flashed his Uncle the bird accompanied by a smile which clued him into the radio.

Growing up Liam had always been in awe of his brother's natural gifts in athletics. He figured it was just because he was older and that when he got to be the same age he would be able to do the same but that wasn't the case, Kyle was just gifted. They all played Hockey and Lacrosse but Kyle was just a Natural at every sport. If he hadn't allowed his high School girlfriend to screw up his head he could have gone on scholarship just about anywhere and maybe rode that wave straight into the pros as seemed likely with Duncan's son Sean.

Dave pulled alongside of the pickup and Kevin hopped down and got the thing started and on the road in an instant. The GPS was still in the pickup so Dave and Liam followed Kevin's lead as they drove back to the family compound with gallons of gas and fuel oil.

The success of both missions far exceeded Jacob's expectations. He was sure that there was a great deal left out of the stories in the telling, they probably edited the events for the benefit of the women. He would get the unvarnished versions later by asking Sean and Kevin, their testosterone wouldn't let them keep the secret from their Grand dad.

57

Kaitlyn found it difficult to work in her grandpa's *'command center'*. She had been spoiled by the state-of-the-art system on her Dad's boat. She felt far more comfortable there. She had made it her place and was very territorial about it. Jacob had deemed it safe for her to continue working there since the river's current made it so remote a chance that any zombies in the water could gain any purchase, and with living quarters being so cramped in the compound, Duncan and his family opted to live on board.

Kaitlyn had been given a mountain of work to do, so she spent most of her time on the boat. She already downloaded a myriad of 'how to' manuals along with survival guides. Titles like, 'how to live off of the grid' and 'how the colonials lived and ate better than we do' were among the most informative. She was combing through the survivor blogs and found several groups in the region, she noted down the URLs and sent them to Jacob in an e-mail. She checked her own, hoping to receive some word from her friends. Long Island was a mess and the information coming from there was spotty at best. It would be some time before anything even remotely reliable was going to come from there. It was too close to the city and ground zero, which now had a double meaning both of which were associated with NYC.

She was able to find a website that was constantly being updated by the Government, that had a map that was tracking the spread of the plague, as well as and more importantly safe havens and established communities, those that were taking in refugees and those that were sealed off, where anyone trying to gain entry were turned away or even shot at. The site even had a bulletin board where communities and havens were advertising for people with specific skill sets, like the newspaper classifieds. These too she jotted down.

There were blogs condemning of the government for inactivity, others pleading for intervention. The scope of the crisis was gargantuan. The whole of the world had been lain waste; the pockets of survivors were just waiting to die, or so read many of the posts. Kaitlyn's every waking thought was consumed with understanding what was happening, she had become obsessed with the news feeds. At least, she lived in America where the net was unrestricted, she couldn't imagine what life would have been like had she been living in China or some other place where the government crushed freedom of information. "Probably dead" she said under her breath.

Each post on each blog was more heart wrenching than the last. She gleaned every piece of information she could from these people who laid their souls bare on the net. So many of the stories spewed the anguish of folks who had people they loved and cherished taken from them, many to return as the ravenous ghouls that they feared, a of children being set upon by the parents who had always protected them. So much anguish and despair and Kaitlyn absorbed it all in her quest for understanding.

Next she checked her aunt Carrie's blog. It always had helpful information. She followed some of the threads and discussions that had been very informative on combat technique and another on the science behind the monsters. This one was a particular favorite of hers, as it somehow made the terror manageable, less supernatural or unholy.

She had been at it for several hours. She was going to break for dinner when she noticed something out of place. She was looking for her aunt's column, when she found it, the by line was from John Roberts. She almost signed off so as to join the family for dinner in the main house, but something wasn't right. A quick scan of the post revealed a eulogy for a pair of fallen soldiers written by the commanding officer.

A lump developed in the pit of her stomach, even before she read the names, she knew her heart was about to break. Part of her wanted to jump out of her chair and retreat from the computer, the other part, the part of her that held the morbid curiosity forced her to remain where she was and to continue reading. The latter won out and she scrolled to the beginning of the post. She read the letter that was delivered to her aunt; John Roberts printed it in its entirety, but the post did not end there.

Tears began to flow from her eyes as she read on, making it more difficult to read, she had to pause more and more often to wipe them away. She read the following, "It is with considerable grief and abject sorrow that I inform you readers of the loss of a friend and colleague; Carrie Sixkiller has passed away. Her loss is a devastating blow to the hopes of mankind, her tireless effort to get life-saving information out to the world. The level of her compassion was beyond compare. She put out on the web all the information from here at the CDC. She has saved more lives and eased more suffering and pain than anyone. It is ironic that her deep compassion is what resulted in her untimely passing. Earlier, she received dire news concerning the loss of her two sons who had been serving in the military. No parent should ever have to outlive their children. This loss was more than any mother could bare and Carrie chose not to go on. Nothing can match the grief of a mother who has lost her child let alone two at the same time. I count myself fortunate to have known Carrie as a friend and colleague and the world is at a loss for her passing. In her memory, I will humbly try to continue her work to the best of my ability. Farewell Carrie, it is my sincerest wish that you and your sons are reunited in paradise beyond the suffering we endure. Rest in peace."

A wail of anguish that started as a whimper and progressed to a level beyond endurance erupted from Kaitlyn as she read of the passing of her aunt. It was loud enough to have been heard up at the main house. Katie and Duncan fearing the worst practically flew out of the house, Duncan with pistol in hand. They were met by screams of grief and loss. However, they could not differentiate them from ones of physical pain or horror. Duncan leaped down from level to level to get to his daughter. Katie's shorter legs were all the caused her to fall behind. Both parents were desperate to get to their child. Duncan got to the dock level and ran for all he was worth finally jumping over the life line on the boat to its deck, calling out to Kaitlyn all the while; whose only reply was the continued cry of despair. He had just cleared the companion way when Katie arrived at the boat and climbed aboard.

Duncan found his little-girl bent in a ball clutching her abdomen rocking in her chair sobbing. He sought anything that could be a danger or the source of the outburst. His eyes fell upon the screen. Katie came down just as Duncan read the news concerning his sister, seeing her daughter safe and her husband not shooting anything, her fear transmuted into anger in a flash. "Kaitlyn, you scared..." Katie began to shout but was cut off when Duncan said one word, "No!" and held up his hand stopping his wife's rant before it got started. He turned and scooped his daughter from the chair. Kaitlyn buried her face in the side of his neck sobbing. Katie saw the tears slip from Duncan's eyes. She knew it was something bad; she saw the screen and read the news.

By this time, everyone else caught up, with the exception of Arthur, who was standing watch in the command center. Duncan printed out the screen and handed the paper to his own father, not trusting his voice, not to break. Jacobs face turned ashen, and he handed the paper to his wife. The post was passed from one family member to the other until they had all read of the tragedy that had befallen them all.

Up until that moment, none of them had realized how lucky they truly had been. Until then, the horrors had left them, mostly unscathed. True they had lost friends along the way, but this was different this was family. These were three of their own, three that they had not been able to save by getting them to the safety of the compound. Keith and Christopher

fell in defense of the country. They fell honorably. This was something that they could rationally accept, soldiers sometimes die doing their duty. Jacob, Patrick and Kevin understood this even better than the rest. Not that understanding made the loss more tolerable, just that it was less shocking, almost expected. Carrie was another case entirely. No one blamed her, sure there was anger but tempered with compassionate understanding.

The climb up the stairs to the main house seemed longer and more taxing than usual. Marie and Jacob seemed somehow frail and smaller than they had only minutes before. The loss that they were experiencing seemed to be draining their life force before the very eyes of everyone. Jacob maintained the stoic facade that he felt was expected of him. He would deal with his personal grief in private; he would be strong for his wife and surviving children; he could I'll afford to give into the depression that would consume him otherwise.

Duncan, like his siblings and parents shared stories about the times shared with each of the fallen, this was for the benefit of his wife and that of Liam's since Carrie had already been living far away before they joined the family, Pamela knew her a little better than did the other sisters in law. In Duncan's heart of hearts, he needed someone to blame so he focused his rage on his ex-brother in law. He secretly wished that he was somewhere still alive and have read the page that Mr. Roberts had written about her, to know that she mattered and that the world would mourn her loss and the loss of his progeny. He then hoped that the Dickhead was caught by some flesh eaters and ripped apart and eaten slowly so that he lived throughout the tortuous pain and know what he was suffering until finally he became one of those things too. "Isn't rage one of the stages of grief" he asked his father, who was too lost in his own thoughts to notice.

The members of the household that were not blood or by marriage retreated giving the rest the space and time that they needed to share in their purgatory of grief. Aaron and Thomas made the rounds of the perimeter without Jacob for the first time. Arthur maintained the watch for a second shift, while Laura and the others busied themselves with the chores that were necessary when you have so many people living together under one roof. Even the weather seemed to be mourning the family's loss as the skies turned a dark grey as pregnant clouds poured forth rain as if the heavens wept.

58

In Atlanta John Roberts exited the Sixkiller's residence, leaving Carrie's grieving husband to question his existence as a widower. No sooner had the door closed when a couple of the couple's neighbors who were solicitous of Jerry's well being asked how he was getting on in the wake of things. John really didn't have an answer for them.

Jerry Sixkiller was awash in grief and despair. He partially blamed himself for his wife's suicide. He really hadn't spent a lot of time with her since this whole mess stared. However, to be fair he had no reason *to* believe anything like this could happen. The boys seemed safe enough, he and Carrie had settled into things here. They had good neighbors. She had meaningful work to do. There was nothing to warn him he would be a widower now.

John Roberts was late for his briefing; he was due to meet with Dr. Hampton, who wanted to share what they had learned about the zombie metabolism. Truth being told John's heart wasn't in it. He too was grieving, not the way, a husband or a lover might but he and Carrie built a strong friendship in a short time. He was determined to live up to his pledge, he would continue to write us articles and to write posts for Carrie for as long as his body allowed, and he was able t o stave off exhaustion.

Dr. Hampton was waiting for John in the same viewing room above the surgical theatre as the last time. He had an assortment of pictures and charts on the smart board already. John entered the room and made a half-hearted apology for his lateness and grabbed a cup off the side board and proceeded to pour himself a coffee from the service there. Secretly, he wished he had a flask of Irish whiskey to put in it. Now, properly fortified he took his seat and waited for the doctor to begin.

"What we have learned so far is remarkable" the doctor began. "These organisms use tremendous amounts of fuel to convert the hosts to zombies, which explains the rapid decomposition rate and why it arrests when it has succeeded in making enough weapons to spread the infection and protozoan. It also explains why they crave flesh. They need massive amounts of proteins to keep the process up. We figured this was likely to be the case; however, it failed to explain why the zombies when faced with the absence of external protein didn't resume rapid decomposition, consuming their own host bodies from within." The doctor paused to allow John to ask questions, which never came, so the doctor resumed his briefing. "The answer we came up with is relatively simple... it hibernates. Not in the way a bear does, but it only reproduces when it detects the pheromones of living mammalians in its immediate area. This also explains why sometimes the zombies devour victims entirely while other times they just bite and scratch a few times then move onto the next victim. It's fascinating really."

John's voice recorder got it all. "Look doctor, I am not at my best right now... I am working through some things. Can I listen to what you just went through and get back to you later with questions and ramifications of what you have revealed?" Doctor Hampton knew about Carrie and that she, and John had become close friends. He could recognize the signs of grief as well as anyone. "Sure John, I will make sure I am available to you whenever you need, even if you just want to talk about the weather." John thanked him and got up and left leaving his coffee virtually untouched.

John returned to his room exhausted. He glanced at the clock on the wall and was shocked to find that he had only been awake for a little over four hours. His visit with Jerry Sixkiller had drained him significantly. He went through the ritual of setting his gear down and docking his laptop. While he was plugging in his voice recorder into the USB slot his computer beeped alerting him to waiting e-mails. He clicked the mail icon and was surprised to find seventy-six new e-mails waiting from him, add that to the ninety-one he had yet to read from this morning that he downloaded we he woke up, "Geeze, I am popular" he said sarcastically. Not long ago, before the dead started walking, he would have had less than a third of the amount, and two-thirds of those would have been ads for Viagra or porn sites. "Amazing, it took an apocalyptic plague to clean up the internet" his sarcastic mind continued.

He looked over at his unmade bed longingly; it took severe self-discipline to stop him from crawling into it. He meant it when he had written that he would do his best to handle Carrie's posts as well as his own articles, but with the volume of reports that he was receiving he was underwater. He went through their subject headings of his Gmail, hoping to get inspired with a starting point, but they could have been written in Greek for all he knew. The hardcore science was even in the titles. He was a reporter who had a faculty for science, not a scientist. He was going to need help. He picked up the phone and dialed Dr. Manis' extension.

The phone rang twice and was picked up on the third ring. He expected it to be the doctor's secretary. He was pleasantly surprised when he heard the doctor's voice give him a personal greeting, he obviously had read the caller ID. "John, how are you holding up? I am sorry to hear about Mrs. Sixkiller. I know you two had become close." John was surprised that the Doctor even knew about Carrie's death, what with all the people housed here now. "I know it's tough, but you have to keep at it; this is too important. So what can I do for you?" the doctor concluded.

"These reports that you have me copied on are too technical for me and there are more than I can possibly get through... I need some technical help. Is there anyone you can spare to help me sort through this, you know help break it down into layman's terms for me?" was John's reply. He didn't expect that there would be, but he had to try. He was already saying he understood the lack of man power before he registered the answer. Dr. Manis had told him he was going to task one of the grad students to help him in the off hours. "That would be great sir, truly ... when and where should I meet him?" Dr. Manis said he would send the help around to his quarters in a couple of hours. John's relief was palpable, he hung up the phone and glanced at his bed again, this time, he opted to grab a nap since help was coming. He set his alarm for one hour and was asleep before his head hit the pillow.

A heavy handed knocking on his door brought him back to consciousness. Blurry eyed, he whipped the drool from the corner of his mouth. "Just a minute" he called out. Fortunately, he was still dressed although his clothes we quite wrinkled, he straightened his bed, and made a half passed attempt to smooth his trousers before he crossed to the door and opened it. Outside was a fellow who was the epitome of the classic nerd. From the white socks and black shoes under high-water pants, to the short sleeve white button-down shirt with a pocket protector chock-full of pens and mechanical pencils, he was the stereotypical nerd, straight out of central casting.

"Mr. Roberts?... I am Randy, Randy Peterson. Dr. Manis said I was to help you with interpreting some research?" the short man with the oily hair extended his hand to shake. On his wrist was a digital watch complete with calculator. "This had to be a joke" he though as he accepted the man's hand and shook it. John stepped back from the doorway, inviting Randy in. Randy reached to the side of the door and pulled a wheeled briefcase in that was teeming with files and papers.

"Wow... you don't share these quarters with anyone else?" the grad student asked innocently. John looked around wondering if this guy lived in a closet or something. In fact in John's apartment in Brooklyn his closet was almost as big as this very room. "Nope, just me here... why don't we set up over at the table here" indicating the only table in the room. He grabbed a couple of days worth of laundry off of one of the chairs and moved it across from the other. Randy took the offered chair and began to pull out the stacks of folders. John asked, "Can I get you some coffee?" "No thank you" he replied as he pulled out a pair of red bull cans. John poured a cup for himself and put it in the microwave sitting on the counter, when he noticed the clock on it showed that he had slept for six hours after his conversation with Dr. Manis.

Rise Fall Rise Again: A New York Zombie Encounter

John sat down across from Randy, he gave him a brief synopsis of what he, and Carrie had been doing and what sort of information they were looking for, what could best help the people out there avoid becoming a meal and survive? John was concerned that Randy might resent having to help a novice or worse a reporter type, but quite, to the contrary, he was eager to help.

"Has anyone been able to nail down a time frame on how fast a victim turns after a bite or a scratch?" Randy paused in his scanning of one of the many reports, "That's just it. It doesn't make any sense... you would think that if the victim was say a healthy 25 year old Caucasian male that he would hold on longer than say an infirm elderly man with a compromised immune system... yet it doesn't seem to follow any rules. We have documented cases that cover most demographics, and no two cases are alike. The most virulent strain of the viral component overwhelms the body's immune response typically in under 36 hours, but there is a significant amount of cases where the freshly infected victim transforms in as few as three hours. Now if the victim already has the toxoplasmosa living within them, it could result in transformation within under an hour, although usually close to 6. So to make a long story short... I know too late... we haven't a clue." He sorted through the pile of reports until he found what he was looking for. "Here it is... spiramycin... is a drug that is used in dealing with toxoplasmosis in India, prior to the zombie strain viral component's introduction. This regiment showed reasonable success with pregnant women infected with the microbes, now current research is focusing on a cocktail that uses anti-radiation meds fortified with anti-malarial meds and spiramycin. The initial data suggests that the microbes can be destroyed and flushed from the tissue, depending on the level of infection. There is no way to cure a zombie! However, we at least have some hope that we can prevent the progression to becoming a zombie given exposure is caught soon enough."

This was truly hopeful news; John was excited by the possibility. That was when Randy let the shoe drop. "So far we have had a nine percent success rate in laboratory trials..." John seemed crestfallen and Randy noticed right away. "But we have also found that certain anti psychotics significantly slow the progression too" he said hoping to put some wind back in John's sails.

Together they went through three-quarters of the pile, and John had some good information to put into some Posts for Carrie's blog and two articles for his own page. They worked well together, and John seemed to have a little more pep about him. They broke for dinner, and John invited Randy to come back and watch a video, and they could pick it up again in the morning. Randy was thrilled at the prospect.

59

The business of survival tolerated no largesse, there was no room for grief, and survival required vigilance. Jacob knew this firsthand and best of all. He was the first to shake the funk, though truth being told it was more a facade then truly rounding the corner. It is written in man's DNA to procreate, from time immemorial a man's measure and worth were what he left behind, largely exhibited by his progeny. Jacob lost his only daughter and two of his grandchildren. A hole had been punched through his soul. Rationally, he knew he had to persevere. He had to overcome his grief for the sake of the rest of his family. He made a concerted effort to compartmentalize his emotional anguish, and to function normally, even when his heart was broken and raw.

Marie was having the worst time of it. She and her daughter had been estranged for so long, and they had only these recent days managed to reconcile the feelings that had so strained their relationship. For Marie, that made it all the more tragic and pushed her further into depression. Were it not for her daughter's-in-law she might have slipped into the abyss? Kristen became her solace, for Kaitlyn was determined to get back in the saddle and return to her task of research and communication. Kristen enjoyed the attention her "Nana " was lavishing upon her. She was a sad and lonely little girl who didn't have a job or purpose since they parted with the children on Liberty Island, and Marie had a hole in her heart that Kristen partly filled. In the days and weeks that followed the two of them were inseparable.

Kaitlyn back at work onboard the Persistence, made an amusing discovery. The largest of the social-networking media's pages were back online after having gone down for a couple of weeks. Her heart soared when she saw status updates of several of her closest friends. She mourned the loss of her aunt still but to find that her four closest friends were still alive although on the move, one through Appalachia trying to get to her Mother's family, the others in a refugee center out in the Hampton's. She was saddened to find out the boy she had been crushing on the last half of the school year had become a ravening beast. This she saw on streaming video.

The boys of the younger generation were hard at work building the tunnels from the out buildings. This work kept them busy and out of trouble, with the added benefit of keeping their muscles hard. Kyle and Duncan stalked deer and other game on the State land that abutted the compound to ensure the supply of meat. Part of Jacob's garage was converted into a smokehouse to cure the venison and other game. When they weren't hunting, the brothers and Dave helped in the tunnels or worked on improving the fortifications. They felled trees to build walls and dead falls. Usually, there were three men working under the guard of two or three with rifles.

They had only a few run ins to speak of with zombies in those first couple of weeks, but they ended quickly and decisively in their favor. Jacob managed to cobble together a reverse osmosis water system based on the one on Duncan's boat. Each and every one of these projects increased their chances of survival by large margins.

Arthur was growing more and more concerned as he kept watch on Google Earth and the Government's site with the map of infected zones. It seemed that down state more and more of the creatures were appearing, which of course meant that fewer and fewer survivors were to be found, and the hordes were growing in numbers. To Arthur's way of thinking, when the creatures exhausted their food supplies, they would likely spread out to find additional sources, and over the course of the last few days his fears were justified. They estimated that NYC, and its suburbs were occupied by more than two million of the undead and the numbers were growing. As their numbers grew the creatures spread out like locusts.

The military carried out hundreds of sorties a day around the more densely populated areas in hopes of containing the threat somewhat. Large urban areas were laid waste under fire bombing attacks, if there had been any survivors there, there weren't any more.

Globally, the United States was faring better than Eastern Europe and Asia. The dead in India and Pakistan were around nine percent and rising. The dead were flooding north into south-east Asia by the millions. It was a tide of death. There was very little information coming out of China but what little intelligence was available suggested that they were not much better off than their southern neighbors, but it was hard to tell and given their military might it was anyone's guess.

North and South Korea had put aside their differences and united with the American forces that were based there and managed to quarantine a couple of the cities where the rest of the county was awash in the dead. The entire continent of Africa was ceded to the dead, aside from small pockets held by this warlord or that, and those pockets grew less numerous with the passing of each day.

Jacob walked out of his office where he had been in discussion with Arthur concerning the increase sizes and number of hordes from south of their position. He sought his sons. They had to formulate some contingency plans while they still had time. Arthur's fears struck a chord in Jacob, so much so that Jacob suspected Arthur was right. He found Kyle dressing two does that he, and Kevin had brought down earlier with crossbows.

Kyle was enjoying the hunting, over the last couple of years he got to go less and less often. The forced conservation of ammunition proved more of a boon than a bane be his measure. It forced him to hunt with alternative weapons, thus adding an element of a challenge to the sport. The next time he went out he was going to try using one of the compound bows. He had been practicing and felt he was ready to try it for real.

"Kyle... I want to talk over some things with you and your brothers, do you happen to know where Duncan is?" asked Jacob of his eldest. Sean and Kevin had seen their grandfather walk up and figured that they would see what was up and wandered over. "Sean, where is your dad and your uncle Liam?" he asked of the newcomers.

"Dad is throwing a stick for Aloha in the yard ... I think Uncle Liam and Aunt Erin are in their place." said the 17-year-old as a touch of red colored his cheeks knowing that his aunt and uncle were trying to enjoy some alone time, which in these crowded quarters was in far too short supply. Jacob was able to read between the lines, but what he had to discuss was far too important. "Listen you two, go and knock on your Uncle's door and tell him I need to speak with him, tell him to meet his brothers and me on Duncan's boat." The seriousness of his tone had them set off right away to deliver his message.

Jacob turned to Kyle and said, "Get cleaned up and come on we have got some planning to do and some decisions to reach." Kyle went over to the picket and turned on the hose and began to sluice himself down washing away the gore from the cutting up of the deer. Jacob waited while Kyle made himself presentable, and then together they walked to join the others at the boat.

Liam caught up with his father and brother on the stairs leading down to the dock and ergo Duncan's boat. "What's this all about Dad?" he asked as he tucked his tee shirt back into his cargo pants. Jacob turned and stopped so that Liam could tie the laces to his boots and not trip and fall to his death in his rush. "I will voice my concerns on the boat and you three will hear them out, and then we can discuss our options so in the interest of me not having to repeat myself let's wait until we are with Dunk." Now that Liam was no longer in danger of tripping himself on his laces they continued down to the boat.

The two heavy electrical cords that provided the shore power were secured to the lifelines on the yacht. A set of fiberglass stairs were bolted to the dock at the stern of the vessel where the gate through the lifelines hung free. Jacob absently grabbed the dangling gate and hooked its end on the line before he stepped aboard the boat. He paused to admire the sleek vessel with its varnished teak bright work then moved aft to the cockpit and companion way followed by his two sons. He noticed that the brass ship's bell was removed. He figured Duncan had taken it down so as to prevent the unwanted attentions of any unread following the acoustical ringing.

They found Duncan below deck in the main saloon. He was sitting in a chair while rubbing his dog's belly with his bare foot. "Kaitlyn, honey why don't you take a break and go up to the house... Grandpa, your Uncles and I have some things to discuss?" he said to his daughter, as a statement posed as a question for politeness' sake. Kaitlyn looked at the grimness in her grandfather's eyes, then collected her things and left.

Kyle was standing closest to the galley so Duncan asked him for a diet coke. Liam took the other chair leaving his father the couch to share with Kyle when he returned with a brace of diet cokes handing Duncan his he sat down to hear what their father was so antsy about.

Jacob deliberated for a moment before he began, "I was talking with Arthur before, and he thinks we are living on borrowed time, that one or more large hordes are going to start moving north in our direction. And to be frank, I agree..." "Erin's pregnant!" Liam blurted out, the gamut of emotions that raced across his features made it impossible to tell how he felt about it. His outburst had everyone stunned. They had to switch gears to process this new information. Duncan recovered quickest. "Congratulation's bro!... It's about time, hell I was going to suggest for you to put a few good men on the job...but I see now I don't have to" They all laughed at that. They each congratulated Liam and shook his hand and embraced him as only family can. Plan's emotional show finally settled into one of happiness as his face fixed itself in a perpetual grin.

The dog pawed at Duncan's foot not understanding why the attention being paid to him had stopped, wanting only for the rubbing to resume. "As you know..." Liam began, "we have been trying to get pregnant for quite some time... Erin saw a fertility specialist and we both had our plumbing checked and well, the doctor said there was nothing wrong it was just we were trying to hard" This statement brought forth a chuckle from his two brothers, and Kyle said under his breath, "no such thing as trying too hard... it's when it's soft that there's a problem" which of course brought about more laughter. Liam continued, "anyhow; we had been trying, with no luck, as you know. It seems sometime just before all of this..." he gestured with his hands, "happened, she came home after a rough shift, and a hard day for me...shut up Kyle...and we just opened some wine, and well, it happened. One of you guys grabbed a pregnancy test accidentally, three, in fact, when you raided the pharmacy. Erin was late but that wasn't unusual, but there were the other symptoms, like her sense of smell and her moodiness... well she took the test, and well, it was blue" Kyle wouldn't resist saying, " like your balls in a few months" Duncan snarffed diet coke out through his nose over that one which added to the hilarity of it. Kyle got up and grabbed Liam's hand and yanked him up into a hug, "all kidding aside bro Congrats again this is great news"

Jacob's inner thoughts were unreadable. He was thankful for that, because he was thinking about the possible repercussions of the news. It wasn't so much the delivery, after all women had been giving birth at home for centuries, but if there were complications... but if they had to move quickly a pregnant woman just couldn't do that and then after the child was born keeping it safe in these times...again he was glad he had a good poker face. Little did he know but Liam shared the same thoughts, which was why his face showed so many conflicting emotions. However, he and Erin had discussed all of it and decided it was a gift from God, and it was not to be spurned.

Jacob stood and addressed his sons once again, "This news makes it even more critical for us to think about the growing number of zombies, up until now, we have been pretty lucky. We have only had to contend with relatively small numbers of the things, but with their growing numbers and fewer survivors how long do you think it is going to be before we are under siege? To add to that possibility we are running low on non perishables and vegetables. At the present, we aren't dangerously low but the supplies, we have won't outlast a prolonged siege." Jacob paused to let his dire words sink in. Kyle made to speak, but Jacob raised a hand t forestall him. "We have made this a very defendable position, but I am not so sure it can withstand a force of such numbers. We might want to consider relocating while we can to a stronger position, which brings us to the crux of why I wanted to speak with you boys... we need to get more supplies, and we have to find an even stronger place to set up home in, while we still can... if it's not too late already." He sat down to give his sons the chance to process his words.

"We can make a few supply runs maybe hit a Costco or some such place... we put the girls and anyone not going on the boat maybe have them loiter off shore while the rest of us go on the supply runs with all the guns and ammo we can carry..." began Duncan. Kyle was nodding following where his brother's thoughts were going. Liam was silent still absorbing the dire prophecy his father had dropped on them.

"I have a few ideas on where we might relocate to, but we need to check them out and see if they are indeed viable... unoccupied and zombie free." interjected Jacob. These words grabbed everyone's attention. "About fifteen miles north of here is an old Revolutionary War fort that was turned into an Armory, the Guardsman kept a lot of supplies there, now I don't know if the Guard even got there for the gear and what not, but the place should have generators and even some semblance of medical facilities, and it's on the water, so we can even have the boats as escape vehicles. And if the Guards haven't claimed the supplies that should give us even more with which to hold out against the hordes almost indefinitely."

Duncan liked the idea immediately and began to expound on it. "Dad is there a U-Haul anywhere near here where we can steal a Box truck?" Jacob had to laugh... his son would have done well in the Special Forces. His mind was quick, and he adapted fast to changes in circumstances. "In fact, fact there is, in the next town about fifteen minutes west of here." Duncan smiled, "Great; we grab a truck that way we can load it with supplies to bring back here, and if we find the Armory to our liking, we can use that and the Suburban to move. I think we should grab the truck first and then scout the Costco and or any supermarkets and wholesale clubs in the area and pick clean the easiest." They all agreed it was a good idea. They decided to bring the younger generation in on the planning, Patrick's input would prove invaluable when they began to discuss strategy. They decided to bring this meeting up to the main house and bring everyone up to speed.

Kristen was in the kitchen with the rest of the women. Everyone was gushing over Erin, who had obviously told them about the approaching baby. There was almost no trace of sorrow in Marie's eyes any longer, the news having acted as a salve on her broken heart. Kaitlyn was in the command center with Arthur whose eyes never left the screens. She had her laptop tied into the wifi network and was chatting with her friends online or at least the couple that she had been able to get into contact with, but to her at least she wasn't alone anymore. Jacob grabbed one of the walkie-talkies and called in 'the NextGen', as the boys liked to be called with the exception of Patrick, who believed himself too old for such sophomoric things.

In came Sean, Aaron, Thomas and Kevin along with Max and Skeela. They were carrying lacrosse sticks as they had been throwing a ball around as the dogs chased hoping to get it away from them. Apparently, they had been having a good time at it. The dogs sure were, they were like puppies again, having teenagers to play with allowed them to play and run out their energies.

The meal was shared by all, although none of them could even recall what they had eaten immediately after finish in it, so engrossed with the two distinctly different conversations shared at the table. The woman and girls were all about the baby where as the men were fixated on the plans that they were roughing out. If the woman were aware that the men were even there it would have been a miracle, neither group was listening to the other.

"... I still think we should put the woman onto the boat while we grab the box truck, this way we can have all the firepower we can muster for the excursion." said Kyle. Arthur had not had much luck in acquiring any laudable skills with any guns, not for lack of trying, nor from competent instruction from a patient teacher, he just didn't have the requisite eye hand coordination to put a projectile even remotely close to his intention. To add to that short coming, his physical stature did not suit this type of action, he could only really be of use driving, which of course was of little benefit to this plan since space was at a premium, if he couldn't shoot or load quickly he was a detriment to their cause. He understood this, no matter how great his desire to contribute his lack of skills put others in jeopardy as they would have to protect him since he wouldn't be able to protect himself reliably. It was suggested that he went on the boat with the women.

Nine heavily armed men would be more than sufficient for the task, or at least they hoped that to be the case. Within the hour after they finished their eating and planning session, they were getting their gear together and the women cast off the lines and were motoring north upriver. Duncan had left nothing to chance. He checked the handheld VHF to be sure it was charged; he cross referenced the chart plotter with physical charts, as well as making certain that Katie was sufficiently comfortable with the emergency systems and gear. He told his wife that they would be in contact off and on at the bottom half of the hour. Everyone was nervous but they at least felt prepared.

The arsenal that the men had with them was impressive, along with the assault rifles, they had modified several of the shotguns. By cutting down the barrels and then welding what could only be described as duck bills to the top and bottom produced a vicious and devastating effect by flattening out and focusing the blast pattern so much so that it would likely sever whatever it hit. In addition to the armaments they were all, each dressed for combat with the living dead. With leather where they could in the form of jackets or welding sleeves, goggles, rip (read bite resistant) clothing, boots, gloves. They were as well prepared as they were able to be. The Suburban pulled out stopping to shut the gate behind them, they then drove to the U-Haul dealer to liberate a step van or better a box truck which they hoped to fill with supplies.

The somber mood and the dire predictions had them all on pins and needles. Dave was behind the wheel with Jacob riding shotgun with his duck-billed shotgun. The rests were jammed in the back listening as Jacob directed Dave on where to go. As they drew near the tool rental/ U-Haul dealer, the hairs on Duncan's neck stood on end as fear one foreboding seized him. Dusk was still more than three hours out yet somehow everything seemed dimmer, as if dark clouds had just crossed in front of the sun. From the backseat Duncan peered through the windscreen searching for whatever doom, he was sure was out there waiting for him. He had never been one to believe in ESP or any such drivel, yet he was sure there was something out there. No one else seemed to be I'll at ease. He was the only one who seemed to sense what was coming.

Dave turned onto the state route that the dealer was on. "Keep on this road, it should be just ahead past the school..."said Jacob his words trailing off as if distracted by something. The Suburban continued along traveling a decent clip. The schoolyard was now in clear view, all within the truck wished it wasn't. Children, or at least what used to be children were trapped thank fully behind the chain-link fence. Their broken and damaged bodies were attempting to get out from the confines of the yard. Faces, some torn and missing features, others ravaged by rapid decomposition, a slime covered stump where a limb once was, yet most of the clothing was intact and undamaged. The horrific sight caused Dave to slow down, everyone's attention was drawn to those poor wretches. An adult zombie came around the corner of the brick building carrying a disembodied limb, presumably the one from the child with the slimy stump. The adult was probably the children's teacher, the emergency procedures, in effect, since nine-one-one sealed the fates of those children, now they have become the things of nightmares. The truck had come nearly to a stop, its idle provided its sole propulsion.

The trapped zombies posed little in the way of a physical threat other than their moans, which could draw the attention of ones whose mobility isn't hampered, but the biggest threat that they posed was the psychological effect that they were having on them collectively. Pat recognized this danger first and slapped the back of Dave's head and shouted, "Move damn it! Don't stop!" Pat's actions shook Dave out of it, and he slammed his foot on the accelerator, and the truck responded spitting gravel from the road out behind as the zombie kids faded in the rear-view mirror.

The tool rental place looked abandoned. The owners of the place appeared to have high-tailed it out with most of the trucks and trailers. The door wasn't locked and the lights were all on still, but by the look of the debris scattered about the owners left in a hurry. A twenty-foot box truck was in the lot; Liam went over to it to begin his magic while Patrick, Kevin, and Dave fanned out around it in a defensive arc with weapons at the ready.

Sean got out of the Suburban and joined his father and grandfather as they were entering the store, leaving Kyle along with the other two boys in the truck. Kyle had moved into the driver's seat as per the plan. Aaron and Thomas were badly shaken by the sight of the children in the schoolyard. Nothing could have prepared them for what they had just witnessed, they were brave boys and they would recover from the shock. It was just that they needed time to come to grips with it.

The three generations of Macgregor's represented enter the store cautiously, Jacob with his Magnum drawn and cocked, Sean and Duncan each had their own pistols in hand. Duncan lead the way in, they each were responsible for their own field of fire. Duncan's was straight ahead while Jacob covered the left and Sean the right. They didn't smell anything other than oil, gas and what could only be described as mowed grass, certainly not death, at any rate. Even with that being the case, they exercised extreme caution, Sean and Duncan had learned their lesson after the narrowly averted disaster at the sporting goods raid. The place was as they thought deserted. Jacob mentally inventoried the place, figuring that if they ever needed equipment to build or refortify with it would be good to know where to get it. Once they had explored the place and were sure that there were no ghouls. They joined the others outside just as the truck's motor turned over. In the cab of the box truck, Duncan saw Liam smiling at his own achievement. Sean opened the roll up door at the back of the truck and found it broom swept, just as it was supposed to have been returned by the previous renters. There were firm points on both sides for the purpose of securing of loads, a small door little more than an access hatch really that connected to the cab, and above that was a grandma's attic... additional storage space over the cab of the truck where you could store lighter items.

They had hoped to have found a thirty footer or even a twenty-six, but they were content enough with the twenty-foot version. Duncan went back into the store and grabbed a hand truck and a box full of ratcheting tied owns and tossed them in the back. Liam climbed through the access hatch at the same time Kevin, Patrick and Sean were climbing the tailgate. Duncan closed the roll up and then walked around and got into the cab after his father. Dave got behind the wheel and asked, "Where do we go now Jake?"

Jacob never liked being called Jake, as far as he was concerned his given name was Jacob, and he should be addressed as that or Sir! However, he had mellowed enough with age that he didn't let his irritation show and gave Dave directions. The truck pulled out of the lot followed by the Suburban heading to the wholesale shopper's club. There was an exit for the shopper's Mecca off of the thruway. However, they opted to travel the back roads to get there. Their experiences thus far with main thoroughfares had made them leery of such roads. Duncan looked at his watch and noted it was time to check in with his wife aboard his boat, so he pulled out the VHF and radio her. "SV PERSISTENCE, SV

Rise Fall Rise Again: A New York Zombie Encounter

PERSISTENCE, this is Duncan. How do you copy over??" He said into the device in his hand. He was answered with a giggle, and his daughter said, "Daddy why do you always speak like a bad war flick when you use the radio?" He had to laugh himself. "Well, honey old ha bits die hard... when you are on the water you are supposed to speak like that it's all part of the maritime etiquette. Tell mom that we've got the truck and are headed for the supplies now, and that I will call her back in an hour or so and not to worry." This time it was his wife's voice that answered him, "What don't you want to talk to me? You better not be going to some zombie trip club or something, all of you men get together, I know what you guys do..." she laughed. The injection of levity eased his spirits somewhat. He couldn't think of any playful banter so he told her, "We are almost there so I will call you in an hour or when we are through okay?" She was fine with that and said good bye. He switched off the radio and hoped he didn't lie to his wife.

The occupants of both vehicles anticipated a sizable undead presence in the massive parking lot due to the fact that it served not only the wholesale club but a Home-Improvement store too, along with several other outlet style store and chain restaurants. They pulled to the shoulder of the road that was slightly elevated in relation to the shopping plaza, for failure of a better word that afforded them a relatively good view of the majority of the parking field. With the aid of 10 power field glasses Duncan was able to get a pretty good view of what was happening down there.

In short, there were perhaps three hundred of the things give or take, just milling around near the home-improvement store. The store's security gates were down, and a group of the shambelers was beating on those gates trying to get in. From on top of the roof, what looked like a grill tank was tossed into a small group of the things, a few moments later there was a loud crack, like that of a deer rifle and the thing exploded in a brilliant flash of orange fire. The concussive force through down the surrounding denizens, there must have been some other accelerant on the ground in that spot because the fire spread and caught

341

ten or so of the creatures a blaze as they were trying to regain their footing, some of the creatures closest to the blast site were not moving, however, the ones that were just milled about oblivious to the flames catching others on fire. There were obviously survivors on the roof of the store, and the zombies knew that they were there. The strategy would have been far more effective on the living than on the undead as zombies are beyond fear, but it did thin their ranks some. If the flames didn't burn out before they consumed the bodies of the unread torches, there would be even less to contend with.

Even from this distance Duncan could clearly hear the haunting moans from the collected zombies. Jacob had another pair of binoculars to his eyes and was taking in everything that Duncan was. "They shouldn't waste their propane that way, first off, they might set their own building on fire, and secondly, they could use it in a more effective way...," said Jacob. Duncan grabbed his smart phone and looked up the phone number to the store and dialed it as his father was speaking. The phone rang a couple of times before an automated message picked up giving the store hours and such. Duncan followed the automated prompts all the way through until it gave him the option for a customer service representative, then it began to ring again. He was about to give up on the tenth ring when a voice on the other end answered, "Hello?" in a puzzled and shaky voice.

Duncan handed the phone to his father. "That was some good shooting, but I have another suggestion on how to better utilize your propane... we might be able to give you some help if you can thin out their ranks a bit more," said Jacob to the voice on the phone. "Who is this?" replied the voice on the line.

"I am Jacob and well, we are survivors just like you. We came to do some shopping and came upon your little battle and figured we could give you a hand." There was a pregnant pause before the voice intoned, " We would be glad for the help, but... we have plenty of room here just not a lot in the way of eats so if you are looking for a place to hold up you are S O L. (shit out of luck). Jacob laughed, "No, we have our own hole we just came for whatever we can find in the Costco. Seems to me if we can get rid of your little problem, we can both get the supplies we need, what do you say?" Jacob didn't have long to wait for an answer. "I say shit yeah! By the way, I am Wayne, Wayne Lewis, you said your name is Jacob? Well, Jacob what do you have in mind? I tell you the last thing I expected was to get a phone call and one offering salvation *to* boot Hell, I just may have to name a kid after you, it won't be one of my own minds you..." he laughed. The relief in his voice was evident.

Wayne and the other survivors had been on their own in there since the whole thing started, and they had been surviving on the candy and soft drinks in the store, and those were almost gone. They were desperate. Wayne wanted to talk, he and his fellow survivors had had no communication with anyone for weeks and the strain that that had upon them was understandable but Jacob told him there would be time for that later. Wayne sounded a bit dejected, but he understood.

"How much ammo do you have for that rifle I heard?" asked Jacob. "three bullets left...not much... just don't leave us" he interjected nervously, "we can think of something we can make some bombs and stuff." Jacob reassured him that they weren't going to leave them without help. Wayne relaxed somewhat. Jacob had a few ideas on how they could thin out the horde some.

"Go down to the plumbing section and get a few black iron pipes and the corresponding caps. Cap both ends and cut the pipes in half...see what sort of fittings you have that can adapt the little propane or map gas tanks and drill out the pipes near the caps for the fittings. You're going to make something like old flint lock guns but instead of black powder, you can use the gas." Wayne caught right onto the idea, "Shit we have got plenty of supplies for that sort of stuff" he replied giddily.

Back at the trucks Jacob and the rest did not have long to wait. Patrick and Kyle decided to recon a little closer they took two of the radios with headsets with them and turned on one of the remaining units and gave it to Duncan before they stalked off silently into the cover of trees, rocks, and tall grass, to get a closer look. It took Wayne less than half an hour to get the first four assembled and put into action. From atop the roof two explosive blasts were heard followed by the delightful albeit gruesome sight of two of the zombie's heads becoming proverbial pin cushions almost like the main monster in those "hell raiser" flicks. A short interval later two more blasts and two less walking dead. Miscellaneous hardware hurled at the tremendous speeds tore through the heads and bodies of the shambling creatures.

Being as the improvised weapons were muzzle loaders, they weren't particularly fast to reload. They were using various cloth type stuffs for wadding since their projectiles were not match fitted to the barrel's diameters. But in a pinch, they were working admirably. They had actually adapted piezoelectric torch assemblies to fill with and to serve as a trigger. They made another eight of the improvised weapons. They could have turned out many more of them. They just didn't have the man power to use them most efficiently. Sure they each could shoot, but then they would have to scurry and find more projectiles to load. This way, they worked as a team some of them shooting, others were loading, and the remainder bringing the hardware and wadding.

Kyle and Pat had moved well away from the group by the time the folks on the roof started volley fire, by no means were they too close, but they could see far better the effects of the improvised weaponry along with a more accurate count of the things. It was Jacob's hope that the firing from the roof would command so much attention that they could possibly gain access to the store they sought, sadly this was not the case. Their only hope was to use up a significant amount of possibly irreplaceable munitions.

Kyle and Pat were of the same opinion of Jacob. They opted to return to the trucks after having trekked far enough to have done a thorough reconnaissance. The plan was simple enough the box truck moves into the lot with the second, third, and fourth-best shots on the roof with the ARs, Kyle who was arguably the best shot, although there was some discussion about it, but it was close enough that I wouldn't cause a change at least they prayed it wouldn't make a difference. He would remain with the rest here with the Suburban to provide cover fire if necessary for those on the box truck.

Patrick, Duncan, and Kevin climbed atop the box truck, and Jacob tossed up a few ratcheting tie downs so that they could secure themselves to the roof and not have to worry about being bounced off during the drive. When they were secured Jacob got into the cab and started the drive that would take them into the Frey of battle. Risking four of the family was more than enough so far as Jacob was concerned, he was at the greatest risk as the fiends did not possess the dexterity to climb to the roof of the box truck, or at least they hoped that they couldn't climb up there, and even though the cab was raised enough that he didn't worry too much about them getting through the glass, he was still closest in proximity to their gnashing teeth and terrible claw like hands.

The circuitous route that they had chosen brought them into the lot from the back side of the buildings, it had been a bouncy ride for the shooters on top, but they had expected that to be the case. Jacob drove around the west side of the stores nearest to the Costco. The loading bays were all closed and deserted, he was thankful to see. As he continued to drive he noticed that within some of the cars in the lot were trapped numerous zombies who were likely infected folks who expired and reanimated in their cars and lacked the mental faculties to extricate themselves from their seat belts let alone their cars. Had Jacob allowed himself to feel any emotions, he surely would have felt a mixture of sadness and mirth at the lights of the creatures, as it was, he only registered the tactical aspects of the situation. He applied a little more speed when he neared the leading edge of the building that would bring them within sight of the horde, as he turned he noted that doors, here were not secured, which of course would be to their benefit unless the store was occupied by another horde within.

As the vehicle came in sight of the horde, a few of the zombies closest to them noticed their approach but their moans went unnoticed by the horde, which confirmed their lack of ability to communicate and work as an organized group, but even with that working in their favor the sheer number of creatures made the chances of success far less certain than any of them would like. They had the fire selection on single fire to conserve their ammo. Firing from a prone position would increase their accuracy as would firing only one shot per trigger squeeze. Pat and Kevin fired almost simultaneously and in a horrifying display, two zombies heads expanded impossibly as the kinetic energy of the rounds was released to the brain tissue inside, ultimately the weak end skulls ruptured in an explosive spray of grey and red tissue and blood.

Duncan took aim at yet a different creature and squeezed producing the same effect, as his zombie went down Pat had fired at another and another, as did Kevin. For every report of a round leaving an assault rifle a zombie went down never to rise again. Wayne and the others on the home-improvement store noticed that they were no longer alone and took heart in their new-found savior's arrival and continued to fire their improvised guns into the horde with vigor.

It was unlikely that the horde reacted out of self-preservation, rather more likely they had caught the scent of new prey closer at hand and perhaps more easily had. The horde turned almost as one to face the box truck and began to move in their direction. The wind had changed direction, and the horrible stench assaulted the olfactory senses of the shooters on the truck. Were it not for the application of the vaporub under each of their nostrils they might have been overcome by the stench? For every step, the horde took in their direction, Pat, Kevin and Duncan carved even more from their ranks. The horde was stretching out and curving around them flanking their sides, as a swath of stilled corpses was squashed beneath the feet of the rest. Kevin switched magazines in his gun and changed over to automatic releasing controlled bursts into the near edge of the line. Pat mirrored his brother's actions concentrating his fire on the opposite edge, while Duncan continued working the middle.

The spent cartridge casings rained down on the roof of the truck sounding like hail, was it not for the distinctive report of the rifles Jacob could have almost have believed it to be exactly that. He was supposed to just drive but he was not a about to sit their impotent, so he chanced to roll down his window after dabbing the menthol paste under his nose and began firing his Magnum at the approaching horde. Each time he felled one of the creatures, he allowed himself some satisfaction of revenge for the losses of his daughter and grandsons.

The awesome carnage unleashed was muted by the relentless press of the zombie horde. Still the fusillade continued. Undead heads exploded; spines were severed, and bodies collapsed. The semi coagulated blood appeared black and with the consistency of mud. The horde was now within mere yards of the truck, their numbers cut by nearly two thirds yet on they pressed. Jacob put the truck into reverse to gain some distance between his own and the tireless fiends who sought to rend the flesh from their bones.

The fire from the store's rooftop had stopped sometime earlier when the horde had moved beyond their weapon's effective range. Wayne and the others just watched as the horde followed after the truck and their saviors. Wayne and his fellow survivors said a prayer for their rescuer's deliverance and wished there was more than they could do.

60

On the Persistence, the women and Arthur waited for the next communication with the rest. Their time had been largely uneventful, although the waiting was taxing in its own way. Katie sat next to her daughter Kaitlyn at the communications station anxiously waiting for word from her husband, worry lines becoming noticeable at the corners of her eyes. Erin in the galley asks Katie if she wants some coffee.

"No" she replied curtly, Erintook no offence, she too felt the strain of not knowing. Katie recognized her shortness and apologized, "Sorry Erin, it's just..."

Erin interjected, "It's nothing sweetie I feel it too."

Katie smiled weakly at her sister in law as she came over with coffee cup in hand. "Don't worry they will call soon" she said as she took a sip. As if commanded to do so the phone rang, and Katie answered it before it had completed its first ring.

"It's about time honey" said Katie into the receiver.

"Umm hello is Duncan there?" said a voice that Katie didn't recognize. "He is out at the moment, may I ask who is calling?" said Katie to the anonymous voice.

"Hi, you must be Duncan's wife...I am Mike Anderson... I met your husband and son and some others, I used to work at the Long Island Outdoorsman... he said he was headed up north somewhere along the west cost of the Hudson... We was headed south towards Kentucky but couldn't get further south than Bethlehem PA. We turned around and have been heading north ever since... figured since we had become friends we would try to link up... you expect him anytime soon?"

Katie didn't know what to say, she told him the general area where they were and Mike said he knew the area well and that he was less than fifty miles away. Duncan had told Katie about the help Mike had given them and for that alone she would forever be in his debt. They spoke for a little while, Mike hadn't had many people to talk to these past couple of weeks other than a few anonymous people on the CB radio, so he was eager to chat. She told him where Duncan and the others had gone for supplies, and he got very excited because he was even closer than he had originally thought. He said that he, and his crew were going to head straight there to see if he could help. She thanked him again and then rang off feeling comforted by the conversation.

Mike Anderson and his family were traveling in relative comfort, in an armored motor coach. They had plenty of food and firepower having brought along almost all of the remaining stock from the store, along with an impressive array of class three automatic weapons and his brother's pride and joy from civil war reenactment, a Gatling gun that stuck out of the back of the bus. Its swivel mount gave it a stunning field of fire. He called Duncan's cell phone, having gotten the number during his conversation with Katie, Kyle answered. Mike mistook Kyle for

Duncan; their two voices were close. Kyle knew right away who Mike was and was glad to hear from him. Kyle began to give Mike a play by play of what was going on. Mike told his brother Richie to step on it, and that they would be there in about twenty to thirty minutes. Just before disconnecting Mike suggested that they give their wives a call as they are worrying, Kyle thanked him for the message and said he would do so when they hung up. After hanging up the phone he lowered the field glasses that he had never ceased looking through and raised the three-thirty-eight magnum rifle and scope on the chance he would have to play 'ma bell' and reach out and touch someone long distance.

With his cheek welded to the rifle stock, he trained his cross hairs on the closest zombie to the group prepared to shoot if necessary, and told his nephew Sean to call his mom. By Kyle's estimation, there were still upwards of a hundred of the things moving around down there, more than enough to cause serious problems if things went bad.

Jacob had to move the truck again after only a few minutes, the zombies seemed to become more aggressive or perhaps insistent would be a better term. The tremendous amount of noise that was being made here was attracting more of the creature that they hadn't seen. Kyle apprised Jacob of the new arrivals and their relative positions; he had still not fired a shot. The plan had called for him to just keep an over watch, and only to shoot if it became necessary, so as not to draw attention to his location. This directive chaffed at Kyle, but the reasoning was sound. As the horde's numbers continued to lessen he was tempted to take a few out despite the plan, but he resisted the urge.

The horde was down to less than thirty, and all spread out. Jacob put the truck into drive to sort of heard the things or more aptly draw them closer together so that they could finish them off all the more easily. It was at that point when the armored motor coach pulled into the lot with what looked like the prow of an ice breaker ship welded *onto* its front. The bus plowed straight into the things mowing them down like tall grass, hurling the things from their feet to fall broken a and damaged as the bus continued past and the rear of the vehicle came into view the Gatling gun came into play, sweeping left and right. Bullets spewed forth from the weapon shredding the bodies, and then there was silence. None of the undead were left, there was no more moaning no more movement, just the stillness of resumed death.

Duncan and the rest changed their magazines and trained their guns on the newcomers, caution being the better part of valor. Their experiences with the pirates were still fresh in their minds, they knew that not all survivors were the type who shared or played well with others but were rather in competition for resources. The buses main door opened and out stepped Mike with an Ak47 in hand held by the fore stock and barrel with as big grin on his face. "Glad you had a few left so that we could make a grand entrance... we were afraid that the party would be over and our arrival would be anticlimactic" he said and laughed.

Duncan climbed off of the roof and jogged over throwing his arms around the man like long lost kin just come home, even though he had only met the man once before and for but a short while at that. The rest of the family filed out of the bus, just as Jacob, Pat and Kevin got out and off of the truck. Mike and Duncan made the introductions, and it was like a homecoming. A few minutes later the Suburban pulled into the lot and the metal roll up door on the home-improvement store opened and out came Wayne the others in his group remained inside a bit more cautiously.

Wayne walked up to the group and stuck out his hand to Duncan and introduced himself. "Boys you guys got here in a nick of time. Things were getting pretty desperate for us in there" Mike didn't know their story so Wayne gave him the abridged version emphasizing their hunger, which brought the whole reason for this escapade back to the fore front. Samantha, Mike's wife went back in. to the bus only to return a few minutes later with a box of MRE*s that she gave to Wayne. She wasn't overly concerned with sharing of theoretical supplies since they were going to be replenishing supplies from within the Costco soon anyhow, and they were looking to join a community and settle in. Life living in a bus was not the life she wanted to do any longer than necessary.

Wayne accepted the hospitality with tears in his eyes, "Thank you" was all that would come out before he became too choked up to speak any further. But that didn't matter the undying gratitude could not have been more clearly expressed. Hunger had weakened them to the point where they would be of no use inside the Costco so Wayne returned to his group to eat the first real food in more than a week, while Duncan and the others hashed out a plan to check out the Costco. The addition of three more automatic weapons was a great boost to their safety.

The newly expanded group gathered in the box truck to formulate a plan while Jacob backed it up to the front doors. Jacob stopped about twenty feet from the door to all low them to extend the loading ramp. As the ramp was fully extended the door sensor opened the doors automatically. "That's not good" said Duncan rhetorically as seven automatic weapons came up simultaneously.

The group entered the store with overlapping fields of fire. Judging by the disarray others had been here before, what was uncertain was if any unread were in here at present. It seemed likely that there would be at least a few inside given that the doors opened automatically. On the assortment of flat screens directly in front of them an animated movie played from some networked DVD system, intended to sell not only the televisions but the movie as well.

"Could have been worse they could have been showing a zombie flick instead" joked Aaron in an obvious attempt to cover his nervousness with bravado. They couldn't smell anything due to the vaporub intended to diminish the debilitating effects of the zombie's stench, so they relied upon their eyes and ears to keep them from becoming dinner. Daylight would soon be fading, thankfully the lights in the store were still burning.

They walked along ever mindful of noise discipline, carefully stepping over debris and discarded items on the floor, side stepping around the shopping carts laden with items that others had loaded and then abandoned for whatever reason. Duncan spotted a decaying arm sticking limply part way out of the inventory cage door where they keep portable electronics, batteries and the replacement razor blades for the more popular razors to prevent shoplifting. The arm twitched and then was still again. They weren't alone that was certain now, but at least this one hadn't noticed them yet and began its moaning that would attract whatever others might be in the store. That one was obviously trapped so they moved away from it hoping to keep it ignorant of their presence.

They slipped up the side aisle giving the trapped zombie a wide birth. They went right past the electronics and then the office supplies followed by the document safes and coffee makers. They decided to cut down that aisle and head up the center figuring they were now far enough away from the one trapped in the cage. Still no sounds betrayed any other lurking denizens. In this part of the store the center area had faux patios set up with a number of different styles of lawn furniture and awnings along with a host of gas grills and barbeques.

They knew that they had to clear the store and quickly. They could split up, which might be a little faster, however, doing so brought with it other possible complications. Duncan made the command decision to stay together, figuring that if there were any large numbers of creepers in here that their combined firepower would quickly overpower their adversaries.

They formed a wedge and began moving up the center aisle eyeing every possible place of concealment. Even though the place had had some looting, the looters had not taken much as a whole. The sturdy steel shelves was still burdened with weighty shrink wrapped pallets of products. In fact, the jewelry cases and some of the electronics were the area's most obviously hit.

"Uncle Dunk... maybe I should climb the racks along that wall taking the high ground. I can move ahead of you guys and see if there are any massing anywhere. It's safer up there so it won't matter that I am on my own" said Pat gesturing towards the racks then ran parallel to the aisle they were in and perpendicular to the aisles that held most of the products.

Duncan though it a good idea and gave the go ahead, and off Pat went. Duncan looked down at his watch. He knew sunset was fast approaching, and he wanted to be out of here quickly. He still had that horrible sense of foreboding. They were approaching the clothing section. The racks of apparel waited for shoppers to buy new outfits for the summer. Duncan had always suspected that the brand-name clothes sold in stores like this were Chinese knock-offs or counterfeit products.

At the entrance, one of the men from Wayne's group came in looking to hook up with the rest. He didn't notice the arm at the security cage and walked right on by. The decomposing hand lunged for him, snaring him by the shoulder with a vice like grip. The pads of the fingertips ruptured booklet, and the boney fingers ripped first into the tee-shirt and then the skin and muscles of his shoulder beneath. He screamed in terror and pain. His screams were joined by the moan of the trapped beast as it tried to slam its head through the wire of the cage door pulling at him trying so hard to bring its prey to its mouth full of gnashing teeth.

The group turned towards the screaming, and at that same moment, a hand shot out from in between the racks of clothing and grabbed Duncan by the forearm. Duncan reaction was one born of muscle memory. He had been a martial artist in his youth. He rotated his wrist outwardly causing pressure on the grip's thumb allowing him to break the grasp, and he stepped back and drought his gun into line and fired a burst into the rack. At the same time, more moans erupted from around the store. The acoustics of the place made in impossible to determined precisely from where or how many for that matter. The creature fell outwardly from within the rack. Black blood oozed from the fresh bullet holes in the thing's torso and neck, but the creature was not yet finished. It continued to reach for Duncan's legs with both hands clumsily

Duncan stepped back out of reach and put a final round through its skull from close range, splitting open the head like an overripe melon spattering the clothes with gore.

The wedge collapsed in on itself as they formed a circle with their backs to its center. Three zombies lumbered out of the pet food aisle drawn by the sound and commotion. These were of the quicker variety and closed the distance rapidly. Rounds from four separate guns ripped through them in an instant, scoring hits all over the pathetic creatures, causing them to dance like marionettes before they fell still as rounds found their vulnerable heads and destroyed the brains that had animated them. An enormously fat zombie, strangely reminiscent of Duncan's fallen coworker Don, waddled towards them. Large ribbon of flesh dangled from his arms and neck where he had obviously been feasted upon by other zombies prior to his demise. Duncan sighted in on the fat gruesome face and put a round through it just to the right of the nose shattering the orbital bone before entering the brain case. "Sorry Flaco," said Duncan as the hulking mass flopped noisily to the floor in an acknowledgement to the man he left behind to be eaten.

A short burst from up and to the right, shot from Pat's gun in his over watch position dropped another. The others found targets as well, and more bodies collapsed as their bullets found their marks. The fire fight had lasted only a couple of minutes. The circled fellows remained poised to resume their assault, but the only sounds were the moans from the one trapped in the cage and failing whimper of the man it had caught.

"You should be all clear Uncle Dunk... I'll go back and finish the one in the cage and put that fella out of his misery," said Pat through the headset and radio. To be sure, they were truly in the clear the group separated into teams who went through the aisles quickly.

"Duncan... you alright in their son" asked Jacob over the radio. "Yeah pop... we are all good. We are going to start hauling the supplies out now." Mike thumped Duncan on his shoulder and said, "Good job there

Dunk, but we better make this quick" Duncan agreed.

Dave found a couple of forklifts, he jumped into one and Liam grabbed the other. They began grabbing pallets of canned goods and moving them towards the front of the store, while Aaron and his brother found a pallet jack and started to pull and push the waiting pallets up the ramp into the truck. The others were filling shopping carts with everything from toilet paper, to coffee, to frozen food. Duncan made his way to the produce section. Much to his dismay he could all the produce wilted and rotting, the breads were all moldy and the meats wrapped in plastic film had turned rancid. On the plus side he did find a bunch of packaged skirt steaks and other meats that had been vacuum sealed that would keep, as would the hard salami and blocks of cheese.

The truck was rapidly filling, they were cramming it full. Mike and his family were moving pallets of foods and other sundries across the lot to the Home store. The parking lot's lights began to come on as they did every night at dusk. Duncan grabbed his cell and called his wife, realizing that he was overdue to call and dreading the reaming he was going to take for that. To his surprise and relief, he found out that Sean had called his mother before thus squaring the deal. "Yeah honey baby we got a ton of supplies, and. made some new friends while we were at it" he said and continued "I think we are going to bed down inside the home store for the night and rendezvous with you guys in the morning" they talked for a little while longer and then hung up.

Duncan made his way over to the home store as the bus and truck were pulling through the oversized roll up door near the lumber section and contractor's check out. He had to laugh as he noticed the priorities in product selection Mike and then joined by Wayne's crew had made, he saw more cases of beer stacked here than could be consumed by a frat house in a semester. There were other things too, cases of water, canned food, the usual. They were moving several refrigerators and freezers so that they could get them power and use them. The overhead door was sealed behind them, and everyone seemed in a celebratory mood.

Someone fired up a couple of the grills and through some steaks and lobster tails on. Duncan found Mike and Wayne talking along with Jacob. "There's plenty of room here, and we can build rooms to allow privacy. You all are welcome to stay, hell, we would like you to stay" said Wayne.

Mike was receptive to the idea, but Jacob was already shaking his head no. "We've got other plans, but we will share your hospitality tonight." The conversation continued and no matter how persuasive Mike and Wayne's words, Jacob was not swayed. The subject eventually changed to where everyone was from and what they did before the apocalypse.

Much beer was consumed and for the moment, everyone seemed glad to be there with each other. Pat was sitting to the side with Lauren getting reacquainted she was still taken with him, and he seemed to enjoy her attentions. The military minds in the group discussed what fortifications and such they would be making, as well as where and how they were going to plant a garden to grow produce.

"They had the beginnings of a nice little community here" thought Duncan, "Just as had the folks on Liberty Island" His father had already explained why it was best that they relocate to the armory or even back to the compound, and it made sense... sort of... "By having small communities close enough that they could help each other, but far enough away that you didn't grate upon each other's nerves. Plus by staying on the cost and waterways it would be easy to help out the folks on Liberty. When things get more stabilized each of our communities is going to discover different needs and there can be trading going on just like the frontier days. It's going to be a long time before the Government gets things under control... if ever. We have to survive as best as we can and I think this is the best way to go about it" said Jacob to Duncan. Whether that would prove true or not remained to be seen but for now it was a start, they could always rejoin one of the communities later, for now Duncan was getting tired. Then he stretched out on a hammock and was snoring peacefully soon thereafter.

61

Duncan woke to the smell of coffee and cooked bacon. Stretching and then rubbing the sleep out of his eyes he got up off of the hammock on which he had slept and joined his father who was sitting with Wayne and Mike, who were sitting by the help desk with a speaker phone talking with the people on Liberty Island. As it turned out, while he had been sleeping Jacob and the others had been discussing forming a confederation of sorts. They were setting up a pact for mutual support and trade guidelines. They had already agreed that they would pool the supplies and share various resources and would barter goods and services with any other communities that they came into contact with. They had established a communications tenement that would use the phones and the internet for as long as those systems remained viable as well as VHF and CB. All in all, it was a good idea that would be beneficial to all.

Duncan and his people were preparing to leave... they were just waiting for Kyle and Pat to come down off of the roof. They were settling once and for all who was the better shot. Overnight a number of zombies had wandered into the lot and there were others milling around on the highway. These provided the targets and the scoring. Kyle came down smiling while Pat looked as if someone pissed in his Cheerios. With that settled, Mike opened the door for them, and they drove off in the box truck and the Suburban, promising to keep in touch. Mike had replenished much of the ammunition that they had used since his impressive arsenal didn't contain any weapons in that caliber, he also told them to save their brass as he had powder and primers as well as the molds to make more bullets.

When they got on the road, they were returning via the same back roads on which they had come, Duncan called Katie and caught her up on the recent events. During the ride, Sean and some of the others busied themselves with reloading magazines so that they would be ready if needed. The drive was a pretty one. The flowers were blooming in their multitude of hues. The skies were clear with small billowing clouds that hung in the air picturesquely, the air was fresh and clear.

There was a feeling of hope and excitement among the group. Just knowing that there was plenty of supplies and that there were other survivors made things seem less bleak, vanquishing the feeling of foreboding that had held *onto* Duncan for so long. Jacob was the only one who didn't show signs of uplift. He wanted to check in with Arthur and Kaitlyn to see if the massive hordes had started to move north to threaten their survival, but he kept that desire in check not wanting to ruin the morale, trusting that Arthur would call with any bad news.

Even from a distance the Revolutionary War era fort looked ideal, with stout stone walls and towers east and west. The former overlooked the great river, where as the latter watched over the land approaches, the land surrounding it had been cleared when the fort had been built giving the watchmen an unobstructed view. The heavy iron banded gates had not been shut in over one hundred and fifty years but appeared to be serviceable and in good repair and sturdy, having been hewn from native hardwood. Portions of this fort had been constructed in the late 17th century by. The French, and it had seen use in the French and Indian war as well as the Revolutionary War. The main building referred to as the French Castle had been converted into an armory in the end of the nineteenth century. The front facade of granite block was largely unchanged however brownstone and brick were used when the military opted to repurpose it. The attempt of fusing the architectural periods was a failure, but as for function, it was near perfect.

The two vehicles passed through the gates onto the parade grounds, which were clear and spacious. They were glad to find things this way. Jacob had been concerned that others may have taken up residence here and might not be receptive to having interlopers joining them. Although the place seemed abandoned, they exited the vehicles with caution, keeping their weapons at the ready. Kyle and his boys were on point and were moving to check out the doors to see if they could gain entry to the armory proper. Dave and Liam were in the trucks keeping them running just I case they needed to make a speedy getaway. Duncan and Sean headed around the left side of the structure while Jacob and Arthur's boys took the right.

"That's far enough" came a female voice from a second-story window as Sean came around the corner of the building discovering a school bus that had seen better days parked in the back. Sean froze in place trying not to make any threatening movements, while he searched the windows for the voice. Duncan moved closer to the building and whispered into his radio letting Jacob and Kyle know that they weren't alone.

The first floor windows had wrought-iron bars on them, which prevented access inside through them. However, they did provide a means of scaling them to the upper level provided there was no one in view of those windows inside. Jacob told Aaron and his brother to hug the wall, and he did the same hoping that they hadn't been spotted. "Kyle... do you copy?" said Jacob into the boom mike of his head set. Kyle and his sons had tried the door and were contemplating how to gain entery when they heard Duncan's transmission followed by Jacob's. They too managed to get out of the immediate line of sight of the windows.

Duncan's back was against the wall, for all he knew there was someone in there with a need drawn on his teenage son. Sean to his credit was standing there motionless trying his best to look unfazed, and succeeding mostly. There wasn't much he could do except watch he had to leave it to his brother and father to do the rescue.

"Put own your gun and get on your knees" ordered the voice.

Sean looked over to his father before complying with the order. This was too much for Duncan, holding his gun by the barrel and butt high over his head he stepped away from the wall into their field of view and stepped in between his son and the faceless voice.

Sean noticed that Duncan had placed his pistol in the back of his waist band. "Hey you inside... we don't want any trouble... why don't you come down here and we can talk this out?" called Duncan up to the window.

Head murmured voices and then the voice called down to them, "There is nothing to talk about... you guys can put your guns down and leave with your lives... and tell Tommy if he shows his face here I will put a bullet in it."

Duncan had no idea who this Tommy was, but he didn't want to piss anyone off by asking. He lowered his rifle to the dirt and told Sean to back away. "They aren't with Tommy that guy is way too old and I never saw the kid before..." Duncan overheard before he backed out of earshot. "Dad, I don't think there's many of them in there... why don't we offer them some food and stuff, and maybe we can... you know to negotiate something." Duncan thought it was worth a try.

Meanwhile, Pat and Kevin were going to try and shimmy up the drain pipe and try to get in from the top down. Jacob envied their youthful muscles and fitness. In his day, he could have done the same thing, now he wasn't so sure. That kind of climbing, looks easy, especially when you've seen it in every action movie, but in actuality, it is very hard to do and even harder on the body. Adding insult to injury his grandsons made it look even easier than the movies. Pat lowered some nylon cord down for Jacob to secure the rifles to so that they could haul them up.

The roof was flat and in the newer section of the building, there were sky lights in the area where the arms and armor would be stored. That was one way for them to enter, another was a rooftop access door and being as they hadn't been spotted on their way up it was their best chance. Pat knew that the easy way wasn't always the best way so they scouted out both options. Investigating the skylights didn't reveal much. First of all, the lexan was badly oxidized making it very cloudy, almost opaque, secondly they didn't want to risk silhouetting themselves from below. They didn't have the ropes and harnesses to make their entrance from there, so the point was moot. They moved to check out the rooftop access door. The door itself was a robust steel door, but since it was a rooftop door it wasn't locked. Pat wished he had his action kit with him in there he had a little plastic bottle of oil that he wanted to apply to the hinges just in case. Kevin grabbed the handle in his off hand, keeping his other on the pistol grip of his rifle, and its butt pressed into his shoulder and prepared to open the door for his brother so that he could enter dynamically.

A window opened on the second floor above Jacobs's head, someone within obviously looking for others. His keen hearing allowed him to hear the chatter as the people inside sounded panicky, "There's two trucks out there so we don't know how many of them are out there... they could throw all of us into the big truck and sell us... what are we going to do?... You should have shot those two and then warned off the others," said one of the more panicked voices.

"Shot him with what... we haven't gotten the locks off of the gun racks yet and do any of you know how to load the things? I didn't think so... we got this one gun, and we don't even know if it's loaded correctly... we did well with the bluff."

Jacob smiled and slipped further away from the window so his communication with the rest wouldn't be overheard. He liked these girls right away. He came up with a quick plan and told everyone their parts in it. Duncan suggested what Sean had suggested about offering food. That fit right into the plan.

From what Jacob had heard there was very little they had to worry about it but there was still some risk so Duncan sent Sean back towards the truck, and he walked back in the direction of the rifles they had left behind in the dirt. Sure enough three girls had come out of a back door cautiously, only one holding a gun; and by the way, she held it. It was obvious that she didn't know how to use the thing beyond what she had seen in the movies. Duncan had his pistol in hand and stepped away from the wall. The guns in the dirt were about halfway between the girls and him. The girls were startled by the sight of him with his pistol drawn.

The one with the rifle raised the gun and aimed it at him..."don't move..." she said shakily.

Duncan smiled and lowered his pistol a fraction and said, "Look you have a gun and so do I... but it doesn't look like you know how to use it, where as I do... now I have no desire to shoot you, but I don't want to get shot either so why don't we both lower our guns and talk... my name is Duncan, and my son Sean I sent back to the trucks so that we can talk, okay?" T

The look on their faces bespoke of their skepticism. Duncan yelled to Sean, "Sean, honk the horn once will you?" Liam in the Suburban complied with the order and honked the horn loudly. Duncan needed not to have yelled as his radio was transmitting the whole time, but it was all part of the show to put the girls at ease.

The girls didn't know what to do. The one with the gun kept it pointed in his direction in her trembling hands. Duncan was pretty sure, that even if she shot the bullets would go wide of the mark. In a show of good faith he lowered his pistol to his side.

"My family and I are just looking for a safe place to ride out this storm... we have plenty of supplies and medicine, food, weapons... you name it. And we are willing to share. My wife and daughters and several of the women in my family are on my sailboat down river. e were planning to seal ourselves up in here, you obviously had the same idea. It's a good plan, and there is no reason why we both can't do exactly that. It's a win win all around..." Duncan entreated.

The girls were still afraid and hadn't answered, hadn't said a word. Duncan was doing his best to keep them calm and win over some trust.

Meanwhile, Pat and Kevin had slipped past the door on the roof and descended the stairs. Their stealth was enough to observe that there were six girls still in the house, and none of them were armed. They remained unobserved, for the moment, not wanting to upset the apple art and maybe get Duncan killed. They doubled clicked their transmit button so to signal to Duncan that they were in place and ready to act if necessary.

Jacob and Arthur's boys slipped around the back virtually hugging the foundation and were in their positions. This was communicated to Duncan by another series of clicks in his ear. Everyone was in place so now it was time to act.

Duncan holstered his pistol. "Tell you what, why don't you two pick up those rifles and follow me out front to our trucks... I will let you see the supplies. The safeties are engaged on our guns so you might want to check that..."

The two unarmed girls looked to the third for leadership. She had never taken her eyes off of Duncan but gave them a nod. The two girls cautiously moved forward and stooped to retrieve the guns. They looked for the safeties and found that Duncan had told the truth. Now at very least they had two working rifles and felt more confident.

"You're taking an awfully big chance mister... what's to stop us from shooting you now and taking all your supplies?" asked the leader as they followed Duncan to the tailgate of the box truck.

Duncan undid the latch and pushed open the roll up door revealing their goodies. "Simple there are three guns behind you and two more in the building" he said "we could have taken you by force but that's not what we want, which is why I let you have two machine guns"

One of the girls looked behind them and confirmed the truth of Duncan's words with a yelp.

"Pat or Kevin come down and unlock the front door" he said at a conversational volume.

He turned and faced the three armed girls and said, "Why don't we all put down our guns and become friends"

The girls looked defeated and lowered the guns. Jacob and the boys lowered theirs and approached. The girls were about to place their guns on the deck when Duncan said that they should hold onto them just not point them at anyone.

The faces of the girls brightened a bit. "Maybe these guys are for real," said one girl to her leader who shrugged as if to answer "could be" A few seconds later Kevin came out with a couple of the girls from within the house looking as though they were good friends as he exuded his 'surfer boy' charm. The others followed Pat out of the building.

Duncan introduced everyone to the girls. The leader was name Veronica, she and her sorority sisters had went to school at Le Roy College not far from here. They had just fled the clutches of some ass holes who they had taken shelter with when everything had gone to shit. The head ass hole was named Tommy something or other, and he felt entitled to whatever pleasures the girls had to offer since he, and his friends were protecting them. They were even going to trade a couple of the girls for supplies... there were some militia wackos that they were in touch with on the internet. The girls didn't go into how they made good their escape, but it was clear that some of the girls had indeed been misused.

Liam and Dave went to the gate to see if they were indeed as serviceable as they appeared, and at that time, Duncan got in touch with his wife and told her about the facilities they now had in their control. The sun was still not directly overhead, and the temperature was already approaching ninety degrees and promised to be a scorcher. There was a smaller portal and gate through the back wall of the fort which led down a stone stairway to a pier below which is where the boats would tie up upon their arrivals. Duncan descended the stairs to the quay and looked through his field glasses at the approaching boats.

Jacob and Arthur's boys stayed with the girls and talked about all they had been through, the girls shared more about their own experiences. Jacob knew that the boys would be trying to impress the college girls, so he stuck around to keep them out of trouble. Patrick and Kevin being more mature although no less susceptible to the charms of pretty girls than their younger counterparts knew that there was going to be a shortage of available women for the foreseeable future opted to go in with Sean to see what sort of supplies they had cashed.

The armory was a treasure trove of hardware and supplies, there were racks of M4s and AR15s along with other guns. There were crates and crates of ammunition and ordinance, even some crew served weapons platforms. There were even two APCs (armored personnel carriers) and a pair of HumVes, the military original version of the popular Hummer SUV. Pat grabbed a clipboard that had an inventory list and brought it out to Jacob with a smile as if he was Charlie and just found out that he now owned Willie Wonka's chocolate factory. Another room housed medical supplies among other things, as they continued to explore they found the generator banks. This place was even better than they had hoped. A few of their team would have to go back down to the family's compound and drive the fuel trucks back and whatever other supplies and gear that they could before the hordes arrived and made such trips too risky to undertake.

The flurry of activity was in full swing as the now larger group made the fort into their new home. The box truck was unloaded, and the food and sundries were inventoried and stored. The now empty truck could go back to the compound so as to transport whatever had been left behind. Patrick and Jacob busied themselves by trying to improve the already formidable defenses of the fortifications. Meanwhile, the sisters of Pi Sigma merged right in with Duncan's extended family and helped everyone settle into what was now their new home. Erin, with the help of Pam and Katie were setting up the 'infirmary ' after all there was little chance that they would come across an OBGYN anytime soon to assist with prenatal care.

Kevin was helping Kaitlyn set up the network, or more aptly rebuild the network. There were workstations in the offices and there were servers that had access to the internet but by Kaitlyn's standards, they were woefully inadequate. Kevin had noticed some SatCom (satellite communications) gear in the warehouse area, so by scavenging some of that equipment along with her laptop and whatever gear that could be brought back from the compound, they should be able to cobble together a respectable system and network. Now if only they could gain access to the military surveillance satellites, they lamented.

Laura didn't like the idea of the sorority sisters joining their group. Her self-esteem issues made fertile ground for jealousy to flourish in. She had been with Dave for these past weeks, and they had shared a lot but how could she compete with Coeds and the supple bodies? She watched for any signs that he might stray at least whenever she could. The business of converting the fort and armory into a home and community required the work of all hands.

Duncan got in touch with Wayne at the home-improvement store and told him of all they had found, and that they would drop by with some of the weapons and ammunition along with a comms system in exchange for some building supplies and some seeds from the gardening section. This barter system would become the means of commerce in this new world, every post-apocalyptic film said so. Duncan felt it could only benefit all by helping and spreading supplies around. After he finished speaking with Wayne, he next contacted the folks on Liberty. He informed them of their good fortune and told them that a boat would be heading down river in a couple of days with their allotment of supplies and gear. Some of the people left there were interested in moving to join Duncan and company, but those requests were tabled, for the time being. Survival was not yet assured for any of the burgeoning communities.

Aaron along with his brother was waiting at the box truck for Dave, Duncan, Sean and Liam. Liam and Dave spent much of their time since arriving at the fort, working on the gates. Liam thought it would have been really cool had there been a portcullis but alas this fort had been designed sans one, so they made do.

There really hadn't been all that much to do save for working the hinges which had seized up due to better than a century of oxidation and lack of use. The native hardwood of the gate measured better than twelve inches in thickness, and the iron banding was still sound. The cosmetic maintenance had served dual purpose by protecting them from rust. The strategically placed holes in the stonework were for the insertion of beams to bar the gates. They had managed to scare up a couple aluminum I beams somewhere to serve that purpose, so now the gates were ready to withstand the hordes indefinitely.

The box truck pulled out, and the gates were sealed behind it. In a worst case scenario they could go over the wall to get back in, as the ramparts of the wall measured short of eighteen feet in height, they could back the truck up and climb over from the top of the truck with the use of a lowered rope, but they hoped it wouldn't come to that. Google earth showed the larger hordes were moving in their direction but at the rate that they were traveling there should be more than enough time to make the journey.

Kevin had finished working with Kaitlyn, so he sought out his sibling. Pat was itching to set up a pair of the crew served machine guns at the front corners of the walls atop the redoubts, so when Kevin showed up they got right to it. Marie had taken it upon herself to get the kitchen in order, and now that the larder was full she had to plan for cooking in far larger quantities than ever before.

Jacob was not overly confident that the nation's fragile infrastructure would remain operable for much longer so he was counting on Duncan to bring back the reverse osmosis rig that he had built at the compound. Apart from being able to desalinate sea water making it drinkable it had the added benefit of removing microbes from the water as well. He went to check on his granddaughters. He was a little worried about Kristen's state of mind. She didn't have an area of responsibility or a purpose like her sister. She didn't have any other children to play with other than her older sister. Maybe he would have to rethink the idea of putting off the immigration embargo and allow a small group with some of the kids whom she had looked after on that first leg of their journey. He would discuss it with Duncan when he returned, meanwhile he figured he would try to get her interested in learning whatever Erin could teach her about nursing and medicine as a whole.

62

They drove first to the home improvement store with the promised munitions and comms gear, and to give them a heads up on the progress of the two nearest hordes. Being as they were considerably further south than the fort they had less time to prepare, and they would need these munitions soon. They were under siege again but by a far smaller group this time. Duncan tied himself off on top of the truck where they had secured a thirty caliber machine gun before they had left in anticipation of just this sort of affair. The swivel mount made it easy to acquire and dispatch targets, it was almost fun if you could forget that the zombies had once been people, maybe friends and neighbors. The worst was when there were children turned fiends. Their diminutive size and shape tore at his heart's strings. He had to remind himself constantly that those were no longer children, there was no innocence left in their bodies.

When the truck pulled into the lot the lookouts on the roof waved to them. Dave flashed the headlights in response and Duncan began dispatching the wretched creatures that were moving about, drawing them away from the big steel doors. The zombies shuffled towards the truck in droves onlookers y to be met by the hellish firepower that Duncan loosed upon them. Burst after burst he loosed into the ranks of the walking dead. Those closest fell first, only to be trampled under the fearless and relentless feet of those behind.

The steel door began to roll up, even while there were still shambelers in the parking lot. Mike, his brother, and his son came out with their own weapons of choice eager to get in on the fun. Many of the fallen were still moving, having suffered crippling wounds. Some worse than others Mike's son walked among them with a sledge hammer shouldered to finish those creatures that Duncan hadn't destroyed. When all was said and done Dave pulled the truck right up to the door and Sean opened the back to facilitate the unloading.

Mike waved to Duncan on the roof of the truck, "Hey Dunk why don't you come on down?" he called up cheerfully.

Duncan kept his eyes scanning the area. "Nah it's too much of a pain in the ass to get untied only to have to tie myself back down in a few minutes... why don't you climb on up though I do need to tell you some stuff" replied Duncan.

With a puzzled expression on his face Mike shrugged his shoulders and climbed the knotted rope that Duncan tossed over the side. It had been Mike's idea to make that modification. They had drilled a hole in the roof and then bolted a screw eye through it giving a firm point to which a rope and a snap shackle could be attached just in case someone needed to get up top in a hurry.

When Mike had gotten up there Duncan gave him his hand. Mike reached behind and into a backpack that he had been wearing and pulled out two beer cans offering one to Duncan who gladly accepted it.

"Listen Mike you guys are going to be receiving company real soon. That's why we stopped here first to bring you these supplies..."

This news had little effect on the unflappable guy. "Well we will just have to get you unloaded and give you guys the seeds and other supplies you had asked for right away. How long do you think we've got?" he asked in a rather nonchalant manner.

"No more than twelve hours probably less" Duncan replied "My dad had an idea he wanted to pass along... we found a pair of APCs that could make traveling a little easier. He suggested that you guys weld up a steel cage that gives a safety zone outside of a doorway with a door that slides up. Shoot it into the ground so it is sturdy. This way in the event that you need to be evacuated we can come and get you. Pull right up and pop the hatch you guys climb right in safely."

This proposed idea shook Mike up more than a little. "Do you really think we are going to need to be rescued? How big are these hordes you are tracking?" Duncan answered mikes query with a question of his own "Aren't you guys monitoring Google earth on the web?"

Duncan was incredulous "Man how many people were there in the NYC area? Most of them are Zombies now, and a fucking lot of those are moving this way... we are talking thousands maybe millions here. Granted they aren't all going to camp outside your door but those that do will be there and trying to get in..." the need for preparation was implied.

Mike yelled down, "Get this truck unloaded and get them their stuff they got to move and we have a lot to do in very little time this aint a social call"

His son picked up right away on the little tremor of voice that went unnoticed by the rest. Wayne looked a whole lot better, as did the rest of the people he had been trapped with. It was an amazing transformation brought on by food and relative peace of mind.

Ten minutes later the truck was ready to leave again. "Get your comms unit going and check in with my dad as soon as you can and for God's sake get someone on the web monitoring the progress of those things" Said Duncan as the truck pulled away.

Fortunately there had been no visitors at the compound since they left it. Duncan unfastened his bonds and climbed over the gate and down the ladder that was set up for that explicit purpose. A few seconds later he had the gate open and in pulled the truck. Jacob and Marie had a list of things that they said were too important to leave behind, so Duncan took it upon himself to retrieve those while everyone else began grabbing the supplies and gear that they could. They packed up everything that they could get their hands on including the meat that Kyle had stored in the garage/ smokehouse. It took some doing to retrieve the cameras that they had installed but they figured a little hard work now could yield life saving benefits later. The last of the items were loaded which was good as they were just about out of space.

Sean opted to ride with his dad, while Aaron road with Liam and his brother with Dave in the fuel trucks. Sean listened at the gate for any unexpected visitors on the other side and then opened the gate wide so that the trucks could pull out.

 Duncan called out of his window to his son, "what are you waiting for? Get back in here don't worry about the gates we aren't coming back here anytime soon" Sean obeyed his father and climbed back in. Out they drove with nary a look back. An hour later they were back at the fort with all three trucks.

At the very same moment, back at the home improvement store haunting moans of hunger form the unread were first heard on the winds. Wayne looked through a pair of 40x binoculars and called out the alarm.

An endless army of the undead could be seen creeping and shambling along the roadway. By nightfall their hamlet would be awash in a sea of ghouls.

63

A frantic call came over the SatCom unit from Wayne informing them that they were soon to be surrounded. This was confirmed by Arthur who was taking his usual post watching the satellite imagery on Google earth. Jacob knew that they were in God's hands now, he hoped that they would be able to ride out the siege, "They are as prepared as we are here" he said to himself along with a quick prayer for their safety.

"Wayne... do not engage them... don't draw attention to yourselves maybe they will pass you by. Just keep everyone inside and as quiet as possible unless you have no other choice" said Jacob in the calmest voice he could muster. It was the best advice he could give.

"Will do, listen Jake if this goes bad thanks for all the help. We will keep you up to date " said Wayne in a voice that was riddled with fear yet tinged with resignation.

"Just keep the faith" said Jacob "We will keep some one listening I'm going to check some things around here... for what it's worth good luck"

Everyone except the kids came together in the great hall. Jacob let them all know the current situation. "We can expect those creatures within the next few hours... I'd give it no more than six... what we have to do now is figure out just how we are going to deal with things."

He looked each of them in the eyes in turn. "It might be prudent to just button ourselves up and sit quiet and hope they pass us by. I think that maybe some may stick around but the longer we stay hidden the more of them should pass us by and besides we are sort of out in the sticks here maybe we'll get lucky." He didn't have much faith in the likelihood of his last statement coming to fruition but he tried to sell it to the rest.

"There really isn't much else we can do... they won't get through the walls so we can hold out as long as our food and supplies. We can watch from inside thanks to the cameras" said Duncan.

Rise Fall Rise Again: A New York Zombie Encounter

Veronica raised her hand to speak, "Can you guys teach us how to use the guns and gear while we can still make some noise?" It was a sensible request and Jacob felt whacked that he hadn't thought of it no less suggested it himself. All of the XY chromosomes in the room under twenty-five years of age volunteered provoking laughter from just about everyone else, even from the sorority sisters although with them their cheeks turned pink in embarrassment.

The laughter in the room stopped when Kristen rushed into the room, "Kaitlyn says that there are a bunch of them approaching, they aren't part of the bigger bunch... those are still pretty far away"

Pat stood and looked over at Veronica and said, " Weapons training begins in five minutes... meet us in the warehouse and we will get you set up... it sounds like some targets will be arriving soon." The girls looked at each other nervously but with great anticipation then got up and filed out of the room.

Pat and Kevin had the advantage of experience and age, both of them had had weapons training paid for by Uncle Sam and they were not above using this to their strategic advantage when it came to selecting their students.

 Kevin stepped aside with Pat and suggested, "Let's allow Sean to help in the teaching he is after all one of us..."

Pat agreed and smiled. "Hey Sean come over here and give us a hand" Sean didn't have to be asked twice, he practically jumped at the opportunity, while Aaron and his brother sulked. Their knowledge base was limited to what they had learned over the past couple of weeks under Jacob's tutelage. All of the girls were cute so it wasn't too bad they would get their chances over time.

After spending some time showing the girls how to load the magazines, and how to load those into the weapons, and how to charge the guns, they explained about how to aim, and how to breathe. Then they showed them how to best hold a gun and how to achieve a good cheek weld. They explained how on automatic fire, the barrels tend to walk upwards to the right. They showed them a little about handguns but stressed far more on using the rifle. Kyle and Duncan had come into the room to make sure the girls were actually being taught, and were glad to see that they were. Kyle picked up his deer rifle and asked if any of the girls was interested in learning distance marksmanship.

Pat looked at his father sternly, "I think they need to learn the basics first... don't you?" Kyle accepted the rebuke with good humor acknowledging his son's point and left with his brother.

"Dunk what are our chances do you think?" Kyle asked of his younger sibling. "I think we are sitting pretty Kyle, we got plenty of food and we are in a safe place...now if only we can use the SatCom to get in touch with the military who knows" Duncan replied with optimism. Kyle laughed, "what if we do get in touch with them and they want their supplies back?" Duncan thought about it for a minute, "They can keep my lottery winnings"

ABOUT THE AUTHOR

C.S. Leon is an Operating Engineer who moonlights as a writer. This is his first published work, and he hopes to be able to reverse the affore mentioned by being a writer who moonlights as an Engineer. He lives on Long Island with his wife and children, where they enjoy sailing with the other members of the Point Lookout Yacht Club.

Coming Soon

Rise Fall Rise Again:
The World In Flames

C.S. Leon

Preface

Daylight creeps in through a small gap between the blackout contact paper and the window frame, the errant ray finds the closed sleeping eyes of Tommy Johnson, the at onetime heralded now disgraced quarterback, making further sleep impossible. Stretching his arms as he makes the transition from sleep to wake fullness, he discovers that his bed is missing an occupant. Rage fills his steroid addled brain as he looks for the missing young girl on whom he wanted to spend his primal and carnal desires. He surveys the slovenly kept room seeing only dirty clothes and empty beer cans and bottles from the night before. Glancing at the headboard reveals the cable he sought still attached. Grabbing it he yanks cruelly and is rewarded with a yelp of pain. He followed the cable with his eyes as it disappeared under a pile of soiled garments.

Getting up from the bed, he walks around to the pile and kicks it none too gently. His size 14 double wide foot made contact with the midsection of the fourteen year old little girl who was hiding underneath. The air exploded out from her lungs and she resumed crying, for she had never really stopped crying from the moment she wound up under the "protection" of this savage.

Tommy grabbed a hold of the cable with one of his large yet exquisitely formed hands and pulled the naked abused child by her ankle where the cable attached to an ankle cuff that bit painfully into her slender leg. He yanked hard on the cable again sadistically reveling in the power he had over her. She groveled at his feet pleading for him to stop. He let go of the cable instead grabbing a hand full of long brown hair and hauled her to her tippy toes, with his other hand he back handed her sending her crashing down on her back on top of the mattress.

Tommy was aroused by the employment of force on this helpless child; he looked towards her crotch where he saw the dried blood of her shame and loss of her virginity. He pounced on her like a hunting cat, she tried to fight him off by scratching at his face and attempting to kick

379

him, this however only seemed to fuel his desire and to illicit greater cruelty. She was badly bruised and unconscious when he had finished with her. He got up and wrapped a towel around his waist leaving his acne riddled torso bare and when down the hall to shower up.

As he stepped out into the hallway he bumped into Tony Girardi, one of his cronies who with seventeen others from his former football team and a couple of other guys who were ROTC ran this palace of suffering like they were royalty and above all reproach. "Tony... take that little one down and put her with the others. We are gonna make that deal with those militia guys tomorrow! Did anyone figure out how those other sluts got away?" Tony shook his head in the negative. "Those ungrateful whores... when we find than I'm not going to be so nice..."he smile lasciviously and continued onto the shower.

Le Roy College was primarily known for its agriculture school if it was known for anything. The small campus was located in upstate New York on the western side of the Hudson River about seven miles as the crow flies from Fort Ramscoe, a Revolutionary War era fort that had been repurposed as an armory by the National Guard in the late 1nineth century. It was to there that the remaining sisters of Pi Sigma escaped to when they fled from clutches of Tommy Johnson and his followers three days prior.

Veronica Charles came from an affluent family that had made its money in a farming conglomerate. She was a lot smarter than her GPA indicated, but like many over privileged trust fund kids, she had been more concerned with partying than with academics. Her father was the majority shareholder in the company and she being his only heir, he expected her to assume a position of authority in the firm. Ultimately his considerable endowments to Le Roy assured her a degree from a respected agricultural school. Staying true to her nature she found herself partying with the bad boys even though they were far beneath her station. She pledged at the best sorority, and ironically enough it was after she became the president of that sorority that she began to think of others before herself.

It was during the spring semester of her junior year when the world took a sharp left turn and the zombies came, devouring society along with the flesh of those who they could ensnare with their claws and gnashing teeth. The school had canceled classes and issued a health advisory, but the students didn't care they looked at it as a chance to start the weekend's partying early. Some of the kids had heard from their parents about the craziness happening at home, some had heard rumors about zombies on the various social media, few of them believed any of it. That was until there was an attack on an Amtrak train that stopped at the station that was within walking or in this case shuffling distance of the campus. Several of the people injured on the train were taken to the infirmary on campus where the predictable happened.

Given the geographical location of the school almost everyone had cars, so when the news started showing the walking dead on the streets of Manhattan much of the school's population jumped into their cars and left. Much of the faculty holed up in their homes. The campus security force abandoned, to a man, their jobs figuring that just above minimum wage was not worth risking their safety or that of their families. As the days passes anarchy became the accepted norm. Ego and attitude spurred a group of athletes to take on the responsibilities of protecting those that stayed, however their lack of character and judgment allowed malcontents to come to power.

Veronica's insightful knowledge of the main players is what allowed her and her sorority sisters to elude the same fate as numerous other females on campus. However she lacked knowledge of what was going on in the surrounding area, so she and her sisters opted to go willingly into the hands of Tommy and his band, hoping that by going willingly they might keep some semblance of freedom so that they could escape when conditions were conducive.

Tommy's right hand man was Karl Metz. Karl's family was closely tied to some fringe type militia people, who could also be called white supremacists, whose fascist views on global governments were far removed from the mainstream. Being the crazy militia types they were however oddly well prepared and suited for the coming apocalypse. When the local emergency and police forces were Co opted from all over the region there wasn't anyone left to prevent fringe groups or other nefarious types from preying upon the weak and helpless. Tommy and Karl were for lack of a better word amoral, therefore more accepting of abandoning the trappings of a society based on the rule of law. As the news from around the world grew graver, the idea of taking by force whatever they wanted. Tommy pressed Karl to reach out to his militia roots for some support and supplies. They had already consolidated the resources to be had on campus, they had acquired the weapons and gear that the ROTC unit trained with. They locked down the food to be had in the cafeteria as well as the drugs and supplies from the infirmary. Together they formed their own little empire. Their barbarous proclivities necessitated the continued crushing abuse of those that dwelled in their realm.

Veronica knew that her freedom was provisional and would end sooner rather than later so she gathered her sisters with her and planned out their escape. She was adamant when she spoke to her sisters, telling them that they had to deceive there would be "protectors". "We have to be duplicitous, and we have to use what god gave us as women to a lay any suspicion. We let them use us... and when they wear themselves out and fall asleep... we sneak out and escape. We go to that armory and arm ourselves."

They knew that if they didn't their fate was sealed, they also knew that Tommy and his band would be coming after them but a chance at survival was better than no chance at all, so they agreed to the plan. That night the sisters of Pi Sigma used all of their feminine wiles to exhaust their captors and then escaped in a tattered and worn school bus to the armory.

1

Pat and his brother Kevin stood within the North Redoubt with nine college girls and the same number of M4 assault rifles. They had explained the mechanics of shooting and given them basic instructions now they were going to get the chance to put the theory into practice.

"Okay Amy you are up first, see the one over there on the right wearing the plaid shirt...I want you to try and hit him center mast" he indicated on his own torso where he wanted her to aim. He gave her an unloaded rifle and a full magazine. "Just like we went over... insert the magazine until you feel it click into place, then charge the weapon by pulling back here..." as he indicated on his own gun, "let it snap home and you are ready to shoot."

Amy held the weapon somewhat awkwardly and did as she was told, the weapon was now ready to fire.

"Now loop your arm through the sling like I showed you and pull the butt into your shoulder nice and tight...good, just like that now get a good cheek weld... that's right... now aim...take a breath and let it all the way out...nice... now squeeze the trigger gradually..."

The quiet was disrupted by the discharge of a round firing from the barrel. A fraction of a second later the zombie's head flew into the air separated from its body. It arced up and away from the torso as the round released its kinetic energy as it impacted on the fiend's neck shattering the cervical vertebrae 6 inches' above where she was aiming.

She very nearly dropped the gun after it recoiled, but the look of accomplishment on her visage was priceless.

"Nicely done. Was that where you were a aiming?" asked Pat of the short Asian girl.

"Not exactly" she admitted sheepishly. "I jerked it at the last second accidentally" she answered.

Pat was happy for two reasons, the first being she knew what she had done, and the second being she was honest about the placement of the round.

"You did great really..." He half turned and faced the other girls, "Who wants to go next?" he asked and they all raised their hands.

Susan Donner, short yet wiry stature hid an inner strength grabbed up a rifle and magazine, a split second later she was locked and loaded and sighted along the weapons rail and squeezed off two rounds in quick succession. The first took the next ghoul dead center and the second drilled a different fiend between the eyes. The creature's head expanded beyond its limits and ruptured in a gruesome display of gore. She was unfazed by the results of her prowess with the weapon and efficiently ejected the mag and then ejected the remaining round from the chamber, and held it out for Patrick to take, smiling all the while.

"My dad was in the Corps" she admitted proudly, "I can shoot V ring up to five hundred yards or so. Pat was impressed, meanwhile Kevin who was standing with Veronica laughed contentedly. He had a feeling that Susie, as she preferred to be called, might have designs on his brother, which was fine with him as it gave him a better shot with the three he had his eyes on.

Pat and Sean continued working with the girls while Veronica walked off with Kevin. He was more laid back than his brother. He exuded a natural charm that put girls immediately at ease. He wasn't making any moves on her, at least not yet but, he wanted to get to know these girls, since they were now living together. Veronica was as curious about him and his family as he was about her, and since he seemed to be the most relaxed of the clan she figured she would strike up some conversation. They headed for the rec room or at least what they were calling the rec room since it had yet to be set up with any recreational equipment. By

Duncan's thinking it was a waste of energy when there were other things that should be of greater priority, but Jacob and the next Gen said that it would be critical for moral if this turned into a prolonged siege.

The room had boxes stacked in the corner and a bunch of canvas camping chairs set up, a flat panel television that had yet to be set up along with other components of the audio visual ilk. Veronica chose a seat that faced only one other, while Kevin grabbed a couple of bags of Fritos out of a box and joined her and offered her a bag, which she demurely declined.

Veronica opted to be direct, rather than beating around the bush and getting the story in dribs and drabs, "So how did you guys wind up here? I mean you and your brother are military right? Why aren't you two with your units?"

 Kevin disarmed her with a smile. "Me, I am a puddle jumper ...err ... Coast Guard ... and I was stationed near where we grew up on Long Island. Now my grandparents, Jacob and Marie they moved up near here a few years ago when he retired. Pat, well Pat was on Medical Leave, he was injured in a training accident... he had just completed *SeAL* / BUDS training and was deploying to the teams when he got his leg and back jacked up when his chute failed during a training mission, his leave was to be up next week, he was supposed to see the doc' on base and get cleared but well that's not going to happen now. Anyhow... my uncle Dunk, he hit the Mega Millions just before the world ended, that's where he got the money for the boat and all, but I digress, He worked in the City as did my Uncle Liam. My dad he's a train guy and he and Pat were at the Garden watching the Islanders play the Rangers when the dead came. Uncle Dunk, he and some of his guys rescued my dad, brother and Uncle Liam, then they escaped Manhattan through the railroad tunnels. The rest of us, we made it to their boat and hooked up with some of the people in Uncle Dunk's yacht club and well we set sail for my grandparents place. We had some run ins with some slime balls who took a bunch of kids and younger woman hostage, we fixed them good"... there was a sudden gleam in his eyes when he got to that part of the story, hinting that there was more to it than he was mentioning, but she let it go and urged him to continue. "Well, once we got to my grandparent's place we were there for a while but we were watching Google Earth and saw some huge hordes headed our way so we came here, and that's our story in a nutshell."

It was a lot of information in a short amount of time for Veronica to process. She told him about her growing up and going to school, and then at last about Tommy Johnson and his band and what they were doing, she was a little vague on how they managed to escape but that was understandable. Kevin didn't press her to elaborate, her body language said there were some painful memories there and perhaps a bit of self recrimination to boot. She seemed to become melancholic, so being the gregarious fellow that he was he slapped her knee playfully and said lets go shoot some dead men, and with that he stood and headed for the door before she had a chance to turn him down.

Rise Fall Rise Again: A New York Zombie Encounter